OCCUPATION

By John Toland

Fiction

Occupation

Gods of War

Non-fiction

Infamy

No Man's Land

Hitler: The Pictorial Documentary
  of His Life

Adolf Hitler

The Rising Sun

The Last Hundred Days

But Not in Shame

The Dillinger Days

Battle: The Story of the Bulge

Ships in the Sky

John Toland
OCCUPATION

Doubleday  **New York**
1987

Library of Congress Cataloging-in-Publication Data
Toland, John.
  Occupation.

  1. Japan—History—Allied occupation, 1945–1952—
Fiction. I. Title.
PS3570.0427O25 1987   813'.54   87-5430
ISBN 0-385-19819-1

To Carolyn Blakemore
and Ken McCormick

Principal Characters

Muk Hun
Colonel Heijiro Iwata
Colonel Oliver Pearson
Major Susumu Watanabe

OTHERS
Charley Harrison
Hiroko Kato
Jun Kato, her cousin
Tomie Nomura
Fumiko Kano Matsutani
Lieutenant Colonel Thomas "Mad Mac" Mulrooney
Jo Mulrooney, his daughter
Ephraim Snow
Chaucy Snow, his daughter
Mariko Tajima
Taro Tajima, her son
Lieutenant General Takeo Takama

HISTORICAL

**THE INTERNATIONAL MILITARY TRIBUNAL
FOR THE FAR EAST (CLASS A WAR CRIMES)**

PRESIDENT	Sir William Webb
JUSTICES	Radhabinad Pal
	B.V.A. Röling
PROVOST MARSHAL	Lieutenant Colonel Aubrey Kenworthy
PROSECUTION	Chief Counsel Joseph B. Keenan
	Sir Arthur Comyns-Carr
	John Darsey
	Robert Donihi
	John Fihelly
	G. Osmond Hyde
DEFENSE	Ben Bruce Blakeney
	George Francis Blewett
	Alfred W. Brooks
	Beverly Coleman
	George Furness
	Ichiro Kiyose
	Aristides Lazarus
	David Smith
	Dr. Somei Uzawa

PRINCIPAL CHARACTERS

DEFENDANTS

Field Marshal Shunroko Hata
Prime Minister Koki Hirota
Lord Privy Seal, Marquis Koichi Kido
Shumei Okawa
General Kenryo Sato
Foreign Minister Mamoru Shigemitsu
Admiral Shigetaro Shimada
Foreign Minister Shigenori Togo
Prime Minister, General Hideki Tojo

OTHERS

Joseph W. Ballantine
Colonel Rufus "Togo" Bratton
Captain Benton Decker
Lieutenant General Robert Eichelberger
Emperor Hirohito of Japan
Lieutenant General Masaharu Homma
Corporal Kiyoshi Kamiko
General Douglas MacArthur
General George Marshall
Manuel Roxas, President of the Philippines
José Abad Santos, Chief Justice of the
    Philippines
President Harry S. Truman
Colonel Masanobu Tsuji
Major General Courtney Whitney

PART ONE

Chapter One

1.

Washington, D.C., September 22, 1945.

Professor Frank McGlynn was packing his personal possessions in a tiny office at OP-16-W, a secret naval operations intelligence agency, while ignoring pleas by an admiral, standing uncomfortably in a cluttered corner, to accept a temporary assignment in Japan for the Navy. He had already spent almost three and a half years away from his teaching job at Williams College. Besides, he had turned down a better offer from the State Department which wanted to capitalize on his expertise in Asian affairs.

"I've made up my mind, Admiral," he said, making him appear—as an ensign in the office once put it—like a marauding hawk swooping down on a helpless rabbit. The professor was tall and slender, with a shock of white hair that accentuated his piercing blue eyes, hawk nose, and pink complexion. His leanness went a long way toward gentility, and helped give him a thistly dignity. Hoisting a heavy carton of books onto his right shoulder, he strode out of the room with a youthful spring despite his sixty-two years.

What asses! he was thinking. Couldn't they understand plain English? How could any sensible man keep working for the government once the war was over?

In an hour he was in his battered Model A Ford en route to his Berkshire Hills in Williamstown, Massachusetts. He had agreed to resume teaching modern history the following autumn when things returned to normal. In the meantime he had a book to write on the tragic six months leading up to Pearl Harbor. His last book, published in the spring of 1941, had propounded the theory that America shared the blame with Japan for their growing differences. Those critics who had highly praised his other histories predicted it was the end of his career. Now he was going to stick his theory down their throats. During his years in Washington he had already collected important new material reinforcing his iconoclastic views.

By late afternoon he crossed into the Commonwealth of Massachusetts and could feel the first welcome tang of fall. What a relief from the sultry, enervating climate he'd had to endure in the capital. At last he could see the top of the college chapel, a ridiculous piece of architecture which he had grown fond of. Soon he arrived at the old house on Hoxsie Street, painted an ugly green by a predecessor. It still reminded him of the setting of a gothic novel. But the inside was cool and restful and at last he could think, since the housekeeper was smart enough to give him a blessedly brief welcome before disappearing into her kitchen.

Then the phone rang and he groaned. Long ago he had thought of fixing it so that calls could only go out, but his four children for once had prevailed. It was an old friend, Harvey Jonas, from the White House. In addition to his work on psychological warfare at OP-16-W McGlynn had been an unofficial adviser to his classmate at Harvard, Franklin Roosevelt. Though why the President had kept asking for advice which he rarely took was beyond understanding.

"Frank, I'm glad I caught you."

"What makes you think you've caught me, Harvey?"

"I see you're still your own sweet self."

"All right, what do you want me to do, Harvey? And the answer is no."

"It's not personal, Frank. I'm calling for President Truman."

"I thought you hated that haberdasher."

"Frank, please don't joke on this line." He cleared his voice. "He wants you to go to Tokyo and help advise General MacArthur on the occupation."

McGlynn laughed. "All right, you've had your fun. Now tell me what you *really* want."

"I'm serious, Frank. Bob Sherwood and Clark Clifford and other people in the know have been telling him how valuable your advice was to FDR."

McGlynn made a derisive noise. "In case you're really serious, the answer is still no. Please give my regards to the President."

"But . . ."

"No, Harvey."

"Frank, please think it over. Call me back any time at the old number."

McGlynn hung up.

It was a ridiculous proposition, but he couldn't get it out of his mind. After graduation from Harvard a good part of his life had been spent in the Orient and it had become his second home. He had stayed seven years in Japan teaching history at Aoyama College, getting married to the daughter of a prominent Scottish missionary and writing a history of the Meiji Restoration which brought renown and an offer to teach at his alma mater. Back at Harvard he became an immediate success, worshipped by many students for his Irish wit. By 1920 he had produced two more books on Asia and was recognized as one of the leading Orientologists in the world. His was a happy and productive life. Then that Christmas Eve Clara McGlynn gave birth to twins—and died. McGlynn, like so many Irishmen, took to drink and soon, by mutual agreement, left Harvard. He already had a son, seven, and a daughter, fourteen, who became mother to the twins. McGlynn took them all back to Japan where he again taught at Aoyama College. Pulling himself together, he became a full professor and wrote two more books; one, a successful biography of the first American ambassador to Japan, was awarded a Pulitzer Prize. This also won him a chair in modern history at Williams. As at Harvard, he was worshipped by those students who could endure his barbs. In 1935 he got special leave to research a book in China where he met Mao, Chu Teh, Chou En-lai and other Red leaders after the epic six-thousand-mile trek in late 1934 of the Red Army from South Central China to their new headquarters in the northwest.

Now, released from his war service in Washington and back at Williams at last, he strolled after dinner around the dark, peaceful campus roiled by thoughts of his beloved Asia. The whole continent was in turmoil. Japan was devastated not only by the firebombings but by Operation Starvation, the sowing of 12,135 mines in Japan's inner waters and harbors. This had put seven hundred ships out of commission, thereby slashing industrial production almost to zero. He had strenuously opposed this operation, which had been designed to bring starvation to seven million people by the spring of 1946; now, unless the Allies—and that meant America—began shipping in massive supplies of food, millions could still die. That was only one problem facing General MacArthur who had also been instructed to show those mis-

15

erable people the evils of their past ways and lead them to salvation via the Western version of democracy. MacArthur was to bring to trial the generals and political leaders for daring to go to war, and to hang thousands of lesser rank for committing atrocities. He also was under orders to change the educational system, replace Buddhism and Shintoism with Christianity, purge the leading industrialists and high government officials, change Japanese laws to fit American ideas of justice, free downtrodden women, bring laborers the dubious benefits of trade unionism, and teach the entire population to eat white bread and Wheaties instead of rice, as well as to drink Coca-Cola instead of sake. Besides all this he was to bring back millions of Japanese prisoners scattered all over the continent while eliminating their army, navy, and air force, in order to make it easier for the Soviets to start gobbling up their islands from the North.

And what about China, which was about to be torn up by civil war? Whose side should we support—Chiang Kai-shek's Nationalists who had already proven to be inept and corrupt, or Mao's Communists? And little Korea, about which America knew almost nothing. That unfortunate country had been freed from Japanese domination only to be split in two by the Allies, with the Russians taking control over the industrial north and America the agricultural south. The Devil himself couldn't have set up a more mischievous and volatile situation. And what was going to happen to the Philippines, India, and the countries of Southeast Asia, all of them tempting targets for communism? The great Japanese victory in Singapore had proven dramatically to all their Asian brothers that the white man could be defeated, and the ending of the war in the Pacific was only a prelude to violent demands that Orientals be freed from Western exploitation.

The possibilities were limitless, the probabilities disastrous. What a terrible task for the poor American Eagle, apparently mighty and all-powerful after its victories in Europe and Asia! Yet already there were civilian demands to bring all servicemen back home as soon as possible and to start mothballing the tremendous American military machine on the assumption that it would never again be needed. Wasn't the A-bomb enough to keep order in the world?

Asia was a tinderbox, ready to go up in flames in a dozen places. It was an incredible, complex mess, and the more McGlynn pondered all its problems and prospects the more intrigued he became. He doubted that he could be of any use, since the egocentric MacArthur would surely be even less susceptible than Roosevelt to good ideas. But he would become an eyewitness to history in the making and the recipient of materials that could be invaluable for future books.

The more he cogitated, the more reasons he could find for accepting Truman's offer. All of his children were in Japan. Floss had married a Japanese diplomat and gone with him to Tokyo after Pearl Harbor. Her husband had been beaten to death by the secret police and her baby had died of malnutrition. Mark, rebellious and quixotic, had enlisted in the Marines, maturing, in spite of himself, in battle. Maggie, his twin, was determined to be the world's greatest woman correspondent; she had already managed to talk her way onto Iwo Jima and Okinawa and become the first woman journalist to travel with the Marines in combat.

The fourth, his older son, Will, after finishing first in his class at Harvard Law School, had been persuaded by Justice Frankfurter to join General George Marshall's staff as a legal officer. Sent to the Philippines in early December 1941 to assess MacArthur's demands for supplies, he had landed at Clark Field moments before the Japanese attack. He had later been captured in Bataan, endured the Death March, Camps O'Donnell and Cabanatuan, then escaped to fight with a guerrilla unit in Cebu. He was recaptured and sent to two camps in southern Japan, the last one in Nagasaki, a thousand meters from the epicenter of the second atomic bomb. Of all his children, Will was by far the closest to the professor whose conquest of alcoholism and depression had turned him into a very private person. And Will would soon be coming back from his harrowing experiences.

McGlynn hurried home and dialed the special White House number. It took half an hour before he got his party. "Harvey," he said. "I'll take the job."

"I thought you would, Frank. Thanks."

"My son Will is coming back in a few days. I must spend time with him. Until after the New Year."

"No sweat. The President thanks you."

"How could he know so fast?"

"I told him I was pretty sure after our talk that you'd say yes."

"Harvey, you're a bastard."

"I know, Frank. That's why I'm still here."

2.

Japan, October 15, 1945.

McGlynn was annoyed to be sitting in a crowded bus bumping its way along the potted dirt road from Atsugi Airport to Yokohama. He had been promised that he wouldn't have to leave for Japan until after the New Year, but an urgent phone call from the White House informed him that MacArthur had requested he be sent at once.

McGlynn could see only beaten, hopeless, despairing people along the road. Gone was the former exuberance of the Japanese crowds he so vividly remembered. What remained was the sad degeneration of a humbled people. Neatness and cleanliness had once been points of honor, but these survivors were slovenly and ill-dressed, with the men openly showing worry and depression. And though their expressionless faces hid their feelings, the women seemed shapeless in their baggy *mompei*. Only the children were lively as they waved and shouted, "Chokoreito! Gummu!" at the professor. But he had no chocolate or gum to throw them, and he winced to see how they had been transformed into little beggars.

The road wound down into the plain between Yokohama and Tokyo. What had once been a fifteen-mile stretch of houses and factories was now flattened debris, a wilderness of rubble. All that rose from the flatlands, like crude memorials to the dead, were the tall, gaunt chimneys of bathhouses, charred metal poles, and a few remnants of stone buildings. Of the wood-and-paper houses only ash remained.

At the outskirts of Tokyo he saw row upon row of tiny shacks constructed from scarred strips of metal and stone, mute remnants of firebombings. It was a vast shantytown, a charred Hooverville. In the heart of the city many hotels and mansions seemed untouched, though surrounded by ruins. But there were few visible landmarks, and he was lost until the car approached the Palace grounds. Then he recognized buildings and streets. Yes, there was the Imperial Hotel and nearby the Dai Ichi Life Insurance Building, and across the avenue the Palace grounds seemed intact. But these survivors in the midst of rubble only turned the incredible into reality. Yes, he thought, this was what remained of Tokyo, and we had done it.

He assumed they would stop at the Dai Ichi Building since practically everyone in the civilized world knew it was the headquarters of the new shogun, MacArthur. As the drab staff car hurried past, the professor complained, only to be informed that POLAD, the Office of the U.S. Political Adviser, was eight blocks away. McGlynn had been told he was to serve directly under George Atcheson who was running the State Department shop in Tokyo, and he had assumed that Atcheson would have his office at headquarters. He was greeted warmly by Atcheson's executive secretary who gave him a tongue-in-cheek excuse for the sad state of the cluttered, overcrowded, dimly lit and heatless rooms before turning him over to a plump, towheaded young career diplomat named Harrison with a disarmingly cherubic face that made him look far younger and more innocent than he was.

"I haven't read any of your books," said Harrison, awed by the hawk-faced professor.

"I don't trust anyone who says they've read *all* my books. Nobody has read *all* of my books." He grinned, and the hawk face seemed less formidable to Harrison.

"You'll soon find out," he said in a high-pitched voice, "that you have just joined the ranks of the damned. We are outcasts, lepers, and undesirables. The President originally set us up as something called 'political advisers,' but the general . . ." (he bowed reverently, with eyes piously shut, toward the Dai Ichi Building) "could not stomach such nomenclature, so they refer to us as the Diplomatic Section. Which only means that we have been very cleverly frozen out of just about everything. Note, for instance, the eight blocks separating us from the Holy Temple." All communications to and from Washington had to go through SCAP. "That stands for Supreme Commander for the Allied Powers. Mac for short. I hope you're not shocked, but I've been here since August and I'm shell-shocked. Every so often one of the general's toadies throws us a few crumbs, but we're barred from all determinations of policy. In other words, we who have been trained to deal with the Japanese are overridden by Army officers whose idea of diplomacy is a machine-gun burst. End of lecture. Let me take you to your hovel. I *do* mean your hotel."

During the hour it took to get transportation Harrison elaborated on the sad state of affairs. "We have just received a War Department film called *Your Job in Japan* for troop information. The commentator starts out by saying, 'Remember! The Japs are not to be trusted!' "

Harrison helped the professor carry his luggage into the Dai Ichi Hotel, a long walk from MacArthur's headquarters. It had been designed to house visitors to the ill-fated 1940 Olympics. Now it was an Allied billet for those of some rank but not high enough to get into the Imperial Hotel. "It's noisy and crowded," he added. "No Japs allowed here except servants and black marketeers." McGlynn started for his room, but Harrison guided him to the hotel PX. "Give me all your Japanese money," he said. He explained that the yen was worth about six and a half cents, and proceeded to buy the professor his quota of cigarettes, chocolate, and soap.

Harrison then brusquely led the way to a small suite. In one room Army and WAC officers were drinking highballs. After introducing McGlynn to the officers, Harrison hustled him along to the next room where a group of rather well-dressed Japanese were huddled in conversation. Harrison quickly traded the cigarettes, soap, and chocolate for thirty times the original cost.

"You just made, in American money, a profit of twenty-five dollars after paying the Japanese traders ten percent commission. That's just chicken feed. I know a G.I. who, on a bet, ran ten cents' worth of soap up to one hundred and fifty dollars in three days. Penny-ante stuff! Did you know you can trade an old pair of socks and shirt for a genuine silk kimono or a piece of jewelry?" He shook his head at McGlynn's look of distaste. "This is not only sound finance, but a true form of philanthropy. The Japanese desperately need our commodities. When we sell a ten-yen carton of cigarettes for four hundred yen we're combating inflation. But a word of warning: Keep your transactions within reasonable limits. Every so often the Army cracks down."

Harrison good-naturedly carried the bags up to McGlynn's room. "Welcome to the good life," he panted. "You know, the Brits have been on this gravy train for lo these many years. Why shouldn't we hop aboard? Why not live like a king? I couldn't get a life like this back in Kansas unless I was a millionaire."

After McGlynn emptied his luggage into dressers and the closet, he asked Harrison to take him to the Foreign Correspondents Club so he could locate his daughter, Maggie. The young diplomat insisted on taking him by way of the Japanese government offices. "We've been wise enough, or perhaps lazy enough, to let the Japs run their own government. Correction, *make a show* of running things. But the general always has the last word. They still have politicians shouting at each other over there." He pointed at the Diet Building, a commanding edifice looking quasi-Egyptian. "Have you ever seen such a monstrosity?"

They passed a drab building. "That's now being shared by the Finance Ministry and the Home Ministry." Their driver had to slam on the brakes to avoid hitting a sputtering ramshackle Japanese car marked "Navy Department." It was belching out a cloud of smoke. "Charcoal burner," said Harrison. "A symbol of the postwar Japanese Government. It's a pitiful sight, but don't let appearances fool you. The Japs were smart enough to appoint their most efficient administrators to prefectural governorships and liaison offices. And all those miserable-looking chaps running all those miserable-looking offices are doing a first-class job." They had been so efficient and cooperative that MacArthur and Truman had not found it necessary to set up a military government like the one in Germany.

Harrison tapped the driver. "Foreign Correspondents Club," he said. In a few minutes they were on a narrow side street not far from the Imperial Hotel. "There are three major Jap newspapers down here so we call it Shimbun—which means newspaper—Alley." Most of the buildings in the area were gaunt shells. Water gushed from a ruptured main. Ahead was a five-story red brick building standing amidst ruins. "That's Number One Shimbun Alley where the correspondents from the U.S., Britain, France, Holland, Russia, China, the Philippines, and Shangri-La hang out. Used to be a restaurant."

Once inside it was a different world, reminding McGlynn of a glamorous spy movie. Men and women of a dozen nationalities were arguing, chatting, whispering, drinking, smoking, laughing uproariously. A Chinese was apparently trying to wheedle some favor from a young man who looked as if he had just graduated from Yale. A British correspondent had wedged an attractive WAC Lieutenant into a corner and, in the din, was propositioning her in a loud, resonant voice. An American was passing something in a fat envelope to a sly Japanese while a Russian nearby was insisting that a beautiful Eurasian girl have another drink. But what intrigued McGlynn the most was the mélange of spirited arguments about the issues of the day: the bashing of the huge financial empires, the *zaibatsu;* the purge of big government officials; retention of the emperor system; and the coming war crimes trial. Everyone had a marked opinion. Everyone had a solution. It was chaotic but invigorating, and for the first time McGlynn felt he was really at the most exciting place in the world at one of the most exciting times in history. A crushed Eastern nation was being recreated in the image of the Western conquerors. An incredible if ridiculous experiment was in motion, and the infectious enthusiasm of both sides stirred McGlynn. A burst of laughter came from a boisterous group at one end of the crowded room where a woman was berating a Russian journalist to the delight of the crowd. It was Maggie! She was making a retort he couldn't quite hear. This brought another burst of laughter. Then she caught sight of the tall, slender man with a shock of silver hair that made his craggy face seem youthful.

"Daddy!" she exclaimed and burst through the crowd, her impish face bright with excitement. There was a pause as they stared at each other. Then they embraced, she exuberantly, he with embarrassment. She was so excited he couldn't get half of what she said in the bedlam. Her black hair, cut short, gave her a gamine look. She wore little if any makeup and her correspondent's uniform was crumpled and stained. It seemed, thought McGlynn, that she was doing everything possible to hide her natural beauty. And he wished she didn't exude so much energy and spew out so many expletives.

After introducing him to half a dozen people, she guided him outside to a battered car. "We're going to see the Todas," she said, and began maneuvering the vehicle through Tokyo's wreckage to visit Floss and their closest friends in Japan.

He was stunned to find Maggie no longer the fresh-faced girl reporter he had last met in Hawaii just before she took off for the war in the Pacific. That was only a year ago but it seemed a decade. In her face were lines of suffering and a strange hardness. She was chattering about her twin, Mark. He was still near Nagasaki with his Marine battalion, the 1/6, but had arranged a leave over Christmas. "How is Will?" she asked with concern. "He was a skeleton when I saw him in Nagasaki."

"He's recovering fast, but he still looks washed out. When I last saw him he seemed content in Boston with his new law firm."

She stopped at the upraised hand of a small Japanese traffic policeman who stood on a platform. Next to him was an American M.P. Although standing on the pavement, he towered a foot above the Japanese.

PART ONE

"Hi, Maggie," said the M.P. "Remember me on Okinawa? I'm the guy that had to arrest you for coming ashore without orders."

"Aren't you the one who told me to give the brass hell?"

"That's right, honey." He nudged the Japanese. "Let the lady through, Tojo."

As they approached the Toda residence in Azabu, they passed piles of rubble. The street was pocked with deep holes, but what appalled McGlynn most was the destruction and the rubbish strewn everywhere. The sad state of the Japanese tugged at his heart. In pre-war days this area had been graceful and dignified with many gracious mansions of high-ranking personages. The famed shopping section of Juban had also been damaged by fire but shopkeepers were back in business in makeshift structures, and the street was lively as swarms of people shopped for food and other necessities. In areas cleared by compulsory evacuation for safety from firebombing, people who had lost their houses had moved in to set up underground shelters as temporary living quarters. Now that peace had come, most of these unfortunates had moved out but some still lived in jerry-built shacks.

The Toda home appeared intact. Leaving the car in the middle of the street, they walked through the aged wooden gate doors and along stepping-stones. The iris pond in the center of the garden was a pool of stagnant water, and the little stream that had wandered gracefully through the grounds was clogged with debris and grass. The surviving garden trees were charred, sad memorials of the lost war. There was little alive except the huge hagi bushes, hardy as the people. These deep-rooted perennials had fattened despite fire and neglect, giving this bleak place promise of shade and flowering beauty in the coming summer.

Floss McGlynn Toda, widow of the eldest Toda son, was at the entrance hall in her getas, wooden clogs. All she could do was say, "Daddy!" and lay her face on his shoulder. Tall and composed, she was the antithesis of her sister. At first glance she seemed plain, but the discerning soon were captivated by her soft blue eyes and warm personality. She was wearing a worn, many-patched dress—but with style. McGlynn hadn't seen his daughter in almost four years. Since then she had barely survived in enemy land, losing a husband and two babies. He held her at arm's length, and it pained him to find her so thin and haggard with much of her once black hair now streaked with gray. On her wedding day she had looked so bonny, like her mother.

Floss turned to the boy who had been standing at her side and said, "This is Masao, your grandson."

Shy, he respectfully held out his right hand. He seemed a lot more Japanese than American. McGlynn could not hide his shock at the sight of an empty left sleeve. It was hard getting the words out, but Floss explained that on the day before the surrender a U.S. Navy pilot had swept down to strafe Masao when he ran out to save a precious chicken. "You never told me . . ." he began.

"There was too much to tell. We lost little Maggie two weeks ago." This baby had been their second to die of malnutrition. She couldn't hold back tears. "Poor little Maggie seemed to fade away," she said.

Maggie, fighting her own tears, embraced her sister.

The professor felt helpless and guilty. Without any complaints Floss had devoted herself, after his wife died, to keeping his family together. And he had let her sacrifice years of her life, treating her, in his own self-pity, more like a servant than a daughter. Now the war had taken her husband and two babies and crippled her son. With some awkwardness he put an arm around his older daughter. "I'm sorry," he said, his throat thick with the emotion he had kept under control for years.

Floss grasped him tighter. For years she had bottled up her own feelings, fearing a rebuff from this strange, reserved man. But a few tears slowly running down his cheeks spoke more eloquently than any words. "Oh, Daddy! It's *so* good to have you here!" He wished he could express his feelings but didn't know how. In her own grief she tried to comfort him. "Everything is going to be all right, Daddy."

Inside, Emi, the mother of the Toda family, was waiting expectantly. Still slight and willowy, as a girl she had been a *moga*, a modern girl. On the eve of her arranged marriage, she had refused to go through with the ceremony. Then, to her family's horror, she had married a Christian, Akira Toda, and embraced not only Christianity but social reforms, and when Akira was sent to China in 1942 to manage a steel mill she alone had kept her little family together. Forewarned that Professor McGlynn might come that afternoon, Emi was wearing a precious kimono. It was their first meeting since 1936, but they greeted each other with "How do you do, Emi?" and "Frank, how are you?" in the style both had borrowed from the English, burying their true feelings under a calmness resembling indifference.

But their feelings soon broke down the barriers of formality and they embraced with spontaneous warmth. Each was so eager to find out about the other that there was a babel of voices. McGlynn insisted first on hearing about Akira, one of his few close friends.

"Last week we finally got a letter brought by a merchant friend." Akira was still in central China. "The Kuomintang troops have taken over the ore mine he managed and he hopes to be home in six months." He was in good health and busy organizing activities for the Japanese employees who had nothing to do.

McGlynn noticed Sumiko, the only daughter, hiding in the background. Neat in her homemade trousers, blouse, and a sweater, the fifteen-year-old girl shyly bowed. "You're not really little Sumiko! You only came up to here!" He indicated a point four feet high and everyone laughed. But when he asked about Ko, her youngest brother whose dream was to be an artist, tears welled in Sumiko's eyes.

"He was sent to Leyte as a private," said Emi. "We haven't heard anything from him. I know many of our men died there but I feel he is still alive." She put an arm around her daughter. "I know he is, Sumiko."

The news about the middle brother, Shogo, was even worse. "He is in Sugamo Prison. You knew he was on Colonel Tsuji's staff." Tsuji had been revered by younger officers as Japan's "God of Operations," the hope of the Orient. He had dreamed of making Asia one great brotherhood, but his hatred of whites had led him to commit many atrocities during the war.

"Maggie told me all about it."

"Shogo's going to be tried down in Yokohama for terrible things Tsuji did in the Philippines and in Burma."

"That's ridiculous!" said McGlynn.

Emi could not bring herself to ask him to help. "Shogo is a good boy and could never have done what they're accusing him of."

"I'm sure of that," he said, humbled by the tragedies and hardships the Todas had endured. All of them had been scarred by a cruel war he had only read about. The historian in him took over and he said, "It is impossible for an American to understand what it means to lose a war and know that enemy troops will soon land and take over your country. What was it like in those first days?"

"We were up in Nagano to escape the bombings when we heard the

Emperor. It was hard to understand what he was saying, but we all knew it meant the war was over. We were in the waiting room of the hospital where Masao was being treated, and we silently rejoiced because we knew what Americans were like. But the others in the room were petrified. They were sure girls and women would be raped and the men beaten or killed."

McGlynn persuaded her to tell of her trip to Tokyo the day after the surrender. "The train was packed, but I found a place on a bench in the third class." People on all sides were wondering what would happen to the Emperor and the high officials. "There was talk of rape and pillage just as a Japanese major came in. Ordinarily people would jump up to give him a seat but nobody moved. He glared at the old man sitting next to me, but the old man just glared back. The major tried to push his way through to the next car but nobody budged. He began to shout and make threats, but people looked at him indifferently and a man shouted, 'Who do you think you are? You lost the war, didn't you?' The major was so furious he drew out his sword. But people stared at him as if he were crazy. No one was afraid. He was so shocked I was almost sorry for him. I was close and his face seemed to say, 'The world has gone mad.' Perplexed, he sheathed his sword and edged his way out of the car. No one in the car spoke for some time as if we were all amazed at our own power. We had challenged and beaten the almighty army."

Everyone had listened in fascination and Emi seemed to have forgotten her own tragedies while reporting the incident. "What happened when you got to Tokyo?" urged McGlynn.

"You never saw such a dead city," said Emi. "It was so quiet when I stepped out of the subway station that it was frightening. The streets were deserted. Such filth! The gutters were clogged with papers and rubble. I strapped on my knapsack and hurried towards Azabu to get a breath of clean air. But the farther I walked the dirtier it became. The air had that oppressive feeling you notice just before a typhoon." She told how the traffic grew a little heavier as she finally neared Azabu. Some of the homes were undamaged, others were mere shells. She was relieved to find their own home intact, if filthy. A neighbor and her son arrived to congratulate her; they too had been lucky. The young man, a former fighter pilot, had survived two crashes. "He told

me he'd never fight another war but at the same time he felt going
into battle had given him a purpose in living. 'For victory,' he told me,
'we were all willing to sacrifice our lives. Now that purpose is gone.' "
Emi sighed. "Many of us seem to have lost our purpose in life."

Chapter Two

1.

Japan, August 15, 1945.

The nation had been stunned that day to hear the Emperor speak for the first time ever to his people. Everyone knew it meant the end of their former way of life. The entire nation was awed, and men as well as women and children sobbed openly. Yet underneath the universal humiliation and sorrow lay relief. The dreadful war was at last over.

The Emperor did not mention surrender in his short talk and the official announcement referred only to the "termination of war." Then came confirmation that the feared and hated enemy would soon land on Japanese soil. The newspapers called this invading horde the "Advancing Army," using a phrase formerly applied to the victorious Japanese armed forces. It was a face-saving device designed to curb panic. Wild rumor succeeded wild rumor: the Chinese were landing in Osaka; parachuting Americans were already looting and raping. Those with means evacuated their daughters and family treasures to the country. The newspapers printed advice that only brought more terror. "When in danger of being raped," women were warned, "show the most dignified attitude. Don't yield. Cry for help." Factories issued poison capsules to women workers. And girls were instructed to wear their bulkiest mompei or cut their hair and pretend to be boys.

Japanese began acting in violation of centuries of form and habit. Some lost their heads, fleeing wildly to the mountains in commandeered vehicles and stealing government gasoline stored in mountain depots. Order, the base of Japanese life, collapsed in many places with people in frenzy driven to the most selfish means to survive.

Yet after the first hours of panic most of the nation returned to general orderliness. Outwardly there was a quiet and restrained atmosphere, for the people were accepting without reservation the word of the Emperor. Yet it was a tense time of waiting, as for an approaching typhoon. The Advancing Army was about to swarm over their nation like locusts. After years of propaganda about the red-haired, blue-eyed savages, the people were resigned to facing overbearing masters, conquerors from an alien culture who would avenge the death of their comrades on the battlefield. They would be callous to the suffering and starvation of their victims. Like conquerors of old they would loot, beat, and take any woman who pleased them. The coming of this horde would be worse than the bombs of the dreaded Bees, the B-29s. These arrogant victors would also regard the obedience of the Japanese to the Emperor as cowardice and think their soldiers had laid down their arms only because they were afraid to fight. These ignorant *gaijin*—these foreigners—would never understand that obedience to their Emperor was a far greater demonstration of selfless devotion than to have fought gallantly to the last man.

Despite the show of calm it was unsafe to go out at night because robbery, once so rare, had become common after dark. Even in Tokyo there was such a scarcity of electric bulbs that the streets were dark. And whenever new lights were installed they would be stolen by morning. Practically every major city in Japan had been devastated by the firebombings, and with the almost complete absence of green vegetation the entire urban landscape was now a monotonous gray, brown, or black. And the variety of smells included the stenches of urine, excrement, garbage, and sewer gas. Worst of all was the over-ruling pungent, sickening stink of burned-out buildings which persisted as lethal reminders of defeat no matter how often the wreckage had been washed by rains or ventilated by winds. Thousands and thousands of stricken areas had turned the nation into a vast, untidy graveyard.

Trolleys still ran in the capital, but there were few cars and trucks. Most of those who had fled to the country to escape the bombings had not yet returned. And so Tokyo, along with other once bustling cities, was eerily quiet. Turning on electric lights was a gamble, as electric failure was frequent and even when a bulb did light it was dim. Because it was almost impossible to find adequate food, survival seemed hopeless for many. Hunger ranged over the cities with the added fear that the Advancing Army would take what was available for themselves.

The farmers feared starvation, for it was predicted the harvest would be poor. Rice, the staff of life, was still unharvested, but it was obvious there would be far too little to last through the coming winter. During the past spring, war had been the nation's chief concern and not much seed had been sown, and a few months later there had not been enough able-bodied men to plant new shoots. And now with complete defeat it was obvious to everyone that Manchuria and Korea were also lost as colonies. Nor would any food be coming from Taiwan and the Asian mainland.

Villagers as well as city dwellers shared the fear of the Advancing Army. Never before had foreign troops invaded their land and now they were about to endure humiliation, disgrace, beatings, and perhaps even death. In one village an hour north of Tokyo when the elders discussed how to survive, one man recommended they select the best-looking women to act as their first line of defense. "Every enemy turns into a friend," he said, "when he's given the right woman."

The children of that village were the most hopeful. On the first day of school after a long absence, they found the school with the windows still broken and the Rising Sun still flying on the flagpole. Then the elderly principal ordered the flag to be lowered, "because Japan lost the war."

As the students entered the main classroom a teacher was taking down the portrait of His Majesty. She placed it on the floor, face to the wall. "Children," she said, "we are now free people. Do you understand?" They no longer had to live and die for the Emperor or for Japan. "Starting today we live only for ourselves." She wrote on the blackboard two ideograms. "One means 'self' and the other 'performance.' Together they mean 'freedom.' And that means that from now on we are spiritually free and what we do is only for ourselves, not the Emperor or the country."

A few days later newspapers throughout the nation showed a picture of MacArthur stepping down from his plane, pipe in hand, like a civilian, not a great general. He was wearing a battered, sweat-stained cap and a plain open-necked khaki shirt with no decorations or insignia except the five-star circle on each collar tab and jacket shoulder straps. Everyone had expected him to arrive with proper pomp and ceremony, in full military regalia, his chest covered with medals, his face arrogant. But he even wore sunglasses! In Japan, only the blind or actors desiring anonymity wore such glasses to hide the eyes.

At last came the dreaded Advancing Army. These were battle-scarred G.I.'s and Marines who were neither threatening nor fearsome. Most of them smiled and waved from trucks. They threw pieces of candy and gum to the children and whistled at the girls. These big soldiers all seemed ordinary, and they all looked alike. They wore their hats the same way, tilted to one side. How peculiar and casual it looked to those used to seeing every Japanese soldier wearing his sacred military cap uniformly straight and his penis to the left. Any deviation in either case would have been severely punished. The only uniformity of these strange men from America seemed to be their friendliness.

They walked through the streets and lanes as if they, like their famous commander, were civilians. Unlike Japanese soldiers who had strutted down the street clattering their swords and stamping their boots, the Americans strolled by as if each man was his own master. Although they had been pictured as brutal and uncouth, one terrified old woman watched in wonder as three huge Marines took off their combat boots before tentatively entering a Buddhist temple. In Yokohama the headmaster of a boys' school, upon abruptly encountering his first G.I. on the street, handed over his precious Leica camera. "Thank you," he said in English, "for not shooting me."

It soon became apparent that the Advancing Army, despite its informality, was efficient and strong. The Japanese watched in awe as long lines of trucks and jeeps spread over the country. Even the lowliest private, it seemed, could drive any kind of vehicle with verve. The Americans did everything with dispatch, from repairing a motor to setting up a Quonset hut. Because the G.I.'s were nonchalant in their generosity, there were few instances of rape or overbearing conduct. And the Japanese responded with universal docility. Some of the occupiers imagined the Japanese were merely opportunistic, but this peaceful acceptance of the American troops was in line with an old Japanese proverb: "Whichever side wins is the Emperor's army. Whichever side loses is the rebel army." During the many shifts of power in Japan, the victorious shogun had always issued his commands in the name of the Emperor, who, being the descendant of the Sun-Goddess, was the one constant source of equation in Japan. Now the Advancing Army was no longer an alien force, and MacArthur had become the new conquering shogun. One old farmer, asked by a foreign correspondent what he thought of the general, replied, "The Emperor could not have picked a better man."

MacArthur had already been flooded with letters thanking him for saving the nation and approving his policies for the future. Captain Mark McGlynn, younger son of the professor, found this same acceptance of the new regime in the town north of Nagasaki where the 1st Battalion of the Sixth Marines was now stationed. A local policeman declared he was grateful to MacArthur for bringing Japan peace. "It seemed as if the war would never end and then all at once it was all over."

"Does everyone around here agree with you?" asked Mark.

"I'd say almost everyone."

"Even the police?"

He nodded. "We all admire how you behave to the people. Your troops are an inspiration to us, and if that is what democracy is I'm for it."

At first the people of Kyushu had been terrified of the Marines, for it was rumored that a man had to prove he had murdered his mother or father before he could be accepted in the Corps. This canard gained credence a few days later when an embittered corporal who had lost his best friend in Saipan gave a boy a carton. He told the youngster to remove the cover and dump the contents into his father's hands. Inside was a grenade with the pin pulled. Both parents were killed, and the boy was badly wounded. Since then the battalion had moved north toward Sasebo and become heroes to the children, who brought them to their homes for dinner. Under the leadership of Gunnery Sergeant Kelly, nicknamed The Beast, money was raised to set up an orphanage similar to the one Marines had founded in New Zealand. Kelly had become revered in the town ever since the battalion had been sent to a nearby coal mine to quell a rioting group of Chinese Communist workers who had captured the mayor, the chief of police, and other officials, demanding transportation back to China. Otherwise, they threatened, they would kill the hostages.

"Tell the mother-lovers," Kelly told an interpreter, "to go ahead and kill those people. And then we'll come in with a flame-thrower to clean up what's left." These few words released the hostages, and the next day Kelly solved another problem after two of the same dissident Chinese started a riot in a house of prostitution. Through sign language and a pocket dictionary he learned that the Chinese wanted their money back on the grounds that the girls had not been satisfactory. Without a word Kelly threw two of them out the second-story window, then came down and told the others that if they wanted to go back to China they'd have to swim for it.

That evening the elders of the town advised their people to accept the inevitable. Their conquerors were no longer enemies but protectors. Henceforth they should be tolerated even though they didn't take off their shoes indoors, ate too much meat, and were so tall.

2.

Tokyo, November 28, 1945.

McGlynn had come to Japan six weeks earlier fearing he would serve no useful purpose and already mentally writing out his resignation. He had done little since except compose useless reports, and spent most of his time searching for material on the six months preceding Pearl Harbor. What irked him most was that MacArthur, who had personally demanded his immediate presence, hadn't even asked to see him. MacArthur's noble experiment, particularly his naïve attempt to impose American-style democracy on Japan, was obviously doomed. The professor's first long talk with Atcheson, who merely bore the title of Minister, had been unsettling. George A., as he was affectionately called behind his back, had been an experienced and able professional diplomat. He had spent most of his time overseas in China, and he spoke Mandarin fluently. Like other old China hands he was bent on imposing an iron-hand policy on the Japanese. "The situation over here is still confused," he confessed. "I'm not even sure what my relationship with GHQ is, and I find it difficult at times to determine what I'm supposed to be doing." He hurried to assure McGlynn that his personal relations with MacArthur were amicable but then he smiled ruefully and added, "Though I must admit they are not as intimate or understanding as I'd like."

The other China hands in the office generally agreed with their chief, and despite rumors at the Dai Ichi Hotel that all these diplomats had been brainwashed by Mao, young Harrison ridiculed the notion. "I'm a hard-rock Republican from Kansas—take my word, these diplomats are just like the other faithful followers of Roosevelt's New Deal, full of good intentions and gullible." Harrison's face broke into an ingenuous grin that was endearing. At first the professor had been turned off by the towhead's breeziness, but he had grown to appreciate the chubby young man's good-natured bluntness. "They're all very decent but so damned sure they're right about everything. I heard one of George A.'s junior cronies talking about you yesterday. 'If you know too damned much about Japan,' this jerk said, 'you might be prejudiced! We don't need any old-time Japan hands around here.'"

What most troubled McGlynn was Atcheson's remark that the Emperor system must disappear if Japan was ever to be truly democratic. "And if it's at all feasible I'd really like to see the old has-been tried as a war criminal." When McGlynn could not hide a look of dismay, the Minister smiled and went on, "I'm afraid that may be out of the question. His trial could cause such a stink that it would be impossible to find any competent men to form a government. I'm still on the fence."

McGlynn forced himself to remain silent, deciding to reserve his advice for MacArthur—if he was ever summoned to the general's office. McGlynn had spent hours wandering around the city looking in vain for old friends and trying to absorb the sheer extent of the devastation. In Shibuya Ward he came upon a former student from Aoyama College and spent an afternoon in his tiny unheated apartment. He had been one of McGlynn's brightest pupils, but was now despondent and confused. His wife and daughter had died in the bombings and only one of his two sons had survived battle. The survivor, Shigeru, arrived with two classmates from Tokyo Imperial University. Although shabby he was spirited and reminded McGlynn of the father when he had been a student. Shigeru laughed when McGlynn asked in Japanese if it was hard to study when hungry. "Every time I try to study the *Essays of Elia* I can only think of a leg of lamb." The other two students laughed at this academic reference to Charles Lamb, and described their own wild visions of food. "But we're not asking for any handouts," said Shigeru in English. The other two asked if they also could try out their miserable English. "I like Makasa," said one.

"MacArthur, stupid," corrected Shigeru who had learned English from his father.

"Do you think he is too tough on you?" asked McGlynn.

The three competed to shout that he should be even tougher. "That's the only way to stop the damned black market."

"Do you think the Emperor should be tried as a war criminal?"

One shouted in the affirmative, *"Hai!"*, the other said it would be an insult to all Japan, and Shigeru shrugged indifference. "Who cares who's tried? I wish they'd hang all the stupid generals."

"What about giving women the vote?"

All three laughed derisively. "They'd all sell their vote for a pair of stockings!" said Shigeru.

What did they think of the Soviet Union? They made sour faces. They didn't think much of China either, and the only good thing about the British was their poets. But they had always liked Americans even when they were supposed to be hating them during the war.

"Why can't America send us food?" complained Shigeru's father. And for once Shigeru agreed with him.

The professor felt useless. His latest assignment was to write a study of the revolutionary Constitution set up by Emperor Meiji, the grandfather of Hirohito, which would have to be drastically changed to make it democratic. What a fruitless task! When the day's work ended he would avoid the Dai Ichi Hotel, except to eat hurriedly and again wander the streets. He seemed driven to view over and over this Tokyo that was no longer *his* Tokyo. Out of fear of germs and catching colds, many men, women, and children now wore nose masks making them resemble grotesque refugees from a vast operating room. What particularly shocked him was the rancid body odor of people once so scrupulously clean and now forced to live like cattle.

Every so often he would come upon piles of tin, tiles, and bits of brick carefully stacked with Japanese neatness for some unimaginable future use. He was fascinated by the unpainted jerry-built frame shops and shacks sprouting amidst the ruins of Shibuya. A new suburb of hovels had grown like weeds over the lifeless wilderness.

Late on the morning of November 28 McGlynn was called into Minister Atcheson's office to be informed that General MacArthur wanted to see him in the afternoon. While sitting in his little cubicle the professor hastily jotted down items to discuss and to save time he ate a sandwich lunch at his desk. He guessed he would have ten minutes and most of that would be spent in listening to the general. Perhaps he'd have two or three minutes for making comments. The Americans he'd met were in no mood to listen to facts that contradicted their preconceptions. Should he bring up the folly of trying to reform Japan in the American image? He was appalled by the problems involved in the effort to import a foreign kind of democracy and the lack of qualified people, moreover, to carry it out. The occupation seemed to be in the hands of young, idealistic Democratic New Deal economists, political scientists, and law graduates with little or no practical experience and no knowledge whatsoever of Japanese customs.

There was only one thing left. Shake SCAP's hand (if that was allowed), listen patiently, and then ask to be sent back home. To hell with him. The stories Will had reported of MacArthur's arrogance and pomposity were undoubtedly true. He hoped he could keep a straight face if, upon entering the great man's room, he found him, as Harrison had predicted, clenching between his teeth the famous corncob pipe.

Harrison insisted on escorting him to the Dai Ichi Building. "Someone must protect you from the Bataan Gang protecting the general." It annoyed McGlynn beyond reason that those cronies from the Philippines who now surrounded MacArthur were given this nickname. To his knowledge not a one had ever fought there. They all had managed to get safely to Australia. It was an insult to those like his son who had suffered through the torture of the Death March.

En route Harrison amused the professor with MacArthur stories. "When local workmen at the Dai Ichi unloaded a huge carpet for the general's office, they found it was too large. They expected the American colonel in charge to order them to cut the carpet to size. Instead he said, 'Move the wall back.' The Japs protested that it was made of steel. 'This is General MacArthur's *personal* property,' said the colonel. 'So move the damned wall back, get the job done by the end of the week, and let me hear no more about this.' No wonder the Japs think he is a god. By the way, don't try to correct any of his pronunciations. He thinks *hara-kiri* should be hah-Rick-ery!"

Harrison explained that the general refused to have a telephone in his room, on the sensible grounds that the ringing would interrupt his conversations. "On the other hand he insists on opening all mail addressed to him. He's the most accessible god the Japs ever had. All they have to do is write him a letter."

As they neared the headquarters, Harrison told how the custodian of the building one morning put a vase of chrysanthemums on MacArthur's desk. The next day General Sutherland, the chief of staff, asked for chrysanthemums, and by the end of the week the diligent custodian was spending hours delivering 'mums all over the building. "When MacArthur heard that the Japanese government was paying for all the flowers, he ordered that any officers at GHQ wishing chrysanthemums would have to pay for them. The Japanese people, he said, had enough trouble surviving without paying for American luxuries."

They were met in the lobby of the Dai Ichi Building by a brisk colonel and taken by elevator to the top floor, the sixth. Harrison pointed to a door that bore no inscription. "The height of pomposity," he whispered. "I'll wait out here. Abandon hope all ye who enter."

The colonel guided McGlynn through a small anteroom and into a spacious but unostentatious walnut-paneled room. MacArthur was sitting behind a large desk covered with green baize. There was no telephone, no clutter of papers, only a note pad and several pencils. The general *was* clenching a long, unlit corncob pipe, and McGlynn had to control a grin.

The general rose and came forward, hand outstretched. He was taller than McGlynn expected and had less hair. In newsreels or photographs he always wore his crumpled cap. He was an extraordinarily handsome man, commanding and vigorous with a look of youthful freshness. His skin was clear and firm, and he appeared much younger than his sixty-six years. McGlynn had expected a domineering, arrogant face. But his mouth, though firm, was sensitive, and while exuding self-confidence he did not seem overbearing.

He did look tired, but he brightened once he began to speak. "I'm certainly glad to see you, Professor McGlynn." He nodded toward a comfortable brown leather sofa. The general sank into a large leather armchair as the colonel left the room. "I imagine you have been told so many things about me that you don't quite know what to expect."

McGlynn couldn't help smiling and was sensible enough to make no comment. Harrison had warned him that the only time to ask questions was when MacArthur stopped talking in order to light his pipe which would keep going out.

"I know you don't agree with me that before the war this country represented an extreme form of fascist feudalism," MacArthur began. "That was the tragedy of Japan's present, and our democratic political ideals are responsible for the strength of America's present." As he spoke he gestured constantly with his sensitive, slim hands, and the one that held the pipe trembled. He delivered his lines sonorously, McGlynn thought, with the effectiveness of a seasoned actor. "In fact, being over here is almost like reading the pages of mythology." He stared past McGlynn as if peering into another world. "These people have little or no realization of how the rest of the world lives. And it is my great mission to make this a vast laboratory for an experiment in liberating the people from totalitarian military rule and for the liberalization of government from within." With head reared back, chin jutting, and an evangelical look on his face, he reminded McGlynn of Moses propounding the Ten Commandments. Abruptly the general vaulted to his feet, took two long steps to his desk, grabbed a box of matches, and rattled it over his head like a saber. "Measured by our standards the Japanese have the minds of twelve-year-old kids. And we must treat them like children who must be brought into democracy, not with harshness but with stern kindness."

He lit his pipe and now was the time—but McGlynn didn't even attempt to ask any questions. What was the use?

"My greatest fear, and you may agree with me, is the sad state of our international relations." General MacArthur shook his aquiline head dolefully. "The Russian Bear! Can we stop Communist expansion? As you know, Stalin first demanded that Red Army troops occupy the northern part of Japan. Fortunately the President refused, but then he suggested that token Soviet forces be employed here temporarily to carry out the surrender terms if I considered this necessary. I had to put my foot down. Politely, of course. Can you imagine the chaos if I had given in?" He got up once more and began pacing up and down, puffing on his pipe. He seemed far away as he spoke grammatically, with deliberation and in carefully phrased sentences, yet managing to round out each idea dramatically.

"My next greatest fear—and I ask you not to repeat this over in your shop—is Washington. Their top priority, as usual, is Europe. I wouldn't put it past Washington to weaken my authority here in order to gain concessions from Stalin in Europe. There is talk of a four-power commission to rule Japan. If that happens, what do you think I should do?"

"Go home."

MacArthur gave a start, then laughed. "All right, what should I do with the Chinaman?"

McGlynn assumed he was referring to China in general. "I'd watch my step."

This also pleased MacArthur. "I never did believe you could trust Mao."

This disheartened McGlynn, who had interviewed both Mao and Chou En-lai after the historic Long March. "I was also referring to Chiang."

MacArthur surveyed him shrewdly. "How do you like your assignment?"

McGlynn replied promptly, "I'm not sure I know what it is. Even if I did know, I'm not sure I could be of any use over here." He was about to ask to be sent home when MacArthur picked up a book from his desk. It was *When East Met West*.

"Bonner Fellers insisted I read it."

McGlynn remembered Fellers as one of the few army officers he had met in pre-war Japan who had any understanding of her problems.

"Some things you wrote disturbed me. But you made me think. That's why I requested you come as soon as possible. I need people like you who are not afraid to go against the tide."

McGlynn felt gooseflesh. "I was on the point of asking you to let me go home."

"I guessed as much. I could feel that you disapproved of a number of things." He held up the book. "I like the way you hammer directly at something."

"I don't believe a historian should be diplomatic."

The general relit his pipe for the tenth time, then gestured with it. "I have enough diplomats—enough yea-sayers. And I could use at least one nay-sayer."

"What about the Emperor?" McGlynn asked abruptly, jutting out his hawk nose.

MacArthur told about their first meeting. "He was extremely nervous, and I was afraid he was going to beg me not to indict him as a war criminal. But instead he said, 'I bear sole responsibility.' And I knew in that instant I faced the First Gentleman of Japan."

"Did you know that Kido had begged him to take *no* responsibility?"

"Who told you that?"

"My good friend Marquis Kido, who did his best to prevent war and who will undoubtedly be indicted as a war criminal."

"I too am disturbed, McGlynn. The principle of holding the political leaders of the vanquished as criminally responsible in war is repugnant to me. It violates the most fundamental rules of criminal justice. But I can assure you of one thing. Despite the insistence of the Russians, the British, the Japanese Communists, and many influential Americans including the New York *Times*, who want him to hang, I shall never allow the Emperor to be tried as a war criminal. Count on it!"

"Does that mean I can see the Marquis Kido if he is arrested?"

"Not *if* but *when*. And when that day arrives I shall consider your request."

As the professor rose to leave, MacArthur remarked how impressed he was with Maggie's unprejudiced reporting. He was also pleased to hear that McGlynn's son Will, whom he had seen several times in the Philippines, had survived. "Your older daughter, I hear, is also quite a determined lady. It must run in the family. I understand she has been making waves at the Public Health and Welfare Section."

"In what way?" asked the puzzled McGlynn.

"She seems to feel that the Japanese should be getting much more food. Colonel Sams assures me there is no famine and won't be. And she wants Public Health and Welfare to sponsor her proposed home for war orphans." MacArthur shook McGlynn's hand, then escorted him politely to the door. "Thank you for coming."

McGlynn left the room with his face a study in stupefaction.

"You're as pale as a ghost," said Harrison. "What happened?"

"I'm staying," he said quietly. "Indefinitely."

3.

Boston, November 27, 1945.

In Boston it was, thanks to the International Date Line, only the twenty-seventh. At the top of General Marshall's letter to Will Mc-Glynn was the address of his farm near Washington. The forceful scrawl of his handwriting brought back memories of those hectic pre-Pearl Harbor days at the chief of staff's office in the old wooden structure containing the headquarters of the Army. During that time his numerous notes to Will were signed G.C.M. This letter, little more than a note, was signed simply as if he were a civilian. Though he had recently resigned as chief of staff, to Will he would always be General Marshall, the man he respected above all others. The two years at his office before being precipitously sent off to the Philippines in December of 1941 to check secretly on MacArthur's heavy demands for more supplies had been the most rewarding in his life. As one of the chief of staff's law officers he had been privileged to observe a remarkable mind at work under pressure. That it had been a demanding assignment only made it more memorable. The general was easy to work for as long as one worked tirelessly and efficiently. But woe to anyone who violated the clock! To Marshall, time was precious and a moment lost could never be regained. Will would never forget the bright young lieutenant who had come up from the South to join the staff. When he arrived two hours late the general peremptorily sent him back to his unit.

Will anxiously glanced at his watch. His taxi was dragging through the crowded streets of Boston that Tuesday morning and his train was leaving South Station in twenty minutes. He was bound for Washington. The general wanted to talk to him about some temporary assignment, probably to edit the notes he had managed to save during his four years of Japanese captivity.

The senior partner of Adams and Snow had summoned him yesterday to say he might expect a letter from General Marshall about an important assignment, adding in his terse and enigmatic manner, "Consult with me later about your course of action."

As he stepped out of the taxi, Will pulled out a two-dollar bill for the

41

fare though he knew the tip was far too large, and put on his gloves. As his long strides carried him across the street into the station, the crisp late autumn air was invigorating, and he even welcomed the momentary swirl of tiny snowflakes that dashed into his face as he broke into a trot. What a delicious feeling after the heat that had oppressed him in the Filipino and Japanese prison camps for more than three years!

He was in his train seat with minutes to spare, but his heart pounded from the exertion. He was relieved but sheepish. Thank God none of his colleagues at Adams and Snow had seen him racing like a West Point plebe late for a class. It was still hard to remember he was a civilian and only going to Washington as a courtesy, not a duty.

On the trip south he read through two Boston papers and the New York *Times*. Back from Japan for almost three months, he still relished the luxury of finding out what was going on all over the world. There was the usual overdose of information on the Pearl Harbor inquiry with the usual Republican efforts to rewrite history. At the Nuremberg war crimes trial the usual ponderous documents were being introduced to show that Hitler had planned to invade Czechoslovakia as early as May 1938. As if everyone hadn't known it long before his troops marched in! It was interesting from a legal point of view, but Will wished that the lawyers at Nuremberg would get down to the main point—the atrocities. What really incensed him was the story on the war crimes trial of General Yamashita in Manila. The butcher in charge of internment camps in Luzon in 1944 was claiming that conditions had been "good" at the Cabanatuan and Santo Tomas prisons and that he had seen no mistreatment or starvation. What crap! Will had been in both of those hellholes and he still hadn't regained all of the seventy pounds he had lost in captivity. The Japanese on trial were no better than the Nazis and they all deserved to be hung!

A grizzled staff sergeant with four hash marks on his sleeve met him at Union Station. He guided Will to a staff car as if he were a walking wounded, and opened the back door but Will got in the front. They drove up the Potomac River, and after some forty miles approached a pleasant farm. The general came out to greet Will warmly. "My boy, how good to see you in one piece!"

Marshall congratulated him on his detailed notes of the last days of fighting on Bataan, the Death March, and the harrowing experiences of the long imprisonment. "We had copies sent over to the Depart-

ment of Justice. They say these will be useful in our war crimes trials."
He explained that the top criminals like Tojo would be tried in an
international military tribunal in Tokyo similar to the one in Nuremberg. Thousands of others of lower rank would be tried for personal
atrocities in lower military courts at Yokohama.

"I asked you here to consider a special assignment. The War Department is selecting a few highly qualified lawyers for the Class A
trial in Tokyo. The Justice Department has already picked most of the
prosecutors, but we'd like to have several men with war experience in
the Pacific who understand the military point of view."

The last thing Will wanted was to return to a country where he had
undergone such hardships. "Sir," he protested, "I had very little battle experience. All I really know about is being a POW."

"Who has a better understanding of the cruelty of the Japanese? I
know what hell you've been through but we need your help." He
explained that influential men like Joseph Clark Grew, the former
Ambassador to Japan, were urging a far less harsh trial than the one
going on in Nuremberg. They opposed not only indicting the Emperor but also trying civilian leaders like the Marquis Kido, the Emperor's chief adviser. "Grew and these other distinguished men . . ."
Including my own father, silently added Will. ". . . such as your
father," said Marshall with a ghost of a smile, "are intelligent and well
informed, yet still are unable to see that nothing is more important
today than teaching the Japanese as well as the Germans that war
itself is a crime. For the first time in history it can be possible to outlaw
war." He spoke of the coming tribunal as a demonstration of democracy to the Japanese people, a sort of crusade for a civilized world.

Despite his feeling of reluctance, Will was moved by Marshall's
quiet eloquence. "I agree, sir, but frankly I have no desire to go back
to Japan even though I still feel it's my second country."

"I don't want you to think we're going to punish the Japanese
people who were just the victims of their leaders," hastily said Marshall, who knew that McGlynn had been raised there by his renowned
father. "We only want to wipe out militarism in Japan, and this will be
for the good of their people. It will be an integral part in the reshaping
of that country, a peaceful crusade for a civilized world."

"I realize that, sir. And I agree that civilian leaders like Kido should
also be brought to trial and punished. But it means a great deal to me
to stay in Boston and live an ordinary existence. Right now I'm pre-

paring a case for a young man unjustly accused of murder during a robbery. His life is in my hands."

"I believe I know how you feel," said Marshall sympathetically. "Just before you arrived I got a call from President Truman. As you may know, Pat Hurley recently spoke out of turn and has resigned as Ambassador to China. Mr. Truman has asked me to replace Pat as special envoy. My wife and I had been looking forward to quiet life after all these years of service. But what could I say?"

"You overrate my importance, sir."

"Not at all. I know how you work and you can take my word that your presence in Tokyo will be felt. As you well know, the President— that is, Mr. Roosevelt—and I had our disagreements with General MacArthur in 1941. Don't get me wrong. I think he is by far the best choice to oversee the occupation of Japan." He noticed the little smile Will couldn't repress. "To be more accurate, the *only* choice."

Will grinned. "You always could read our minds, sir."

"Despite our differences, I sincerely believe MacArthur can do more to straighten out that country than any other man. Yet he has already shown a willingness to be a bit soft. This is for your ears only, but I understand he is the one most instrumental in persuading President Truman not to indict the Emperor, who was just as responsible as Tojo for the war."

Will agreed but was still reluctant.

"You won't have to leave for two months, which will give you time to wind up your work in Boston. The Justice Department tells me you'll be back within six months. And I've already been told by Mr. Snow that I was to feel entirely free to discuss the matter with you. He assured me that if you decided to take the assignment it would not prejudice your position with the firm, which has always tried in any way to be useful to the United States." Marshall studied him with concern. "I'm indeed sorry to put you through this, and I don't want to press you into an immediate answer. Think it over for a week and if you decide you can't go to Japan I won't urge you further. You have already done enough for your country."

As the staff car headed toward Washington, Will felt relieved. He'd wait a week and then send in a polite refusal. But on the train back to Boston he was unable to read. His thoughts were crowded with memories of the years of captivity and his vow to make his captors pay for what they had done if by a miracle he survived.

The following afternoon he requested a few minutes of the senior partner's time. Ephraim Snow was tall and spare. His mere authoritative appearance in a courtroom seemed to spell success. Grandson of one of the founders of Adams and Snow, his skill in presenting evidence, along with his powers of persuasion, had won numerous seemingly hopeless cases. He dominated a courtroom with his calculated strategy, ingenuity, and carefully disguised plans.

After reporting Marshall's proposal, Will asked for advice. Snow stroked his long chin thoughtfully, then said slowly, "You should decide this question entirely in the light of your own judgment as to where your duty and your opportunity lie. You have unique qualifications, and the tribunal in Tokyo would be an extraordinary opportunity to see law in the making. On the other hand, you must ask yourself if you are yet physically fit for such an arduous assignment. What you have gone through in prison camps must have sapped your strength." He got to his feet and walked to the window.

"Is that the only advice you can give me, sir?"

Snow turned around. "The decision must be yours. Whatever course you take will meet with the approval of the firm. We old-timers are all acutely aware of the vicissitudes of life and the risks of choices made by you young people. That's why we hesitate—properly, I think —to urge a particular course. The disposition around this office has always been to make it plain to someone in your position that you are quite free to take an opportunity of this kind without prejudice to your future." He paused slightly as if addressing a jury, then added, "as long as you feel it both your duty and an opportunity for development of your skills."

"Thank you, sir." Will was gratified by his attitude and yet had hoped the decision would be taken out of his hands.

"My daughter has been going through somewhat similar soul-searching. As you may know she's over at Ropes-Gray."

Everyone in the office knew all too well about the legendary Chaucy Snow who had finished third in her class at Boston University Law and was already reputed to be one of the most aggressive defense lawyers in town.

"She was asked to go to Tokyo as a defense counsel. I wouldn't give her any advice either." He smiled. "If I had, she might well have done the opposite."

That night Will could not sleep. It would be easy to say he hadn't gained back all his lost weight. But the truth was that he felt almost normal, and by February he would surely be fit. Scenes of pain, misery, and shame at the camps in the Philippines flashed in his mind. One haunting incident kept recurring. At Cabanatuan the Japanese had organized the prisoners into "shooting squads" of ten each. If one man tried to escape, all would be executed. Four of Will's squad had made a break for it one night. They were shot promptly. The other six were imprisoned, and after a terrifying week of "meditation" the prison commander announced that as a lesson to the rest of the camp, one of the six would have to be publicly punished by being tied to a pole just outside the barbed wire in an area feared for its voracious red ants. No one volunteered and Will, the tallest, was selected. No sooner had he been stripped naked and tied to the pole than a long line of red ants had started crawling up his legs. He writhed in his bed remembering the stinging bites, then the blazing sun rays with not a drop of water to relieve his thirst, followed by the welcome rain at night bringing such a chill that he longed for the beating sun. By the third day he knew he could no longer stand the torture and banged his head against the pole in a fruitless attempt to kill himself. He prayed for death and meant it. But that night a fellow prisoner named Popov risked his life to sneak under the fence and bring him water, rub his swollen ant-riddled body with lotion, and feed him evaporated milk as if he were a baby. The irony was that Popov, who ran a thriving black market, was the most hated prisoner in camp. He had come, he said, because Will was the only one who didn't treat him like scum. Will's strength and hope had flowed back. He begged forgiveness for praying to die and vowed he would escape somehow to bring back proof of the atrocities committed by the Japanese.

He had already turned over such proof in his little battered notebooks, but was that enough? Reliving the terrible nights tied to the pole awakened the bitter hatred he had felt toward the Japanese. He had carried this hatred for all things Japanese to his last prison camp in Nagasaki. Then on that August day when the second atom bomb exploded, he had undergone the same terror and pain suffered by the people of that city. This brought vague feelings of guilt and shame for being an American. With the anguished shouts of those who had died in Nagasaki haunting him, his hatred of the Japanese was burned out. Or so he thought until memories of Cabanatuan had aroused once more the old hatred, and at the first gray light of day he knew he had to repay all those comrades in prison who had died. He had to go back to Japan and not only help see justice done but join the crusade to outlaw war.

When he told Snow of his decision, the senior partner only said noncommitally, "So be it," and then hoped Will might give his daughter, Chaucy, a few hints on Japanese customs when they met in Tokyo. Will promised to do so, inwardly wincing at the thought of having to drag around the redoubtable Chaucy Snow, who in his imagination looked exactly like the lantern-jawed Snow with a gaudy wig.

Chapter Three

1.

Tokyo, December 2, 1945.

Upon arriving at the office that day the professor was informed by Harrison that fifty-nine more Japanese were to be arrested as war criminals. They included prominent government officials, diplomats, and business leaders but not the Marquis Kido, and McGlynn surmised that MacArthur, after their talk, had taken him off the list along with Prince Konoye, the former prime minister who had tried in vain to meet with Roosevelt in 1941 and work out a peaceful solution.

But McGlynn was disillusioned two weeks later when both of these men were named. He hurried to the Kido home to console his old friend, who had just finished packing a few clothes for the trip next day to Sugamo Prison. "It was bound to happen," said Kido philosophically. When the professor wondered how Konoye was taking the news, Kido observed, "The Prince never carried a wallet or squeezed his own wet washcloth when he took a bath. He couldn't take prison life for a week. *I* can and I will."

Next morning McGlynn found the office in a hubbub. "All hell's broken loose!" exclaimed Harrison. "We just got word that Prince Konoye took poison!"

"Is he dead?"

"Yes. His wife found him stretched out like he was sleeping." An empty bottle lay next to his pillow. "I'll bet they're running around like scared rabbits at the Dai Ichi Building."

"How did Marquis Kido react when they took him to prison?"

Harrison chuckled. "I understand he acted as calm as if he were going out to play golf. He was carted over to the prison in the limousine reserved for the Imperial family and walked in like he owned the place."

Upset, the professor grabbed the phone and asked to be connected with General MacArthur's office. Harrison was horrified but McGlynn ignored his protests and to the surprise of both in a few minutes SCAP himself was on the other end of the line. Controlling himself, McGlynn said, "General, I apologize for not going through channels but I would like to ask if you would consider letting me visit the Marquis Kido at Sugamo Prison."

There was no answer for a long moment but then the answer came slowly, "For personal reasons?"

"Not exactly, sir." He took a deep breath. "I know he keeps a detailed diary and I would like to advise him to use it at the tribunal." Again there was a brief silence. "General, I'm convinced his diary will substantiate the fact that both he and the Emperor had no involvement in starting the war."

"I'm not surprised to hear such a suggestion from you, Professor." MacArthur's voice was friendly, and McGlynn imagined he was smiling and trying to relight his pipe. "I'll inform Keenan, the chief prosecutor, that you're going to check in with him."

Joseph Keenan, noted for his prosecution of gangsters, greeted McGlynn that afternoon with Irish affability. He was a stocky, square-jawed, combative Irishman with a florid face. A vital man, he exuded energy and confidence. McGlynn hoped Keenan's bulbous reddish nose was not an indication of too much drinking. If so, the coming trial could become a shambles.

First Keenan expressed his delight that young Will McGlynn was soon coming out to join the prosecution, and then he announced that he'd already planned to send someone out to Sugamo to interrogate Kido. "You could act as an interpreter," he said and then stopped as if something had just occurred to him. "It might be a good idea if you could go out to Sugamo and bring Kido back to Hattori House for the interrogation." This was the mansion where Keenan and the other prosecution lawyers lived. "After all, he was the Emperor's chief adviser." McGlynn approved, and wondered if it had been MacArthur's idea.

Late the following morning, after a twenty-minute drive accompanied by the colonel who would do the interrogating, McGlynn could see what looked like a drab factory. The white wooden entrance gate was certainly not very imposing. Ten feet high, it was topped by barbed wire and a sign:

SUGAMO PRISON
APO 500

There were two small guard shacks on either side, one for those entering, the other for those leaving. The main building was three stories high. Atop flew an American flag. McGlynn could see a complex of grim buildings beyond.

Marquis Koichi Kido, a briefcase in hand, was waiting in the commandant's office. He was a small man of fifty-six with an immaculately trimmed mustache. He had changed from his oversized prison garb and looked neat and compact in his own clothing. He smiled to see his old friend.

On the trip to Hattori House McGlynn said, "I mentioned to General MacArthur that I felt sure you had kept a diary of your association with His Majesty."

"Yes, I have been keeping a sort of private diary, not a diary as a government official."

"What's he saying?" asked the colonel.

"Later," said McGlynn peremptorily, and turned back to Kido. "It seems to me it would be extremely helpful to use this diary in your own defense." Kido nodded. "It should also clarify His Majesty's true role regarding foreign policy and military matters."

"No doubt," said the Lord Privy Seal, as composed as if he were still in charge; and McGlynn felt sure that he was as regulated and organized in prison as he had been when he was one of the most important men in Japan. Everything about Kido had always been direct, decisive, and precisely carried out. McGlynn smiled to remember how Kido had brought these characteristics to the Sagami Country Club where, a model of perfection with his golf swing, he was called Kido the Clock. He was still Kido the Clock.

It was noon by the time they reached Hattori House. During a leisurely lunch in the dining room the prosecution colonel led the discussion, making sure that no serious business was brought up. At two o'clock Kido was escorted up to Keenan's room. The chief counsel greeted the Lord Privy Seal politely and listened intently as the interrogation by the colonel began, with McGlynn interpreting. After a few queries on Kido's duty as chief adviser to the Emperor, he was asked about the causes of war.

Kido patiently explained the situation: the Navy was pressed for oil, and certain young aggressive officers were calling for retaliatory action.

"Will you name some of those young officers?" interrupted Keenan eagerly.

Kido listed three men who had not been important enough to be indicted, and Keenan lost interest.

"When did you first learn about Pearl Harbor?" asked the prosecution colonel.

"When I heard about the raid on the radio," was the answer. Nor did the Privy Seal know that the two envoys in Washington had not given Hull the war warning until after the bombs fell. "I took it for granted in those days that a warning had been sent to Washington prior to the attack."

"Can you tell us how the Emperor felt about the war?" asked McGlynn in English and to the surprise of the others Kido replied directly in Japanese. "Always from beginning to end His Majesty tried his best to avoid war. He was extremely regretful when the attack was launched. It was particularly painful to fight Great Britain because of his long personal relations with the Royal family."

After an hour Keenan excused himself, and the prosecution colonel called attention to Kido's briefcase.

"During the period that you were an official, did you keep a diary?" asked the colonel.

"It was a sort of private diary, not official."

"That is the very thing I'm getting at!" said the colonel eagerly. "Where is it now?"

"I have it at home."

"Can you give it to us?"

"On the trip from the prison he told me about it," said McGlynn. "He also said he would be willing to let us have it."

"Please urge them to get a proper translation," said Kido. "I have seen so many documents mistranslated into English." The colonel assured Kido this would be done. Kido took a sheaf of papers from a small briefcase. "Here are some other things I have been writing in prison, my memoirs." He showed McGlynn the first page. "You see I begin with the Manchurian Incident." He thumbed through the pages. "I did refer briefly to the negotiations before Pearl Harbor at this point. But it's still far from complete."

The colonel was eyeing the papers avidly. "Are these available?"

"Yes," said Kido in English.

"Do you have any other papers that might clarify matters?" asked McGlynn, again in English.

Kido stroked his chin. "I did write a sort of memoir on the transition from the Konoye Cabinet to the Tojo Cabinet," he said in Japanese. "You know—in October 1941. That might be of interest."

The colonel leaned forward. "I shall inform Mr. Keenan," he said, "that I have complete confidence that you want to give us all the information in your possession, either as an individual or a former official since you have nothing to hide. I'd appreciate it if you would tell Dr. McGlynn where all your papers are located at home. You know—the different papers, the diary, the memoirs, your private files. All that valuable information. And I would like Dr. McGlynn to get all that stuff and bring it to us so we can read it and learn what really happened. As soon as we digest this material we'd like to have several more interviews with you."

Kido looked questioningly at McGlynn who said, "I'm sure the Marquis understands that we are only looking for the truth. But I'd like you to assure him, Colonel, that the Supreme Commander is neither threatening him nor promising him anything if he cooperates completely."

"I couldn't have said it better, Dr. McGlynn. We neither threaten nor promise and I again assure you, Marquis Kido, that I am convinced you want only to bring out the true facts. And we'll handle things in the customary way."

"I think you might add," said McGlynn, "that all these papers and diaries are turned over to us merely as a loan."

"Absolutely! Once this material has served its purpose, every page will be returned."

Kido, understanding the gist of this, nodded to McGlynn.

"We may have to keep the papers awhile," said the colonel. "But they will be safe in our hands and I promise he will get everything back."

"Tell them that the files in our home were destroyed by fire," said Kido. "And I personally destroyed all the files in my office at the Imperial Household Building during a mutiny of the guards on the night of August 14. That was when I had to hide in the cellar." He explained that the private diary wasn't very methodical about reporting political affairs. "But once I have the diary in my hands, it can refresh my memory on more details." Kido stood up. He bowed to McGlynn.

"I shall see you again soon," said the professor.

Later the prosecution colonel thanked McGlynn for "loosening up" Kido.

McGlynn grimaced at such words. "He only wants to tell the truth and we must keep all our promises."

"No sweat, no sweat." The colonel beamed. "We're going to nail the bastards with that diary!"

McGlynn didn't reply. The lawyer could not conceive that Kido's principal reason for turning over the diary was to save the Emperor from any involvement in the waging of the Pacific war.

That night the Privy Seal began writing a letter to the American authorities. "I should like to define my fundamental belief and attitude, which is nothing more than to speak the truth. I am therefore anxious to produce openly whatever materials on hand, to bring the truth to light. Now that the war is over, my belief impels me to leave on the world's record the truth, free from subterfuge and strife, to contribute to the peace of the world."

This belief, he continued, he owed to an American, Walter Page, the ambassador to London during the First World War. In 1931 he had read a book in English about Page. "I was much impressed by his firm belief in the development of democracy, as well as his dauntless courage." He had read the book many times and had it in his cell. During the war he had been spurred by Page's example to keep advising the Emperor to do his best to end the war regardless of the danger to Kido himself. "It is indeed my comfort and satisfaction to have succeeded in saving the lives of at least twenty million innocent Japanese civilians, as well as several hundred thousand American officers and soldiers, for to this task I have devoted my heart and soul." He ended with a confirmation of his intent to state only the truth in future interrogations.

2.

Late the next morning McGlynn was ordered to report immediately to MacArthur's office. En route he guessed that he would be scorched for dominating the interview with Kido. The hell with them! MacArthur had instructed him to see Kido, and if they didn't like the way he operated they could send him back to Massachusetts. By the time he entered the general's outer office he was bristling, only to find himself greeted with enthusiasm by a bright-eyed colonel who escorted him down the hallway a short distance to another waiting room.

"You've been reassigned to the Government Section," said the colonel. "The general believes you'll be more useful here." He was being put in a branch of the Public Affairs Division. "I hope you can work with Red Mulrooney. Just try to get used to him. He's a real diamond in the rough. In fact, he was one of the most decorated battalion commanders in Eichelberger's army. He should have made full colonel long ago but he always managed to talk his way out of it. The men called him Mad Mac. The screwball led them into battle wearing a Brooklyn Dodgers cap."

Lieutenant Colonel Tom Mulrooney was waiting in the next office. He was a big man with light red hair. Grinning like a huge Cheshire cat, he shoved a ham hand at McGlynn. "Heard a lot about you, Professor," he said in a slow Texas drawl. Once they were alone he added, "I guess that smoothbar warned you about me."

"He said I'd like you once I got used to you."

"I'm one of those problem children surviving a war. What do you do with the animals you've trained to be killers? Someday they'll learn how to keep us in a deep freeze until the next war. Now let me introduce you to the zoo. You are about to get a glimpse of the strangest collection of weirdos ever put in one section. Half of them are red-hot Democrat New Dealers out to magically transform this country into our forty-ninth state. The other half are diehard conservatives who wonder how the hell it can possibly be done."

They entered a large room that had once been a ballroom. Individual offices had been set up on all sides. Never had McGlynn encountered such a concerted hubbub. Above the clatter of typewriters was the subdued din of chatter from small groups.

"It's a regulated madhouse," said Mulrooney. "Not only are these people set on making the Diet democratic, giving the vote to women, purging the top politicians and business tycoons, and bringing civil liberties to a nation that might not want some of them, but you have managed to arrive during an unholy crisis." He explained that MacArthur had just turned the Government Section over to one of his closest cronies, Brigadier General Courtney Whitney. "He arrived from Manila a few days ago expecting to be made the general's special civil affairs adviser. But this place has been spinning its wheels so Mac sent him over here to get things rolling."

An office door opened and they could hear a choleric blast of oratory. "That's Courtney. They've already nicknamed him the Terrible-Tempered Mr. Bang of Tokyo." A portly red-faced man appeared, shaking a finger at a pale-faced victim. "Himself," said Mulrooney in an undertone. "Note the well-rounded phrases and courtroom style. Made a million dollars as a lawyer in Manila before the war."

The various conversations in the place lapsed until Whitney abruptly ended the lecture with a stinging phrase and returned to his office, banging the door behind.

"One thing you've got to give him. Things are moving already. Personally, I like his style. Behind the fancy words is a lot of common sense. He knows he's the general's watchdog and he believes the sun rises at SCAP's command. If Mac told him to fly out the window he'd be out like a flash, flapping his wings."

The groups were once more engaged in voluble arguments. Their enthusiasm, even in dispute, was infectious and McGlynn again was glad he was at one of the most exciting places in the world at one of the most exciting times in history. Both the ardent New Dealers and their opponents seemed to be working in mad harmony to reshape an entire nation and doing it the American way. What a comedy-drama this would make on Broadway! These industrious, ardent reformers, despite all their preconceptions and egotism were at work demolishing an ancient structure with its financial empires, the *zaibatsu*, its archaic Emperor worship, its Shinto State religion, its feudal sharecropping. Once the nation was cleared of these hindrances the reformers intended to erect a brave new world with all citizens, even women, voting; with children being educated according to democratic and humanitarian principles; with the huge slave labor force led by genuine unions; and with the nation at last freed from an oppressive military regime.

Both the idealists and the pragmatists in the vast room had no doubts about their mission or their ability to carry it through, and even though McGlynn feared that much that was good in the old Japan could be lost in the process, there was no other place in the world he wanted to be.

While he was observing, he was being observed by a tall, slender Japanese interpreter who appeared to be a college girl but had a sixteen-year-old son. She was Emi Toda's neighbor, a Bryn Mawr graduate whose diplomat husband had died of a liver ailment. Mariko Tajima, having read two of McGlynn's books and many of his articles, was surprised to see him tall and slim like a young man, striding in her direction. The silver hair above the bright, searching blue eyes and strong features only made him more attractive. The first time she saw him in the office he had reminded her of a magnificent eagle. But when he smiled he appeared affable and sympathetic. It was hard to believe this was the man noted for his gruffness and biting wit. She hoped he was going to speak to her but, ignoring her as if she were part of the furniture, the American eagle soared past.

The next day McGlynn did little but observe and listen to Mulrooney's comments. The entire Government Section was still in such a state of flux with the arrival of Whitney that Mulrooney suggested to McGlynn that he spend his time wandering through the city to see for himself how the people were reacting to the first stage of the great experiment.

He ranged the city, one evening accosting a middle-aged man named Shimura to ask for a direction, but looking for a conversation. After a few minutes Shimura invited McGlynn to his room to have a drink of sake. They entered a darkened, dingy office building, made their way up four flights of rickety stairs, and entered a large room dimly lit by candles. There were several chairs, a wobbly table, and a dozen dirty *futon* (bedding) scattered on the floor. Shimura explained he shared this refuge with other homeless. His wife and daughter had died in a firebombing and his son, a lieutenant, was somewhere in China. He hadn't heard from him in over a year. The only heat was from a charcoal fire in a brazier. As they sipped warm sake to help fight off the cold, three young women and a thin old man entered, rubbing their bare hands to restore circulation. All complained of the bone-chilling temperature in the room and gratefully sipped sake. After one of the girls complained that it was going to be a miserable night, Shimura offhandedly said, "If you slept with me we'd both be warmer."

She was not at all embarrassed and her casual "Not tonight" made McGlynn laugh. The others joined in, laughing more at the American who could understand Japanese than at the situation. In any case, barriers were down and the professor felt he could ask what they all thought of the growing fraternization between Japanese girls and the G.I.'s.

One girl shrugged her shoulders. Another said it depended on the G.I., and the third thought it was a good way to end the war hatred. But the old man was bitter. "You Americans only want the girls for one thing and by the end of the year we're going to have a big crop of Occupation babies."

"And then the G.I.'s will go home to their own women," said Shimura.

All three girls solemnly joined in the nods of assent and the old man began criticizing MacArthur's attempt to turn their country into a democracy. "It's just a lot of hypocrisy. You people always talk about equal opportunity but don't give it to us. You let us sleep in tombs like this and go hungry." He hugged himself to stop shivering. "I'll listen to you preach democracy if you give me a warm bed and some food."

"General MacArthur is going to do that," promised McGlynn. "Give him time."

Shimura tried to soothe the old man. "That's right, Mori-san, give him time. You were the one who said the Americans were going to kill us all. They're not so bad." He tended some sliced sweet potatoes on the brazier. "Have some," he offered to McGlynn.

"I've had dinner," he said. He thanked them all for their hospitality and left feeling guilty that he was bound for a clean warm room.

He went out as usual after dinner on December 23, stopping to observe a ragged woman bending over a public water fountain so she could scoop handfuls of water into her baby's mouth. It squealed with delight and she smiled.

It was growing darker and the professor wandered to the Ginza, the Broadway of Tokyo and the only animated place in the city. He could hear hundreds of Japanese, crowded around the windows of a U.S. Army Post Exchange, exclaiming in wonder at the G.I. sweaters, battle jackets, and shoes made of genuine leather. Children and young women were pestering the American soldiers waiting in line. Some wanted gum, some candy, some chocolate, some money for favors offered.

Peddlers had set up shop along the curbs but the prices were so high that almost all customers were G.I.'s. "Hell, it's just yen!" exclaimed one rosy-cheeked teenager in uniform, picking out poorly printed naughty postcards for the folks back home. Shoddy goods were also on display in the rubble-covered ground floors of two bomb-wrecked department stores.

Even so there was a festive spirit. A boarded-up dance hall now featured a large sign: "Merry Christmas, G.I. We soon open here with beautiful hostesses." Two scantily clad, shivering girls, heavily made up, were passing out leaflets advertising the grand opening. "Merry Christmas, Joe," chanted one to McGlynn while the other was offering him immediate service. "Very good, Joe. Look at this! Very cheap."

He walked briskly toward the Dai Ichi Building. On the front a thousand electric lights spelled out a hugely grotesque MERRY XMAS. Its glow spread over the outer wall of the Imperial Palace and was reflected in the waters of the great moat. "MacArthur's Christmas card to his twelve-year-olds," he thought, not realizing he was muttering aloud.

"Good evening, Professor McGlynn." It was Mariko Tajima, the best interpreter in the office according to Mulrooney. He tipped his hat to her and was immediately annoyed to find himself trying to make a good impression. He pulled in his stomach, stood straighter, and wondered why he was making such a fool of himself. And then to his surprise he was asking her if she would like some coffee. There was a good place nearby.

But she said her son was expecting her and she was already very late since she'd had to work overtime. He offered to take her home in a taxi. She protested but again to his own surprise, he was insistent. As their charcoal-burning cab rattled toward Azabu, he learned that she had graduated from Bryn Mawr. Her husband, a diplomat, had died in 1944, and she lived alone with her son who went to Ichiko, the most prestigious government preparatory school in Japan. He would enter

Tokyo University in two years. She looked far too young to have a son that old. When he had first seen her gliding toward him in the office he had guessed she was in her late twenties. She had seemed, in her grace, to step out of the pages of *The Tale of Genji*—a subtly elegant and cultured court lady of pre-feudal days. But he had not accosted her, fearing she would turn into a *moga*. Now he discovered that she spoke excellent English. At the same time she sounded totally Japanese and his interest was aroused.

As he started explaining who he was, she laughed softly. She knew him well, she said, from his books. "I particularly enjoyed *When East Met West.* You didn't write at all like a Westerner."

He found himself telling her about his four children. All but his older son, Will, were having dinner with him at the Imperial Hotel on Christmas Day. "Would you like to join us?" he asked impulsively.

To his relief she thanked him but declined. As she gave further directions to the driver he said, "Perhaps you know friends of mine, the Todas?"

"We are neighbors but not so fortunate as they are." She explained that only part of her house was habitable. She pointed to a dim heap of ruins as she stepped lightly out of the taxi.

"Please, don't," she said when he followed her to the street. "I can find my way." She had a small flashlight.

But he told the driver to wait and in his efforts to help her over or around rubble kept tripping. She laughed and told him it would be safer if he just followed her.

"My son Mark would say I was being a Helpful Henry." He tried to explain what this meant as he stumbled his way through the wreckage of a garden. Then the moon came from behind a cloud and he could see ruins like those of some feudal castle, and the graceful form in front of him again became a lady from *Genji*. The debris of the stone foundations and walls were covered with weeds and looked vaguely romantic. The rear portion fortunately was intact, and there were dim lights inside.

A boy of sixteen opened the door to stare insolently with black, piercing eyes at McGlynn. "This is my son, Taro," said Mariko with embarrassment. "Won't you come in and have some green tea?"

But the professor, chilled by the boy's hostility, declined, and though Mariko had looked forward to further conversation with the professor, she too was relieved. She had hoped that Taro, going through that difficult time of lost identity experienced by other bright young Japanese boys, might be influenced by such an urbane and learned man.

As McGlynn prepared for bed, mixed feelings succeeded one another. For the first time in years he had felt a stirring in his loins. After Clara's death there had been several brief, unsatisfactory encounters. But he had never felt like this. Then he cursed himself. Thank God she'd had the taste not to accept the invitation to Christmas dinner. What a farce that would have been! He could just see the stunned looks on his children's faces to see him with a woman young enough to be his daughter. Here was the classic old fool in his dotage, about to replay *The Blue Angel.*

In the morning McGlynn had a closer look at the man who had, in a few days, seemed to completely take over for MacArthur. Courtney Whitney had been abruptly put in charge of the most important section in the Dai Ichi Building and had the only door that led directly to the general's office. And it was already common knowledge that he could use that door whenever he pleased. No one else had the access of "Dear Court," as the general called him. Whitney looked completely undistinguished. A plumpish man in his late forties, he reminded McGlynn of a sharp businessman who had become president of his local Kiwanis Club.

Now he was gloomily surveying his entire staff and everyone expected that they had been assembled to receive a temperamental tongue lashing. Instead he began to speak softly, solemnly. "General MacArthur views the Occupation as one of the greatest events in the history of American foreign policy and considers the Government Section the backbone of the Occupation."

McGlynn could feel the sudden electricity in the room, for everyone agreed with every word.

"What this section does or fails to do, he told me a few evenings ago, will be of tremendous significance to the United States and to Japan for generations to come. This means we have a grave responsibility which we must shoulder together. We must work as a team. I need your help. The door of my office is open to you. Drop in any time, even for a chat." He turned and ponderously stumped back to his office.

McGlynn felt like applauding and he could feel the excitement around him. People were looking at one another in wonder. Whitney's words seemed to have been uttered by MacArthur himself. Those who had come that morning with reluctance or cynicism, expecting to be lectured at, were as deeply stirred as McGlynn was.

Everyone was surprised to hear Whitney mention not a single word about secrecy or security, the watchwords of his predecessor. Instead he made everyone feel he had MacArthur's supreme confidence. Here at last was someone who wasn't afraid of anyone, even the general.

To McGlynn the entire staff seemed to be returning to their little alcoves inspired, to tackle their jobs with renewed vigor and confidence. He guessed that these little Pygmalions, already eager to transform Japan into a model of democracy, felt they at last had a chief who would back them to the limit. McGlynn hoped that in their zeal they wouldn't turn out to be Frankensteins unwittingly creating monsters that would destroy their masters.

He saw Mariko coming toward him and imagined she wanted to speak to him. Should he ask her to share a coffee break, or was that inviting complications? But she only said "Good morning" and hurried past. Feeling piqued and a little hurt, he derided himself for reacting as a human being.

3.

The Imperial Hotel didn't look particularly large since the front half was a mere four stories high. Tall Americans would automatically stoop a bit as they entered. But once inside they found the main ceiling was three stories high, and they could appreciate the grandeur of Frank Lloyd Wright's design. Of course, Mr. Wright would have grimaced at the condition of his beloved hotel in late 1945. The south wing had been gutted by incendiaries. The furnishings were threadbare. All the rooms and corridors needed painting. Moreover the walls, though in their original state, were a gloomy brown brick trimmed with oya stone, a volcanic rock perforated like Swiss cheese.

It all reminded McGlynn's son Mark, just arrived from Kyushu, of a poorly run penitentiary; in fact it had already been nicknamed "the morgue." But despite all this the meeting of the McGlynn and Toda clans in the main dining room on that Christmas Day was festive. All they needed was Will, thought the professor, who was feeling an unaccustomed sentimental glow, remembering past holidays in Williamstown.

Until Mark had become a Marine, he and his father had always been at odds, perhaps because both were born rebels, impatient and impetuous. Mark had turned down Harvard in favor of Williams and then insisted on working and living on campus in the poor boys' dorm. He had preferred riding freight trains in the summer to staying at the family cottage in New Hampshire. And after making considerable money as an entrepreneur while at college, he had turned down an offer to work for Standard Oil after graduation in favor of going to New York and joining the Communist Party. When war came he had quit the Party and enlisted in the Marines. It took the battles of Guadalcanal and Tarawa and a tough but understanding battalion commander to straighten him out. The transformation brought him closer at last to his father whose only regret, a silent one, was that to cope with his bloody battle experiences he had found it necessary to convert to Catholicism, the religion McGlynn himself had abandoned soon after he had entered Harvard.

Maggie and Mark seemed to have been made from the same mold. Each had black curly hair, a bright mischievous face, and an irrepressible sense of humor. At the festive table they were now joking with each other like college sophomores. Their older sister Floss, their second mother, was delighted to see them so unrestrained. It was just like old times back in Williamstown, when even Daddy had let freedom ring on holidays.

Floss's son, Masao, insisted on sitting next to Mark and kept pestering him to tell how he won his medal on Iwo Jima.

"I did what everyone was doing," he said lightly. "Trying to save my a—my behind." He suddenly turned serious. "Every snuffy who landed on that beach deserved a medal." Maggie wanted to know if it would be worthwhile to go again to the Nagasaki area for a story. He doubted it. The battalion was now in Sasebo and was about to push north. "Things are going fine."

McGlynn, proud of a son he had never really known before the war, observed that he was disturbed and said so.

"The fact is, Dad," he said lowering his voice so the others could not hear, "the fact is that some of the new replacements from the States are a piss-poor lot. They've never heard a shot fired in anger and now act as if they won the war single-handed. They act like conquerors. And some of the new officers are no better. They're not only chicken-shit but arrogant. Some of these characters race through town in a jeep shouting obscenities and calling the Japs 'Gooks.' It's pitiful." There was a big difference between the combat Marine and the noncombatant. "The crap we all went through at Tarawa and Saipan made us a family. The new officers seem to have chips on their shoulders."

"What are you two gabbing about?" said Maggie. "How about letting us in on it."

"I was just telling Dad that the hardest duty I've had so far was being officer in charge of a trainload of Marines bound for several weeks of R and R in Kyoto." When they finally straggled back to the train they had brought with them about two hundred women. "It was going to be a three-day ride and I knew there'd be a riot if I didn't let the girls come along so I decided to let them stay. But at every stop I'd have some sergeant sneak a bunch of them off. We still had about thirty left when we reached Sasebo and I turned them over to the Red Cross so they could be taken back to their villages. I tell you, that trip was as bad as hitting the beach at Saipan. But it was worse for the poor captain in charge of R and R at Kyoto. You should hear what he had to go through!"

He was about to expand on the story when Maggie saw the look of concern on Floss's face to hear about such antics with Sumiko and Masao present. She kicked her brother under the table, then changed the subject by asking what they all thought of the recent charges by Colonel Sams, the chief of the Public Health and Welfare Section, that the Japanese Government had started a whispering campaign alleging the country was on the brink of famine. "Sams says it's a lie to say that scores die every night here in Tokyo at Ueno Station."

Maggie didn't notice that Floss was bristling.

"You know," Maggie added, "We've been sitting on this 'whispering campaign' story for weeks. Thank God SCAP has finally come out to show it's a fake."

"How can you believe such nonsense!" Floss exploded. The family had never before seen her lose her temper. "You correspondents sit around at your club being fed pap by MacArthur's staff and you think you know what's going on all over Japan! But you don't know anything! You drive around in jeeps like little gods but you don't see a thing! You have no idea what it is to be a Japanese. For them every nail, every rag, every tangerine peel is valuable. While we sit here stuffing ourselves the Japanese are starving. A Japanese has a cupful of rice and a rotting fish—if he's lucky. Our men don't even have enough matches to light the three cigarettes a day he gets. On a sunny day you see them leaning out of windows trying to light a butt with magnifying glasses."

They had never seen this Floss and her father, recalling Operation Starvation, knew she was right. She spoke with authority.

"Most of us survive by the black market," Floss continued. "But what will we do when the last kimono is gone, the last piece of furniture, the last dish? Shall we send Sumiko out to Hibiya Park to pick up some G.I.?"

Mark put an arm around his sister. "Floss," he said, "what can we do?"

She pushed back her chair and stood up, her militant attitude reminding her astounded father of Joan of Arc. "You can all come down to Ueno Station with me and see the truth for yourselves!"

On the way to Ueno, Emi whispered to McGlynn. "She is obsessed about starting a refuge for war orphans. It is almost a madness. I think the death of her two babies has affected her."

In pre-war times Ueno Station, on the north side of central Tokyo, had been the largest, busiest, and most efficient railroad station in Japan. Practically untouched by the bombings, it had fallen into disrepair; what the McGlynns saw that evening was a dim, poorly ventilated, filthy structure swarming with returnees from rural areas where they'd been sent for safety during the war. There was incessant pushing and shoving. Babies cried, older children whined, and parents faces were marred by worry. The din was unsettling and the smells overwhelming. Some toted bulging reed sacks on their backs. Others pulled handcarts piled with trunks, wooden chests, and sacks. Ragged children tagging behind were deeply tanned. Their scalps looked bluish, for even the girls' hair had been shorn because of lice. Their ranks were swollen by thousand of refugees from Hiroshima, Nagasaki, Kobe, and Sendai. Fifty special trains and nearly three hundred local trains came and went every day, serving as many as half a million passengers.

It was already dark by the time Floss led the way down a stairway. They heard a shriek above the hubbub as a one-legged man, whose crutches had slipped, plummeted down the steps. There was such a seething mass of people they never saw what happened to him, but all traces of disturbance were gone before they reached the lower level.

Floss explained that the refugees from other bombed-out cities had come to Tokyo, the seat of government, looking for food and shelter. Then they passed a bandaged, badly scarred woman lying on the floor, her begging box open. Next to her sat a dazed little boy who looked up at them with hopefully questioning eyes. "But there's not even enough for those who live here." On all sides people were looking for a place to set down their possessions so they could sleep. "During the day," she said, "they spend most of their time across the street in Ueno Park. But when it gets chilly they have to come down here for warmth. You're the reporter," she said to Maggie, whose eyes were big with disbelief, "ask that man why he has to sleep down here." Maggie stooped and in Japanese began questioning a wan-faced, shivering man of about forty-five. He looked up as if she were crazy. His home had been destroyed, his wife and children killed in the great bombing of April. He had worked in a machine shop but it had been destroyed and he could find no work. And because he was unemployed he wasn't eligible for ration coupons.

"How do you eat?"

"I beg. I scavenge." But he was too proud to hold out a hand to her.

"What hope do you have?"

He looked up at the McGlynns with dead eyes. "No hope."

Floss led them deeper into the corridor. "Here is where I come every day," she said, "to see my war orphans." The stink was even worse down here. They came upon a girl, probably ten, carrying on her back a crying baby. The girl skipped every so often to comfort the baby.

"He is crying because he's hungry," said Floss.

Just ahead two teenage boys in dirt-matted rags were grappling fiercely for an empty K-ration can. The victor ran a dirty finger inside the can and sucked a few fragments.

Other children, recognizing Floss, flocked around her crying, *"Obachan!"* Mark saw their haunted eyes brighten. She told the clamoring children she would be back in the morning with some food.

Upstairs they passed a Red Cross girl passing out doughnuts and coffee to American servicemen. Mark noticed that several ragged Japanese were eyeing the sight with apparent indifference, but when one G.I. tossed aside half of his doughnut there was a frenzied scramble.

Mark went up to the girl, who had a plain, pleasant face. "You're making quite an impression on the Japanese," he said. She was surprised. "Am I?" she laughed. "I never see them. Hey, how about a doughnut, Captain?" she said cheerily.

Chapter Four

1.

Tokyo, December 1945.

What Maggie had seen at Ueno Station aroused both her pity and indignation. But for Floss, she might never have learned what was really going on at such places. Was she getting like too many journalists, hanging around the Foreign Correspondents Club for stories instead of wearing out shoe leather? So the next evening she was back at bustling Ueno Station with a photographer. While interviewing several of Floss's war orphans she learned that the toughest gang of young beggars was run by a big girl known as Fatty who ruled them like a czar. She found the girl outside the station. She was porky, towering above a dozen boys who hovered near her waiting for orders. A G.I. passed by, flicking his cigarette into the gutter. Fatty imperiously snapped her fingers and a boy rushed to the cigarette, beating a middle-aged man by a few seconds. He carried the live butt to Fatty who puffed at it in the grand manner. A jeep stopped and as a Marine sergeant leaped out, she gave another signal and two boys ran out to beg. They made such a to-do that the Marine, digging in his pockets for change, didn't know that a third boy was snatching his wallet from his back pocket.

Maggie grabbed the boy, gave the Marine his wallet, and told him she would turn the thief over to the police. The boy began weeping. The police would beat him up. "Shut up!" Maggie said in Japanese and shook him until he quieted down. She said she'd let him go if he told her about the gang. The boy put on another display of tears. "Fatty will kill me!" Maggie shook him until he reluctantly told how the tough girl trained them to steal, beg, and beat up other gangs. Their main occupation was filching food and money at the flimsy open air black-market stalls near the station. It was easy, he boasted, since

67

there were such big crowds that a couple of boys could cause confusion by fighting or bumping into people while others were snatching the goods or money that most blackmarketeers kept in the open under a paperweight.

"Why don't you get into an orphanage?" asked Maggie.

"Have you ever been in one around here? They're like prisons. The food is bad and there isn't much of it. And they make you wash your face and brush your teeth and sleep in beds." It was more fun living on the streets. "Out here we're free!"

"Aren't you afraid of Fatty?"

"Sure, but she protects us. She's really tough." He looked around as if hoping to be rescued. "She treats us good too. We get plenty to eat and every night she takes us to the Hibiya Park swimming pool so we can get clean."

"Did you have a bath last night?" Yes. "How did you get so filthy in one day?" He shrugged his shoulders. She gave him a pack of cigarettes. He couldn't believe his luck and ran off before she could change her mind.

She felt a light tap on her shoulder. She turned to see a small Japanese. "Excuse me," he said apologetically, "but aren't you Maggie McGlynn?"

"That's right."

"I'm Jun Kato." They shook hands. "I'm a friend of Ko Toda."

She vaguely remembered hearing of the Nisei who had been brought to Japan as a young boy by a father who couldn't afford to support more than two sons. Her interest was aroused. Perhaps there was a story. "Weren't you the one who was here all during the war?"

"Yes. After I graduated from Ayoma College in forty-three I worked as a reporter in the foreign department of Tokyo *Shimbun*. I'm still with them." He didn't tell how he had managed to stay out of the army with a fake heart ailment.

"It must have been rough for you to be caught in the middle."

"When Pearl Harbor came I didn't know what to think." His feelings had been complicated by divided loyalties. "I couldn't help being proud of the great victories like Singapore. But something inside me didn't want to accept them. I could still remember with a thrill 'The Star-Spangled Banner' and the pledge of allegiance every morning in the third grade."

It could be a very good story and she guided him to a little place for tea. "When the B-29s flew over Tokyo I listened over a shortwave radio in the closet as the fliers talked. I was not scared—just fascinated —to hear English spoken by Americans for the first time since the war started! And the jazz music. It was really exciting!" When he learned she had just been interviewing a gang of war orphans he wondered whether she would be interested in a nice story about Japanese women surviving by buying soap and cigarettes from G.I.'s just arriving in Japan. "I hear they swarm into the military train taking the G.I.'s up to Camp Zama and what goes on is like a movie." He suggested she do the story, since Japanese reporters were not admitted to U.S. facilities.

"Sounds good," said Maggie. She thanked him and urged him to tell more of his experiences.

"All during the war I had to smell rotten fish. Then the Americans came with their books and I would just riffle the pages to smell the wonderful American paper! It smelled just like it did when I was in elementary school! It was so American." His greatest desire, he said, was to return to the United States and reinstate his citizenship. But he feared that if he applied he might face charges as a war criminal since he had written several articles about the American terror-bombing campaign. "I was told I might be treated as a traitor. Look what happened to Iva Toguri. You know, she was only one of three or four Tokyo Roses. Her folks made her come to Japan just before the war after she graduated from UCLA. And she was persuaded by an American POW—an Army captain, an ex-radio commentator—to make fifteen-minute daily broadcasts to the Allied soldiers. Nothing's happened to the captain or other POW's who were also broadcasting propaganda since they had been threatened, so they said, with death. But poor Iva, who used to sneak them extra food, is going to prison— and so will I if they catch me. And they never would have caught Iva if she hadn't asked to have her American citizenship reinstated." This was the first time he had felt free to talk of such things, and he even revealed that he had been persuaded by his old radical mentor on the paper to become a delegate from Tokyo *Shimbun* for the newspaper labor union. "It's been very exciting. I've met some wonderful men. I even got to know Nosaka!" He was the brilliant strategist of the Communist Party. "He told me about his close relations with the Russians and how he worked five years with Mao! What a sharp mind!"

"Aren't you taking a big chance to get lined up with the Reds?"

"I'm careful, and besides it was General MacArthur himself who let all the Communists out of prison and made the party legal."

Maggie felt guilty for having led on this simple, trusting soul. "Take my advice. If you ever want to get your U.S. citizenship back, stay away from that crew."

"But you don't understand. Nosaka-san only wants a true democracy in Japan. He's not for bloody revolution or any of that nonsense. He told me he is going to insist at the Fifth Party Congress that the Party wage only a *peaceful* revolution and so become the lovable Communist Party."

"You're kidding!" Maggie laughed.

But he was deadly serious. "He used those very words. He wants the people of Japan to realize the party is not only for the working class but for everyone and is going to bring social justice by building a democratic Japan through peaceful revolution. That's what he meant by making the party lovable."

Poor fool, she thought, but she knew he had been bitten by the virus of idealism just as Mark had been briefly bitten before Pearl Harbor. She had already written a piece on the lure of communism to the young people of Japan who'd had their minds blasted by war. And now that it had been made legal it seemed safe. The new leaders of the party like Nosaka were appealing to the average Japanese by pressing vigorously for solutions to the problems of daily life—food, housing, traffic jams, unfair taxes.

Two days later Maggie, following up Kato's tip, watched newly arrived G.I.'s board a military train near Yokohama. It was dusk. Although exhausted by the long sea trip, the soldiers were excited by the sights and smells of the strange new land. There was a raucous cheer as the train finally began pulling away. Soon it jerked to a stop and there were moans, groans, and shouts of protests.

Suddenly out of the darkness more than a hundred women came streaming up to the train, many with babies or small children strapped to their backs.

All along the military train the G.I.'s were opening the windows to see the strange sight of women waving paper money and shouting, "Cigaretto, candy, chewing gum!"

"What are you trying to do?" Maggie asked a middle-aged woman in Japanese.

"We try to buy something."

"Isn't it dangerous coming out here at night? This is a troop train with more than four hundred men. Aren't you afraid?"

By now there were transactions going on all along the train.

"No, we do it all the time. So you please sell me a bar of soap or a cigarette or something American. Please!"

"But that's black marketing," said Maggie. "You might get caught."

"We buy things and take to the town tomorrow and we charge a little more for it. Is that bad?"

Maggie tossed her a pack of cigarettes.

Her face was incredulous. "This is enough to feed my family for two weeks! I am very happy!" The train jerked to a start.

Maggie would never forget the beatific look of gratitude on the haggard face of the woman as the train pulled away.

"Can you tell me if this is any good?" a redheaded private asked, and showed Maggie a yen note he'd received for a pack of cigarettes.

"What'd you pay for the cigarettes?" she asked.

"Six cents."

"Well, the yen is now about seven cents. So you made a big profit of a penny. But that woman will have enough money to feed her family for a week."

The G.I. grinned as he carefully folded the yen note and put it in his wallet. "Good deal."

Half an hour later the train again stopped and the train was once more besieged by shouting women. This time the red-haired G.I. received a larger piece of paper for his pack. "How much is this worth?" he asked.

Maggie examined the paper. "It's no good," she said.

"What do you mean it's no good?"

"It's a war bond. Japan lost the war so war bonds are no good."

The redhead grinned. "It'll look nice on my wall."

At the third stop he traded a tube of toothpaste for another bank note. "This is also no good," Maggie explained.

"What's wrong this time?"

"It has no seal on it. The first yen note you got was the new yen and has a seal. This one is illegal. Obsolete."

The soldier was still unperturbed. "It's worth it," he said.

"Why?" asked Maggie.

"I've learned the value of Japanese money just for a tube of tooth-paste and two lousy packs of Camels."

Maggie leaned over and kissed him on the forehead. "Welcome to the land of the Rising Sun, soldier. Enjoy it."

At Zama the troops were billeted in a converted military academy. Maggie had no trouble in getting a private room, formerly an office. In the morning she ate in a huge messhall. Breakfast consisted of dehydrated potatoes, omelets, bacon, bread, and coffee. Maggie noticed a crowd of about thirty women standing outside near large drums filled with the garbage from breakfast. She went out through the kitchen. Now she could see that each woman had an empty half-gallon can.

"What's going on?" Maggie asked a K.P.

"They get a can of this garbage to take home."

Maggie peered into one of the drums at a mass of brownish slop. "What are they going to do with it?"

"Eat it, lady," said the K.P.

Maggie called to a woman who had just filled her can. The woman turned away, but Maggie caught up to her. "What are you going to do with this when you get home?" Her friendly voice reassured the woman.

"We make a fire and cook it very slowly for a long time. And then we eat it."

The thought was nauseating.

"It tastes strange," said the woman. "But it is all good food."

2.

On the last day of the year Whitney once again summoned his entire staff. In his impatient, blunt manner he announced, "This will be a regular affair. I want all of you to be conversant with what goes on. I want your reaction to every proposed directive to the Japanese Government prepared in this section." McGlynn felt as if Whitney was talking directly to him and from the rapt looks in other faces it was apparent that everyone felt the same sense of personal communication. "The junior officers are as well if not better qualified to pass judgment on our moves as the higher-ranking ones, including myself." Mulrooney nudged the professor and whispered, "I think I might like this bird."

"I mean exactly what I say." Whitney glared around. "And I look forward to the time when a lieutenant has the guts to barge into my office, bang my desk and say, 'Goddammit, general, such-and-such a proposed directive is preposterous, and you would be out of your mind to ask General MacArthur to approve it."

McGlynn, Mulrooney, and a few others laughed outright, and Whitney grinned as he surveyed the room like a searchlight. "I see I'm getting across. I mean every damned word. Now you take the Japanese election law as amended by the Imperial Diet. Our expert on politics, Major Roest, believes that we should not meddle with it, that a fair election can be held under it as is. He may be right, but I want a section hearing on the matter anyway. Accordingly I have asked the head of the Public Administration Branch to appoint a staff member to marshal all the opposition he can find to Roest's position."

"That's going to cause a real donnybrook," Mulrooney remarked as he escorted McGlynn through the crowd to their own cubicle in the farthest corner of the room. The major was grinning as broadly as a big cat about to swallow a mouse. "It's about time they cut off those Democrat Brain Trusters at the knees." There was a bloodthirsty quality in his voice that gave credence to the story going around the office that Mulrooney had taken emergency leave right after the surrender to go back to California and put an alligator in the swimming pool of his former division commander. This general had given an apparently unnecessary order for Mulrooney's battalion to capture an obscure hill. That order had cost a hundred casualties.

"Is it really true about the alligator?" McGlynn impulsively asked. The big cat grin again transformed Mulrooney's face. "You should have seen the bastard shoot out of that pool like Johnny Weissmuller." A few minutes later he radiated good nature as he brought out a picture of his twelve-year old daughter. "Jo's coming over to join me in a few weeks." He proudly told of the girl's prowess on the field hockey team and in the classroom. He didn't mention his wife and it was a month before McGlynn learned that she had divorced him, and had recently died.

"I've got a dinky room over at the Peers' Club. Where do you think I could find a decent place for the two of us?"

"Have you thought of renting part of a Japanese house?" Mulrooney liked the idea. Could the professor recommend someplace? "I'll look around," he said, already thinking of the American section of the Toda home.

While McGlynn was taking a coffee break alone at the cafeteria, Mariko passed with her cup of coffee.

"Won't you join me?" he said and quickly got to his feet.

She smiled as she sat across from him before he could hold her chair. How effortlessly she moved, he thought. Like a dancer. Fortunately she didn't have the bandy legs of so many Japanese women. Hers were straight and slender.

"I'd like your advice," he said and told about Mulrooney's request. "How about Emi Toda's place? I know she could use the money and there's plenty of room." He was surprised at her lack of enthusiasm.

"Perhaps he wouldn't fit in," she said.

"I've found him to be not only amusing but thoughtful. I know his reputation around here, but he's really a decent fellow and I think Emi might enjoy having the girl around." She said nothing. "You're probably thinking of that alligator story. It's not as bad as you think." He told her Mad Mac's version and she had to laugh. "He only did it because of all the men he had lost so uselessly."

"I didn't hear that part of it."

"You have to forgive the Irish for doing the unexpected. For instance, will you have dinner with me tonight?"

She was indeed surprised and pleased. "I'm sorry but Taro is expecting me."

"What about tomorrow?"

"I'd be happy to," she said, convincing herself it would be a good means of getting his advice on Taro who was going through a crisis experienced by so many Japanese boys. They resented the Americans for beating Japan yet were impressed by their strength and their machines. First Taro had been crushed by the surrender, then elated to read one of the pamphlets dropped by dissident Japanese aviators saying, "We are not defeated. We are going to keep on fighting." But nothing had happened and he felt ashamed of his subservient countrymen. He felt humiliated living in a home half destroyed by an enemy who was now passing out gum and candy. And like so many other youngsters he had fallen for the lure of communism and spent most of his free time with a Communist Youth League group. And that was why she had so readily agreed to have dinner with this white-haired historian. Or so she told herself.

Two days later twenty-one Government Section officials, including McGlynn, assembled to hear Major Roest debate another major on the merits of Japan's election laws. Roest spent his twenty minutes defending the law, pointing out that all the party leaders—Liberal, Progressive, Socialist, People's Cooperative, and Communists—approved the law in its present form. He admitted there were no printed ballots, that candidates were not allowed to canvass door to door, and that newspapers could not support or oppose individual candidates. This might seem quaint and undemocratic to Americans, but all the Japanese, from conservative to Communist, insisted the law was not partial to any particular party or faction, and that not a single press or radio commentator believed a democratic election could not be held under it.

The second major, a conservative Republican, disagreed. A truly democratic vote must follow American election practices. "Otherwise," he concluded, "the Imperial Rule Assistance Association, the fascist organization, will be returned to power." After a five-minute rebuttal, Colonel Kades—already the de facto assistant to Whitney and a man so good-looking he was known throughout the building as the American Charles Boyer—called for questions and comments from the audience. After a lively exchange of opinions, a vote was taken. Fifteen, not including the professor, voted for changing the law.

Mulrooney was amused. "How in hell could you support anything so undemocratic?" he asked.

"What makes you think the American way is the only democratic way?"

"Aw, nuts," chided Mad Mac, "you're evading the issue. Didn't the Potsdam Declaration call for the establishment of all really democratic institutions. Anyway you can bet Court will knock it down."

McGlynn agreed. General Whitney, as a matter of military routine, was bound to approve the majority view. But when Whitney later summoned his staff and read out a memorandum addressed to MacArthur advising him to make no changes in the present law, everyone was shocked. There was a hushed, tense silence until Kades said good-naturedly, "Well, my head is awfully bloody but not bowed." Everyone laughed. Then Whitney marched down the hall and into MacArthur's office. Minutes later the word was passed from cubicle to cubicle. MacArthur had backed Whitney.

While some were shocked, many like Mulrooney were delighted. "Things have really changed," he told McGlynn. "Until Court arrived, every memorandum we prepared in this section got bogged down in red tape. I got so pissed off I wrote out my resignation. I was going to hand it in on the day Whitney made that first speech to us. Now I'm going to tear it up."

Even those who opposed Whitney's decision shared his enthusiasm. All rejoiced at finally having a chief who was not afraid to throw his weight around and get things done. It was now obvious, thought McGlynn, that Whitney was not acting egocentrically but as the strong right arm of MacArthur. The former Manila lawyer knew what SCAP wanted and was seeing that it was done promptly. This was bound to give the discouraged Government Section at last a sense of accomplishment and prestige. McGlynn guessed that MacArthur was using his faithful and efficient friend to backstop the programs of all the other GHQ sections. Granted that it was an unprecedented and perilous procedure, in practice it could be the only way to accomplish the monumental task of occupation. And the architect of this peculiar system would probably get little if any credit.

Whitney probably would go down in history as the terrible-tempered Mr. Bang, a choleric and autocratic bully. In truth, concluded McGlynn, excited at the new developments, Whitney's only desire was to serve his master well. It was apparent that he was able to anticipate MacArthur's needs without explanations and had become his alter ego. Their close relationship had already created an undercurrent of ill will among others in the hierarchy, but Whitney was stolidly ignoring their envious barbs. He didn't care that he was labeled arrogant, rude and crude. He was going to do anything to carry out his boss's wishes. Thank God, thought the professor, that he himself was on hand to view this backstage maneuvering that could very well bring about what he had first imagined to be unlikely—a successful occupation. In his mind McGlynn was already constructing a book to follow the one on pre-Pearl Harbor. This would be on the triumphs and failures of the noble experiment.

3.

Back in the United States it was a day earlier because of the time change. The professor's older son, Will, was climbing into a plane at Hamilton Field in California. Marshall had promised he wouldn't have to leave until late February but apparently they needed him at once. Undoubtedly another case of hurry-up-to-wait. Will McGlynn's brand-new flight bag, bulging hugely, contained the Class A uniforms he'd had to buy in Washington. He was clad in an Eisenhower jacket and wool khakis. Other officers were traveling in their blouses and pinks but Will liked the feel of the new jacket, which unfortunately made short officers look like bellhops. He was very good-looking and, being unaware of it, was always surprised when women found him attractive. He was blond, unlike the twins, and even taller than his father. His gawky Jimmy Stewart walk was deceptive, hiding an athletic agility that had made him the national squash champion.

He was still self-conscious about the too shiny gold leaves on his shoulders, and he hoped no one from prison camp in Japan ever saw him with a major's insignia, because no one else there had been promoted. On the plane there were only a few seats left, but he found one halfway down the aisle beside a civilian.

By the time they were airborne Will had learned that his name was Donihi, he had served in the Coast Guard Temporary Reserve during the war, and until recently was a trial lawyer in Nashville. He had gone to Japan in early December as a counsel for the prosecution in the International Military Tribunal for the Far East. But he had returned home on a family emergency. While there he had helped recruit additional counsel and personnel for the prosecution.

"That's my destination too," said Will. "I'm with Adams and Snow in Boston."

"Prosecution or defense?"

"Prosecution."

"That's a relief," Donihi said with a grin. "Now we can be friends." It also helped that Will was Irish. The chief prosecutor, Joe Keenan, was as Irish as Paddy's pig. "I think that's why he made me his temporary envoy."

During the next five days, after layovers in four islands, Will learned from Donihi that Keenan, as Assistant Attorney General of the United States in charge of the Criminal Division, had prosecuted Machine Gun Kelly and his wife for kidnapping during the Depression. In a landmark case he not only got life sentences for the Kellys and four accomplices but also got long sentences for one of the defendants' lawyers and a number of harborers. This helped end the wave of kidnappings that had terrorized the Midwest. Keenan became one of the most influential men in Washington, pulling more strings than a master puppeteer, and was given the nickname "Joe the Key" by Roosevelt because he had influence with such as the Chairman of the Senate Finance Committee. Just before his death, the President had slated Keenan to head the prosecution in Tokyo.

"Unfortunately Joe has already made enemies in Tokyo," said Donihi. "He and the former number two man in our group, John Darsey, are usually at odds. Joe has a short temper, loves the limelight, reduces some of the girls on his staff to tears, and is his own worst enemy." It was too bad because Keenan was brilliant and, if you got to know him, very decent.

By this time Will's feeling of repugnance on returning to Japan had been succeeded by anticipation at the chance of helping bring to justice those who had committed such fiendish atrocities. The thought of all those comrades who had been murdered or brutalized and starved made him eager to get at the task. And when this task was completed he hoped he'd purge his feelings of hatred toward the millions of Japanese who had not committed atrocities. He and his new friend, Donihi, were driven to the large, rambling mansion called Hattori House where Keenan and other prosecution lawyers were billeted. After unpacking, Will lay down to take a nap before dinner. He was wakened by loud knocking. It was Mark. They stared at each other as if they were strangers, not having seen each other since 1941. "What the hell are you doing in uniform?" asked Mark. "Dad said you'd come over as a lawyer."

Will explained as he tried to adjust to this Marine before him who was not the impetuous kid he remembered. Mark, in turn, was stunned to see a gaunt man with haunted eyes, not the completely self-assured big brother who used to lecture him on the importance of being on the winning team and knowing the right people at the right time. During the last four years in prison camps Will had certainly not met the right people at the right time. Impulsively Mark seized his brother's hand and squeezed it until Will winced. "My train is leaving at midnight so I can't stay too long."

Will looked at his watch and saw to his amazement that he had slept through dinner.

"I had to tell you," said Mark, "about your friend Mrs. Goto."

This was a young woman victim of the atom-bombing of Nagasaki. Will had helped her escape and they had had a brief affair. "She's dead?" he asked with a pang of remorse. He hadn't kept in touch.

"She died soon after my last visit."

Will hung his head in sorrow and self-condemnation.

"I went out to see her last week," Mark said, "We've been bringing the family food. Tullio's president of the staff NCO mess and always orders more than they need. The big trouble was getting the proud little lady to accept anything. We have to hide the stuff in the kitchen."

Will could see the Goto farmhouse and the relatives staring coldly at Michiko for bringing disgrace to the family. He could still feel the hatred directed at him, and that was why he had tried to erase all memory of those days from his mind.

"There's a good chance I'll be transferred to Yokosuka Naval Base," said Mark to get his brother's mind off Michiko Goto. "Then I'll be close enough to help."

"Help?"

"Masao lost an arm. Some gung-ho Navy fly-boy strafed our little nephew. We've got to get him one of those prosthetic dinguses. There's a good Navy hospital at Yokosuka and we can work out something."

"I should have done something about Michiko."

"Big brother," said Mark patting him on the back, "there's nothing you could have done about Mrs. Goto. We *can* do something about Masao. From now on you're going to have to listen to your little brother."

The next morning Will accompanied the other prosecutors living at Hattori House to headquarters at the Japanese War Ministry Building on Ichigaya Heights. The trial would take place in the large hall in the center of the building where military academy graduation ceremonies had taken place before the war. Will soon discovered there were two factions, one comprising those men selected and paid by the

Department of Justice and the other those selected and paid by the War Department. The former supported Darsey; the latter, Keenan.

Darsey had been making no secret of his dismay that Keenan had been selected as chief prosecutor: he talked too much and antagonized too many people. Darsey had also protested making the prosecution subordinate to MacArthur, arguing with reason that since both the prosecution and MacArthur were on presidential orders, the prosecution should remain aloof from SCAP, and so keep the trial an independent criminal tribunal. From the beginning Keenan was charmed by MacArthur who, in turn, was so impressed by the flamboyant Irishman that he treated him as a member of his own staff.

Soon after Will had been introduced to the other prosecutors they were all summoned to the auditorium for a staff meeting. Standing on the stage was a sturdy, ruddy-faced man. The man sitting to Will's left whispered, "Joseph B. Keenan, crime buster! W. C. Fields in the flesh —including the nose." Will guessed correctly that his neighbor was from the Department of Justice.

But once Keenan opened his mouth he seized everyone's attention; even those who didn't like him were gripped by his dynamic personality. He reminded Will of Knute Rockne giving an inspirational locker-room speech. Theirs was a formidable task, he said. They must do a thorough, professional job of investigating those who would be indicted; the trial should be carried out under the highest standards of justice and fair play in accordance with American legal standards. At the same time they must not neglect the right to justice of those victims of Japanese oppression who had been maimed, tortured, or murdered. "To accomplish all this each and every one of you, regardless of personal beliefs, must put your shoulder to the wheel and give a hundred and one percent effort. Each and every one of you must spend every possible moment in the great task that is going to prove to the Japanese exactly what democratic justice is." Even the Department of Justice people left the auditorium inspired, until one of their number happened to go backstage and see Keenan sneaking down the rear stairs with his golf clubs.

Will returned to his quarters feeling a stir of renewed vigor and confidence. At last he was being driven not by his emotions but his mind. He was back in Japan not seeking vengeance but only to help see justice done. He was not being impelled by secret, dark thoughts of soul-destroying revenge. He was joining the crusade envisaged by his idol Franklin D. Roosevelt, the crusade to end war and free the Japanese people from those who had enslaved them. And to do this they must now go to the root of the problem, something his own father seemed unwilling to do. The trial must outlaw war itself and sentence not only the military leaders who had waged it cruelly but those civilians who had helped the generals and admirals instigate it. The crime had started in Manchuria where Japanese capitalists had seen military conquest as the golden opportunity of expanding the nation's economy. The crime had continued in China and then in the drive into southeast Asia which led to the sneak attack on Pearl Harbor. And friends of his father, like Kido, were just as responsible as Tojo himself. Kido, as much as Tojo, had advanced the conspiracy of aggression. He too was a nationalist who had secretly operated behind the throne for military victories. Why couldn't his father, brilliant as he was, see that Kido was a shadowy, sinister figure, an oriental Machiavelli? Even his father had written that it was Kido who had chosen Tojo to be prime minister. And wasn't it obvious that the wily Marquis was also an ally of the *zaibatsu*, the Japanese cartel that financed the militarists? Kido must hang alongside Tojo and the other military war criminals.

Chapter Five

1.

Japan, February 1946.

A week later as dusk was falling, the civilian sitting next to Chaucy Snow on the plane reported they were approaching Japan. They had left Guam before dawn in their C-54 after a six-hour layover to make sure their battered craft was in good enough shape to combat the ice they would probably meet off the Japanese coast.

Chaucy could see nothing until the plane made a sharp turn. From the ringing in her ears, she guessed they were fast losing altitude. Then through a break in the clouds a familiar snow-capped peak suddenly appeared on the left. Mount Fuji! She recognized it from pictures. Her heart beat faster. But the dramatic peak disappeared once they began circling for a landing. They plunged into a cloud and she could see only an occasional dim pile of what appeared to be rubble, but even these indistinct objects had a touch of romanticism. This, at last, was the Orient. The Far East!

After the excessive heat of the plane, the first blast of cold in her face was invigorating and the large flakes of gently falling snow made her feel as if she were about to walk into an old Japanese woodcut. Even after more than a week of flights over a vast ocean and tiresome waits at dingy airfields, she felt a thrill as she stepped onto Japanese soil. She peered into the fading light, hoping that her father's new acquisition, Will McGlynn, would not be there to meet her. The last thing she wanted was to have her first impressions of Japan influenced by some old hand. She wanted to feel for herself, to see for herself. She was tall with a turned-up Irish nose and wore her dark hair cut short. She had the eager look of a bright child opening a Christmas present. She had come far in her profession because of her industry, intelligence, and an insatiable need to show her father that she could be his equal in a courtroom. She was aware of every waking minute, constantly assessing, reviewing, and adjusting herself to whatever situation faced her.

There was little to see from the bus as it rattled and banged its way toward Yokohama, eighteen miles south of Tokyo. Occasionally she managed to glimpse Japanese people but they all looked alike, the men in a sort of people's uniform of olive drab, the women in ugly clothing that resembled floppy Gay Nineties bloomers.

Though all others in the bus appeared bored, as if they were touring the Bronx, she had never felt so alive. The oriental mysteries that lay hidden intrigued her. Dark rising shadows ahead, she guessed, were the buildings of Tokyo. She could hardly wait her turn to get off the bus and stand on a real Japanese street. The snow was now coming faster, but it melted as soon as it touched the sidewalk and, encumbered as she was with two heavy suitcases, she almost pitched over in the slush. She followed others into the headquarters of Army Transport Command. It had once been some sort of large tea shop, for its name was still printed in gold letters on the glass door. As she was wrestling her luggage through the door a tall American officer approached her hesitantly. She knew who it was because she had once caught a glimpse of Will McGlynn in her father's outer office. Now that he was not as thin or frail as he had been, he reminded her a bit of Gary Cooper.

"Excuse me, are you Chaucy Snow?"

He was as stuffy as she had imagined, but she was grateful to be relieved of the two heavy bags. Then an energetic young woman with a pert, saucy face was pumping her hand.

"I'm Maggie McGlynn. Welcome to the madhouse we call Tokyo!" She appropriated Chaucy's right arm and guided her outside to a dilapidated car. "Sit up front with me so we can have some girl talk instead of a travelogue from my darling brother." As Maggie guided the car rapidly through the snow the two were soon chattering like old friends.

In the back seat Will was grateful Maggie had taken over. He had not looked forward to this meeting, for the last thing he wanted was to talk about the coming trial. Chaucy Snow obviously was intent on setting free those who should be hanged. He had expected her to look like Old Man Snow but she wasn't bad-looking. Still, her voice *was* annoying—she sounded so sure of herself.

Maggie was informing Chaucy that someone had used a lot of influence to get her a room at the famous Imperial Hotel, but by now Chaucy was so entranced by the passing sights that she was paying little attention. There was a real ricksha in the fluttering snow! And sitting in it was a made-up doll of a woman! It was just what she was hoping to see. Maggie was asking her what she thought of the Emperor's New Year's Rescript renouncing his divinity. Chaucy hadn't heard about it but thought it was a good idea.

Good idea! thought Will. Couldn't anyone see this was a monumental hoax? Just before renouncing his divinity, Hirohito had praised his grandfather, the Emperor Meiji, for issuing his famous "Charter Oath," which purportedly provided for a genuinely democratic regime with the participation of all classes, high and low, in the affairs of state. What a fraud! This was the same Emperor Meiji who had set the feudal mold for today's Japan. He had battled with China and Russia, overrun both Formosa and Korea and established "special rights" for Japanese in Manchuria.

"I can hear brother grinding his teeth in the back seat," said Maggie. "He thinks Meiji was a rapscallion because he fought wars with Russia and China and gobbled up both Formosa and Korea."

Will could not keep quiet. "He also set up the feudal pattern for today's Japan."

"You should read Daddy's books more carefully, big brother."

He was silent.

Chaucy was intrigued by a large group of people eagerly huddling around some sort of a stove. "What are they doing?"

"Roasting sweet potatoes," said Will and laughed. "Remember, Maggie, how you and Mark used to run out in the street when the sweet-potato man came by pushing a cart and chanting his wares?"

"Weren't they the most delicious things?" she said. "I tried one the other day and it was awful. I guess I lost my taste for them. But about the Emperor's Rescript, Will. You'll have to admit he wound it up with a nice ode for the New Year."

" 'The pine is brave, That changes not its color . . .' "

When she hesitated he finished it, " 'With the weight of snow.' "

It was lovely, thought Chaucy, particularly on that magical first night. And she had liked the way Will had finished it, not with sarcasm but with appreciation.

Will was thinking of that part of the Rescript which Maggie apparently had not read, lamenting the spread of "excessive radical tendencies" which were weakening the people's sense of morality. What was that but a step backward?

Maggie let Chaucy sleep until midafternoon, then took her to a meal at the Foreign Correspondents Club, and later the time-weary Chaucy couldn't even remember what she ate. Maggie guided her back to the Imperial Hotel where she gratefully clambered back into bed, blessing her new friend for her thoughtfulness. The following morning Will escorted her to the War Ministry Building headquarters of the counsels defending the Japanese war criminals. On the way he made no secret of his distaste for those on trial. Even civilians like the Marquis Kido, he said, were just as guilty as the generals. When she retorted that each man on trial was a separate case, he was about to retort but controlled himself. His silence was more insulting to her than anything he might have said; it made her feel that he thought a new woman lawyer couldn't stand the heat of argument.

He introduced her to the coordinator of the defense, a Nisei, George Yamaoka, a member of a leading New York law firm. He was effusive. "We need all the help we can get."

"Even from a lady lawyer?" said Chaucy, unaware that some of her resentment had stemmed from jealousy of her father's extravagant praise of Will.

"I think you'll find most of us not concerned about your sex," said Yamaoka. He took her aside and confided that there was already a split in their ranks. Beverly Coleman, a Navy captain, had just been brought up from the atrocity trials already in session at Yokohama to be chief defense counsel. He wanted them to concentrate on a common defense instead of merely pleading individual cases. "But those two men in uniform, Lazarus and Furness," he said, pointing at two men, one a Marine lieutenant, the other an Army captain, "won't go along." It could weaken their clients' cases. "There's something to be said for both views and I hope you take some time before making up your mind." Chaucy nodded but had already decided to plead one case only. "We have another problem," continued Yamaoka. "Few of the Japanese defense counsels really understand our legal system. In America we consider a man innocent until proven guilty. The Japanese feel that if a man is indicted he is guilty, and their duty is to get the best possible deal." He was particularly concerned about the defense of Marquis Kido, the Lord Privy Seal. "He has only one counsel, a Japanese who is also going to represent Togo, the Foreign Minister at the time of Pearl Harbor." The Nisei feared there would be a serious conflict of interests and had asked one of his law partners in New York to come over to help Kido, who was obviously unpopular with the military defendants.

Chaucy found the slim and gracious Captain Coleman to be a charming Southern gentleman. His father was a lawyer, like his grandfather, the famous cavalry raider Colonel Mosby. Those opposed to Coleman were equally affable. Marine lieutenant Aristides Lazarus, a dynamic Greek never at a loss for words, gave off an aura of pent-up energy. And George Furness, a graduate of Harvard Law School, was tall and quietly impressive. Upon learning that she had graduated from Boston University Law, he insisted she lunch with him at the nearby Quonset hut which served as a dining room.

"Things are not going well at all," he said. "Do you know anything about the Yamashita and Homma trials in Manila?"

"Only what I read in the papers. Both were tried and convicted of atrocities and are going to be hanged."

"In Washington the Supreme Court is still reviewing the Yamashita case but I have no doubt they'll uphold the verdict. What troubles me is the effect this will have on our trial. Will General MacArthur again interfere as he did in the Manila trials? I know, because I helped defend Homma, a very decent man who was convicted unfairly. We only had two weeks to prepare our case although the prosecution had been working on it for months. Furthermore, the trial was not conducted according to accepted legal procedure. We couldn't even cross-examine the deponents." For the first time in modern history a commanding officer had been held criminally liable for acts committed by his troops. The court itself concluded there had been no criminal intent or even gross negligence. "The court's findings created a *new* crime," he said. "It was ridiculous." Homma had been tried by authority of the man he had defeated in battle and by whose authority both defense and prosecution personnel were appointed. "And so, of course, a fair trial was impossible. What is going to happen over there?" he asked, nodding toward the War Ministry Building. "That trial isn't going to be run internationally the way they're doing at Nuremberg. The Charter here was drawn up only by Americans and primarily by that great libertarian Joe Keenan! It is an executive

decree of General MacArthur acting under orders from the U.S. Joint
Chiefs of Staff. Believe it or not, our Allies were consulted on the
Charter only after it was issued!"

A prosecution lawyer joined them. He laughed. "Don't get yourself
in an uproar, George. You know damn well the Charter is almost
exactly like the one at Nuremberg. Tokyo is going to be the Nuremberg of the Pacific."

"I'm not sure even that means the defense is going to get a fair
deal," said Furness gloomily. "Besides, there's no one like MacArthur
in Germany."

After lunch Chaucy talked with one of the Japanese defense lawyers who could speak English. "Our policy," he said, "is to maintain
the line of no responsibility of the Emperor. Secondly, the defense of
individuals should only be within the framework of the national defense."

"That could present some problems for individual defense," said
Chaucy.

The Japanese agreed. "Your legal process is not easy to understand.
Your prosecutors are very courteous. And the questions they are now
asking those in Sugamo Prison who will be indicted sometimes seem
naïve. They stumble as though they're asking for advice. It gives our
clients a false sense of security. They don't know they're being
trapped by clever men. Some of these Americans have been public
prosecutors, some connected with the FBI. And you know how *they*
work. They make a defendant feel superior so they can trip him up.
And they've planted spies in Sugamo and are treating war crimes the
same as a big murder case. Keenan had a lot of experience with
Chicago gangsters and the Mafia; he thinks he can deal just as successfully with what he calls Japan's international political gangsters."

During dinner at the Imperial Hotel that night with Maggie and
Will, Chaucy talked guardedly about the problems facing the defense.
It was going to be difficult to reconcile the Japanese lawyers to Western legal ways. She also brought up Furness's fears after the unjust
trials given to Homma and Yamashita.

"Lawyers who lose a case often think they've been robbed," Will
said. "And what does Mr. Furness really know about Homma? Was he
on the Death March? Was he a prisoner of war at Cabanatuan when
Yamashita relieved Homma to take command of the Philippines? Do
you think Furness would make as good a witness on the stand as

someone who was there?" His tone was without rancor and Chaucy was impressed by his logic.

All three went outside. The streets were almost clear of snow. Will was silent as they walked through Hibiya Park past the pitifully made-up girls leaning against a long wall displaying their wares for the passing G.I.'s. Will's two companions, leaning toward each other in confidence, suddenly burst into laughter. He wanted to know what was so funny.

"I was in the infirmary this afternoon to give blood," explained Maggie, "and this young Japanese doctor came up to me with his syringe and said, 'May I suck your blood, madam?' " Will joined in the laughter and the three, with Chaucy in the middle, went off arm in arm.

In the next two weeks Chaucy saw Maggie almost every evening. One Sunday Maggie took her to Kamakura to family friends whose ancestors had been feudal lords for two hundred years. The Kondos—grandfather, father, mother, two aunts, and three children—were waiting in formal silk kimonos decorated with the family crest. Maggie and Chaucy had come in their heaviest clothing, but they found a charcoal fire glowing in the tatami guest room; Maggie felt guilty to see Kondo-san liberally adding charcoal which was so precious.

"If you are using all this charcoal for us, it is not necessary," she said. "I wanted Snow-san to see how Japanese live in these difficult days."

"Please do not concern yourselves," said Kondo in English. "The town council office allowed us a special ration of charcoal and sake for our honorable guests." He poured warm sake into their cups.

Chaucy's legs ached from sitting cross-legged so long on the tatami but she hid her discomfort from the Kondos who were eager for information about America. She finally managed to turn the talk to Japan. "I've heard that Emperor Meiji set up the feudal model for today's Japan."

"*Naruhodo*, really?" said Kondo, sucking his teeth and turning to his father who did the same. "It is very interesting. I never thought of it that way but it could be true."

"Do the people blame the Emperor for the war?" she asked.

Maggie gulped at such a question, but the Kondos nodded to one another and finally the father said, "Perhaps a number of young people or radicals believe His Majesty is to blame but I hope you understand that it was not his role to interfere in politics. The same as in England. No one blames King George for the war with Hitler, do they?" He added that he was happy to find Americans so interested in Japan's problems. "It is a great honor to meet a lady who will take part in the International Tribunal." He laughed nervously. "Quite a shock to some of my friends but I find it very progressive—I mean that a lady should take such a role."

"What wonderful people!" said Chaucy on their way home. "They're so friendly and open."

"They were just as delighted with you. They've never seen a lady lawyer before. I hope you didn't believe that nonsense about getting special rations for charcoal and sake. They probably used up a month's supply tonight."

Since as yet there was relatively little to do at the War Ministry, Chaucy spent much of her free time wandering around on her own. She wanted to see Japan without Maggie on hand to explain everything. Before coming she had read several books, but she had already discovered that the mysterious East they portrayed did not exist.

She wrote long letters of her experiences to her father and described how stoic but innately curious she found the Japanese. As they scurried around carrying their lunches of rice balls and bits of fish in little metal boxes, apparently intent on saving every second, they would suddenly stop to watch a young American soldier deftly move a huge pile of debris with a bulldozer, fascinated to see such a huge man with such a baby face accomplish such wonders and then smile down at them.

Chaucy was amused by the way the people bowed at everything. They bowed if she bumped into them, bowed when some tipsy American berated them, bowed when they said hello, bowed when they said good-bye. She even saw a group of country women carrying vegetables bowing whenever a jeep passed. Perhaps they thought the jeep was the symbol of the new shogun, MacArthur. Every day more signs in English would appear. One of her favorites was a large billboard:

YOUR KIND DARN
AND POLITE
LAUNDRY WORKS
SUN RISE CO.

Then there was the curio shop sign: THE HOUSE OF THE REAL MCCOY: and one curious one over a little food store: V.D. Will explained that a mischievous G.I. had told the owner that it meant "Welcome Allied Forces." The most mystifying misunderstanding of English was the printing on the bags of a fruit store: FRESH FARTS. But the sign that gave the biggest laugh was the one a defense counsel from New York told her he had seen in a public toilet: DON'T THROW CIGARETTES BUTTS, CHEWING GUM AND OTHERS INTO THIS URINAL.

She spent hours walking past the Occupation buildings opposite the Palace, American flags waving above them all. Strange sights became common—pedicabs, charcoal-burning taxis spewing acrid smoke, little trolleys bulging with people. She spent a whole afternoon exploring the Ginza. Despite its crumbling sidewalks and rubble, it still maintained some of its pre-war gaiety. It was crowded by Japanese who remembered it as a romantic symbol of the outside world with its neon lights, boutiques, coffee shops, Western-style dance halls, restaurants, and movie theaters. There was little left, yet the magnet of Ginza still drew ragged people who somehow found money to pay exorbitant prices for food and household utensils. She found it at first unsettling to be the object of so much curiosity. Men, women and children openly gaped at her. She finally realized she represented to them not only the conqueror but the symbol of freedom from hunger and deprivation. She was the child of democracy, the strange, emancipated woman wearing stylish clothes—a super being from the puzzling West.

Her most memorable excursion was a train trip to the north. Ueno Station was packed so tightly it was almost impossible to move. She was the only American and she was almost exhausted before she got her special Allied ticket with the help of an elderly man who spoke some English. She had said she just wanted to go to any town that was about an hour away. The car was packed and at first she feared her fellow passengers might resent her presence, but once the train started those nearby who knew a little English began asking her questions. A courtly elderly gentleman was astounded to learn she was a lawyer. "I never heard of such a thing!" he said and when he passed on this information it caused a wide buzz of comment. Some had relatives in New York and Chicago and wondered if she knew them. Others wanted to know if food was rationed in the United

States. When her station was announced, several passengers began passing up their calling cards and she barely got out in time.

A number of women from Tokyo got off with her. They were carrying goods for barter—kimonos, valuable scrolls, prints. "We call it our 'onion existence,'" one of them told Chaucy. "We cry while we peel off successive layers of our remaining possessions." The town was relatively undamaged and the outlying farmhouses were still intact. Here the rhythm of life appeared to be placid. She spent two hours wandering through the picturesque streets until she reached the edge of town. There she paused to drink in the beauty of the fields beyond, unscarred by war and made even more memorable by the background of austere mountains in the distance. As she returned to the little station she could see the Tokyo women returning with bags filled with vegetables. Chaucy had read how the middle-class city dweller had traditionally looked down on the farmer. Now the rural people were far better off.

The train was even more crowded on the trip back to Tokyo and the foul odor of unwashed bodies mixed with the strong smell of vegetables being carried to the city for sale. The train lurched and swayed but the other passengers seemed oblivious, accepting the discomfort as normal. One woman, unable to take her baby to the toilet, simply held him out the window, his bottom exposed to the open air, then calmly brought him back to nurse at her breast.

Chaucy got yet another view of Japan from her visits to the Todas with Maggie and Will. She always cherished these trips not only for the privilege of seeing Japanese in their own home at complete ease with *gaijin* but also for the privilege of participating in the close relationship of the two families. Although she had not yet met Shogo, Ko, or their father, she felt she knew them. She appreciated Sumiko's quiet acceptance of poverty and respected Emi's strength and endurance. But one day she and Will found the little household in a state of mild confusion. An American officer, Emi informed them, had just arrived with his daughter to take over the western section of the house. Maggie was particularly upset to learn that it was her father who had persuaded Mrs. Toda to rent the rooms. But Emi said it was an answer to her prayers. They had a dwindling supply of clothing to barter for food. Furthermore Lieutenant Colonel Mulrooney was such an agreeable man and his daughter brought new life into the house.

While they were drinking tea Emi apologetically brought up the subject of her middle son, Shogo, who was going to be tried for atrocities.

"They allowed Sumi-chan and me to visit him a few minutes at the Sugamo Prison. He was looking so well, almost contented. But that is what worries me. He doesn't seem interested in getting a good lawyer. 'Oh, they cost too much,' he joked. 'Besides, I don't need one. All I have to do is tell the truth.' "

She asked if he meant about Colonel Tsuji, his former commanding officer who had committed so many atrocities during the war. "And he said, 'About myself only. You and father would not respect me if I betrayed my superior officer.' I said that Papa and I expected him to tell that he was not at all involved in Tsuji's unspeakable atrocities. He just took my hand and said gently that all would be well. He had the face of a little priest who had purged himself of self." She looked up appealingly. "Forgive me, but could you possibly go see him?"

Will hesitated. "I don't know if I'd be allowed to do so." He explained he was assigned to the prosecution for the trial of the principal war criminals in Tokyo, and Shogo would be tried in the individual trials for atrocities in Yokohama. But on seeing her look of despair for being so bold as to ask such a favor, he said he would ask Mr. Keenan, his superior. "Perhaps he will allow me to see Shogo if there is no conflict with my duties."

2.

To Will's surprise the chief prosecutor had no objections. Talking with Shogo would involve no conflict of interest and might be very useful. It would give Will the chance to query Shogo on the whereabouts of the infamous Tsuji, one of the most wanted war criminals. Keenan, in fact, became enthusiastic. Colonel Tsuji had exerted an insidious influence on the Japanese military. What a witness he would make on the stand! Keenan suggested that Will go to Sugamo Prison with the prosecutor he had selected to interview Tojo. Will could sit in on this interview and then see Shogo.

That afternoon Will and the prosecutor, John W. Fihelly, followed by an interpreter and a secretary, were brought to a small interrogation cell in Sugamo Prison. While waiting for Tojo, Fihelly remarked that few of the other prisoners would speak to the general, who spent most of the exercise time alone strolling slowly around the yard, puffing on a cigarette. Unlike the other prisoners, Tojo usually started an interrogation with a few complaints. Wasn't it possible, he would say, to prevent the G.I. guards from swiping his pipes and handkerchiefs for souvenirs? They even took buttons from his shirt and his Buddhist rosary. "But you'll find him quite affable even though we call him Old Razor Blade because he's so sharp."

Tojo entered, bowed, and sat down. He complained about the poor treatment being given the Class B-C prisoners which comprised military officers, enlisted men, and civilians charged with the personal mistreatment of prisoners of war. They were being tried in Yokohama. Will felt his gorge rising at the man's arrogance in demanding that these criminals get more consideration. Then with a little smile Tojo noted that his cell had the ominous number 44. Since four in Japanese meant death, wasn't double four a little too much? And, moreover, the cells were too cold.

Will had been instructed to say nothing but couldn't help remarking, "You made it that way for the folks you put in it, so I guess it'll have to be cold for you too."

Tojo laughed. Coffee in large mugs was brought in and Tojo gratefully took a long sip. He drew out a little notebook and rubbed his hands as if eager to begin the session. But they were interrupted by two Japanese plumbers who began pounding large wrenches on a radiator giving off too much heat. After a minute of this the secretary said to them, "Hubba, hubba!" and pointed to the door. Understanding the American slang for "Hurry up," they bowed and left.

Tojo turned to the interpreter. "Every day when I leave here the guard pokes me in the back with his billy club and says, 'Hubba, hubba!' Until now," he added with a little smile, "I thought it meant, 'Remember Pearl Harbor!' "

On his way with a male Nisei secretary to interview Shogo, Will had been startled to see an old friend of his father scrubbing the corridor. The Marquis Kido looked up but he hadn't seen Will since he was a boy, and only wondered why the tall American officer was staring at him.

The interview with Shogo was confusing and unsettling. They both spoke in Japanese with the secretary desperately trying to keep up with them. Shogo did not have any complaints. He appeared to be completely at peace, and only answered questions about Tsuji with praise for his former commander. Nor did he seem at all concerned about his coming trial in Yokohama. *"Un o ten ni makase masu,"* he said.

Noticing that the Nisei secretary was stumped, Shogo said, "My fate is in the hands of Heaven," and affably switched to fluent English.

But Will was not impressed, figuring Shogo was putting on an act of cooperation and friendliness. They had never got along as boys, and when Shogo had gone to military academy and then become a worshipper of the notorious Tsuji, Will had lost all respect for him. As an aide he surely knew about the many atrocities committed by his idol, and had probably participated. What bothered Will most was the searing memory of that day on the Bataan Death March when he had collapsed from exhaustion, then vaguely saw, just before losing consciousness, a Japanese officer who looked exactly like Shogo leaning down to help him.

"According to your record," said Will, "you and Tsuji were both on Bataan during the Death March."

"Yes, sir. The colonel was sent from Singapore to help plan the final attack on Bataan but we arrived late. The American and Filipino prisoners were being rounded up."

"Did you know I was one of those prisoners?"

"I heard you were."

"I passed out near Lubao and when I came to a Catholic chaplain told me a Japanese officer brought me in and wouldn't leave until the priest promised to take good care of me." He stared at Shogo. "Were you that officer?"

"What makes you think so?"

"I got a glimpse of the officer. He looked like you." Will was almost positive it had been a hallucination, and he was sure Shogo would now claim credit for this act of humanity.

Shogo *had* saved Will because it had been the right thing to do. But out of pride he said, "I was not the man who helped you, Major McGlynn."

Will was taken aback. Somehow he was disappointed. Shogo's face was expressionless. Was Toda even more clever than he imagined? What was the point of all this? Will had assumed that Shogo and the other young zealots who had served Tsuji were so dedicated to his cause that they were still willing to die for him like the celebrated forty-seven *ronin*, *samurai* forced to roam in feudal days when they lost their master. The history of Japan seemed full of such fools.

Will had planned to ask Shogo a series of seemingly unconnected questions that would reveal the depth of Tsuji's war crimes. But Shogo's refusal to take credit for saving him perversely made Will think there *was* a slight chance he was his savior. Abandoning his subtle plan, Will now bluntly said, "What part did you play in Tsuji's murder of six thousand innocent Chinese in Singapore?"

"I know nothing about any such murders," was his honest reply. He had later heard stories about the murders but had not believed them. Nor had he believed the story that Tsuji had persuaded key officers on General Homma's staff in Bataan to put to death Filipino and American prisoners of war during the Death March. It was not until 1944 when he and Tsuji were transferred to Burma that he realized he'd been deceived. It was then that he heard Tsuji give orders to execute several captured Allied airmen, and cut out their livers. In disgust Shogo had requested a transfer to Tokyo.

And now, though he had never participated in any atrocities, he felt guilty for having unwittingly helped Tsuji. Nor could he forget Tsuji's remarkable accomplishments as Japan's God of Operations. He himself was guilty by association and deserved to die. And it would be contrary to the *samurai* code to testify against a former commander.

Completely frustrated, Will asked a few more questions, got similarly unsatisfactory answers and finally left, displeased with himself and disgusted with Shogo. How could any responsible person ever have been drawn to Tsuji in the first place?

It was snowing hard by the time Will left the camp with Fihelly, the gate sign now spelling out in large letters: DRIVE CAREFULLY. Will turned to see a woman and six children standing outside the barbed-wire fence staring at the prison, unaware of the snow covering their bare heads. What were they thinking? Would their loved one behind the grim, gray walls be hanged at the gallows-house that had recently been, as *Stars and Stripes* reported, "set for business"? God knows, most of those behind the barbed wire would deserve what they got. Kido and Tojo certainly but for some strange reason Will still felt, despite his repugnance, that Shogo might have been the man who saved him. In his three years of captivity he had encountered a number of other Japanese who had shown him kindness. How many behind those gray walls were victims of circumstance? It was a disturbing thought for a prosecutor.

That evening Will reported to Keenan at his room in Hattori House. The chief prosecutor's face was flushed as he greeted Will effusively. When Will mentioned seeing Kido at Sugamo and wondered if he was on the list to be tried, Keenan finished his drink and got one for Will. The executive committee of the prosecution, he explained a bit thickly, had already conducted long sessions to select those to be indicted. "We haven't chosen any civilians yet but you can bet your last dollar Kido will be on it." After all, wasn't he a sinister figure plotting behind the throne?

"Yes, sir."

Keenan escorted Will to the door. Across the hall they could hear laughing in Donihi's room. "Helluva racket," complained Keenan and slid the door open. Donihi was chatting with MacArthur's chief political adviser, George Atcheson, and several men from the Political Affairs Section. Keenan motioned Donihi to come out and then said in a loud stage whisper, "Who are those bums in there? Throw them the hell out!" Then the chief prosecutor spun around and headed unsteadily toward his own room.

Will was appalled. Brilliant as Keenan apparently was, how fit was he to lead the prosecution?

Chapter Six

1.

Tokyo, March 1946.

Ever since their first dinner together several weeks earlier McGlynn had thought of little except Mariko. Never before had he felt like this. Even as he struggled with the fascinating problem of turning the old Meiji Constitution into a democratic organic law he kept envisioning Mariko's *komugi-iro* complexion, that subtle wheat color which to him was the essence of femininity. And his notes would become marred with the Japanese characters of her name. It might be asinine, yet he had never been so alive. Why, at age sixty—well, sixty-two— had he been so abruptly obsessed (there was no better word for it) by this young women's image? It was like a delicious brain disease. It was ridiculous, unfitting, embarrassing, and to normal observers indecent to be mooning over someone young enough to be his daughter.

Perhaps there was something in the air of a nation going through major surgery that was setting the doctors of the massive operation awry. Or could it be because he had never before met anyone like Mariko, and long-imprisoned emotions had been stirred up? He knew most of his colleagues would not regard her as beautiful or even desirable. And yet he never tired of watching her. Her eyes could light up and her modest face be transformed by a thought which suggested a mysterious world within. It was like seeing some distant mountain in his beloved New Hampshire reveal, in a change of light, an indescribable beauty. Behind her simplicity lay a poem of unmatched loveliness, as rhythmical and eloquent as a clear stream to the man fortunate enough to fathom it. She obviously wore makeup but it was subtle with no attempts to glorify any feature. He had never been interested in such things so could not analyze what he appreciated, but he did know that what he surveyed was without guile or art.

She reminded him of Wordsworth's tribute to his wife. "She was a Phantom of Delight!" Yes, Mariko was just such a phantom, a lovely apparition from a far more gracious past. "A dancing shape, an image gay, to haunt, to startle, and waylay." When she smiled or laughed it was not for effect but a natural expression of joy. Nor was he ever conscious of any feminine ploys. There was no affectation in either her good humor or her anger, no attempt in gesture or gait to impress. She always was exactly what she was without effort.

She seemed to possess something that was only hers and could never be corrupted. She was a born princess in her everyday movements, the essence of tranquillity in her self-possession. Even when she had bridled at some of his insensitive remarks about Japan, she never lost her composure. But what he admired most was the revelation that behind her innate modesty was a granite fortress. She could not be tempted by any material rewards to abandon her sense of what was proper, nor won by compliments, nor cowed by force or threat. She would be a very good ally in stress and danger. He realized his adoration would seem extravagant to others, but his feelings for some damned reason were extravagant. He reveled in their extravagance. If only he were twenty years younger! Even ten years!

She had made it apparent that she respected him highly for his books, and that she felt at ease with him because of his understanding of things Japanese. But as yet he had not dared to hold her hand, let alone kiss her. He had thought long ago that any such experience was over for him. Now his pulse pounded as soon as she approached— which she did late one afternoon to have dinner with him for the fourth time. Tonight they went to the Dai Ichi Hotel where he found it difficult to hide his feelings. At last they climbed into a rickety taxi and headed for her home. Taro would be staying overnight with a friend and he would not have to endure the insolence of that young snot.

It was obvious that Mariko liked him but did it go beyond admiration for his accomplishments? He was probably a fool to have such hopes but tonight he was going to risk the embarrassment of repulse. But how to start? He tried to think of something witty to say, but he could only come up with a forced observation: "Wasn't it Wilde who said you should commit follies in youth in order to have something to regret in old age?"

Mariko couldn't think of any sensible answer, and he felt foolish.

"My only folly has been an obsession for work," he said, "and so my personal life for years has been deadly dull. I wish I weren't so boring!"

Boring! she thought. Didn't he know everything he said was fascinating, including his own false perception of himself? She wished she could express herself out loud but lapsed into silence. Finally she decided to bring up a subject that troubled her. "I want to apologize for Taro's rudeness to you. I told you he was staying with a school friend tonight but I didn't tell you the reason. He's attending a very late session of the Young Communist League. His history teacher at Ichiko has persuaded many of the boys to become Communists. I'm so worried!"

"It's only logical," he said, relieved to be back in an arena where he shone. "These youngsters are looking desperately for something to cling to. Some hope for a decent life. The appeal of communism to the brightest and most idealistic is irresistible. My son Mark went through the same phase just before Pearl Harbor. Only the Communist Party seemed to be for peace, and against Jim Crow and anti-Semitism. So he had a grand time making street speeches in upper Manhattan and picketing the White House for peace." He chuckled. "I was as worried as you are, but Franklin Roosevelt gave me the most practical advice. 'Better a Young Red,' he said, 'than a Young Republican.' And the day after Pearl Harbor, Mark enlisted in the Marines. The best thing you can do is nothing. Above all don't try to argue with that young rascal of yours. Be patient."

She felt reassured, and wondered if he was going to try and hold her hand. Their driver, obviously a former kamikaze pilot, seemed to be seething with a resentment McGlynn had noted in other young cab drivers whenever an American was riding with a Japanese young woman. After narrowly avoiding an oncoming Kamikaze by inches, the driver took a sharp right turn at full speed, throwing Mariko into McGlynn. He grasped her firmly in protection but as the car straightened up he didn't let go. Her face was inches from his. It had been, as Mark would call it, "a benefit curve." He kissed her lightly and she made no protest. In fact, she said nothing but neither did she try to free herself.

McGlynn wondered if he would be wiser to leave well enough alone since she had not responded to his kiss. But it was no time for wisdom. He kissed her again, this time more forcefully and to his amazement she *did* respond. He did not want the kiss to end—and held it as long as his breath lasted.

She said nothing but did not resist when he held her tighter. Indeed, she huddled closer. Too soon they were rumbling over her bumpy street.

"May I come in?" he said.

"Yes."

Always before, he had told the driver to wait but this time he paid him. Led by Mariko and her flashlight, he started down the path. Stumbling over a stray rock, he had to grab her to keep from falling. They managed to stay upright but she dropped the flashlight. She started to giggle and soon the two were in paroxysms of laughter as they groped to retrieve it.

"Shhh!" she said. "The neighbors will hear." But this only caused both of them to resume laughing. At last they found the light, made their way to the door and were inside, the door closing, thought McGlynn, with a satisfying finality.

Tentatively, daintily, she approached the bed and there was enough moonlight for him to see she had an astoundingly young, trim body. She cautiously slid into bed, shivering even though it wasn't that cold. The artificial barrier between them suddenly broke. Within him had previously lurked the fear of rebuff. That was why he always had been guarded with himself, guarded with his associates, guarded from the world. Mariko had sensed this, for she instinctively fathomed his sudden moods. Schooled by stoic upbringing to distrust show of emotion, she was as proud as he. But in a magic moment they were stripped of the armor which years had built around them. He pressed against her avidly and she responded by going limp in sweet surrender. Their warm lips met. "My darling," she whispered in English since there was no word for this in Japanese. He abandoned himself to her, but she took no advantage of his defenseless position. Their last reserve melted simultaneously and they blended into each other in an extremity of passion neither had ever before attained. She kissed his sensitive hands which she had admired, and this simple act raised his ardor in a last untying of bonds.

As they rested, McGlynn felt no sense of lassitude or regret. But neither he nor Mariko knew what to say. Then to his wonder—and hers—they were once more simultaneously aroused and their mutual enjoyment and fulfillment were even more exquisite.

Upon waking in the morning from a deep sleep McGlynn was pleased to find her cuddled up as close as possible against him. She was asleep and her face, innocent and trusting, was beautiful without any makeup at all. How could I ever have deserved all this? he thought. At last her eyes opened and she showed no false modesty or regret. She kissed him lustily and soon they were again locked together in tender coupling.

After a hasty breakfast Mariko left the house with her customary composure, looking as if she had spent the usual prim and proper night in bed. He followed a minute later, feeling as if the eyes of all Japan, and particularly those of the neighboring Todas, were upon him. She had suggested he keep behind her at a respectable distance to the bus stop and they sat far from each other on the bus. Twice their eyes met. The first time, she hastily looked away, but the second time her face was transformed by a faint Mona Lisa smile. She was thinking, "How can such an unusual man see anything in me?" while he was wondering what magic spell had come over her last night. They also sat far from each other on the subway, nor did they use the same elevator to the sixth floor of the Dai Ichi Building.

When he arrived at his office there was a young woman, an American, waiting next to his desk. It was Chaucy Snow. She apologized for intruding and then bluntly asked a favor.

"What?" he asked, feeling little desire to help her since he had observed she seemed to have reservations about his older son.

Chaucy still did harbor resentment toward Will for allowing his mistreatment as a prisoner of war to affect his judgment as a lawyer. But she held his father in high esteem. "I could use your advice. I've been thrown into a case involving people I know little about. Perhaps—"

He interrupted her as if she were one of his less bright students. "Young lady, I'm afraid you're going to have to learn about the Japanese on your own. There's no such thing as a *Readers Digest* condensed version."

She smiled and he couldn't help realizing she was attractive. "May I have fifteen seconds to present my case, Professor?" Just then Mariko passed, carrying papers, and he appreciated that she had come by a roundabout course. What a delightful rear end she had! The memory of last night made him affable. "Shoot," he said with a grin that had nothing to do with Chaucy, and glanced at his watch.

"In the little time I've been here I've realized that everything I've ever read about Japan is hogwash, except your books. I rest my case."

He had to laugh. "By God, young lady, you made it with one second to spare." He surveyed her pert, bright face. "Your mother must be Irish."

"She died when I was twelve."

"So you have your father's brains and your mother's looks. Scotch-Irish, not a bad blend. My own children are similarly gifted.

"I can give you half an hour this morning and perhaps we can continue later. First thing you have to do is empty from your brain all the garbage that has been dumped into it by the Japanese 'experts' over here who have been brainwashed by academicians, psychiatrists, anthropologists, and politicians. I can give you a few guidelines but you must learn on your own in the streets, the trains, the markets and, whenever possible, in the homes. Research with your feelings and instinct, not your mind. Appreciate the differences. In everyday life, for instance, Japanese instinctively practice the concept of the contradiction of opposites, and the means of harmonizing with them. Right and wrong, spirit and matter, God and man—all these opposing elements are harmoniously united in a Japanese. That's why a thing can be good and bad at the same time. We Westerners think in terms of black *or* white. This is how I always explain it to my students: Western logic is like a suitcase, defined and limited. Eastern logic is like the *furoshiki,* that cloth the Japanese carry for wrapping all sort of things. It can be large or small according to needs, and afterward can be folded and put in the pocket." He reached in his desk to draw out a worn book. "This explains Buddhism, and you must understand Buddhism since it is the guiding force of almost all Japanese, including most Christians. You won't be able to understand the people you're going to defend unless you digest this. Within almost every Japanese, metaphysical intuition and instinctive animalistic urges lie side by side. That's why they can brutalize their philosophy and philosophize their brutality. The assassination and bloody acts in Japanese history were usually inspired by idealism. And the soldiers who sailed across to Manchuria and China to save the Orient for the Orient ended up by slaughtering thousands of fellow Orientals in places like Nanking. Who is responsible for the murders? The soldiers, their field officers, their officers in Tokyo, their diplomats, their politicians, the Emperor, the ordinary citizens?"

She was taking notes, desperately trying to keep up with him. "Don't take notes, Miss Snow! We'll go over this again and again. Try to get the essence. Try to realize that during the war there was no buffer zone in the thinking of Japanese soldiers between the transcendental and the empirical, between the chrysanthemum and the sword. They were religious but had no God in our sense—that is, a single Divine Being. They had sympathy but little humanity. Try to imagine their past. They had clans but no society in our sense. They had a rigid family system which gave every person security but took away individuality. That was why the Japanese in our recent conflict were driven by opposing forces, often trying to go in opposite directions simultaneously."

He stopped to observe her radiant face and was pleased. "You'll see so many petty differences today. If you ask, 'This isn't the road for Tokyo, is it?' the average Japanese will bow and say, '*Hai!* Yes!' What he means is, 'What you say is correct. It is *not* the road to Tokyo.' You must already have been confused when a Japanese agrees with you just to be agreeable or to avoid embarrassment, or even give you wrong information rather than admit his lack of knowledge.

"We look at a Japanese and conclude he's utterly inscrutable. Look at the way Japanese workmen handle their funny-looking tools. All wrong. He squats at an anvil and pulls rather than pushes a saw. His books start where ours end, and the writing goes up and down instead of horizontally. He sits on the floor instead of in a chair. He eats raw fish and live, wriggling shrimps! Ugh! He can tell you his stupid wife just died, and then grin. He can fall in the mud with his best kimono and come up with a smile. He will often attempt to convey his ideas to you by misdirection, discussing details in a devious, tortuous manner. He can treat you with exaggerated politeness in his home and rudely shove you aside to get into a train where he'll take off his shoes and put his stocking feet on the seat in front. He has even been known to assassinate a man and later apologize to the servants for messing up the house." He looked at his watch. "In short, what you must realize above all, my dear, is that underneath the veneer of modernity and Westernization, Japan during the war was still oriental. Japan had plunged so precipitously from feudalism to imperialism that the great Meiji, the present Emperor's grandfather, had neither the time nor the inclination to develop liberalism and humanitarianism. Meiji and the Japanese leaders had been interested solely in Western technocracy and methods, not Western values."

There was, he said, a clear difference in the sense of morality between the two cultures. "Beliefs rooted in the Judeo-Christian tradition dictate that once you commit a crime, you must bear the consequences for as long as you live. Oriental teachers, however, preach that if you admit your wrongs, apologize and atone for them, you can start fresh. We Westerners always remember our errors and sins, but the Japanese is taught that his errors are predestined. He must cleanse himself of past mistakes, so he will be able to adapt himself to new possibilities." McGlynn grimaced. "You and your Western colleagues have come across the Pacific to try the Japanese for war crimes with reference *only* to Western justice. For the proper defense you must think Japanese, feel Japanese, and almost *be* Japanese. Even so you'll undoubtedly not prevent them from being hanged with Western rope or put into a Western prison for life."

"Not if I can help it, sir," she said and felt an almost irresistible impulse to lean over and kiss the old fellow on the forehead.

He pushed back his chair with an awful screech, and gallantly helped her to her feet as if she'd been an invalid. "Here endeth the first lesson. Don't forget to study the book on Buddhism." His own flow of words had made him expansive. "Now let me get back to work in this monster laboratory." He gestured grandly. "In this room are some of the finest brains of America. All dedicated to turning *furoshiki* into briefcases. This place often reminds me of the opening of *Macbeth*. Here we are witches all, stirring our kettles of reform and progress known as democracy while chanting, 'Bubble, bubble, toil and trouble, cauldron burn and something-or-other bubble.' See that group?" He pointed. "They've just added eyes of newt. Those over there—toes of frogs! Delicious smell, isn't it?"

As if by magic Mulrooney appeared to escort Chaucy out of the room before the professor could launch into another lecture. He returned a moment later to beg McGlynn to finish their segment of the revised Constitution before Kades had heart failure.

Two weeks earlier the portly Whitney had summoned his entire staff to the conference room to announce solemnly, "Ladies and gentlemen, this is a historic occasion. I am pronouncing you a constitutional assembly. As you undoubtedly know, the most pressing issue facing Japan is a new Constitution. All the Japanese drafts have been completely unacceptable and the Supreme Commander"—he pronounced it Com*mahn*der—"feels he must intervene." He beamed. "I am greatly flattered that he considers our Government Section capable of drafting such a Constitution." Teams, he concluded, would be immediately set up to compose segments of the document.

The deadline for these final drafts was that very afternoon of Chaucy's visit. Two days later Whitney and two assistants marched to the office of Foreign Minister Shigeru Yoshida, who increased his slight resemblance to Winston Churchill by smoking huge cigars. With pomp and circumstance Whitney exhibited to Yoshida and two advisers copies of the American model of the new Constitution.

"Gentlemen," he said dramatically, "the Supreme Commahnder has studied the draft of the new Constitution prepared by you. But he has found it completely unacceptable. I have here a document which has the complete approval of the Supreme Commahnder. He feels it safeguards the Emperor." He handed one copy to Yoshida. "Read it. I'll return in fifteen minutes and we can discuss it." Followed by two assistants, Whitney stepped onto an adjoining porch where they watched the Japanese huddling with perturbation over the documents.

A low-flying American bomber thundered overhead and Whitney grinned at his associates. After checking his watch, he led the way back into the room. "Gentlemen," he said as if addressing a jury, "we have been basking in the warmth of the atomic sunshine."

The three Japanese were agitated. Finally Yoshida, his face a black cloud, picked up the American draft. "It is of a revolutionary nature," he complained. One of his advisers rose swiftly from his seat as if he had sat on a tack and the other sucked in his breath. All three Japanese were visibly surprised and disturbed at the scale of the proposed reforms. One stated that while the Emperor was to be the hereditary head of state, sovereignty was to reside with the people; another renounced war and the possession of arms, and a third abolished all aristocratic privileges.

To Japanese conservatives in the government the idea of popular sovereignty was anathema. It would throw the basic orientation of Japanese society into wild disorder. How could you then distinguish between superiors and inferiors? How know where authority lay? For centuries the people had unquestioningly obeyed those officials who controlled the Emperor.

"Gentlemen," said Whitney impatiently, "General MacArthur will not consider any document which does not include the features we've drawn up."

The Japanese conferred.

"If you are not prepared to sponsor a similar document,"said Whitney, "the Supreme Commahnder will go over your heads to the Japanese people. If you support a Constitution of this kind, General MacArthur will support you."

Though the reforms were thoroughly alien and many of them objectionable, the three Japanese bowed politely and set to work drawing up a draft Constitution incorporating what they believed to be the basic principles of the Government Section's version. On March 4 it was presented to Whitney, and Government Section translators, including Mariko, began working with Japanese Ministry officials and Government Section lawyers. They worked through the night and, despite several heated debates and numerous arguments, late the following afternoon the job was finally completed to everyone's satisfaction.

Mariko was too exhausted to have dinner with the professor, who escorted her home, thoughtfully refusing to stay even a minute. He too was exhausted but his mind was in such turmoil that he slept little that night. It was extraordinary what had been accomplished in so short a time, and he felt that the greatest credit should go to the indomitable Whitney who had shepherded the project through like a shrewd businessman rather than a general. During the ordeal he had never barked commands or thrown his weight around. Contrary to news stories that he was a terror to underlings, he had shown consideration for the welfare of the lowliest worker in his office and had listened patiently to both complaints and compliments. What McGlynn liked was that without fuss he was doing what was necessary promptly and without red tape—but always with MacArthur's approval. In a few short weeks he had brought standing and prestige to the Government Section and turned it into MacArthur's strong right arm.

McGlynn awoke in the morning from fitful sleep prepared for a storm of protest once the new model Constitution was revealed to the press by the Secretary of the Japanese Cabinet. The professor was so curious that he was present with Mulrooney when the bushy-haired Japanese Secretary—clad in Western-style striped pants, black coat, and stiff wing collar—declared that the new Constitution was an epoch-making document. "In it the Emperor himself proclaims the people sovereign. In it we declare militarism dead." Henceforth His Majesty would become a symbol of the people and they would realize this was their own government.

Answering questions in fluent French, the Secretary declared, "We're in a very dangerous situation and in order to avoid a bloody revolution we must take revolutionary steps, such as this Constitution. Some people say this is a government of peers. But I myself was a coal miner, and I began work at the age of fourteen. I think I know what the people want."

McGlynn was surprised that some liberal American journalists regarded the new constitution as a disaster, an alien document foisted on the Japanese Government as a native product. Such criticism was reinforced by a joke popular among Japanese newsmen:

FUJI: "Have you read the new Constitution yet, Yoshi?"
YOSHI: "No, has it been translated into Japanese?"

The new Constitution, argued these critics, should have come from the grass roots. And its worst feature was the ineffective renunciation of the armed forces, a provision which obviously could never be reinforced. Anyone who had ever studied Japanese history knew that the moment the Occupation ended, the Japanese would find some excuse for rebuilding a strong military force. Such critics concluded that MacArthur had jammed the new Constitution down Japanese throats on the theory that anything could be accomplished by military order.

"How long do you think this Constitution will last?" McGlynn asked the foremost of these critics.

"It will die before MacArthur does."

Later in the day the professor called on Kido's former second secretary, Tomohiko Yabe, to pick up a file to be turned over to Keenan for use in the trial. As he was leaving, McGlynn asked what Yabe thought of the new Constitution. He shrugged his shoulders. "It pretends to be a draft by our government but it was made in Washington. It is a cowardly thing, perpetrated by the present Cabinet which is composed of opportunists and liars. How MacArthur must laugh to see the government in the hands of tottering bureaucrats!"

The new Constitution, he said, disregarded the fact that for centuries the life of Japan revolved around the Emperor. He smiled wryly. "Perhaps all will work out for the best by doing it the American way. You know we never regarded the Emperor as a god but as a divine ancestral figure. Our great mistake before the war was to erect a protective barrier around him. Whenever he appeared in public he was surrounded by police, and the streets were cleared. There is no need for this. He was always loved by the people and still is. Now perhaps he will become accessible to leaders of all walks of life, even Communists. Remember the old proverb, 'Environment is more important than birth.' It's the environment of His Majesty which fits him to rule, since his lineage goes back three thousand years. He should still rule, perhaps not through the Constitution but through his relationship to the people. You know he has no personal ambitions, no desire for glory, no material desires, no ambition. He has always disliked militarism. Mark what I say: Out of the great mistakes of the new Constitution and other alien reforms could come an even greater love and power of the Emperor. And you will see it begin in a few weeks."

McGlynn was intrigued. "What do *you* know that *I* don't?"

"At the Imperial household they are secretly planning his first visit to the people—not as a god but as a benign father figure."

2.

At eight o'clock on the morning of March 26, a large black Mercedes-Benz emerged from the Palace gates. Maggie could see Hirohito sitting stiffly in the back, staring straight ahead. His car turned to the right. Then, in a long procession led by white American M.P. jeeps, the Mercedes started down almost empty streets. Maggie, in a jeep behind the Emperor, could see him looking curiously to right and left like a child on an outing. At street crossings Japanese traffic police turned their backs. People were bowing, first to His Majesty, then hurriedly to the white jeeps.

At a suburban railroad station he and his retinue transferred to a shiny train bearing the crest of the Imperial chrysanthemum. Maggie and a few other journalists were allowed to enter the car behind the Emperor's. As the train proceeded through the vast wasteland between the capital and Yokohama, crowds at crossings pressed against the lowered barriers waving little flags to greet their monarch. At every station railroad officials were lined up at rigid attention.

Upon stopping at Takasaki, Maggie edged forward to get just behind the Emperor. She was almost deafened by the shouts of "Banzai!"—ten thousand years. She saw him bow stiffly and, apparently impassive, step into a Mercedes. Inwardly the Emperor was in torment but he had been taught since childhood to hide his feelings. He had suffered deeply at having to tell his people on that fatal day of August 15 that Japan had surrendered. It had been agonizing because he held no real power either as superintendent of state affairs or as commander in chief. "Let me say a word about the causes of surrender," he wrote his son, Crown Prince Akihito. "Our military placed too much emphasis on the spirit, neglecting science." The generals and admirals, he continued, "did not regard the broader aspects of the situation; they knew only how to attack and not how to fall back."

The Emperor also thought it unbearable to remain on the throne while some of his subjects were about to be put on trial as war criminals. He could be heard talking to himself as he paced back and forth in the Palace. He blamed himself over and over for the great damage Japan had caused to other nations, and was determined to abdicate and mount the scaffold himself. Instead he had been forced to keep quiet and let others suffer for his guilt.

Maggie joined the other journalists in a U.S. Army truck. Crowds lining the streets shouted excitedly as the Mercedes crept by. After a visit to a hospital the cavalcade continued southward along a dusty dirt road. Those living in hovels built from the ruins lined the highway and greeted their monarch with bewildered reverence. Recently he had announced that he was not a god, but it was difficult for them to accept such heresy.

Once he stepped from the car to inspect the Kawasaki branch of the Showa Electric Company near Yokohama. Maggie could see that he wore a dark business suit, blue shirt, striped tie, and pointed tan shoes. His tweed overcoat was too large and his soft felt hat was not only too small but crumpled. He walked with quick, mincing steps to meet the manager who explained quite unnecessarily what damage had been suffered by the plant. Face twitching constantly, the Emperor shifted uneasily from foot to foot. Then the Mayor of Kawasaki began a stilted report as photographers crept to within a few yards of His Majesty who sniffled and bobbed his chin up and down. At last he spoke. *"Ah, so,"* he said in a high, squeaky voice. This unnerved most of the Japanese and one, holding a high silk hat, whispered to Maggie, "What an honor! The people will rejoice."

While stiffly walking through the wreckage past long lines of work-men, he would occasionally stop and ask a question and give the same remark, *"Ah, so."*

The workers bowed their heads in awe.

One middle-aged woman was so overcome when asked how long she had worked at the plant that she shook with emotion and wept.

Taking off his hat, he politely asked another woman, "Are you working hard?" She nodded and he put on his hat, bowed. *"Ah, so desuka."*

Soon after entering Yokohama they stopped at a long wooden build-ing that reminded Maggie of a barracks. It was occupied by bombed-out people, and as the Emperor passed down the corridor the people inside the rooms knelt down. Several times he almost spoke but al-ways hesitated and passed on.

Outside, several hundred G.I.'s were waiting with cameras. They pushed forward, dogging his hurried steps. One G.I., ridiculing his high-pitched voice, said loudly, "He's Charlie! He's Charlie McCar-thy," referring to the popular ventriloquist's wooden dummy.

Maggie flared as several reporters laughed and started calling out, "Charlie!" She felt like kicking the bastards! The poor man was having a painful enough time. Next came a visit to a shelter for the homeless. The Emperor looked pale and sick as he trudged from one room to another. The people bowed low, weeping to see a deity looking at them with sympathy. By this time his jaw sagged and he looked as if he were crushed under a heavy burden. At one room he stopped to talk to a woman whose husband had a wooden leg. "Where did your husband get wounded?"

"The Philippines."

"Ah, so. In the Philippines. *Ah, so.* You have children? I'm very sorry. How long have you been here? The place is rather cold, but it will become warmer. I hope you will cheer up." It was his longest speech of the day.

The woman wept.

Maggie could see the pain on Hirohito's face as he hurried away and she had to restrain herself from assailing several fellow journalists who were openly calling him "Charlie." The one she detested most was a Japanese who proposed they now nickname His Majesty "Ah-so-san!" —Mr. Is that so. She bet that fellow had been a royal ass-kisser in the days of victory.

At dinner that night with her father, Chaucy, and Will, she predicted that this shy, ill-at-ease little man with the twitching face and crumpled hat would soon become dearer than ever to his people. Will was silent, thinking how shrewd the old men at the Imperial Household had been to make this trip the first step in the manufacture of a new myth—the democratic ruler sensitive to his people's sufferings and needs. What a travesty to force upon the nation! And all done in the name of democracy with the blessing of the new shogun in the Dai Ichi Building. His father was thinking how prophetic his friend Yabe had been, and out loud agreed with his daughter that a surge of love for the Emperor would ensue. Chaucy was regretting she had not been with Maggie. What a thrilling sight it must have been!

3.

A week later Whitney informed McGlynn that he was to see the general in half an hour. "He wants to talk to you about the Allied Council." This was the organization of the four principal Allied Powers created to advise SCAP. Even though MacArthur had vigorously protested its formation, the first meeting was soon to be held. It was no secret in the office that Whitney feared the meeting would cause mischief, since it would undoubtedly be used by the Soviets to attack the Occupation itself. "Enjoy yourself," said Whitney, grimacing.

McGlynn had only a few minutes to prepare to face the general who already enjoyed unprecedented authority. Never before had such absolute power been placed in the hands of a single American. Despite some gaffes, the Occupation *was* working surprisingly well, and that was primarily because the general always got his way.

He was staring out his single window at a blank wall. He turned, strode dramatically toward McGlynn, hand outstretched; then after maneuvering the professor into the worn leather divan he himself lunged into a chair.

"Let me review my thinking first," he said. Then he sprang up to begin pacing. "Not quite a month ago, a man of vision told the citizens of Fulton, Missouri, 'An iron curtain has descended across the Continent.'" He gave the words such intensity that one might have supposed he himself had originated them, not Churchill. "As you well know, half of Europe is occupied by the Soviets. The grand wartime alliance between East and West has crumbled. The Cold War has begun!" He swung around and pointed a finger at the professor. "And I am expected to allow these people to turn this so-called Allied Council into a forum for Russian propaganda. It's bad enough to be criticized by American officials, but I cannot allow SCAP to become the target for ill-informed and unfair criticism. I shall attend the opening session, speak a few words, and do not plan ever to return." He looked questioningly at McGlynn.

"Sounds sensible," he said. "The Japanese would call it *mokusatsu*, to ignore with silence."

MacArthur waited a moment, expecting more. Then he almost smiled. "I'd like you to attend several sessions and then give me your thoughts."

It was well known that the Soviets hoped to make these Allied Council meetings an open forum for criticism of MacArthur's policies, and that the other members of the Council might support such criticism. How, wondered McGlynn, would MacArthur handle this touchy problem without alienating his Western allies?

On April 5 the Council met in the paneled second-floor boardroom of a building within walking distance of GHQ. Military police guarded every entrance, screening those who swarmed to enter. The Japanese were told they could attend, but the security was so formidable that few entered, and those who did, to their humiliation, were forced to enter through the back door.

The room was jammed with correspondents, cameramen, Allied officers, and influential Western civilians. The four Council members and their staffs sat behind a large mahogany table that faced glaring movie lights. A mild-looking major general was the American representative. A burly lieutenant general, looking like a professional football lineman, represented the Soviet Union. At parties in the embassy he was always a jovial back-slapper. Now he was aggressively puffing a pipe and looking around, thought McGlynn, for someone to eat. The

British were represented by a brilliant Australian professor who, like so many of his countrymen, thought MacArthur was too gentle with the Japanese. And the fourth man, representing Chiang Kai-shek, already looked bored.

MacArthur made his usual effective appearance dressed as always in the plain khaki uniform, without the decorations that he wore every day to the office. His hair was slicked down to cover the bald spot. Affably he shook hands with the three foreign delegates, and then began to read his speech. He spoke vigorously and with well-trained emphasis. "As the functions of this Council will be advisory and consultative," he said, "it will not divide the heavy administrative responsibility of the Supreme Commander as the *sole* executive authority for the Allied Powers in Japan." In plain words *he* was the *sole* authority in Japan and the Allies would merely advise and consult.

Mulrooney nudged McGlynn in delight upon seeing the Russian puff smoke even more intensely and glare more fiercely while the Australian looked even more impatient and the Chinese even more inscrutable.

Although the general spoke in his self-confident, flowery manner, McGlynn noticed that one hand was trembling. MacArthur summarized the achievements of the Occupation, then castigated those critics "who would exploit as slaves a thoroughly defeated nation and a people," words that were apparently aimed at both the Russian and the Australian.

The Council should not concern itself with past actions, MacArthur continued with feeling, and then asked that its meetings be held in public. "The suspicion, the distrust, and the hatred so often engendered by the veil of secrecy will thus be avoided, and in the undimmed light of public scrutiny we will, therefore, invite full confidence in the sincerity, the high purpose, and the rectitude of our aims. As Supreme Commander, I can assure you that I entertain no fears that such an opportunity for public discussion will have the slightest adverse effect upon the discharge of my responsibilities."

MacArthur had promised to speak only "a few words," but he continued with a warning to the Council against "sharp and ill-conceived criticism of our Occupation policies" and concluded, in a voice trembling with emotion, with praise of Japan's renunciation of war in the impending new Constitution. McGlynn was impressed by the sincerity of these last words which faded away into silence. There was

113

an uneasy hesitation. Someone cleared his throat and MacArthur, coming out of a momentary daze, strode from the room.

His exit was followed by a wrangle among the members of the Council over the rules of procedure for future meetings. But this was mild compared to the imbroglio during the second Council meeting two weeks later. The professor would never forget the wrangling, rudeness, and bombastics, later observing to Mulrooney that it was topped in bad taste only by the recent crowning in Nagasaki of "Miss Atom Bomb," who had been elected by three Marines, six Japanese, and one Frenchman in a citywide contest sponsored by Nagasaki's newspapers.

Whitney appeared at this meeting to give a progress report on the political purge that had been requested by the Soviet general, who urged the report be "as full as possible." Whitney more than obliged with a three-hour dissertation. But first he indignantly asserted that the Russian's demand for the report endangered the success of the Occupation. When he stated that the Japanese Government was already complying with the purge directives the entire press corps broke into guffaws, but Whitney was used to rough and tumble set-tos as a civilian lawyer and was unperturbed by the open ridicule. "I shall now reply to General Derevyanko's request," he said, turning to the Russian, "even if it takes all summer." He began reading off the names of those organizations purged. His voice was calm as he slowly enunciated every word. Occasionally he would mispronounce a Japanese name and stop to apologize and slowly reread an entire passage. An hour passed; everyone fidgeted. McGlynn felt embarrassed at this childish performance and he could see other Americans shriveling with shame. It reminded them all of the time-honored custom of filibuster in Congress. Whitney had taken over complete control of the meeting.

After lunch the filibuster resumed. To McGlynn's annoyance, Whitney droned on, stopping once to remark, "There are thirty thousand members of these organizations I've listed. I must apologize to the Council for not having the names with me. That was an oversight of mine. If I only had them with me I should read the names with the greatest pleasure."

McGlynn took mental notes of the remarks overheard from those walking out of the meeting. There was almost universal criticism of Whitney's performance. One American colonel noted, "Whitney managed to skillfully walk on the borderline between permissible insult and the point where you get punched on the nose."

At the next meeting two days later Whitney peremptorily announced, "The Supreme Commander will reserve the right at any time to send representatives before this Council." It was an open declaration of war. "The Council" he added, "is here only for the purpose of constructive assistance." He bludgeoned down protests from the Russian and Australian representatives, and ended with a combative announcement.

"The Council," he insisted, "is not set up for the purpose of prying into SCAP affairs, attempting to find some weak point in SCAP armor, or probing for something by which to create national sensationalism."

"Well," confided Whitney to one of MacArthur's aides after the meeting, "that took the claws out of the lion's paws."

The aide, after sitting through the two days of wrangling in absolute shame that Americans could carry on so rudely, was unable to answer. McGlynn too was distressed. "The Council could have been very useful," he told Mulrooney as they headed back to the office. "MacArthur might have used the wisdom and experience of the Chinese general and the Australian to present to the Japanese a front of unity. Now both the Australians and the Chinese are antagonized."

But Mulrooney, who had sat through the long sessions grinning like the Cheshire cat, said, "I'm surprised, Professor. You're Irish and you didn't see all this has been an orchestrated performance? Dear old Court was only doing what his boss wanted. The Commahnder is convinced, and I agree with him, that this Council could screw up the entire Occupation. And Court, the faithful hatchet man, was just doing his duty."

McGlynn shook his head and said ruefully, "Sometimes you amaze me, Red. You're absolutely right. I feel like a fool."

"It's good for all of us to feel foolish occasionally. Of course, there are times when I abuse the privilege."

On their return McGlynn got a phone call from MacArthur. "What do you think?" he said eagerly.

"It was quite a performance, General."

"So I heard. But what do *you* think?"

"Well, sir, I think the Council is as good as dead."

"I hope so. They'd only be a nuisance."

Of course, thought McGlynn, Mulrooney was right. After the extremely adverse press reaction Whitney gathered his people in the conference room and informally pointed out the previous Russian attempts to embarrass General MacArthur. "It's plain that the Russkies want to use the Council as a sounding board to discredit the Occupation. If they want a knock-down drag-out, we can play that game. If they insist on long speeches so will we. If they read long reports so will we. If they push us we're going to push back. And let me assure you that Washington has been assured of this course of action."

Someone mentioned the sharp comments of W. M. Ball, the Australian member, on General Whitney's "boorish" performance. "Ball," he observed good-naturedly, "always sides with the Soviets. He's a farmer who speaks his own opinions rather than those of the Australians. Did you know that when GHQ gave him a twelve-room house he said it was the biggest one he ever had? And he asked us to relax the regulations forbidding foreigners to buy Japanese clothing so he could get striped trousers and a formal coat. He's a farmer, I tell you, but you have to like him."

By the time Whitney finished, it was evident to everyone that his hammer tactics had been dictated by MacArthur. This realization heightened the interest of all his listeners, liberals and conservatives alike. What would this unconventional and unpredictable pair of generals do next?

PART TWO

Chapter Seven

1.

Tokyo, April 18, 1946.

By now Keenan felt so much at ease with Will that he would occasionally stop off at his room evenings to discuss the trial. Just before midnight that day, Keenan dropped in and, after a brief discussion of the donnybrook at the Allied Council meeting, poured himself another drink and confessed that they were preparing their entire case in the dark. "Few of our people know a darned thing about the Japs or even realize what a monstrous job we have. It's like hunting rabbits in the dark with a slingshot. Thank God you're working on the Nanking massacre, McGlynn. I'm counting on that segment to nail down the China phase of our case."

He refilled his glass and in an expansive mood told of his interview with President Roosevelt just before he died. "He called me Joe the Key, you know. He said, 'Joe, I want you to be my mouthpiece at the war crimes trials in Japan.' He wanted me to hang bastards like Tojo—but also to see that the Japs got the best possible defense because the trials should be a showcase for democracy."

Abruptly changing the subject, he asked for Will's help in preparing his opening statement which would set the tone of the entire prosecution case, and he also suggested that Will accompany Fihelly on his next interrogation of Tojo. As usual Fihelly's tactics the following afternoon induced the former prime minister to talk freely. "These are important matters for Japan and for world peace," said Tojo. "What happens to me is of slight importance but the matters themselves are important." He admitted he had known the prearranged date of the Pearl Harbor attack but none of the details.

Did he realize, asked Fihelly, that he would be charged and tried as a war criminal because of the attacks on American and British possessions? Completely self-possessed, Tojo surveyed the Americans with a knowing little smile that infuriated Will. It reminded him of Humphrey Bogart in *The Petrified Forest*, as he nonchalantly took a drag on his cigarette in his gangster style. "It's already been decided that I am a war criminal," he said as if he were still in command. "The truth is that I am the person with the chief political responsibility for starting the war. This is going to be a trial of the righteousness or unrighteousness of my actions. So be it." He deftly flicked ashes from his cigarette. "I also hope that during this trial the hopes, the feelings, and the outcries of Asiatics will be heard. That is, if you want peace in the future for this continent."

Despite his distaste at sitting in the same room with Tojo, Will was at first impressed by these words. Then he asked himself, Are these only words to give the prosecution a false sense of security? As he left Sugamo, Will was determined to be as wary as ever of this keen-witted man.

That afternoon Dr. Ichiro Kiyose, a prominent attorney who had recently agreed to serve as Tojo's chief defense counsel, told a reporter he believed his client's case was defensible on the grounds that no single group could have been responsible for the Pacific War. "His role was only that of igniting a room already filled with gas. The war was the outcome of destiny made by many men other than Tojo; he merely happened to light the match." Kiyose said he had never been an intimate friend of the Tojo family but had accepted their request to defend the ex-Premier because he was convinced that the Tokyo Tribunal was seeking the truth and not vengeance. "I am sure Mr. Keenan, who is a well-known lawyer and a Christian, is able to understand my viewpoint."

Chaucy had little to do. There were still only six American members of the defense in Tokyo and they didn't know who would be indicted or what the charges would be. Nor did any of them have a client as yet. Furness, who had helped defend Homma in Manila, expressed his concern that the Yamashita and Homma convictions would influence the Tokyo Tribunal. The U.S. Supreme Court had upheld both convictions even though Chief Justice Stone had earlier written a friend of his displeasure with Associate Justice Robert Jackson, who had become chief prosecutor at Nuremberg. Jackson, he said, was conducting a high-grade lynching party in Nuremberg. "I don't mind what he does to the Nazis, but I hate to see the pretense that he is running a court or proceeding according to common law. This is a little too sanctimonious a fraud to suit my old-fashioned ideas." Ironically this was the same Stone who later maneuvered a 6–2 decision against Yamashita. Justice Murphy had dissented vigorously. The Americans, he claimed, had done everything possible to destroy Yamashita's lines of communication. "To use the very inefficiency and disorganization created by the victorious forces as the primary basis for condemning officers of the defeated armies bears no resemblance to justice or to military reality."

Despite this, Yamashita had been hanged, said Furness, always the Harvard gentleman despite his bitterness. And Homma, whom he had helped defend, had also been executed even though Justice Murphy had said, "Either we conduct such a trial as this in the noble spirit and atmosphere of our Constitution or we abandon all pretense to justice, let the ages slip away, and descend to the level of revengeful blood purges."

Furness shook his head dolefully. "Homma was a decent man. He treated the Filipinos so well after the battle that he was fired and brought home in disgrace. He was thankful to us for getting him shot, not hanged." MacArthur, he said, was paying him back for beating him in battle. "And so I ask myself, can we get a fair hearing in Tokyo?"

Something occurred to Chaucy and she interrupted. "Just a minute. It seems obvious that in the Yamashita case the majority opinion in the Supreme Court attempted to bypass the Fifth Amendment issue in the case of a military tribunal having jurisdiction by Act of Congress."

"What's your point?"

"In the broader Tokyo trial, the basic issue, I think, will undoubtedly be whether Japan engaged in a war effort required by its legitimate self-interest as defined by its government."

"You think like a man," said Furness.

"I think like a lawyer."

He started to apologize, but she was already talking again. "Listen, George, if I'm right, how could a tribunal composed of judges representing the U.S., British, and Dutch governments possibly be qualified to pass on this issue?"

"A good lawyer named Blakeney is joining us in a few days. We've got to get together on this."

Chaucy continued her protest. "And how could lawyers in U.S. uniforms on active duty like you and Artie Lazarus defend a case which would require accusing your own commander in chief of provocative and warlike acts?"

"You're going too fast," he said, stimulated by the prospects.

"And is a built-in anomaly a matter which a lawyer representing a particular accused can urge other than by motion to dismiss at the outset? And if this anomaly is a condition rooted in the proceeding, what is the effective time of defense?"

"Lieutenant Lazarus!" Furness called frantically. "Will you come over here?"

"Don't get me wrong," she said. "I realize a lawyer needn't like a client to represent him properly. The lawyer doesn't even have to believe in his client's moral or legal innocence. When I accepted this job I detested the defendants and I was morally sure they were guilty." She smiled wryly. "But I'm already getting an itchy feeling that some of our clients may be innocent."

That evening Chaucy and Will dined with the professor in a little Japanese restaurant. McGlynn was pleased that she and his son were getting along better. McGlynn was still in a thoughtful mood because of today's Allied Council meeting. MacArthur, he said, was constantly surprising him. One day he would be extremely reasonable, the next day arrogantly imperious. "Some of my Japanese friends are quite taken by him, however. One who teaches the tea ceremony told me, 'His imperious aloofness and lordly graciousness are establishing the prestige of the Occupation.'" McGlynn shook his head and continued. "He's a walking set of contradictions. A right-wing superconservative who has opened the jail gates for all Communists. He's now thinking of turning over most of the land to the peasants." Then he related how Whitney had performed MacArthur's dirty work at the Council meeting. He chuckled. "A couple of weeks ago I was in the lobby of the Dai Ichi Building with the Supreme Commander when a Japanese, obviously from the country, forced his way toward us. He then belligerently placed a wooden sword wrapped in a newspaper at the general's feet. We expected the general to explode at such insolence, but he simply took the Japanese by the arm and led him to the M.P. 'Take this man downstairs,' MacArthur said, 'and give him a lecture on good manners and then send him home.'"

PART TWO

"That's the first good thing I ever heard about MacArthur," said Will.

"Don't write him off, son. He may become a great man. He's certainly a great damned fool but every really great man has a damned fool lurking inside him." Will had never seen his father so tolerant. The past few weeks he'd been acting like a different man. What had happened to the argumentative, iconoclastic gadfly? "I came over here prepared to return on the next plane," continued McGlynn, and then told of his hope after the first meeting with MacArthur. "For a moment today at the Council meeting I felt things were impossible and I'd never be of any use. But then I began to realize what a rare opportunity I've been given. On the way over here I saw dozens of eager American men and women. Some young, some gray-haired. I saw schoolteachers and dietitians and G.I.'s and doctors and chemists and economists—all of them here in this great laboratory to help build a new life for people with strange faces and strange customs, enemies we hated a few months ago and that we're beginning to like. It was like a scene from H. G. Wells or Shaw. I realized we had experts in all fields seeking perfection, trying to bring religion, ethics, hygiene, proper nutrition. We're building a modern telephone system. We're introducing proper toilets. My God, is there anything we're not trying to impose on these starving, tattered, war-weary folks? At first I ridiculed it all. I saw little chance of any success. But tonight it came to me in a flash that success is not only possible but very probable. You know why?"

He had their interest and mischievously paused.

"Because of that Japanese disease known as conformity. *Deru kugi wa utareru.* That's an old Japanese proverb. 'The nail that sticks out is the one pounded down.' Both at home and in school every Japanese child is taught to fit in, not to stand out. That's why I am convinced we can make a success of the Occupation. The Japanese will accept whatever is the thing to do. Most G.I.'s and Marines were amazed to meet no trouble when they landed. They found no feeling of rebellion because the Emperor had told his people to submit. And so they all surrendered as a group."

Chaucy's rapt attention was appealing. She was slender and looked slight but he could see she was a shrewd, forceful young woman. McGlynn could see her in a covered wagon on the Western plains picking off marauding Indians with her rifle.

"What every Japanese seeks is what they call *wa*, harmony," he continued. "Unlike the Koreans, what they need above all is no conflict. Japan is the land of *wa*. As a prefix it means Japanese: *washoku* means Japanese food; *wafu* means Japanese style. Japan's greatest battleship in the war was the *Yamato*, 'Great Harmony.' This could never happen in the United States but Japan is monoracial, and therefore monocultural. *Wa* is only for people who conform to the same standards. That's why, Chaucy, there are ten times more lawyers in the United States than over here. Japanese rarely sue each other. That is *fuwa*, 'discord, strife.' Their whole system of justice is based on *wa*. If a man is indicted he is assumed to be guilty and the lawyer only tries to get the best possible deal. And so the prisoner almost always confesses right away, apologizes to the victims of his crime, and hopes for forgiveness. End of lecture." The professor hurriedly pulled on his overcoat. He spoke rather awkwardly. "I've got an appointment with an old friend who has some official documents on the Imperial Conferences. For my new book on 1941 when I get a chance to write it."

When Chaucy set out the next morning for another exploration of the mysteries of Tokyo, she looked at passers-by with more understanding. Here and there people stopped to greet each other, and invariably they smiled and bowed over and over. When she first arrived in Japan she had been amused by the incessant bowing. But now she understood. This was *wa* in action. She found herself smiling, and she wanted to bow to someone. She wandered into the section near the Toda home called Moto-Azabu. There was some destruction but many of the houses were intact. At the top of the hill she stood to admire the view of a temple down below. Two girls in blue school uniforms gave her surreptitious looks. "Is that Buddhist or Shinto?" asked Chaucy, indicating the temple. The two girls put hands to their mouths, giggled and fled.

"It is Buddhist," said a rather tall, elderly Japanese in English. He explained it had become the first American legation in 1856 but was more famous for its ginkgo tree which was more than thirty feet in girth. From his debonair manners she guessed he was a diplomat. "According to legend a renowned priest planted his staff in the ground more than seven hundred years ago. That staff grew into what you see. It was hit by firebombs but miraculously is recovering." He introduced himself: Mr. Obata, and presented his card. By now she could reciprocate with a card of her own: English on one side, Japanese on the other. Would she do him the honor of sharing a meal with him and his wife?

The house looked modest, but once she discarded her shoes, put on slippers, and saw the inside, it was obvious the Obatas were wealthy, or at least had been at one time. Obata apologized for the sparse furnishings and lack of heat.

A petite, wizened woman entered with a startled look. Obata introduced her, apologizing for her lack of English. He said something which made his wife turn pale and Chaucy guessed that having a *gaijin*, a foreigner, for lunch was terrifying. But Obata said his wife was delighted to know she could stay if Miss Snow would forgive her poor cooking.

"You will be warmer here," he said as he led her into a small room which was equally cold. In the middle of the room was a strange-looking table three feet square and a foot high covered with a colorful quilt. Atop the quilt was a wooden board. "This is a *kotatsu,*" said Obata. "In the winter this is how we eat in comfort." He lifted one end of the quilt, and Mrs. Obata placed a cushion for Chaucy to sit on. She saw there was a hole in the floor. "There's a charcoal fire underneath but don't worry. Your feet are protected by checkered wooden slats."

She sat on the tatami and tentatively put her feet down until they touched the slats.

"The family and guests sit around the *kotatsu* with legs under the covering to keep warm." Chaucy pulled the quilt over her lap and felt delightfully warm all over. "Here we take our tea and meals in primitive comfort. With so little fuel nowadays our winter life centers around the *kotatsu*, which probably came to us from China five hundred years ago."

Obata explained that he had attended Columbia University before returning to the family business, and apologized for the meager repast. "I have recently been purged," he said almost as though it were a joke. "But perhaps I can be of some use in the future."

While they were eating, a boy of ten in a student's uniform rushed in, stopping aghast at sight of Chaucy. "Our grandson," explained Obata and said something to him. The boy, embarrassed and a bit frightened, extended his right hand. She shook it. Remembering that she had a bag of Hershey's Kisses in her coat pocket, she offered one to the boy. He intently undid the wrapping of a Kiss, and said something with distaste.

Obata laughed. "He says he does not want to eat mud." He told the youngster to at least take a nibble. He did and his eyes shone. He gobbled it down. "He wonders if he can have another."

Chaucy gave him the entire bag which he accepted with awe. On the long walk back to her hotel, she passed other Americans strolling in the sun. Most of them were smiling. Because they were conquerors? Probably not. Probably like herself they were enjoying freedom from all ties and limits of home. Here she was free even from herself, for she had left one way of life for a completely different one. She was trying to acclimate herself to this new life whereas most Americans were just riding with the tide and had no deep interest in understanding their hosts. They were having too much fun being away from home in an exotic country where every day was an adventure and there was no one on hand to restrict or reprimand them.

The ruins of Tokyo seemed to have been transformed into a sort of devil's playground where a person could be as reckless as he wanted. All social barriers and conventions were lowered in this strange, destructive wilderness where cars and handcarts collided throughout the day and death was commonplace. She wrote all this to her father almost in confession, while vowing inwardly that *she* was going to keep close rein on herself.

2.

In the morning Chaucy complained to Captain Coleman, chief counsel for the defense. The prosecution apparently was already well prepared but only Japanese defense lawyers had been selected by those prisoners most likely to be indicted. There was nothing Coleman could do. But more help was coming from the United States, he said, and the indictment should be announced shortly. Only then could something be done.

Despite outward appearances Chaucy was aware that all was also not well in the prosecution. Chaucy wrote her father that Keenan's behavior was causing the British prosecutors acute anxiety. "Their chief prosecutor, Comyns-Carr, has already written a furious letter to the British attorney general revealing that he had found everything in chaos on arrival. Great piles of documents were yet to be translated and when Comyns-Carr protested, Keenan promptly made him chairman of an executive committee to sort out the mess!" Another colleague was even more explicit, complaining to London that there was a disgraceful lack of coordination and direction on the part of Keenan, who treated Comyns-Carr like an office boy.

The British, continued Chaucy, were openly expressing concern that Keenan would be unable to show judgment during the trial, not only because of his eccentric behavior but because of his excessive drinking. "He is, in one man's opinion, 'a disgrace' and, in another's, incapable of distinguishing between black and white even when they come out of the same bottle!"

At present, she said, the British and the other Allies were hopelessly struggling over which war criminals should be tried. "Comyns-Carr, a very bright lawyer, told me the whole Japanese situation was infinitely more complicated than the German, as the Japanese politicians, soldiers, and sailors were continually squabbling and double-crossing one another all the time, and that was making it even more difficult to pick the right ones to indict." Selecting those to be tried was made even more difficult by the limitations of time, space, and expense. "All the Allied prosecutors agree they could try only about thirty men at most. And since each ally is submitting its own list, the wrangling goes on and on."

The objects of their labors were stewing at Sugamo Prison, thinking of little except the coming indictment. Those who had been most frequently interrogated assumed they were bound to be selected but kept their concern to themselves. To pass the time they had been constructing things. Tojo made small paper boxes to hold the precious four cigarettes a day they were issued. An admiral made intricate little chests of drawers from magazine paper and passed them on to his comrades.

The lives of all those in Sugamo were made endurable by certain events. One was mail, even though all letters were photostated, then discarded for fear the original paper had been impregnated with poison. Another was the monthly visit of a relative for half an hour. The bathing and shaving period was a special highlight. Twice a week the Class A men who faced trial in Tokyo would bathe in small wooden tubs with the less important Class B-C inmates who would be tried for atrocities in Yokohama. Speeded up constantly by M.P.'s, they were given only twenty minutes in the tubs.

By now open resentment was expressed by the Class B-C men toward their superiors. "It's because of you Class A fellows that we're here today!" one told Tojo. "Because there are people like you, we will not be understood and will all be tarred with the same brush."

Tojo good-naturedly ignored such comments. He had become friendly with one Class B prisoner who never was critical, Shogo Toda. They often talked of death. "Death is peaceful," said Shogo, "and in no way painful, if one knows how to choose the time to die." Everybody was going to die. "Hitler died, Mussolini died, President Roosevelt died, and so did Japan's Mr. Konoye. Stalin, too, will die one day, since he is a human being."

That afternoon Will spent an hour with Tojo asking questions about the letter Premier Konoye had sent to President Roosevelt late in August 1941, requesting a meeting to settle their differences. Tojo's self-confident entry into the room and his nonchalant lighting of a cigarette irritated Will, but he tried to hide his feelings. "As Minister of War," said Will, "I assume you were privy to this letter?"

"Of course."

"I understand you were opposed to sending it."

Tojo took a long drag on his cigarette, blew out the smoke slowly, then said, "By no means, Captain. Excuse me, Major." He expertly tapped off the ash of his cigarette. "I felt both of these leaders were gentlemen from distinguished families and they might possibly reach an honorable settlement." He smiled faintly. "Am I correct in thinking you don't believe me?" He shrugged his shoulders so good-naturedly that Will felt insulted. "I have no need to lie. I am near the end of my life and my teeth and hair are almost gone. If a man's life expectancy in Japan is fifty years, then I've already had ten extra years. It will make no difference as far as my fate is concerned whether I take responsibility for one thing or everything. I shall therefore, Major McGlynn, take the responsibility for as many things as I can. I want to make it evident that it is I, and I only, who am responsible for the Pacific War."

It was a noble statement and at first Will was impressed, but then came doubt that Tojo would have the courage to do as he promised in court. Again Tojo smiled. "Far more important than your opinion of me is the unhappy result of the refusal of your President to accept that invitation. You are, of course, aware that Prince Konoye sent a second message on that same day, an official proposal to your government offering to abide by Secretary of State Hull's four basic principles for negotiation. You look surprised. Didn't you know about that?"

Will blushed from embarrassment. In the mountain of official documents he'd studied he had not seen that.

"I can still remember some of the wording. We stated that the Hull principles were the prime requisites of a true peace and should be applied not only in the Pacific area but throughout the world. You wonder I can remember? After all, I had to approve and this offer of ours was a negation of the policies we had championed for months." He snuffed out his cigarette as if ending the discussion. "A far better witness on this subject is the Lord Privy Seal. Is that all?"

Keenan approved Will's request to interrogate Marquis Kido again. He was as self-assured as Tojo, and equally irritating. He confirmed Tojo's story. "The general approved the summit meeting even though he thought it only had a thirty percent chance of success. We later learned that the President at first made plans to spend three days or so with Konoye but then was convinced by Hull and others that we were not sincere in our offer." Kido spoke crisply with an air of authority that Will felt bordered on arrogance. "We waited almost a week but no answer came, and Navy chief of staff Nagano said, 'We are getting weaker and weaker with each day, until finally we won't be able to stand on our feet.' The Army chief of staff agreed. 'We must try to achieve our diplomatic objectives by October 10. If this fails we must dash forward. Things cannot be allowed to drag out.' "

The situation was so desperate, explained Kido, that the Cabinet approved this deadline policy without argument, and an imperial conference was called on September 6 to make the policy official. "Just before we met I advised the Emperor to remain silent at first and let Privy Council president Hara question the military. Once the discussion was over, His Majesty should then break the precedent, similar to that in England, to reign but not rule. That is, he should cease to reign, and momentarily rule. 'Instruct the chiefs of staff to cooperate with the government in making the negotiations with America successful,' I advised His Majesty. Only through such a dramatic break in tradition could the disastrous deadline policy be reversed."

Although Will was listening politely he was not impressed. What an actor! he thought.

"Everything worked as we planned. The more the military explained, the more it bothered the civilian officials. Finally Privy Council president Hara asked the military directly if they were going to place emphasis on war or diplomacy. There was an embarrassing silence and then the Emperor did the unheard-of. 'Why don't you answer?' he asked loudly. I was the only one who was not astounded to hear his voice. It meant he had abandoned his traditional role as emperor. And then he read a poem of peace written by his grandfather Emperor Meiji. Everyone sat awed by his censure. 'I make it a rule,' he said, 'to read this poem from time to time to remind me of Emperor Meiji's love of peace. How do you feel about all this?' "

Kido wiped the sweat from his brow. "I have never experienced such a moment, Major McGlynn. The Navy chief of staff bowed his head humbly and apologized. So did the Army chief of staff. They both agreed to continue to seek an honorable peace with America. Of course, that meant the end of the Konoye Cabinet. And I used my influence to have War Minister Tojo appointed as the next prime minister. And I assure you that he did his utmost to achieve that peace. But he can tell you more about that than I can." He gathered his papers, like Tojo, ending the discussion.

Will thanked the Lord Privy Seal, politely bowed and left still convinced that Tojo and Kido were the chief architects of war and both deserved the noose.

3.

Death became a reality at Sugamo on the night of April 26 with the execution of the first Class B prisoner convicted in Yokohama. Rain was falling softly and once those prisoners near the American-constructed death house heard the crash of the trapdoor, word went from cell to cell of the passing of their comrade to another world. Two days later a message circulated that someone on the first floor had gone mad. In the exercise yard it was finally confirmed that it was Shumei Okawa, a propagandist and ultranationalist, one of the civilian Class A prisoners. His cellmate, General Matsui, who had commanded the Kwantung Army in 1937–1938, said nothing when asked if his cellmate was insane. He only smiled sardonically. Another Class A man wondered if someone of Okawa's undoubted intelligence could really have gone mad, and Tojo surmised there was only a hair's breadth between genius and madness. "Since he is a genius, that hair has presumably snapped."

The Class B-C inmates had much to gossip about that morning: it was rumored that their superiors were finally about to be indicted. They argued about who would make the best appearance in court. One thought Matsuoka, the controversial foreign minister, but he was sick and didn't look as if he'd last too long.

"We can't expect much of Tojo-san. He's not in as good spirits as he used to be."

Another wondered about General Suzuki. "He groans in a most peculiar way every morning. Will he do that in court?"

At 8:30 the next morning, April 29, the prison commandant allowed the prisoners on the third floor to celebrate the birthday of the Emperor. Led by General Suzuki, the alleged groaner, they sang the national anthem.

Later in the day the prisoners learned that eighteen military men and ten civilians had finally been indicted and would be arraigned in four days. No one was surprised that the list included Tojo and Kido, but almost everyone was taken aback to learn that a diplomat known for his opposition to war, Shigemitsu, was also named.

After the evening meal those indicted were brought to a room in the basement. An M.P. called their names in alphabetical order. Each was handed a large envelope containing the charges against him.

"It's like getting a diploma at graduation," joked one general. But there was solemnity once Tojo's name was called. And the Americans were impressed that everyone, including those who detested him, stood at attention.

"It's a mean thing," commented an admiral, "doing this on the Emperor's birthday!" They all agreed it was no accident that all this had been scheduled for the 29th of April.

Throughout the corridors that night there was no singing, not even by the Class B-C inmates.

4.

When Chaucy and the McGlynns arrived at the Todas that evening
for dinner, Floss was glowing. She hugged her sister. "Something
incredible has happened!" she said. "I have a place for the orphanage!" It had all come about through Colonel Mulrooney. He, Colonel
Kades, and several others from the Government Section had been
invited to a lavish party at the requisitioned mansion of the president
of the Bridgestone Tire Company. "It was sponsored by State Minister Narahashi," said Floss. He had collected a group of lovely Japanese
ladies to meet prominent Occupation officials. After the most elaborate dinner there was dancing and Colonel Mulrooney had found
himself whirling around with the Baroness Megata. Floss was so excited her words ran together. "You remember her, Maggie, and just
by luck Tom happened to mention that I wanted to start a home for
war orphans but nobody at the Dai Ichi Building seemed to be interested, and you won't believe it, but the baroness offered to let me
have their old summer home on the shore, Maggie, the place along
the bay near Chigasaki!"

After Floss and Emi had spent five minutes praising the colonel for
his many thoughtful little presents and for the fun he brought into the
house, Floss told of more good news. Mark was being transferred from
Kyushu to the Yokosuka Naval Base which was only an hour or so from
the Megata beach house. "He says the Marines are used to helping
orphans."

Will had brought food from the commissary and the women, except
for Chaucy who was no help in a kitchen, began preparing a meal. She
was learning much about Japan. Previously Chaucy had used the
Todas' Western bathroom but now that the Mulrooneys had moved in,
she was forced to have another challenging experience with a Japanese toilet over which she had to squat precariously.

During the festive dinner, attended also by Mulrooney and his
daughter, the professor explained that the party sponsored by
Narahashi had historical precedents. Several times in feudal days
when a clan was soundly defeated in battle, their women of high rank
had helped win the peace by entertaining the victors with wit, grace,
and sex.

"I can vouch for the wit and grace," said Mulrooney, "but my partner, the baroness, was at least seventy-five!"

The next day during their coffee break Mariko told McGlynn she was concerned about the colonel.

"What do you mean?" he asked.

"He could be a disturbing element at the Toda home," she said. According to office gossip, he played poker for money with the enlisted men. He laughed. "Emi doesn't play poker."

"It's not funny," she said. "He's not a proper man."

"He's harmless and he's good-natured."

"Did you know he's also in the black market?"

"So is practically everyone else."

"I mean big black market. Buying and selling money."

"Where do you get all this juicy gossip?"

She explained that the enlisted men told the Japanese civilians everything that went on. Mulrooney had lost a lot of money at poker and couldn't pay his bills.

"Well, it's none of my business," said McGlynn who wanted to talk about his paper on land reform, not this nonsense.

"It should be."

"Why?" he said impatiently.

"Because Floss is interested in him."

"What utter nonsense!"

"He's an attractive man and all the Todas are taken by him too. He's been down at the orphanage with his daughter several times. That's a long trip and he must be serious."

"MacArthur should have your Intelligence network." He was upset and, taking his annoyance out on her, said nothing more.

"Don't you think you should tell Emi?" she finally said.

"Oh, all right," he promised reluctantly, adding to himself, when the proper time comes.

Emi Toda was reading a letter from her husband delivered by a repatriate just arrived from China. Her husband, Akira, was safe and under the protection of the Nationalists. He had withdrawn to headquarters on the Yangtze River all those Japanese supervising work at the mines. There was plenty to eat, and he was keeping the entire Japanese delegation busy with sports, special classes, and exercise sessions. Apparently the Red Army was inactive in their area and so there was nothing to worry about. It looked as if they all would return home before the New Year.

Emi wrote a letter which she doubted would ever reach him, but told nothing of their dire straits. She did reveal that she had rented half of the house to a wonderful American officer who had a lovely thirteen-year-old daughter named Jo. She and Sumiko were having none of the problems of others who were renting to those Americans who wanted to paint everything in sight, clog up the drains of Western toilets, leave the kitchen in a piggish mess every day, play jazz on Victrolas and bring pompom girls or permanent mistresses into the house. When Colonel Mulrooney had said his only requirement was privacy, she asked, "Does that mean you want to bring a girlfriend here at night? This is our home and it is sacred to us." And he had replied gravely, "Madame Toda, my only girlfriend is my daughter. I want to experience life in a sacred Japanese home."

Chapter Eight

1.

Tokyo, May 1946.

The skies were gray and threatening that morning, but soon after breakfast crowds were already flowing into the Imperial Plaza to celebrate the first massive Communist May Day rally in the history of Japan. Jun Kato was there, purportedly to cover the story for his newspaper but actually as an active participant. When he first joined the press union he had been uncertain what a union could or should do, but under a Communist delegate they had already achieved a pay raise and there was even talk of overtime pay. Thrilled by the display of strength of thousands acting as one, Jun had become convinced that Japanese industry would survive and flourish only under the control of labor. He had been persuaded to take over leadership of his little delegation at his newspaper and this had led to an invitation to attend a Communist study group where he met so many dedicated intellectuals that he had taken the next logical step—joined the Party. Now he was in the tiny three-member shop cell at Tokyo *Shimbun*, living an exciting double life. Since childhood he had lived a passive existence, hiding his aspirations and trying to adjust to his conflicting loyalties to both America and Japan. But the Party had offered him a new involvement where he could take an active role. Who would have believed that he would be out in the Plaza today carrying a banner and celebrating this great day of liberation? A group of young men shouting labor slogans passed, and he enthusiastically joined them.

The professor was with Maggie, whose eyes were bright with anticipation. Never had either of them seen in Japan such a buoyant gathering that was not religious or patriotic. Japanese were waving posters and flags, cheering, singing, talking excitedly.

The McGlynns forced their way through the moiling but well-behaved crowd toward the decorated speakers' platform. Maggie pointed out the two most important leaders, Tokuda and Nosaka. The first, a vigorous man who liked to pound tables and shout at meetings, had recently been freed from ten years in prison; the latter had spent the war years in Yenan with Mao and Chou En-lai, the intellectual mastermind of the Chinese Reds. Nosaka was a slim, thoughtful man who reminded McGlynn of a professor. One of his hands was deformed from a police beating. He had conceived of a startling new approach for the Party: "peaceful revolution" and the rebuilding of a "lovable Communist Party." An astute strategist, Nosaka had based this plan on Mao's "New Democracy," and persuaded the Party to agree that it would have no direct liaison with the Soviet Union and would simply be a party of the Japanese people.

Maggie thought this was just a ploy, but her father disagreed. On his last trip to China in 1936 Chou En-lai had told him in confidence they were already having trouble with Moscow, which was trying to direct the Chinese revolution according to Marxist dogma. " 'We don't have an industrial proletariat,' Chou told me. 'Ours will be an agrarian revolution.' "

"Oh, Daddy, you were taken in! Stalin and Chou share the same goals."

"Maybe they do but anyone sharing a border with the Soviets has an enemy." She looked at him with the pitying smile which the young address to their doddering elders, and he did not react. After all, neither had MacArthur taken him seriously on China.

Tokuda, the fiery secretary general of the Party, was being pressed by Japanese cameramen for pictures while Nosaka sat stiffly as if reviewing his thoughts. The huge crowd pressed closer, squirming with impatience. At last the first speaker, another union leader who had been imprisoned, rose and began shouting into the microphone. This resulted in a mechanical shriek from the amplifier that did not at all deter the speaker. Other speakers shouted and only half of their words could be heard. All the politicians, right-wing and left, had the same demand: more food and a democratic government. Tokuda spoke last and he kept his voice at a level that could be heard. He spoke calmly with no oratorical frills, but his words were effective as he told of the rice hoarded by speculators and the rich in contrast to the meager cupful allowed to the people. The crowd cheered but the sound was nothing compared to the roar that went up when he suddenly raised both arms and exclaimed, "Down with the Emperor!"

Afterward a young man in a shiny serge suit stopped McGlynn. "You American?" He excitedly pointed to the crowd. "We won war!" he exclaimed. "Year ago no can do this. Now we shout, sing and strike. We won war!"

It began to rain and the cardboard signs began to grow soggy and collapse, but the crowd, including Jun Kato and young Taro accompanied by equally exuberant classmates from Ichiko Preparatory School, started home still in high spirits, singing the "Marseillaise," the "May Day Song," and their favorite, "Akahata" (Red Flag):

> The people's flag, the red flag, wraps the bodies
> of our dead:
> Before the corpses turn cold, their blood dyes the flag.

Americans hearing its cheerful tune had no idea the words were so morbid.

"Why are you demonstrating?" Maggie asked a farmer glowing with enthusiasm as rain swept down his face. "I am very excited!" And a mail carrier said, "This is my day, and I consider it an honor to participate." Another man answered, "Because I believe that in democracy the power should belong to the people."

For an hour and a half the McGlynns watched the noisy passing procession, its fervor undampened by the downpour. Every so often a small group of the younger converts would cavort in a dance performed at shrine festivals, but there were no fights, no attempts to destroy property.

"Only the Japanese," mused McGlynn, "know how to be raucous in an orderly fashion."

At Sugamo Prison the Japanese lawyers defending the indicted Class A prisoners were having their first meetings with their clients in the family reception room. Tojo arrived, dressed in a gray jacket and carrying a bag filled with numerous notes and the full text of the indictment. Dr. Kiyose, his counsel, explained the procedure of the arraignment which would take place in 48 hours and how Tojo should reply. They conversed for an hour and Kiyose was impressed that the MP on guard, a Nisei, neither took notes nor even attempted to listen.

At the War Ministry, Chaucy was steaming. Here it was two days before the arraignment and the American lawyers still had no clients. Never had she imagined such confusion could exist. The defense was supposed to have at least thirty American attorneys and fifteen secretaries but there were only three secretaries, and others would not arrive for two weeks. The Japanese lawyers were also in bad shape, impeded as they were by the language barrier. More important, their basic legal concepts and training were making it difficult for them to understand Western law, which would rule the Tribunal.

The day of the arraignment dawned cloudy and threatening. Just after 8 A.M. on May 3, the indicted prisoners filed somberly out the main door of Sugamo Prison guarded by M.P.'s with loaded submachine guns. A small crowd of workmen and passing schoolchildren watched curiously, few realizing this was a historic occasion. The prisoners quietly boarded a waiting bus, its windows covered by sheets of paper. The public session on Ichigaya Heights was not scheduled to begin until 10:30 A.M., but the spectators were already lining up at the northern entrance of the former War Ministry, the headquarters of the Imperial Army and symbol of Japanese militarism. McGlynn had been offered a seat in the section reserved for distinguished Allied personnel but he preferred to sit next to Maggie in the press section.

Mariko, who like other civilian workers in the Government Section had permission from Whitney to attend, was in the long waiting line just behind a group of American and British officers who were chatting as if they were queueing up for a Broadway show. The Japanese in the line talked in an undertone. Each pass was checked by white-helmeted American M.P.'s. One M.P. was a young woman and this caused a quiet stir among the Japanese who marveled that such a thing could be.

Three hundred Allied spectators were seated on the eastern side of the balcony and two hundred Japanese on the other side. Mariko recalled that the auditorium had formerly been used for graduation ceremonies of cadets from Japan's West Point. For months workmen had been transforming it into an impressive courtroom. The floor was covered with thick carpets to muffle footsteps. On a high platform at the left were seats for the judges; behind stood the flags of their nations. Court reporters were already seated in a row just below the judges. Farther down were the witness box and tables for the prosecuting and defense attorneys. To the right of the witness box were the glass booths for simultaneous interpretation, occupied by four translators, a monitor, and a court clerk. A middle-aged man next to Mariko explained that the defendants would be seated in the elevated section on the western side of the room directly facing the judges' bench. High above Mariko was a small booth occupied by newsreel cameramen. In front of the defendants she could see the defense counsel, and guessed that the pert-looking young woman was the Boston lawyer the professor had told her about. Just below, she made out Frank himself in the section reserved for correspondents. He was talking to a dark-haired girl. It must be his daughter, Maggie. And across the room from the balcony, on rows of seats rising up from the stage of the auditorium, were places for the distinguished. There Mariko recognized the general who had represented China at the Allied Council, and General Eichelberger, Commander of the Eighth Army.

McGlynn was intrigued by the spectacle. It reminded him of a courtroom play he had seen on Broadway with the curtain open as the audience arrived, and minor actors preparing the courtroom for a session. He could picture the prisoners and their counsel tensely waiting off stage. The drama was about to begin. He had decided it was not wise to sit with Mariko but they would have dinner tonight at her place and if luck was with him Taro, the pest, would again be out with his Red friends.

The ringing of a bell stilled the buzz of the courtroom at exactly 11:13. The room was hushed as the massive doors to the main entrance of the courtroom were closed and Keenan, his square face red, led the other prosecution members to the center of the courtroom. Then the voice of the marshal announced the opening of the session and the defendants began filing into their raised, fenced-in dock. First was Lieutenant General Kenryo Sato, a close friend and trusted adviser of Tojo, followed by twenty-five others. Two defendants had just arrived from Bangkok but were not present. Four American M.P.'s and their commander, the provost marshal of the tribunal, guided the defendants to their seats. Foreign Minister Matsuoka, a graduate of the University of Oregon, looked deathly pale and emaciated; he had shaved his head and grown a scruffy beard. Foreign Minister Shigemitsu, who had signed the surrender on the *Missouri*, needed a cane. Kaya, Minister of Finance under Tojo, looked around the court and up into the spectators' balcony like a curious student. All wore shoddy olive-drab wartime suits except General Oshima who was smartly dressed, sporting a raffish bow tie. Some wore geta, one was barefoot. Tojo was most impressive, however. He strode in as if he were still Prime Minister and head of the army. Although this was the very room where he had often addressed his generals and planned the strategy of the war, he remained composed.

Chaucy was enthralled and disturbed. In the prisoners' dock was someone she was supposed to defend. She didn't know who it would be or even whether any of those miserable-looking individuals would choose her.

In the balcony Mariko was wondering what the American attorneys were thinking about. It was the business of lawyers to defend known criminals as well as the innocent. But what a strange sensation it must be to have to defend men who recently were hated enemies! She herself found it difficult to believe that those insignificant-looking defendants once controlled the fate of a hundred million people. She became so indignant she wanted to slap Tojo and those who sat placidly as if they had done no wrong. The men in the dock surely had planned the war—but wasn't she also guilty for allowing them to do so? Leaders alone couldn't start a war without active or passive support of the people. And even those like herself who were against war had done nothing at all to stop it. The painful truth was that by doing nothing she had helped to wage the war. The arrest of Prince Konoye, a liberal, had seemed unjust to her. But hadn't he been a tool of the militarists even though he had tried to make peace with President Roosevelt? And couldn't she herself have done something concrete? Wasn't every mature Japanese guilty even if only in a small way? About the only ones who had vehemently opposed the militarist adventurers were the Communists, who wound up in prison.

At 11:20 A.M. the marshal ordered the court to stand, and solemn, black-robed judges representing ten nations slowly filed in noiselessly on the plush carpet. Maggie was scribbling notes on the judges: B.V.A. Röling of the Netherlands—lean, white-haired with a sensitive, humorous face; the erudite Henri Bernard of France; McDougall of Canada—little, worldly, gentle; Lord Patrick, a Scottish Lord Justice, handsome and spare but reported to be a woman-hater; a Soviet general—blond, jovial; and the Chief Justice, Sir William Webb of Australia—an alert man with a warrior's aggressive nose, and keen blue eyes that surveyed the room like searchlights. Still in India was Judge Pal who had been selected at the last moment.

"We fully appreciate the great responsibility resting upon us," said the hawk-nosed Webb. "There has been no more important trial in all history." Tojo, who had slumped in his seat, sat erect and attentive as the Japanese translation was read. "The crimes alleged are crimes against the peace of the world, against the laws of war, and against humanity, and conspiracy to commit these crimes. They are so many and so great that it was decided the appropriate forum would be a military tribunal of an international character . . ."

Behind Tojo was the civilian, Okawa, who had recently acted as if he had gone mad at Sugamo. When the M.P. colonel, Aubrey Kenworthy, politely ordered Okawa to remove his clogs which were making a clatter, he also took off his black coat before slouching down in a crumpled light-blue pajama top.

When Webb finished, McGlynn noticed that several defendants began looking around the courtroom, like actors in a play waiting for applause. It was then that Keenan rose and presented to the court his fellow prosecutors from Britain, China, Russia, France, the Philippines and the Netherlands, whereupon court was recessed until 2:30 P.M.

At 2:30 Keenan again led out the prosecutors and ten minutes later the marshal, a captain, began reading the indictment which accused the defendants of participating in a conspiracy with Germany and Italy to dominate the world.

After ten minutes, Shigemitsu's Japanese counsel raised an objection, pointing out mistakes in translation. The language arbiter, an American major, admitted there were typographical errors. "But as far as we can see there are none that change the meaning for anyone who understands the difficulty in transcribing and typing the Japanese language."

"We will proceed to the reading of the indictment and the translation that has been prepared," ruled Webb despite a number of obvious inaccuracies.

The defendants were listening intently, all except Okawa who kept unbuttoning his pajama top and scratching his chest. This became so distracting that Webb ordered Colonel Kenworthy to button him up. No sooner was this done than Okawa unbuttoned himself again. The

M.P. officer gently but firmly put his hands on Okawa's shoulders and restrained him whenever he made a move. Okawa finally turned back with a reassuring smile and the marshal continued reading the indictment. But a moment later Okawa suddenly leaned forward and slapped Tojo's bald pate. The court was in an uproar. Tojo turned around affably and smiled at Okawa and movie cameramen cranked away. Kenworthy gently but firmly led out the tall, gaunt Okawa who was grinning, and took him to the defendants' room where he was soon besieged by correspondents. Maggie, one of the first to arrive, asked in Japanese, "Why did you do it?"

After looking around, he answered in slow, distinct English, "Tojo is a fool, must kill him." He held out a hand. "Give me a cigarette. I am in excellent health because I take nourishment only from the air." He demonstrated how he did so, then declared he was in favor of democracy. "America is *not* for democracy. She is demo-crazy." He winked mischievously at Maggie. "Get it? Demo-crazy." He stretched out on a couch as photographers took pictures. "I'm all right," he said and sat up suddenly to explain more about his theory of atmospheric nutrition. "I am right now preparing a deadly poison from the air."

More correspondents entered and asked why he wanted to kill Tojo. "It will be good for my country if I do," he replied, and gave a rambling explanation of his motives. "I was double-crossed in the past." Did they want to see how he slapped Tojo's head? He began banging the head of a Japanese journalist, pounding harder and harder as the flash guns exploded.

"Are you guilty of the war crimes charges?" asked Maggie.

"Me and 'Happy' Chandler are good friends." He was referring to the former Senator who was now Baseball Commissioner in the United States. "We're going into business together." He puckered up his face as if about to cry. "My eighty-one-year-old mother has just come to Tokyo and I want to see her."

2.

Most of the American correspondents reported that the opening session was low comedy at best. *Time* compared it to a Hollywood premiere with its glaring Klieg lights. "Nuremberg's impresarios had used simpler furnishings, relied on the majesty of the concept to set the tone." And whereas Nuremberg was Wagnerian, the Tokyo affair resembled Gilbert and Sullivan. It was "a third-string road company of the Nuremberg show." The twenty-eight Japanese war criminals, according to *Time*, had "shuffled into court like schoolboys carrying their primers to class. In the shadow of reckoning and doom, they giggled and gossiped." With his big red nose, Keenan reminded one correspondent of W. C. Fields; another related that Tojo "picked his nose unconcernedly and flirted with an American stenographer," and that Oshima "affected the dandy, with white pocket handkerchief, smart bow tie and black-ribboned pince-nez."

But such observers had missed the underlying drama and tragedy Maggie cabled in her report. Nor did she make the mistake of stating that twenty-eight defendants had marched in when there were only twenty-six. The last two had arrived from Bangkok too late, and that was why the opening had been delayed forty-three minutes. She also had visited Sugamo several times and had seen the "war criminals" as human beings under almost unbearable pressure.

Will too was upset by the condescending stories and the snide remarks about Keenan. But the most incensed was Chaucy who openly commented in the Dai Ichi Hotel dining room that too many Americans had brought to Japan their outdated belief in racial superiority. The professor was only amused. "Time will take care of all this," he said. The correspondents were not really racist, he added, predicting that within a few years they would be overpraising the Japanese. What tickled McGlynn was Chaucy's combative reaction. She was a warm young lady. Her own young lady. Too bad Mark hadn't found someone like that.

"It's a shambles, Dad," Chaucy angrily banged out on her typewriter. "I'm surrounded by incompetents who think I've been brought over here to get them coffee. I feel like quitting, but don't worry. I won't! I'm here to stay."

At Sugamo those Class A criminals not yet indicted gossiped about the outlandish behavior of Okawa, but what concerned them most was their own fate. With the trial at last in motion the suspense was almost intolerable. "I always had the feeling that I would be released," one told Shogo, "but now I feel worn out by the suspense. They surely must let me go! I can't take this any longer."

The sun appeared in the morning of Saturday, May 4, to greet the second day of the trial. Today McGlynn was sitting in the balcony just behind Mariko, blissfully unaware that Will and Maggie had been aware of his "secret" romance for some time. They had decided to pretend ignorance since the affair would obviously run its course in a short time.

The session featured delivery of the charges against defendants by a speech from Keenan. This had been prepared by Donihi, Will, and others on the staff, but the chief prosecutor had added his own personal touches and he was compelling from the first sentence. He charged that all the defendants had entered into a common conspiracy to conquer Manchuria and use it as a base to dominate Eastern Asia as well as the Pacific and Indian Oceans. The accused had taken the law into their own hands to force their will upon mankind. "They declared war upon civilization." The prosecution's task was one of prevention and deterrence, not "the small, meaner purpose of vengeance or retaliation." Individuals were now being "brought to the bar of justice for the first time in history to answer personally for offenses that they have committed while acting in official capacities as chiefs of state." In that sense, he conceded, these trials were without precedent. "However,,it is essential to realize that if we waited for precedent and held ourselves in a straitjacket by reason of lack thereof, grave consequences would ensue without warrant or justification." Because of recent scientific developments, another war would mean the end of civilization. "We have no particular interest in any individual or his punishment. They are representative in a certain sense of a class and a group. These defendants are being prosecuted because they were converts to the rule of the tooth and claw."

Keenan was surrounded by fellow prosecutors congratulating him on his bravura performance. He drew Donihi and Will aside. "How did it really go?" he asked like an actor on opening night. Truthfully they both assured him it was convincing, solid and moving. But he spent the evening going from place to place "to feel out the sympathetic aspects of the address," as he confided to Will. He ended up at the Dai Ichi Hotel in the apartment of a Justice Department woman attorney. After a drink he suddenly excused himself and went to the bathroom. Returning in a state of panic, he revealed that he had thrown up and somehow lost his false teeth. They were either flushed down the drain or misplaced somewhere.

A friend quietly asked the assistant night manager to make a discreet inquiry about the whereabouts of the missing teeth. He misunderstood the word "discreet" and placed a notice on the bulletin board. Word was passed to MacArthur, an admirer of Keenan's and the general's personal dentist hurriedly set about making new teeth so the chief prosecutor could make a dignified appearance at court on Monday morning.

That session opened with another incident. Someone had secretly placed on the desk of each of the judges a pamphlet entitled "Japan's Record." Chief Justice Webb, the president of the Tribunal, angrily termed the action improper and warned that any future attempt to influence the judges with such anti-Japanese propaganda would not be tolerated.

Then came a minor sensation. Tojo's counsel, Ichiro Kiyose, speaking as deputy chief of counsel for the defense, challenged the propriety of Webb and eight other judges to preside. Webb was so visibly perturbed that the little gray-haired Kiyose said, "It does not mean that I have any lack of respect for this court, but it is because of the historical importance and historical purposes for which this trial is being held that I speak."

Webb bristled. "I want you to tell me whether you are challenging the individual members of the Court personally?"

"Yes, sir," said Kiyose stoutly. He was little and middle-aged but he stood as straight as a soldier. "But first I wish to present the challenge to Sir William Webb, president of the Tribunal."

"On what grounds?"

"First, that it is not proper, from the standpoint of justice and fairness, that Sir William Webb should conduct this trial. Second, that it is improper for Sir William to conduct this trial in accordance with the Potsdam Declaration of July 26, 1945."

"You must be more specific in stating your grounds," the Australian Chief Justice said. Will noticed that Webb's face was reddening. Chaucy leaned forward expectantly, knowing what Kiyose was going to say.

"That I shall now present," said Kiyose. "There is the fact that Sir William Webb has investigated the case of Japanese atrocities in New Guinea and has submitted the results of said investigation to the Australian Government."

Jutting his hawk nose forward like some winged predator, the ruffled Webb declared he would take no part in the decision on the matter. "I think that point should be decided immediately. The court will now recess and will reassemble when the decision is reached." He repeated himself angrily, "I will take no part in the decision."

Such a hubbub broke out in the room that the marshal exclaimed, "May I ask the spectators to remain quiet!"

"The president," continued Kiyose, his voice rising to a high pitch, "has now called for a recess of this session. However, after the recess it is my desire that his excellency, the president of the court, *calmly* listen to the objections I will have to raise." He waved a copy of the charter of the Tribunal. Chaucy thought Webb was about to fly out of his chair.

But Kiyose was not to be daunted. Webb's reports on the New Guinea atrocities, he continued doggedly, were not without connection with this trial. "They have a relationship. However, if any references to such incidents in New Guinea are withdrawn from the indictment, then I shall withdraw the objection at that point."

This was too much for Webb. "I can make no conditions!" he shouted. "I think the court had better recess."

After an intermission of fifteen minutes, the prosecutor from New Zealand announced, "The members of the Tribunal are of opinion that no objection to the person of any member of the Tribunal can be sustained." They had all been appointed by SCAP.

This decision was immediately followed by the moment the spectators had been waiting for. "I now call on the defendants to plead," said Webb. First on the list was the elderly General Araki, idol of the reformists in the army, and well known throughout the world for his outspoken remarks on social reforms and his ferocious handlebar mustache. He stood at attention.

"Araki, Sadao. How do you plead, guilty or not guilty?"

The answer, in Japanese, was completely unexpected. "That question will be replied to by my counsel," he said defiantly.

"He should answer for himself," said Webb impatiently, but Araki insisted he could not submit to the charges of crimes against humanity and peace because he had never committed any such crime throughout his seventy years. Not waiting for a translation, Webb exclaimed, "We want a plea, not a speech!"

This was translated to Araki who said, "I plead not guilty."

"May we have a translation of what the accused said before?" asked one of the defense counsel.

"Not at this stage," said the exasperated Webb.

Keenan rose. "I ask the court to strike from the record everything that was said by the accused other than the words 'not guilty.'"

"To which we object," retorted the defense counsel. "Counsel has not been informed what he said. If we do not know, we cannot protect his rights."

"Neither does the Tribunal know," retorted Webb and asked the next man, Doihara, how he pleaded. He and all the others simply said "Not guilty" except for Matsuoka who said in English, "Not guilty of all the charges charged in the indictment," and Tojo who stepped forward confidently to declare in his familiar authoritative manner, "On all counts I plead not guilty."

Court was adjourned until May 13.

3.

The recess at the Tokyo trial increased the tension of all the prisoners, including those still not indicted who had imagined they would be released. "It's a mental torture," said one former prime minister. Others took out their frustration by submitting a joint written complaint concerning the jerry-built dance hall that had been constructed near the gallows chamber for the entertainment of the M.P.'s. Every night they could hear jazz music and the laughing voices of girls and even "unbecomingly suggestive squeals."

They felt that the single line of barbed wire between themselves and the dance hall was a boundary between heaven and hell, and that those red-haired brutes were deliberately taunting them just because they had lost the war. It made them seethe. But within a week even the nightly jazz and laughing ceased to bother most of them. "After all," reasoned Tojo to one admiral who still boiled, "What's so strange about red-haired M.P.'s having a little fun?"

The prisoners soon lost their resentment of the pompom girls who would come up to the barbed-wire fence every day, puffing away on American cigarettes and negotiating with the M.P.s by sign language. "They must have been forced to make this kind of living," said Tojo, who had daughters. "Who can survive on the rations we get without the black market and such ways of earning money?"

By now the defense realized that the challenge of Webb's right to be a judge would be turned down by the other members as they concentrated on a second challenge: the right of the Tribunal to try the defendants for "crimes against peace" and "crimes against humanity." It was agreed to let Kiyose, who had already proved himself, launch the attack. Chaucy had come to admire the short, aggressive Kiyose, who now wore military boots, and when she followed him into the courtroom on the morning of May 13 she looked forward to the battle he was going to fight. As he strode purposefully toward the lectern he looked like a boxer about to enter the ring.

Looking boldly at the president he said, "This Tribunal *is* empowered to make charges and try what are called 'war criminals' in accordance with the Potsdam Declaration, but *not* so empowered to try those who cannot be considered as war criminals." And if the Allies did not have the authority to try those cases, neither did MacArthur. "To grant authority or powers to others which one does not possess himself is, in the light of international law, unfounded." Even Will had to admit it was a telling point.

"And speaking of 'crimes against peace,' " little Kiyose continued, slightly raising his voice for emphasis, "whatever the nature of the war or character of the war, the planning, the preparing, the initiating and waging of war cannot be considered as 'crimes against peace' in accordance with the conception of war held by the civilized nations of the world up to July 1945." He startled everyone by banging the table for emphasis.

He then eloquently pointed out the very great difference between the way in which Germany and Japan had surrendered. With Germany it was literally unconditional surrender. But the Japanese Government was in full control when the Allies proposed that Japan accept the Potsdam Declaration.

And since the Potsdam Declaration had been accepted by Japan to end the war in the Pacific, war crimes must then be confined to that war. It was therefore unthinkable that incidents such as that in Manchuria, which had already been settled in the past, should be brought within the range of this trial.

It was another sound point and McGlynn, again in the balcony with Mariko, noted the intense interest shown by American as well as Japanese spectators. Many seemed impressed by Kiyose's eloquence and forcefulness. He wondered how Keenan, whose neck was already red, would reply. In the well of the courtroom Will was concerned that his chief might lose his temper, and he prayed that Keenan would not add any more hyperbole to the prepared statements they had all worked on so assiduously. Keenan appeared nervous, but once he stood up he began to bask in the heat of the Klieg lights.

"Mr. President, members of this International Military Tribunal," he boomed as he launched into a marathon sentence, "can it be that eleven nations representing this Tribunal, and in this prosecution and in themselves representatives of orderly governments of countries containing one half to two thirds of the inhabitants of this world, having suffered through this aggression the losses of a vast amount of their resources and deplorable and incalculable quantities of *blood* due to the *crimes* of *murder, brigandage,* and *plunder,* are now *totally impotent* to bring to trial those responsible for this worldwide calamity, and must now stand *idly* by and permit the perpetrators of those offenses to remain without the reach of any *lawful* punishment whatsoever?"

As he paused for breath, Webb politely interrupted. "Mr. Chief Prosecutor, do you think those rhetorical phrases are fitting at this juncture?"

"Mr. President, in answer to that remark from the president of this Tribunal, I regard the motions as being addressed to the body public of the world, as they are being published, and I do not desire . . ."

My God, thought Maggie, this was vintage W. C. Fields. But her father was seeing the telling effect of such a performance on those in the gallery as Keenan flamboyantly presented the prosecution's case. As the crowd was leaving for lunch, McGlynn was interested to hear a number of Americans arguing among themselves. It was like a play, he thought, but wished the whole thing could be trimmed down in an out-of-town tryout.

To McGlynn's delight the hyperbole resumed at 1:30 P.M. No one could pump up the English language like an Irishman. Keenan bemoaned the horrible fate of millions of innocent Japanese crushed by the orders of their leaders whom the defense wished to free from punishment. "Such a contention is as revolting as it is unsound. And the broader point is raised by the accused's motion, whether mankind will place itself in a straitjacket of legal precepts (which are without foundation or logic) by bowing to the force of such wormwood legalisms, and leave those responsible criminals unpunished and at large?"

Will noticed President Webb moving restlessly. If Keenan did, he ignored it, for he became even more Irish in his hand and body gestures. Oh, Barry Fitzgerald, thought McGlynn, what have the movies done to you! "And is it supposed that in the meantime organized society must remain *supinely quiescent,* with the soft folded hands of indifference, and await its own destruction in a very literal sense? It is tantamount to the assertion that mankind is without lawful power to save itself."

Then despite Webb's attempt to cut him short, Keenan insisted on quoting Franklin D. Roosevelt in a radio address on the birthday "of the Great Emancipator, Lincoln," at the Cairo Conference. At last Kiyose was given the chance to retort. It was a welcome change of pace as the feisty little Japanese fought back with logic and bangs on the table.

Webb showed his annoyance when Kiyose briefly quoted the Potsdam Declaration, interrupting to say, "I suggest to you that 'unconditional surrender' means free from any terms imposed by the Japanese. Go ahead."

Kiyose would not be intimidated. "Mr. President," he said in English, "will you wait for me to finish my opinion of the term 'unconditional surrender' before giving your own? Will you allow me to give my *own* opinion in a *calm* manner?"

Webb fumed. "You should know what is troubling this court in your arguments, but you may proceed without any interruption as far as I am concerned."

To Chaucy's delight Kiyose continued to make valid points. The unconditional surrender of the Japanese troops was recognized in the Instrument of Surrender. "But there is no provision whatsoever made for the unconditional surrender of the Japanese Government or the Japanese people." This was something Chaucy had asked him to accent, since it was proved by the fact the Japanese Government, unlike the Nazi regime, was still operating under the guidance of MacArthur.

Late that afternoon, after an objection by Keenan had been heard, the distraught president said, "The debate is closed. As far as we can judge, nobody has anything to add."

Whereupon Kiyose began speaking in Japanese.

"You are speaking out of order," interrupted Webb peremptorily.

"No new matter has been introduced in the reply, so you are not entitled to reply to Mr. Keenan."

What a chilling note to end the session! thought Chaucy. It was obvious that Sir William Webb, ruffled at Kiyose's challenge to his own authority to be a member of the Tribunal, was going to give the defense a hard time. The reason, she wrote her father that night, was that Webb had become so sickened by the overwhelming evidence of Japanese brutality to Australian prisoners of war that he was determined to see that those in command of this evil regime be brought to stern justice. She feared, therefore, that the trial might turn out to be only victors' justice. She told how Furness and Blakeney had recently gone to Sugamo Prison in defiance of their chief counsel, and asked if any indicted prisoners wanted also to be represented by Americans. "Shigemitsu," she wrote, "chose Furness and General Umezu chose Blakeney. Then representatives of Field Marshal Hata heard of Artie Lazarus's remarkable record of acquittals in the Yokohama Class B-C trials and requested his services. Three other Americans were also selected, and one of the less important civilian defendants did request your daughter. But he did this so disdainfully (whoever heard of a lady lawyer?) that I turned him down. Instead I've accepted an offer from Kiyose (he fights as if he came from County Cork) to assist him in the defense of Razor Blade Tojo. I'm not to appear in person in this benighted male-oriented chamber. I'll be only a glorified law clerk, but it's better than nothing."

On the eve of the next session, Chaucy had dinner with the professor and Will. Lately the three had gotten together at least twice a week. The professor had grown fond of Chaucy, and she had come to esteem his son. The arguments between her and Will were still lively, but now they were genial duels. During the miso—bean paste—soup she told them how surprised Tojo had been to learn from Kiyose that a prominent American attorney, George Blewett, had offered to represent him. " 'I'll only accept him,' Tojo said to Kiyose, 'if he agrees my defense rests on three points. First, that the great East Asian war was a war of self-defense; second, that the Emperor is not responsible for the war; and third, that the objective of the war was the liberation of the Oriental peoples.' "

Will was not at all impressed by such words, but his father exclaimed in delight, "Vintage Tojo, children!"

In the morning the defense continued its attack on Keenan's opening statement by pointing out the inadequate time they'd had to prepare their case. The work, Furness told Webb, had to be divided up among the few American counsel who now represented defendants. "We all wish to stress the fact that our motion is supplemental to the motion argued by Dr. Kiyose. We think it was a valid motion and a brilliant presentation."

"I think we can omit the compliments," said Webb, as testy as ever. "It is quite unnecessary."

Furness argued that the members of the Tribunal were representatives of nations who were the accusers. And regardless of their personal integrity, their judgment could not be impartial and could never be free from substantial doubt as to its legality, fairness, and impartiality. "We say that this is not necessary and that the accused should be tried by representatives of neutral nations free from the heat and hatred of war."

At this juncture Major Ben Bruce Blakeney, the Oklahoman who had represented General Umezu—Tojo's successor in 1944 as chief of staff of the army—took over the common defense. A good-looking man, he moved to the podium with the ease of a polished actor, giving off an aura of restrained energy. "My first point is that war is not a crime." He spoke with persuasive clarity, rarely raising his voice but making every word count. A product of Harvard Law School, like Furness, he was dramatic without being flamboyant. "The very concept of war implies the legal right to use force. Indeed, the very existence of the entire body of international law on the subject of war is evidence of the legality of war." Never in the history of civilization had the planning and waging of wars been tried as a crime. There was thus no precedent for the present proceeding. "The establishing of a precedent which results in ex post facto definition of crime, in the imposing of a punishment upon the doing of an act *not punished when it was performed,* has always been abhorrent to every system of civilized law."

Killing in war, Blakeney continued, could not be called murder since war itself was legal. "This legalized killing—justifiable homicide —however repulsive, however abhorrent, has never been thought of as imposing criminal responsibility." By now he was speaking with more force and those in the gallery were leaning forward expectantly, completely entranced. "Nor has it ever been asked whether such killings occur in a just or unjust war, in a legal or illegal war, a war of defense or a war of aggression. Men have been tried, within recent memory, for responsibility for killing in war in violation of the laws and customs which have grown up to regulate the contest of war. But the trial and punishment of those men was no judicial novelty."

Many of those in the prisoners' dock had feared that the generous offer of American counsel was merely a ploy to weaken the defense. But here was an American speaking out boldly on behalf of the defeated and against American interests.

"If the killing of Admiral Kidd by the bombing of Pearl Harbor is murder, we know the name of the very man whose hands loosed the atomic bomb on Hiroshima." A restrained sensation was felt throughout the room. An American had dared bring up the atomic bomb and even mentioned the man who had dropped it! "We know the chief of staff who planned that act, we know the chief of the responsible state." Everyone was shocked. How dared he mention Marshall and Truman as men sharing the same blame of atrocities committed as those in the prisoners' dock! McGlynn felt goose pimples rising as he watched Blakeney standing there, bold, erect, without tremor, and recalled Dryden's apt line, "Ev'n victors are by victory undone." "Is murder on their conscience? We may well doubt it. We may well doubt it, and not because the event of the armed conflict has declared their cause just and their enemies unjust, but because the act is *not* murder." How magnificent, thought McGlynn, who had imagined himself impervious to such feelings. "Show us the charge, produce the proof of the killing contrary to the laws and customs of war, name the man whose hand dealt the blow, produce the responsible superior who planned, ordered, permitted or acquiesced in this act, and you have brought a criminal to the bar of justice. But let us forgo this attempt also, by the so-called 'murder' counts of the Indictment, to impose responsibility for them upon men innocent of any specific connection therewith."

Moments later Blakeney concluded with quiet force, "And now, Mr. President, I am through, with one last word: The chief prosecutor presumes to speak for America in urging upon this Tribunal the acceptance of this Indictment as drawn. Those of us American defense counsel who wear the uniform of the armed forces of our country, I think, may also have the right to speak for America. We speak for American, for Anglo-Saxon, for Anglo-American, for democratic views of justice, of fair play. We speak for the proposition that observing legal forms while ignoring the essence of legal principles is the supreme atrocity against the law." The entire room was dead quiet. "The responsibility of all those playing their several parts in this Tribunal," he said, raising his voice imperceptibly, "is tremendous, awe-inspiring. If, from this trial, a better world, which we all hope for, and a more perfect system of law, are to emerge, the proceeding must be so conducted that no man shall be able to say that justice has been outraged. By a trial founded upon such a dubious jurisdiction as this, we may, indeed, prove anew the power of the victor over the vanquished; but we cannot hope to add luster to our reputation for attachment to justice and law." As Blakeney returned to his seat, Chaucy felt like applauding. Never had she felt so proud to be an American.

Will warred with himself. When Blakeney had mentioned the atomic bomb, the horrors of Nagasaki roiled in his mind and left him weak. Blakeney was speaking for him and all those he had met on the terrible day of the bombing. But that was no excuse for permitting those Japanese in uniform in the dock to go free. They were as guilty as Homma and, God knows, it was right and just that Homma had been shot.

It was Keenan's misfortune that he must answer such an inspiring address. He tried a little Irish humor, noting that to have the defendants tried by "neutral nations" they must wait until scientists could perfect a safe rocket ship to go up to Mars and other planets to find "neutral" peoples to sit upon judgment of those responsible for aggressive wars. It fell flat, and he called the challenge to the fairness of the Tribunal a misconception. "The test of the fairness and of the impartiality will be manifest in an open court where every proceeding is subject to the scrutiny of the press and the observers and the Japanese people and the visitors and the wide, wide world." This was going to be a fair trial, something unknown to the Axis powers. He too was an actor and he looked up at the gallery. The Japanese people, he said, will see a fair trial—which, we dare say, perhaps they have never before enjoyed in the fullness, in all their past history."

Most of the Japanese in the gallery, except the families of the defendants, were already convinced of this. And few had much sympathy for Tojo and the other men in uniform. All of them had brought Japan into ruins and deserved the hangman's noose.

After court was adjourned, Chaucy noticed Will going up to Blakeney. Was he bringing some reprimand from Keenan? To her surprise, Will was shaking Blakeney's hand. Only much later would she learn that he had been so deeply moved by Blakeney's reference to the atom bomb that he could not resist the impulse to shake his hand.

Three days later the Tribunal met for seven minutes. The most notable event was the presence, at last, of the judge from India. Radhabinad Pal was a lawyer with far more experience in international law than any of the other judges. He was tall, dark, and distinguished. Before sitting down Pal held palms together and bowed deeply to the prisoners. This caused the only mild sensation of the day, one that went unnoticed by about all in the room except the prisoners themselves.

The clerk of the court asked for judgment on the three motions raised by the defense, but no one was surprised when Webb peremptorily dismissed all three. "I propose to adjourn," he said. "Does any counsel wish to raise any objection?" There was no reply and the court was adjourned to a date to be fixed. The later the better, prayed Chaucy.

Chapter Nine

1.

Tokyo, June 3, 1946.

Despite Kido's suggestion that the best witness of the actions of Tojo once he became prime minister in 1941 was the general himself, Will McGlynn had not yet got around to interrogating him on that subject. The reason, he finally admitted to himself, was his utter dislike of the man, and so on the eve of the formal start of the prosecution case he went back to Sugamo.

The general was as ever chipper and composed, and even while Will was taking out his notebook Tojo began to complain. "Several of our enlisted men claim they're not fed properly when they have to appear in the Yokohama Class B-C court. Sometimes they arrive too late for lunch and get back to Sugamo too late for a decent meal."

It was a legitimate complaint. "I'll see what I can do," said Will. It was decent of Tojo to be so considerate of his subordinates, he thought, and then wondered if it was just another grandstand play. "Is it true," he asked, "that you were the one most responsible for the fall of the Konoye Cabinet in October 1941?"

Tojo lit a cigarette, then calmly said, "Yes. That man was too weak to be a prime minister at such a critical time. He told me we should proceed with great caution since America had such superiority in resources." His face grew stony in memory. "I told him, 'There are times when we must have the courage to do extraordinary things—like jumping with eyes closed, off the veranda of Kiyomizu Temple!' "

This, Will knew, was the famous Buddhist temple in Kyoto located on a steep hill at the edge of a ravine. Will hid his delight. The man was going to hang himself with his own rash words!

"Yes, I was responsible for the fall of Konoye. He didn't even have the nerve to keep his own promises. A prime minister must have courage. After Konoye resigned I went to my quarters to pack. I was sure they'd relieve me as War Minister. Then I got a phone call from the Grand Chamberlain to report to the Palace at once. I knew this was the end, and put some papers in my briefcase to support my position. I expected to be admonished by the Emperor and was amazed when he said, 'We order you to form a Cabinet. Observe the provisions of the Constitution.' " He drew himself erect. "I was so awed I could hardly speak, but finally asked for time to consider in the waiting room. Then Marquis Kido came in and explained what His Majesty could only imply. 'It is the Emperor's wish,' he said, 'that you make an exhaustive study of domestic and foreign conditions—without regard to the decision of the September 6 Imperial Conference.' " Tojo shook his head. "This was unheard of in Japanese history! No Emperor before had ever rescinded a decision of the Imperial Conference. The Lord Privy Seal then said, 'You are ordered to go back to blank paper.' That meant I was to start with a clean slate and negotiate seriously with America for peace." Tojo stared into space. "I couldn't really understand what had happened but I managed to tell the Marquis that I would accept the responsibility thrust on me. I had myself driven out to Yasukuni Shrine." This was where the souls of Japan's war dead were enshrined. "The head priest brought me to the Hall of Worship where he expelled evil spirits by waving the branch of a sacred tree. Then we marched up the stone steps of the main hall." His face paled. "I bowed twice, clapped my hands, and bowed again. I told myself I now faced a completely new life. From this moment I must think of myself as a civilian, not as a soldier. Mine must be a national, not a military cabinet. Above all, I must follow scrupulously the wishes of the Emperor." He stopped. "Since I was a boy I had never cried but now tears flooded out of my eyes, and I vowed to have the Emperor as the mirror of my judgment. I would take every decision to the Emperor. If His mirror was clear, I would proceed, but if it was clouded even slightly, I would reconsider." Tojo had let his cigarette burn to his finger. Without any evidence of pain he snubbed out the tiny butt.

Despite himself Will was impressed.

"From then on," said Tojo curtly, "I did my utmost to bring about peace with America. Some of my former colleagues considered me a traitor to the military. But I kept on this course until your government turned down our reasonable offer and forced us to go to war."

Will's momentary sympathy evaporated, and his distrust was obvious to Tojo. "You can verify everything I've told you," said Tojo, "in the records of the Liaison Conferences." Which he pretends to believe we intentionally destroyed, thought Will, and left the prison convinced Tojo had twisted the truth.

That evening Chaucy and Will found themselves alone in the dining room at the Dai Ichi Hotel. At the last minute Maggie had been called to her office and the professor excused himself, saying he must finish a report on land reform. He was, in truth, spending the evening with Mariko whose son had been unexpectedly summoned overnight for an emergency meeting of the Young Communist League.

Neither Chaucy nor Will relished a discussion of the morrow's session since it would inevitably lead to an argument. Chaucy, in some desperation, asked what Will thought of the recent article Mark Gayn of the Chicago *Sun* had written on the indicted war criminals. As soon as the words were out of her mouth she wished she could withdraw them, for it was obvious that Will would heartily endorse everything the noted liberal correspondent had written. At the same time she was secretly tickled at the way he quickly shot out of the water to take the bait; this made her realize how the perverse Irish in her had once again taken subconscious control.

Will should have responded coolly but occasionally his own Irish half would also rise to the surface. "On target!" he said enthusiastically. "You're going to hear more of the same when Keenan delivers his opening statement. Is there any doubt that the military-financial oligarchy in Japan took over in 1931 with the seizure of Manchuria? And then plunged the country into adventures that finally ended at Pearl Harbor?" He didn't give her a chance to answer as he went on to graphically describe how paranoiac fear of the Soviet Union had driven the Japanese expansionists into an anti-Comintern pact with Hitler and Mussolini. He spoke and gestured with an energy and conviction that impressed Chaucy even though she disagreed with nearly everything he had to say. This was certainly not the frail, haunted man she had first seen in her father's office. He was going to be a worthy opponent and for the first time she could see why her father had brought him into the firm.

Fascinated, she let him go on about the conspiracy between militarists like Tojo and civilian leaders like Kido. "As Gayn said, they both had faith in Japan's destiny and they both connived independently to drive Japan into aggression. And the conspiracy grew along with their own personal power, so they were able to devise new intrigues both at home and in Washington and London. Both were drunk with power and both became tools for the *zaibatsu* which hungered for new markets and new sources of raw materials." He suddenly stopped. "Why are you grinning?"

Impishly she took a battered book out of her briefcase. It was *When East Met West.* "Your father seems to disagree with you."

He flushed and then suddenly laughed. "Do you remember that cartoon of Thurber's where a duelist has just amputated his opponent's head with a wild swing and cries, *'Touché!'?*"

She laughed. Such a good-natured reaction was appealing.

"Dad and I never did agree about politics. But he never agreed with anyone about anything." He hefted the book. "It's a wonderful book. And I can go along with most of it. But he knows Kido so well that he can't admit even to himself that the illustrious Privy Seal could be involved in conspiracy with Tojo."

"May I ask a personal question?"

"Go ahead."

"What did you say to Blakeney after his reply to Keenan?"

"I was just congratulating him on having the nerve to bring up the atom bomb."

"I could see you shaking hands with him but I couldn't imagine why you did."

"I was at Nagasaki," he said simply.

"You mean after the bombing?"

"Before, during, and after." He was about to comment that FDR would surely *not* have dropped the bomb, but instead excused himself. "Busy day tomorrow for the prosecution. Enjoyed our talk." He bowed slightly and left. She watched his tall, lanky form weaving through the crowd with awkward grace. She walked slowly to the Imperial Hotel musing on how there was much more to Will than she'd first imagined. Once in her room she began another letter to her father.

"Tomorrow the Big Show really starts and I expect Keenan will try to blow us all out of the water. He can be brilliant but I don't think he's big enough for the job. He doesn't see that this trial is going to be a series of anomalies. How, for instance, can we pour decades of history into the mold of an adversary process with conventional litigation techniques? How are the judges, all representatives of the victors, going to accord justice to the vanquished on the premise that it was a crime for the vanquished to attempt to disturb an existing status quo of the victors?

"By the way, you'll be happy to know that Will McGlynn is physically in good shape. We had dinner tonight and I had a hard time getting a word in. I'll finish this later. Must be in good shape myself for tomorrow. . . ."

But she couldn't get to sleep. She kept tossing from side to side realizing how poorly prepared the defense was. Their office was still unfurnished. There weren't enough desks or stenographers. Eleven new counsel had poured in from America but none of them knew anything about the case and all had been trained in the Anglo-American system.

Few of the new American defense counsel knew anything about Japanese history, customs, and government, and fewer still had any knowledge of the Japanese language. Witnesses would have to be examined primarily through Japanese interpreters who, being Japanese, hated to say "no" and often said "yes" when they meant "no," or "yes" when they meant they didn't know. The Japanese of course had the same trouble understanding Westerners, whose idiosyncrasies were equally unreasonable.

But Chaucy's main complaint was that the defense had not had enough time to find material and prepare its case, and she knew that the Japanese defense counsel also had their problems. Some doubted the sincerity of their American colleagues' intentions to present an aggressive defense. Even the defendants who had already chosen American counsel were suspicious. Why would the Americans provide free U.S. legal aid unless it was for a mere show of what they called democracy? It didn't make sense to be defended by officers who had tried to kill you a few months earlier.

Chaucy got out of bed and began pacing. What worried her most was the increasing tension between the Southern gentleman, Captain Coleman, the chief counsel for defense, and those like Furness and Blakeney who wanted the freedom of defending their own clients individually. She admired all three men but it was obvious they would never agree. There were no heated arguments and Coleman simply reiterated that he had been chosen by MacArthur as chief counsel and it was his understanding that he was to put together a united common defense.

Coleman also made it apparent that he was distressed by the poor quality of most of his associates. He felt they were incompetent or blowhards. He had tried to train the newcomers but the task was too formidable. For example, one new counsel was a law school dropout, and there were several newcomers who were stubbornly planning to defend *two* clients. They could easily have conflicting interests!

Coleman confided to Chaucy that he was so appalled, he had recently sought an audience with MacArthur. As Coleman began presenting his complaints, the general had interrupted angrily. He thought Coleman, who had fought against the Japanese, didn't want to defend them, and launched into a lecture. When MacArthur finally simmered down, Coleman pointed out his real reasons. "I'm afraid this could be an unfair trial. I don't like such vague charges as 'war as crime and conspiracy.' They should be more specific. I'm also concerned that the inexperienced defense people sent over here will give America a bad name. Americans have always stood for a fair trial with every defendant getting the best possible defense. It could be a blot on our entire legal profession."

"I sympathize with you," said MacArthur.

Wouldn't it be possible to postpone the trial a few months so more competent men could be brought over from the States?

"It's a good idea but impractical. We cannot delay the trial."

"In that case," said Coleman regretfully, "I will have to ask for a different assignment. It is against my principles to be involved in an unfair trial."

MacArthur regretted his decision. "I hope you change your mind."

At Sugamo Prison the indicted Class A prisoners were being told by an interpreter that they were to appear in the Ichigaya court the next day. A little after eight the next morning they filed out the front door of Sugamo. Guarded by M.P.'s with machine guns, they were herded into a bus. At exactly 9:30 the marshal announced that the Tribunal was ready to hear any matter brought before it. The defense requested that Okawa and Matsuoka, both in the hospital, be struck from indictment. After Judge Webb said he would consider the matter, a newly arrived defense counsel made an eloquent plea for a delay. The newcomers, he said, had come on short notice, unprepared. "We ask only a reasonable time to acquaint ourselves with the situation." Since arrival they had been busy with billeting, processing, vaccinations, and recovering from the vaccinations. Office quarters were not ready, and they hadn't seen a single secretary or stenographer until that morning.

After Keenan urged the Court to advance the proceedings in their proper order as designated, the new counsel appealed for a two-week delay. "I say that seriously because in the short time we have been here we have learned that everything we do is a time-consuming matter." Talking to a defendant through an interpreter was time-consuming—it took about four times as long as it did back home. They simply had to have more time. "We have not had it," he said and then, realizing his plea was futile, added distraughtly, "I wonder why we are here?"

The following morning eleven more American defense counsel were introduced to the court. They would defend Kido and ten other prisoners. Today Mariko was in the gallery. In the row ahead she recognized the two daughters of former Prime Minister Hirota, who was staring up at the balcony from the prisoners' dock. He greeted his girls with a little wave of the hand.

McGlynn was in the press section with Maggie. She nudged him when Judge Pal bowed to the defendants just before sitting down. Then Keenan stepped forward into the glare of the Klieg lights, relishing his role as star performer, for today he would deliver the prosecution's opening statement over which he, Donihi, and Will had labored many hours. After surveying the courtroom he began reading from a sixty-five-page document. "We are waging a part of the determined battle of civilization to preserve the entire world from destruction." His voice was strong, his presentation effective. By now earphones had been installed throughout the room and at last the defendants could hear a simultaneous Japanese translation as Keenan presented an outline of the prosecution's theory of law and the facts which would prove that each of the accused was guilty.

"They declared war upon civilization!" he declared. "And to this end they joined hands with the Hitlerite group; they did it formally, by way of treaty, and they were proud of their confederacy. Together they planned, or prepared and initiated, aggressive wars against the great democracies enumerated in the indictment. They willingly dealt with human beings as chattels and pawns. That this meant murder and the subjugation and enslavement of millions meant nothing to them."

Will was concerned: Keenan's face was beet red and his legs wobbled. But he gathered himself together and declared with renewed vigor that the defendants' purpose had been to loose a terrible force upon the world. "In this enterprise millions could die; the resources of nations could be destroyed. All of this was of no import in their mad scheme for domination and control of East Asia, and, as they advanced, ultimately the whole world. This was the import of their conspiracy."

The defendants were listening attentively but without show of emotion. Maggie nudged her father. "Some show!" she muttered.

"There's method in his madness," he said.

"Perhaps madness in his method," replied his daughter.

McGlynn tried in vain to check a laugh and was chided by a stern look from a British correspondent.

"Is civilization," Keenan was saying, "compelled to stand idly by and permit these outrages without an attempt to deter such efforts?" The purpose of the prosecution was "prevention or deterrence" of future wars, and had nothing to do with vengeance, he asserted, calling Tojo and his mates "common felons."

He argued that a war of aggression *was* a crime under international law, and that the war in the Pacific was illegal since Japan had broken treaties in waging war. Therefore every Allied killed during the conflict was the victim of murder.

He vowed to produce irrefutable evidence proving that each of the accused was directly guilty "as a responsible military or government official, or as a leader, organizer, instigator, or accomplice in the formulation or execution of a common plan or conspiracy, of violation of practically all of the recognized rules and customs of war."

After orating all morning, he resumed in the afternoon for another hour and a half. Then after a short recess the defense was given half an hour to make objections, all of which were overruled by Webb.

Mariko had been gripped by Keenan's flowery but forceful words and when he said, "We now come to the point where we shall show the acts of Japan to be among the most treacherous and perfidious of all time," she blushed with shame. "In 1904," he continued, "Japan opened the Russo-Japanese War with an attack on the Russian fleet at Port Arthur without notice or warning. The civilized nations of the world recognized that a continuance of this practice would be intolerable."

This last sentence turned her from shame to indignation. How dared he say such a ridiculous thing! None of those "civilized nations" had accused Japan of a treacherous act at the time. Instead, Americans sympathetic to an underdog highly praised the Japanese for their pluck. The whole civilized world, in fact, had accepted the Japanese victory for almost fifty years. Now all at once the "pluck" of 1904 had been turned into treachery. Was this the fair trial MacArthur had promised?

Yet by the time court was adjourned for ten days and the defendants began filing out of the courtroom Mariko felt no sympathy for any of them, particularly Tojo who turned to the judges to make a curt little bow which reminded Mariko of the way Japanese men and children leave a room of their superiors.

Will, who was standing in line to congratulate the tomato-faced and exhausted Keenan, saw in the background a grinning Chaucy tap her head with a finger. He wondered whether she was doffing her hat to the chief prosecutor or indicating he was mad.

2.

As Maggie was collecting her papers after the historic session she heard someone behind her saying, "Wow, wasn't that some circus!" She turned to see little Jun Kato, who said he hoped the trial wouldn't take all summer.

"I'm afraid this thing is going to last a long, long time," she replied and offered him a ride to Hibiya. On the way they argued about the May Day rally. Maggie felt it was a flash in the pan and that the enthusiasm for communism would soon die down. He tried to convince her that many young Japanese saw in the Party the new direction they had been searching for and that the labor unions were the belt linking the Communist Party to the masses. When she laughed he protested vigorously. First he revealed that he had become chief delegate of his shop union, and then in a burst of enthusiasm proudly confessed he had joined the Party.

She was so startled she almost smashed into the car ahead. The utter damned fool! "I thought you wanted to get back to America and regain your citizenship?"

"I still do—at the right time." Then, like almost all new recruits to love and politics, he couldn't restrain from talking at length about the momentous decision. "I had to join the Party because I can't help being on the side of justice and also because there now is within me a desire to examine things and understand their true nature." He blushed. "I know I'm not someone who can play a great role in the revolution. But I didn't want to be an obstacle in its path. I know I'm only a little cog in the machine, but can't you see that by joining the Party I do contribute something to the cause? And joining the Party at least means that I'm not joining the enemy. This is all new to me, and from now on I must work and learn. I realize I must concentrate on my profession, but by writing good articles and maybe later a book or two I can help the Party and participate in the revolution. Only that way can I grow as a human being."

Maggie was moved by his naïveté. What a pure soul he was, a gentle soul, and he would be mangled in the machine.

He was reciting earnestly, like a religious acolyte:

> "Within the ranks
> of comrades in the march,
> I take my place."

"I know you think I'm a fool, Miss McGlynn." He blushed. "Will you do me a favor?" She nodded. "There's a Party rally about to start at Hibiya Hall. Will you come with me and please just listen?"

They parked at the Imperial Hotel and walked across to the distinctive Western structure at the end of Hibiya Park. On the way he told of the study group he had joined. His class was in the process of analyzing Stalin's book on dialectical materialism. "But don't think we are slaves to Moscow, Miss McGlynn. We only want to bring about a peaceful revolution and we regard the American Occupation as a liberating force. Nosaka-san insists we cooperate with MacArthur. All we want is a classless utopia."

They passed several white M.P. jeeps parked outside the hall. But the M.P.'s merely sat watching the crowd flow into the building. In the lobby shabby young men were selling Communist papers and magazines. "I write some articles in the *Red Flag* daily," he confided.

"Under your own name?"

"Oh, no. Not yet. I call myself Searchlight. Do you like it?"

"Very good," she said.

An excited but orderly mob was pouring into the huge hall and it took time to find empty seats. Maggie was surprised to see mostly middle-aged, poorly dressed men. While she read in the dim light a handbill outlining the new Party program, Jun was peering around in vain for friends.

At last the meeting began. A youngish man, smaller than Jun, sidled onto the stage as if he didn't belong there, bowed nervously and began speaking monotonously of what they hoped to accomplish in the next year. He introduced another man who also bowed several times and started reading the Party program from a large scroll. His voice was shrill and so high-pitched Maggie had difficulty in understanding the words. The audience became restless and Jun whispered, "It takes time to get going. Wait till you hear Shiga-san, he's next."

Maggie had already interviewed Yoshio Shiga, the theorist of the Party. Younger than Nosaka and the fiery Tokuda, the Secretary General, he impressed her as the brainiest in the Party. Easy to interview, he had revealed to her without embarrassment that once his wife had renounced communism under torture, he could not forgive her. "That day I gave up my wife." But they couldn't break *his* spirit. "The prison guards slapped me until I lost hearing in one ear. And my eyes are bad from malnutrition." He had smiled grimly. "I spent seventeen years in jail and, as you see, I've come out alive—the same man who went into jail."

The crowd came alive as soon as Shiga, slight and weather-beaten, stepped to the podium. He thrust out his right arm in salute and spoke in a loud, confident voice. Every word was clear and his tone was not at all grim. Instead he spread cheer and hope; Maggie found herself strangely uplifted by words she would have satirized if she had read them.

Then he abruptly turned to a different subject, the indictment of the war criminals. Gripping the lectern he cried out, "The time has come to name all those guilty; to list the men who brought Japan to ruin, who made her a place of terror and oppression." The twenty-eight men named at the International Military Tribunal were only the beginning. "Our list is long. It has thirteen hundred names." There were hundreds in both the Lower and Upper Houses of the Diet who had voted as their taskmaster dictated. "There are one hundred and sixty-eight murderers and ruffians who masked their crimes with patriotism. There are one hundred and thirty generals and admirals; eighty-six men of the *zaibatsu* who made war pay profits; one hundred and fourteen labor leaders of the so-called unions . . ."

This brought a raucous jeer.

". . . formed to do the army's bidding. There are seventy journalists and fifty scholars who betrayed science and journalism." He shouted that there were also twenty-three officials of the court, and named Admiral Nomura and the diplomat Kurusu as militarist connivers in Washington before Pearl Harbor. The crowd cheered. He began listing famous premiers and ambassadors, each name bringing a shout of approval.

"There are more names on our list. We want to include all adult members of the Imperial family." The audience shouted louder than ever. "Including Empress Nagako. She led Japan's womanhood on the path of reaction and feudalism. She is the symbol of the half-slave status of our women."

The crowd laughed with delight, but Shiga did not smile. As the laughter died he kept staring at the audience. What showmanship, thought Maggie. He waited until the silence became almost unbearable. Then he boomed out, "We now come to the last name on our list —the Emperor!"

The crowd stamped their feet, cheered and shouted while Shiga, his face cavernous, stared back, the symbol of the angry oppressed.

In a state of exultation Jun led Maggie through the crowd to backstage. "You must meet him," he said and she didn't have the heart to say she already had. "He's the editor of *Red Flag* and I know him!"

Although Shiga was still sweating from his speech he was already smiling and exuding good humor. He grinned to see Maggie and she hurriedly gave her name and paper before he could reveal he knew her. "What was the most memorable event of your prison life?" she asked.

He laughed. "The day we were finally released by General MacArthur. Did you know we prisoners had accumulated so much property in jail, we had to get seven trucks to cart it off? We even had a sewing machine."

This was too much for Maggie. "Is that a fact?" she said.

"Of course it's a fact," said Shiga indignantly. "You Americans, all you want are facts, facts, facts."

Chapter Ten

Yokosuka, June 14, 1946.

On the day the Tokyo Tribunal adjourned, Captain Mark McGlynn was just arriving at the Yokosuka Naval Base. He was met by the former commandant of the 1st Battalion 6th Marines, Lieutenant Colonel William J. Sullivan. They had seen action together at Guadalcanal, Tarawa, Saipan, and Tinian.

Colonel Sullivan, better known as Billy J., was presently commandant of the Marine detachment at Yokosuka, and it was he who had arranged Mark's transfer. The base, established at the time of the American Civil War, was located twenty-two miles south of Tokyo on Miura Peninsula and had been the headquarters for the Imperial Japanese Navy's Yokosuka naval district. Here the most powerful carriers and battleships had been built. Consequently it had become not only one of the largest and best-equipped bases in the Orient but the naval defense core of the Japanese Empire. But there had been no time during the last two years of war to repair buildings damaged by usage, minor bombings, strafing, and civilian looting, and so the Americans had to take over an area in shambles as their major naval base in the Orient.

The present commander, Captain Benton Decker, a stocky, hearty man brimming with enthusiasm, had arrived in early April to find a massive junk pile peopled by naval personnel whose main goal was to get home. No one was interested in the inhabitants of Yokosuka, the great majority of whom were unemployed and hungry. The best officers and most experienced enlisted men had already been rushed back to America, leaving behind few experienced enough to handle the tremendous task of disposing of Japanese war materiel in addition to salvaging and identifying huge amounts of U.S. surplus equipment pouring in from the southern islands.

Decker regarded as an opportunity what others would have looked on as an unmitigated disaster, and he tackled the job of reconstruction with an energy and ingenuity that had already brought frowns from shorebound superiors in Washington who resented his disregard for protocol. He was appreciated by the admiral commanding Far East Naval Forces, who requested the Bureau of Personnel to promote him to commodore. But Washington replied, "Not at this time," which meant "Never."

Once Mark had mastered the basics of being assistant provost marshal, he took the train to Tokyo where he found the Toda home in disarray. Floss was preparing to take the first detachment of children to her orphanage. Upon seeing Mark she hugged him and to his surprise she was close to tears.

"What the hell's the matter?"

She was so distraught he couldn't understand half of what she said. It appeared that the summer home on the beach turned over to her had been half destroyed by a bomb, and money promised by MacArthur's Welfare section was being held up. Moreover, the children at Ueno Station were getting wilder and more desperate, and she had a cold. "And we can't even get proper transportation to take them to Chigasaki."

But Marines were used to catastrophes. "No sweat," he said confidently, and this brought another hug. "When do you want to leave?"

"Tomorrow," she said more as a question than a statement.

"No sweat," he replied.

When he presented the problem to two other former members of the old 1/6 Battalion they also said, "No sweat." Gunnery Sergeant Harold "The Beast" Kelly had control of the motor pool and First Sergeant Tullio Rossi left to set up a work detail. By midmorning of the next day four Marine trucks had pulled up to Ueno Station. An Army M.P. came over to protest but The Beast placated him with a carton of cigarettes, and in half an hour Floss and a hundred ragged, filthy, wild-eyed boys and girls were scrambling into the vehicles.

There was a moment of crisis when a fat girl of fifteen rushed out, mouthing Japanese obscenities. This was the gang leader Maggie had earlier encountered. Fatty roughly corralled five cowering young boys over whom she towered and arrogantly demanded that Floss return them to her. They were her gang of beggars and petty thieves. The Beast, after one disdainful look at her, flung aside a lit cigarette. Fatty snapped her fingers and one of her boys sprang forward to retrieve it. She puffed it in her grand manner, seized two of the boys, and started off. The Beast grunted, peeled off the boys, picked her up like a sack of potatoes, and dumped her in a pile of rubbish.

At last all the children were aboard. They couldn't believe their luck when sandwiches were passed out while they rumbled down the bumpy streets. It took more than three hours to reach Chigasaki. A few minutes outside of town on the road along Sagami Bay they came upon a large wooden structure standing in the midst of a desolate stretch of small trees along the sandy, windswept seashore. "That's it!" said Floss who was sitting between the driver and Mark in the first truck.

At first it looked in good shape to Mark, but he could soon see there were great holes in the roof. To the children it was a dream come true and they raced into the run-down structure despite Floss's attempts to control them.

"Holy shit!" exclaimed The Beast when he saw the condition of the house. Then, to Mark's amazement, he blushed. "Excuse me, lady. I think we gotta make some repairs. But don't worry, lady. No sweat."

The children and Masao were roaming through the house, exclaiming in wonder at the dilapidated furniture and filthy rugs. What had seemed utterly depressing to Floss on her previous visit was transformed into a haven by the children's awe and joy. Never before had she seen them so happy.

The Beast nudged Mark. "That sister of yours would make one helluva gunny and that kid of hers is okay too. Gutty little pisser. What happened to his arm?" Mark explained, and The Beast growled, "Just like the fucking Navy!"

By now Tullio and his work detail were clearing out debris, making repairs, and setting up emergency latrines with a dispatch and efficiency that made the children gape as if watching a miracle.

Other Marines had brought fresh water, powdered milk, Cheerios, rice, meat, and vegetables. They began preparing a meal which was served just before dusk. Afterward Floss gathered everyone inside the house, and in candlelight one of the older girls led everyone in a Japanese folk song and then sang a lullaby.

As the children were being bedded down in folding cots, one boy asked Mark why some of the Marines called the big Marine "The Beast." It was, Mark explained, because he looked like a bear. This delighted the children who shouted over and over, *"Kuma! Kuma!"* The Beast obligingly growled at them, which caused more shouts.

Floss put her arm around Mark but was unable to put her thanks into words.

A week later Floss was watching a dozen Marines construct a wooden building. By now, Billy J., after a session with Captain Decker, had made the orphanage a semiofficial responsibility, and it was no longer necessary for Tullio and The Beast to commandeer work parties. Since there was little in the budget for such charitable work, Tullio was already collecting contributions from the detachment to buy lumber and supplies; and The Beast substantially enlarged each truckload of legal supplies with government-issue material at the base warehouse.

Late in the afternoon work stopped and a meal of hamburgers and potato salad was served outdoors to all the children and Marines by three cooks and half a dozen helpers from the mess hall. Each Marine was the center of a group of entranced children. What an incredible sight, thought Floss, to watch the conquerors treating as their own kin the sons and daughters of soldiers they had so ferociously fought!

The next morning the Marines resumed their duties at the base. Mark had been selected as assistant provost marshal because he could speak Japanese. One task was to supervise the M.P. patrols in the city of Yokosuka and coordinate actions with the Shore Patrol from visiting ships and the local police. The primary mission was to keep off-duty sailors and Marines out of trouble. Mark would be driven in a jeep to Honcho Alley, a street just outside the main gate replete with bars and beer halls, to prevent brawls between Marines and sailors, if possible settling arguments without arrest. Their first stop would usually be the Shit Slinging Saloon, a name bestowed by The Beast to the owner who had requested something "Wild West." It boasted a little band playing Country and Western music. Mark never tired of hearing one heavily made-up girl sing "Souser dah Bohder."

Since his principal task was to keep peace in Yokosuka, he spent much of that Monday morning patrolling the demoralized city in a jeep. The people were half starved and most of the jobless men prowled the streets scrounging for fuel and food. Since there was no sewer system or any public toilets, Captain Decker was cleaning out the flies, mosquitoes and fleas that plagued town and base by dusting every street with DDT. Areas inaccessible by jeep were sprayed by Marine fighter planes which swept down the narrow valleys following pathways. By now the children had become so used to the Americans that they dashed into the clouds of DDT, screaming delightedly and throwing wide their jackets.

As Mark drove around the town he was greeted as usual by children waving and shouting "Herro!" At one corner he nodded to a husky young Japanese standing by a rickshaw on which was a large sign in English: "Wellcome, Sir, Round trip by this Omnibus Cheerfully." He passed a department store whose windows showed only a few pieces of merchandise, wondering what the crowds of women, many carrying babies on their backs, were going to buy and how they could pay for it. Probably they were only window-shopping. The shops along the way spoke of general poverty. They were small unpainted shacks without windows or doors. Over each entrance hung the short curtains called *noren*.

After making a quick survey of the suburbs where hordes of ramshackle homes provided pitiful housing for 230,000 human beings, he returned to headquarters to learn that Marine private Brown had finally been caught and put in the brig to await a general court-martial. Brown, a tall, impressive man who looked older than his twenty-five years, was already a legend. Several weeks earlier he had promoted himself to colonel, strapped on a .45 pistol, and made off with a truck. After altering its number he headed for the biggest bank in Yokosuka. Looking impressive, he strutted into the bank to announce he had been sent by General MacArthur as bank inspector. The bank officials panicked. At last the president emerged in top hat, striped trousers, and tails—the only proper attire to meet such an important American official. Brown announced crisply that all records and money were to be taken to SCAP headquarters for a bank audit. The Japanese scurried to comply and soon the money and records were loaded into the Marine truck. With the bank president sitting beside him, Brown took off. Once outside the city limits Brown stopped the truck, ordered the president to dismount.

"This is as far as you go, buddy," said Brown, and took off for Kyushu where he spent money lavishly before being picked up by Army M.P.'s on a tip from the Japanese police.

By the time Mark arrived at the brig he had learned that Brown had outdone himself. After complaining of a terrible stomachache, he was taken to the base hospital. There he had asked to use the head, which had a window. And so he had disappeared into one of the twenty-eight miles of caves under the base.

Colonel Billy J. Sullivan took immediate action. "There will be no more liberty given to any Marine until Brown is returned to the brig," he announced.

Mark complained of the decision to Tullio, but he disagreed. "It makes sense. Billy J.'s judgments come from the burning bush. He's never wrong. It's like he can see the future. I'd just like to stand under him and let his dandruff fall on me so I can get some of his wisdom."

He was right. Within forty-eight hours Brown was turned in and back in the brig, and the Marines could continue their nightly sprees on Honcho Alley at the Yokosuka Beer Hall, the Fuji Cabaret, or the Shit Slinging Saloon. But a much more serious problem than Brown flared up the following day with the arrival from Washington of the Marine Inspector General. Navy headquarters had heard that too many regulations were being bent at Yokosuka and there was evidence that large-scale black marketing was going on. Colonel Henry A. Evans was sent to clean up the mess. A burly, crude man notorious for his bad taste, he had been passed over for promotion twice, nor had he ever been recommended even for a Bronze Star. It was disgusting, he vocally protested at the officers' club, to see lesser men displaying fruit salad on their chests when all he had were the ribbons given to men who commanded PX's and motor pools. To those who met him casually at the club he appeared to be good-natured if bluff, but this mask of fellowship came off after several drinks when he became obnoxious to those junior to him, and at dances attempted to pat the bottom of every girl present. That was how he had earned his nickname, "Heavy Hand Hank."

While Evans was checking in at Colonel Sullivan's office, Mark entered with the evening report. "Heavy Hand" flushed visibly, for of all the junior officers he found McGlynn the most detestable. Their feud had started in late 1944 in Guam where the Marines were training for the landing on Iwo Jima. At the Christmas party in the officers' club, under the influence of three or four drinks, he had pulled rank to get a dance with Maggie. After a few stumbling trips around the dance hall, Heavy Hand had pulled Maggie onto the porch. She had attempted to joke her way free but he began his usual pawing and she kicked him in the shins. He grabbed her, and while he was manhandling her out the back door Mark's best friend, a lieutenant named MacDowell, had poured a pailful of ice water over the colonel's head. To make matters worse, the mild-appearing MacDowell, who later became Maggie's fiancé, politely apologized: "I spilled my drink." While Evans was being hustled out of the club by Marine officers, he noticed in his alcoholic haze that Mark was laughing. He never forgave Mark and in time was convinced it was he who had doused him with water. A week later as an officer of the Court of Inquiry into the so-called mutiny of Negro sailors, Evans had noticed that Mark recognized one of the defendants and he insisted on knowing why. The disclosure that the two had met at a left-wing seminar brought the further revelation that Mark had briefly been a Communist, a fact he had not revealed when he had enlisted. With the help of the redoubtable Billy J., Mark had survived this breach of discipline, and now the sight of captain's bars on McGlynn brought out Evans's ugly nature faster than liquor. How dared this Commie get a promotion!

Mark excused his interruption, nodded politely to Evans, and told Colonel Sullivan he was escorting a truckload of supplies for the orphanage purchased with money donated by the Marines. Once he left, Evans excused himself. He smelled a rat. This could be a black-market operation. Evans trailed Mark to a truck and ordered the driver of his staff car to follow. In the truck Mark was telling The Beast to head for the base warehouse so they could pick up an additional "donation" of government supplies. Fortunately they were stopped just before reaching this destination when the staff car swerved in front of them.

A few minutes later Evans stormed into Billy J.'s office demanding the arrest of Captain McGlynn for black-market operations. But after Sullivan inspected the truck, he explained to Evans that this was an authorized shipment to an orphanage sponsored by the Marines.

Evans's face grew a fiery red and his eyes seemed to bulge with repressed rage. Nor was he mollified when Mark suggested that he accompany them to Chigasaki and see the good work being done by the Marines. Inwardly he vowed to come back in six months and catch the Commie red-handed the next time. Obviously McGlynn was using the orphanage to cover his own operations. Just a look at the ugly driver of the truck was enough for Evans to know that both belonged in the brig.

2.

Despite Mariko's increased uneasiness about Colonel Mulrooney, Mc-Glynn only laughed at her anxiety, so she finally warned her friend, Emi Toda, that he might become an embarrassment. He not only gambled with enlisted men but was rumored to be deeply involved in the black market. And his language was at times outrageous. Just yesterday she had overheard him advise the professor, "Never have a pissing contest with a skunk." Of course, she cited no such examples and Emi did not take the office gossip seriously. She found the Colonel a gentleman, a breath of fresh air. He always had a joke and kept bringing them presents that were so little they didn't feel embarrassed to take them. He also made it a point to see they always had staples such as coffee, salt, and sugar. No one ever saw him deliver them and it would have been pointless pride to have refused such desperately needed little items.

Her main worry was Shogo, who still greeted her as though he had not a care in the world. Though he still showed little interest in his own defense, he did not object when she said she wanted to get a prominent Japanese lawyer. She had asked three but all were "too busy." She interpreted this to mean they either thought his case was hopeless or they feared to be associated with a case that would surely get unwelcome publicity because of Tsuji's involvement.

And so she appealed to her old friend McGlynn, who said his son had already spoken to his superior about the matter but had been informed it would be a conflict of interest. Even so, the professor felt sure that Miss Snow would accept.

Chaucy did and wrote her father an exuberant letter. "At last I've got something I can sink my teeth in! I'm going to defend the son of Mrs. Toda down at Yokohama. That doesn't mean I won't continue my work on the Tojo defense. There are so many recesses at the Tokyo circus that I'll have plenty of time. The prosecution has just started its case and probably won't finish until autumn. I've already been out to Sugamo Prison to see my client. He's a bright, likable young man but for some reason shows little interest in his own case. I'll have to build a fire under him. First let me explain the setup." There were three classes of war criminals, A, B, and C. The A people, the leaders like Tojo, were being tried in Tokyo. They were charged with responsibility for the policy decisions leading to Japan's "crimes against peace." Class B and C defendants were high-ranking military officers charged with command responsibility for troops that had committed atrocities, as well as lesser officers, enlisted men, and civilians charged with the personal mistreatment of prisoners of war. Hundreds were already being tried by the British, Dutch, Chinese, French, and Russians all over Asia from Rangoon to Siberia and the Americans were holding B-C trials in the Philippines, China, and the Pacific islands.

"About a thousand will also be tried by us in Yokohama and many of these prisoners, like my client, are kept in Sugamo Prison with the Class A men. As I wrote you before, we're again in recess and tomorrow Will McGlynn and I are going down to Yokohama. He has been asked to testify in person to atrocities committed in a prison camp in Kyushu even though he'd already submitted an affidavit. He thoughtfully suggested that I go with him so I can see how the U.S. Eighth Army handles these B-C cases. More later. Must rush off."

The trial was to start the following morning and Will would not be called to testify until the afternoon. They drove to Yokohama in Maggie's car and were met outside the city courthouse, where the trial would be held, by Captain Jim Burns, a friend of Keenan's.

A small, aggressive Irishman, Burns reminded Chaucy of an intellectual Jimmy Cagney. "The trials down here are like nothing you've ever seen," he said as he escorted them to a nearby hotel. He explained they were under the jurisdiction of General Eichelberger, commander of the Eighth Army. Eichelberger was not only in charge of enforcing SCAP directives over a vast area but had been ordered to establish facilities for the confinement, interrogation, and safekeeping of suspected war criminals and unfriendly witnesses. It was also his responsibility to appoint military commissions for the conduct of the B-C trials.

"As you know," Burns continued, "there have already been many similar trials conducted by the Allies throughout Asia." But the most important cases, those of an international nature, were to be tried in Yokohama and they covered every type of crime from misuse of Red Cross gift parcels to the most brutal atrocities. "The defendants include women, soldiers from generals to privates, and sailors up to admirals. We get interpreters, farmers, teachers, doctors, nurses, Shinto priests, and college professors." He struck his forehead. We must have two thousand suspects! So darned many that we sometimes try four, five, or six at once. You're going to testify at a trial for a private, a corporal, a sergeant, and a major."

"Major!" Will was astounded. "There was no major involved in the Camp 13 atrocities."

"There is now—Major Watanabe, the commander of the camp."

Will was appalled. "He was the most decent guy I met in prison camps! He saved my life."

"Then it's too damned bad you didn't come down earlier and testify for him."

"Why can't I testify for him this afternoon? What kind of a rigged deal is this?"

"In the first place, Major McGlynn, there is no rigged deal. I've been down here defending for six months and we run a fairer court than you do up in Tokyo. It's screwed up, yes. But I'd a damned sight rather be tried here than up there." He calmed Will down by assuring him he would be allowed to have his say for Watanabe. "There is a president of the commission whose only object is to see justice done, not to get newspaper headlines." There were at least three other officers on the commission to help the President come to a decision. "When I first came here it was a mess. Some of the defense attorneys had been picked up in the boondocks and hadn't even finished law school. Others had never tried a criminal case. At first there were so many convictions that even the prosecutors protested. It was like shooting fish in a barrel. They wanted better opposition." But the greatest difficulty was the difference between Japanese and Western law. "In their court the defendant usually confesses immediately in hopes of being treated more leniently. In my first case I was taken by surprise when my client immediately confessed and blew the case. After that I had to plead with the defendants to be quiet, and at first they thought I was trying to trick them."

Another problem was the refusal of many Japanese witnesses to testify for a defendant. " 'This is none of my business,' one witness told me. 'These are the sacrifices a man must make for losing a war.' "

"Very opportunistic," said Chaucy.

"Perhaps. It's also very Japanese. If you help a person in the Orient you become responsible for him." Burns lit a cigar but snuffed it out when Chaucy coughed. "One of the most serious things we contend with is the different view of the Japanese toward punishment for an offense. Sometimes we use the word 'correct' to imply 'punish' or some kind of chastisement. The Japanese usually use the word in that sense. So the Japanese sergeant thinks it's proper to hit one of his men who makes a mistake, meaning only, 'Don't do it again.' But if there is a very serious offense, he will not be struck. Instead his commanding officer will write him up on the theory that this will put the offense on record for the future. See what I mean? He was doing a favor to the first man by striking him. It ended the matter." He checked his watch. "We'd better get moving."

The sun had come out and it was already hot. On the way to the courthouse Burns said, "Probably the greatest obstacle is the Japanese language. In one of my cases the prosecutor asked my defendant, 'Didn't you see the victim get beaten to death? Answer briefly, please.' When the defendant said, 'Yes,' I was petrified—it meant a sentence of death. 'Ask again!' I urged the prosecutor. He did and the defendant again said, 'Yes.' I almost shouted, 'You saw the victim beaten to death?' 'Oh, no,' said the defendant. 'Didn't you just say you did?' I said, and he replied, 'No, Burns-san. I said, "Yes, I did not see the beating." ' "

They all burst out laughing.

The outside of the courthouse was a grim, forbidding relic of the late nineteenth century. But inside they were met with welcome coolness because of the high ceilings and stone floors. They climbed a wide staircase to the courtroom, which surprised Chaucy by its spaciousness. Above was a skylight. It would have been a perfect setting for a courtroom play. At one end was a dais on which were three large old-fashioned leather chairs. In front was a handsome curved wooden table.

"That's where the president of the commission will sit with two assistants," explained Burns.

Facing the dais at the other end of the room were seats for a hundred visitors. At least fifty Japanese were adjusting earphones. In front of the visitors was a wooden barrier. A row of seats facing the judge was on the other side of the barrier. "For witnesses," said Burns and told them to sit down. "I'll be in the back."

A captain without battle stars came up to Will. "Major McGlynn?" he said. "I'm Captain Branch, the chief prosecutor." Will stood up and they shook hands. "You cut it close. I was afraid you weren't going to show up. Your affidavit was excellent, but your testimony will clinch things."

"I didn't know Major Watanabe was also being tried."

"We have a very good case against him."

"But he had nothing to do with the atrocities. He made life endurable for us."

Captain Branch, who had seen no combat, was not impressed. "Two American sergeants testified against him this morning. They were convincing."

Chaucy stood up. "Major McGlynn would like to testify for him this afternoon."

"Well, if you feel strongly about it, I won't object. Colonel Pearson, the president, is very tolerant." Branch eyed Will closely. "I can count on your testimony concerning the other three men?" After Will nodded, he left.

"I've met his type before," said Chaucy. "He could be mean."

Will began making notes as four prisoners filed in from the right. Watanabe, looking much older but still with the stride of a young man, nodded slightly on sighting Will. The vindictive guard they had called the One-Armed Bandit, his left arm cut off at the elbow, glared insolently at Will who felt a chill, remembering how this man would shout at a prisoner he'd just beaten, "You Americans no good! You lie to us! You steal from us! You call us monkey people behind backs! When I punish you, you show no proper respect and humiliation. You no willing to do better! You no repent! We slap and beat you! Do you appreciate? Hell, no! You just sneer and say, 'Fuck 'em!' You all no damned good!"

Another guard, Billy the Kid, walked by as arrogant as ever, not even deigning to glance at Will. Big for a Japanese, he had several times made Will the victim of his brutality. The third man, a private, had been in charge of the guardhouse. It was he who had hung up poor Harris by the fingers.

The two defense attorneys joined their clients at the defense table. Both looked harried and the senior officer, a first lieutenant, reminded Chaucy of the White Rabbit. "They're going to be eaten up by that prosecutor," she whispered to Will. Finally the president and two members entered from the judges' chamber at the back. A bailiff called, "Hear ye, Hear ye! The court is now in session. All rise."

Everyone stood, the Japanese politely bowing to the bench.

"Please be seated," said Colonel Pearson in a Southern accent. He was a heavyset man with two Purple Hearts and the infantry rifle badge. "Continue with the witness, please," he drawled.

The witness, a staff sergeant, looked familiar to Will. When he began telling how Major Watanabe had punched an American private, Will placed him. He had worked in the mess hall for Colonel Abbot who had collaborated with Billy the Kid.

Will nudged Chaucy. "That sergeant was one of Abbot's toadies," he whispered.

The sergeant glanced at Will as he was leaving the courtroom, then quickly looked away.

"Sergeant Mason's testimony clearly corroborates what the three affidavits reveal about Watanabe," said Branch.

"Please reserve your comments for your closing statement, Captain," said the president coldly, but his next words were friendly. "We are fortunate to have with us today Major McGlynn, who has kindly left the big show up in Tokyo for our little shebang. I am curious, Major, about the young lady sitting beside you. I'd heard you were the only new witness."

"I apologize to your honor but I took the liberty of bringing along Miss Chaucy Snow who is presently helping defend General Tojo. She has agreed to defend a Class B defendant and wanted to see your procedures."

Chaucy stood up. "Your honor, I too apologize and will retire to the back of the room."

"By no means, Miss Chaucy," said the colonel gallantly. "The commission recognizes you as a colleague and we are happy to have you observe our antics from as close as possible. I can only add that I hope I preside at your hearings down here. You are the first lady counsel we have seen in Yokohama." He bowed his head as if taking off a hat. "Back to the business at hand, Major McGlynn. As you have already observed, this is not Tokyo and we have different regulations. For instance, the officer who helped the prosecutor interrogate the last witness is our law member. He assists the commission in rulings and clarifications. You might say he is sort of an amicus curiae, as you lawyers say. I am not a lawyer nor is any member of this commission, but we all do know military law and despite what you may have heard some kind of justice *is* administered. Our only purpose is finding out the truth, and to do so we often extend liberties not allowed in a civilian court. We are also forced to make compromises and that is why we accept affidavits as good evidence. Otherwise we would never get anything settled, since most of those testifying to Japanese atrocities are now back home where they belong. That is why we are so happy to have an eyewitness. And so, Major, please take the stand and talk freely."

Will had already written down what he intended to say about the guards. The president's little speech, ending with an invitation to speak freely, would also give him an opportunity to speak for Watanabe.

With no waste of words but in graphic detail he told of the countless beatings administered by the One-Armed Bandit and Billy the Kid, and how their reign of terror was openly sanctioned by the first camp commander. Will was tempted to contrast this man with his successor, Watanabe, but decided to concentrate first on the guards. He told how fear swept the camp when the Americans began bombing Japan, describing how Corporal Banning had been put on bread and water for two weeks by Billy the Kid for selling rice he'd bought from the Japanese to his fellow prisoners.

The law member interrupted. "What evidence do you have that he was being starved?"

"I was one of the officers selected to speak up for the men. One of our Japanese informants told me that Banning had just died in the guardhouse. So I informed the senior American doctor—his name I believe was Pruitt. Well, he insisted on seeing the body and told me he was shocked to see a man normally weighing about 170 pounds down to only a third of that. Billy the Kid ordered Dr. Pruitt to write on the death certificate that death was from malaria. He refused but another American wrote down Pruitt's name."

Next he told of the case of Private Harris who had stolen a bun from the kitchen. "A dozen of us saw Billy the Kid drag Harris out of the mess hall and beat him with his sawed-off club. Then he ordered two of his men to continue the beatings. One of these guards was the sergeant we called the One-Armed Bandit. The short, squat man sitting there." He pointed at the defense table. "During the next week poor Harris was tortured. Corporal Franklin saw him forced to kneel on sharp bamboo rods while the One-Armed Bandit and Billy the Kid lashed him with their belts. I myself, while on the way to the

181

mines, saw Billy the Kid suspend Harris by his fingers outside the guardhouse. And a day later when I went to the guardhouse to make a protest I found those two men"—again he pointed—"Harris was soaking wet and had an electric wire around his neck. And I saw Billy the Kid turn on the power! It was awful to hear the poor devil yelling."

Chaucy was revolted. Such raw evil was impossible to imagine. But Billy the Kid kept insolently staring at Will.

"They cut down Harris's food to nothing and a week later I saw him lying senseless in the mud outside the guardhouse. We were told by a Japanese doctor next morning that Harris had died of heart failure." He finished with a description of Billy the Kid forcing him into a jujitsu match. "I let myself be thrown twice. The third time he kicked my feet from under me, kneed me in the jaw. I knew he'd break a bone the next time and so I threw him to the ground. He was furious when the prisoners cheered. I tossed him over my back but he grabbed his club and came at me." He paused. "I would have been a goner except for the new camp commander. He ordered Billy the Kid to take me to his office. That afternoon he sent me to Camp 14 which was run by a friend. The man who stood up for me was Major Watanabe." He pointed. "He not only saved my life but he had previously done his utmost to make our lives at Camp 13 passable." He stopped. "Mr. President, may I say a few more words on behalf of this man?"

The colonel conferred with the officers on both sides. "I don't see why not."

Will told of Watanabe's many reforms. How he increased the food rations; how he improved working conditions in the mine; how he let the men play baseball and football and put on amateur shows and singalongs. "We called him Gentleman Jim and it is impossible to imagine him striking a prisoner as Sergeant Mason recently testified. And I can guess the names of those men who wrote affidavits accusing the major. I knew Mason well. I knew all those over at the mess hall who worked for Colonel Abbot."

"Major McGlynn," said Pearson sharply, "You're on dangerous ground!"

"It is Abbot who should be tried. He was collaborating with Billy the Kid and—"

Major Branch objected.

"Major McGlynn," said the president, "I don't want to hear another word about Colonel Abbot."

"May I say a few things about his toadies Mason and Cresswell and—"

"Don't try our patience, Major."

"I apologize for my outburst, sir. I had no intention of trying your patience."

"I accept your apology, Major." He sighed heavily. "Aren't you aware that Colonel Abbot is going to be tried in Washington for collaborating with the Japanese?"

"No, sir. But I am glad to hear it."

What a defense counsel McGlynn would make! thought Chaucy, and how ironical that he could fight so ably and vigorously for Watanabe and yet still be convinced that Shogo Toda, also a victim of circumstances, should be guilty.

"The commission thanks you, Major McGlynn, for what must have been a trying ordeal." The president turned to Branch. "Are there any more questions?"

"No, sir."

"Apparently none. The witness is excused. Anything further by the defense?"

"No, no sir," said the White Rabbit hurriedly. "The defense has rested, sir."

"Prosecution?"

"Nothing further, sir."

"The commission is now ready to hear the arguments of the prosecution and the defense. Do you wish some time?"

The White Rabbit was about to ask for a recess but once the chief prosecutor had replied, "No sir, we are ready," he hastily squeaked, "So is the defense, sir."

The prosecution's opening argument was clear, concise, and convincing and made no mention at all of Will's defense of Watanabe. The White Rabbit rose hesitantly and spoke stumblingly, every so often glancing at a fistful of notes with a page occasionally falling to the floor. It was one of the most inept arguments Chaucy had ever heard and she felt embarrassed for the White Rabbit.

The chief prosecutor then delivered his closing argument, again without wasting a word.

"The commission will retire," said the president. "The verdict will be announced in open court at 0900 hours tomorrow if it has been reached by that time. If not, further announcement will be made as to the time at which the verdict can be expected."

Burns had a big smile. "Nice going, Major. You played our dear president like Isaac Newton."

"I thought he got hit on the head by an apple," said Chaucy who was still wrung out by the session.

"You're a city slicker, counsel, and don't know beans about Newton. First, it was his cousin who was hit on the head and second, I was referring to Isaac's abilities as a fisherman."

"Don't you mean Izaak Walton, *The Compleat Angler?*"

Burns laughed. "Right you are. Let's have a couple of drinks in celebration."

"Do you think I did any good for Watanabe?"

"Wouldn't be surprised. I heard from a friend that the morning session was a field day for the prosecution. But you may have saved the major from a very long sentence."

At exactly 9 A.M. Colonel Pearson announced, "I will read this fully. The accused will stand forth."

The four Japanese stood before the commission.

"Ryunosuke Shiraishi, Tsunesuke Ichiba, Fukujiro Ohno, and Susumu Watanabe, it is my duty to inform you that this military commission in closed session, two thirds of the members present at the time each vote was taken, concurring in each finding of guilty, has arrived at the following verdict."

Chaucy, sitting next to Will in the visitors' section, instinctively reached for his hand but then quickly drew back.

The first three, the three guards, were sentenced to be hung at Sugamo Prison. "Susumu Watanabe," continued the President, "you are to be confined at hard labor at such place as the reviewing authority or higher authority may direct for twenty years."

Will paled. How could this happen to an innocent man?

As Watanabe left the courtroom under guard he turned toward Will, his face showing no emotion, and gave a little nod. Burns tapped Will on the shoulder. "I think a *good* lawyer can get him another trial and another verdict. All these cases go to a reviewing board. We've won a number of reduced sentences."

The White Rabbit sidled up to them apologetically. "Thank you for what you did for Watanabe," he said. "I wish I'd known . . ."

"It's not your fault, Harry," said Burns.

"My specialty is really probate and real estate." He looked around furtively. "I never even was in court until I came here."

"Are you going to ask for a new trial?" asked Burns.

"Oh, no!" The thought was frightening. "I was hoping that Major McGlynn could take over."

"I'd be glad to do so," said Will.

"I can't tell you how much this means to me," said the White Rabbit, clutching Will's hand. "It's a big relief."

"How about that drink," said Burns and escorted Chaucy and Will into the hall and down the wide staircase. "Miss Snow, I understand you are going to defend Shogo Toda down here. You should know that Lieutenant Colonel Henry Chestnutt is prosecuting. Around here we call him Hanging Harry. Apparently piling up a record so he can be a district attorney back home. Since Toda's case involves Colonel Tsuji, he's pulling out all the stops. He's asked for a long postponement so he can send researchers everywhere from the Philippines to Burma." He turned to Will.

"Loved the way you handled old Pearson. You went right up to the last inch with him. What's your secret? Was he also a prisoner of war?"

"Not with two battle stars. What sold me was his infantry rifle badge. My brother Mark is a Marine and he told me the only G.I. worth sharing a beer with wore that badge."

Chapter Eleven

1.

No sooner had Will started back toward Tokyo than he brought the car to an abrupt halt. "Let's go down to Yokosuka and see my brother Mark. It's only a few miles. He's a character. You'll get a kick out of him." Having heard so much about Mark from Maggie, Chaucy had no objections. As they headed south he recounted some of Mark's exploits: how he had ridden freight trains; how he had picketed the White House in the spring of 1941 for peace; how he had joined the Marines and gone into caves to rescue Japanese on Iwo Jima and Okinawa. They arrived at the naval base just as Mark was leaving BOQ for dinner. Chaucy was startled. His dark hair, blue eyes, and grin reminded her of Tim, her twin who had drowned in Squam Lake trying to save their mother. During dinner at the Officers' Club she couldn't keep her eyes off him. His gestures, his quick sense of humor made him seem like Tim grown up.

Mark had led them to a large table but within a minute Marine and Navy officers crowded it like bees drawn to a honey pot. She never would remember anything she ate in the hubbub that followed. Colonel Billy J. Sullivan managed to get a seat next to her and regaled her with stories about Mark as a private. "He was on report more than anyone in the battalion. The first time I saw him he was wearing a belt around his neck for coming to inspection without cartridge belt or bayonet. And a week later he missed Monday morning roll call claiming he missed the last bus from San Diego."

Someone else recalled how Mark had missed the last boat to the transport that was taking them from New Zealand to the Battle of Tarawa. "What did you do to him?" Chaucy asked Billy J.

"Just gave him a little lecture," he said innocently.

"And made me shovel coal in the engine room for a week!"

"He made it all up by saving my life at least half a dozen times. Will you ever forget the first time, Mark? We were climbing the cargo nets of the *President Adams* after we finished at the Canal. We were all carrying transport packs which must have weighed a hundred pounds."

Someone shouted, "Seventy pounds."

"Eighty," corrected Mark. "I ought to know."

"Well, it felt like more than a hundred," said Billy J. "I didn't know it but I had jaundice and by the time I was halfway up I didn't think I'd make it. Mark was ahead of me and kept stepping on my hands."

"Never happened," said Mark.

"Anyway I finally could see the rail. And I reached out for it but missed. I could imagine myself hitting the water and sinking like a rock, but as I began to topple backward an arm grabbed my pack. Then I felt myself being dragged over the gunwale. How the devil did you ever manage to do it, Mark?"

"Sheer desperation, Colonel. I did my best to let go but my hand was tangled and it was either go into the drink with you or pull you back." Everyone laughed.

Then they talked about Saipan but only remembered the funny things: how the Catholic chaplain kept calmly passing out fried chicken and whiskey as they hit the beach. How "Mad Dog" McCarthy led an attack wearing no helmet and waving a large banner on a bamboo pole. "It was a homemade flag of bright red with heavy tassels and yellow stripes spelling out 'A 1/6,'" explained Billy J. "And Mad Dog was howling like the Hound of the Baskervilles. It sure was a stirring sight but then I got a call from Regiment asking what was that damn flag doing flying along my front lines!"

Navy officers interrupted to tell stories about their commander, Captain Benny Decker: how he had saved Yokosuka from going to pot; how he insisted that the local police commission women in their ranks; how he put local women on the parole board when their jail got too full.

"It was Edwina's idea," said a booming voice. This was Captain Decker himself taking a quickly emptied seat facing Chaucy. "My wife organized a group of Japanese women who kept eagle eyes on every man paroled. The record of violators went down to zero. The women were in their glory and my problem was solved." Then he told how he had ordered a hundred cartons of Puffed Wheat. "But the storekeeper left out in his order the syllable 'Car-' and we got a hundred tons!" This brought a roar. "I sent out a message canceling the order but the factory reported the ship was already on its way. We served Puffed Wheat cookies, Puffed Wheat candy, Puffed Wheat cakes and Puffed Wheat biscuits and even tried Puffed Wheat with ice cream until the men had Puffed Wheat coming out their ears. Well, I knew we were about to have a mutiny so I got permission to sell it to the Japanese and then use the yen from the sale to pay our men. But this was easier said than done. The Japanese didn't want to buy any Puffed Wheat. I said, 'Use it for chicken food.' They said, 'No chickens.' I said, 'Teach your people to eat it.' They said, 'No sugar, cream, or even milk. No sale.' "

By now a crowd was around the table listening to a master storyteller. "Well, Miss Snow, you must know that the Navy has never had a problem it couldn't solve." There were some rude remarks apparently from Marines which Decker ignored. "I remembered that we had twenty tons of chocolate dumped on us from the Pacific islands from the roll-up after the war ended. It would last twenty years and was already getting moldy. And then Edwina said to me, 'The Japanese haven't had any chocolate for years so why not sell this to them in a tie-in deal with the Puffed Wheat?' Well, Miss Snow, the Japanese made candy balls out of the mixture and they sold like hot cakes. We got rid of our chocolate and Puffed Wheat at cost. Then we sold the yen to sailors at the official exchange rate, and the Japanese had a big bargain. That's what I call good Navy business."

There was a round of applause.

No one wanted to leave, and drinks were brought in. The stories went on until ten o'clock and by that time Chaucy's concepts of the Navy and the Marines had been shattered. The Navy weren't a gang of snobs and the Marines weren't a gang of boneheaded idiots. As she and Will were leaving, Mark asked if she'd have dinner with him in Tokyo. "When?" she said.

"Tomorrow night."

"Can you get off that easily?"

"Billy J.—that is, Colonel Sullivan—is an understanding man." As they fixed a time and place, Will was surprised to feel a stab of resentment. It wouldn't, of course, be that he was jealous since there was nothing to be jealous about. Nor that he in any way thought Mark was poaching on his territory. Admittedly he himself had gained a new appreciation of Chaucy after what had taken place during and after the Camp 13 trial. But he certainly had no romantic illusions, and to prove it spent much of the long trip home telling her of Mark's good qualities.

She listened with interest for she had never been so attracted to a man. Mark could laugh at himself. It was also obvious from the good-natured mockery he received from his colleagues that he was not only well liked but respected. They hadn't exchanged any thoughts or ideas or even many words, but she felt as if she'd known him for years. She tried to analyze what had happened to her, but for some reason her pulse beat faster just to think of him.

A message from the professor was waiting for her. He would be free in the morning about ten o'clock for an hour or so if she wanted to continue their discussions of things Japanese. He took her to the downstairs cafeteria. "In the coming months you're going to be faced with a contradiction—the natural politeness and friendliness of the individual Japanese at home and his brutality abroad." Over coffee he explained that in Japanese society there was an amazing similarity in the manners of all classes. "This is the ancient way of Japan, the culture of a web society. It turns almost every Japanese into a model citizen, held in bonds tight enough to give him security. Yet it is a security which causes strain since he is the slave of honor, loyalty, and *sekinin*—responsibility. You must always be conscious of this during the coming trial. The defendants at Ichigaya, whether civilian or military, well-born or from the lower classes, have been molded by *sekinin*. Each one has been accustomed to accepting responsibility without question, yet does his best to avoid taking on a new responsibility. For example, the man who saves your life considers himself responsible for your future. And that is one reason Westerners are amazed to find few Japanese rushing to the aid of someone who has an accident. The Japanese are not callous or cruel, only avoiding an additional responsibility."

He sipped his coffee thoughtfully, wondering whether her relationship with Will would go beyond friendship. It would be just what Will needed to bring him back to normal. "Where was I? Oh, yes. A Japanese tends to avoid responsibility. That's one reason he is so often a poor drinker. He is only trying to free himself for a few minutes from the crushing bonds of responsibility. It is for the same reason that he often makes a fool of himself when traveling abroad, for he has been brought up with the proverb 'A man away from home need feel no shame.' Once he was outside his islands he could relax. The Japanese soldier who was rigidly self-disciplined in the homeland had no responsibilities in China, since his code of morality was national and all the frustrations he experienced in Japan were suddenly released— so he joined his mates in pillage, rape, and murder. In Nanking he had no web to restrain him.

"Of course something similar to this also happened to the German soldier in Russia. But what you must understand at the trial is that there is a great difference. I'm afraid the prosecutors are going to equate Japanese atrocities with those committed by the Germans merely because they both were members of the Tripartite Pact. The Japanese would have been incapable of designing gas chambers and conducting mass racial murder. Their atrocities were not ordered from above but committed by individuals out of fear, rage, and a lifetime of restrictions and group responsibilities. Island people tend to have tight societies. Consider the atrocities committed by the English in India while preaching humanitarianism at home. Unfortunately Japan has only recently broken out of her medieval days, but she too is on the road to humanitarianism. It is going to be a terrible shock to the people when they hear at the trial the horrible crimes committed by their sons overseas. It is up to you people on the defense to put atrocity in its true perspective and disprove the prosecution's attempt to condemn the defendants by association with the Nazis."

Chaucy returned to Ichigaya Heights still somewhat dazed by the prospect that lay ahead, but when Mark arrived to pick her up for dinner her problems dissipated. Later she couldn't remember much of what they had talked about, only that he made the most commonplace topics sound interesting. He took her to her door, asked and was granted another date in two days, kissed her once and left. She couldn't get him out of her mind even as she prepared for bed. And once inside the sheets she thought of him and not the trial.

On June 13 four more U.S. defense counsel were introduced to the Tribunal. To the amazement of almost everyone, Keenan announced that he was returning to Washington. Rumor fed upon rumor. Few believed he was really going back home on leave. According to some journalists a growing feud with Webb was the cause. Some guessed that the Department of Justice wanted to give him new instructions. More likely, said others, he was being brought back to be dried out; he was an obvious lush. Stories were circulated of rages with his secretaries, losing his false teeth, and gross insults to big shots.

When Will stoutly defended Keenan his father replied, "I also happen to appreciate Keenan. Perhaps because he's such a damned fool. He reminds me of that poem of G. K. Chesterton. I believe it goes like this:

> The Gaels are men the Gods made mad,
> For all their wars are merry
> And all their songs are sad."

During a stopover at San Francisco, Keenan told reporters that he didn't expect to return to Tokyo for a month. And when someone chided him on the stern punishment he had sworn to inflict upon the Japanese war criminals he replied indignantly, "If you don't establish a punishment for such crimes, you might as well admit that orderly government among nations is impossible."

The prosecution case began without benefit of its chief prosecutor, but the greatest blow to the defense came that afternoon when Captain Coleman, the chief defense counsel, revealed to his associates that he'd had enough. He was leaving for another assignment. He refused to talk to newsmen. He didn't want the Japanese to know the defendants had been treated so badly, and he was afraid his words might be taken out of context. With him went five other defense counsel.

Keenan told reporters in Washington that the so-called wrangle among American counsel for the defense was inconsequential. "Nothing serious, just a sharp difference of opinion on how the trials should be conducted." It was simply a matter of able U.S. attorneys disagreeing over the manner in which the defense should present its case. More important was the recent announcement in Washington that the Emperor would not be indicted. Trying him, said Keenan, would be a "distinct mistake since it was clear from the evidence that the Japanese warlords had employed the Emperor for their own evil purposes." He added that he was happy to report that the entire trial was proceeding without a trace of friction among the eleven prosecuting nations—not mentioning, of course, that England, Australia, and Russia were still extremely disturbed that MacArthur and Truman had unilaterally removed the Emperor from the list of war criminals.

The next day's session was marred by an unpleasant incident backstage where toilets had been installed for the justices and Western counsels. There were separate but inadequate facilities for the Japanese lawyers, and Kiyose in desperation after a long wait hurried into one of the Western toilets. An officious M.P. rushed over and dragged him out by force before he could finish.

"What's going on, Corporal?" asked Will who was conversing nearby with Chaucy.

"This Jap was using one of our johns!"

"Take your hands off him!" ordered Will sharply. He apologized to Kiyose and opened the toilet door. Little Kiyose, steaming with rage, bowed rapidly twice just as Colonel Kenworthy, the M.P. chief, appeared. He also profusely apologized.

"Racial discrimination!" exclaimed Kiyose. "What about the way they keep searching our briefcases?" Yesterday when a watch was discovered missing from Judge Webb's desk, every Japanese counsel had been carefully examined. "But not a single American! And that was the third time!" Kiyose was so incensed that he had lapsed into Japanese and Will had to interpret.

"I assure you, Mr. Kiyose, it won't happen again," said Kenworthy quietly, and managed to smooth over the fracas just before the arrival of two reporters who had heard there was trouble.

"This afternoon Will prevented an international incident," Chaucy wrote her father. She turned it into an amusing story, but couldn't hide her admiration of Will's prompt action.

2.

By the end of the month Foreign Minister Matsuoka had died of illness, and Okawa, who had slapped Tojo's head, was in an insane asylum; the remaining twenty-six major war criminals had been transferred from Block 4 to Block 6. This, the abrupt departure of Keenan, and the resignation of six defense counsel, had a disquieting effect on the defendants. There were new rumors every day: Keenan also was quitting—no, he was being chastised in Washington; Webb was also on the point of being dismissed. As the defendants strolled around the exercise yard the talk was usually about the trial. One civilian had high hopes that something Churchill had said in Parliament just before Pearl Harbor would be helpful to the defense. It was rumored, for example, that he had declared that the British had made many concessions to prevent war in the Pacific but Roosevelt was sticking to a policy that would force the Japanese to stand up and fight.

A change had come over the guards at Sugamo Prison. At first openly antagonistic, now they looked upon their charges with some pity; and occasionally an M.P. guarding a work party would take a nap with his rifle in his lap, often asking the prisoners to wake him up if an officer should approach. But such relaxation never tempted the Japanese, who could not betray such a trust, to lie down on the job. It was too bad, they thought, that men like the M.P.'s who had lived for months with the prisoners were not the judges at Ichigaya.

This was a time of great uneasiness, with former prime ministers and generals scrounging for cigarette butts carelessly discarded by the M.P.'s and devouring every newspaper brought into the prison. That almost all Japanese outside of Sugamo took little interest in their fate was crushing. When Chandra Bose was being tried in India by a war crimes tribunal, remarked one general, many Indians, including Gandhi, objected on the grounds that he hadn't fought for Japan but for the independence of India. And in Germany some young men were demanding that Goering be released. "Yet no one," he said, "has asked for the pardon of Tojo-san. In fact, the people seem to hope that a lot of us will be hanged."

"In Germany Goering seems to have retained his greatness," observed a civilian not yet indicted. "But not one of the Japanese leaders can still be regarded as a great man without his title and position. The proof is right here in this prison. It is very apparent, isn't it, when you look at the men who once led us but are now in here."

Someone laughed. "If we had won the war and Churchill and Roosevelt were here in Sugamo scrounging cigarette butts, they wouldn't look so great either."

That afternoon Will came to Sugamo to confirm Tojo's version of his purported efforts to negotiate a peace after he became prime minister. He found Kido in a serene mood even though he was still the target of insults from some of the military defendants. "There are only two types here at Sugamo," he said with a faint smile. "Those who start chanting the sutra as soon as they wake up, not because they are at peace but because they desperately want peace of mind. And so it's sutra in the morning, sutra as soon as they finish a meal, sutra before going to bed. Sutra at all times. Their spirits waver up and down all day long. And so their entire existence is pitiful and helpless."

Will listened patiently, hoping to give him a false sense of security. "Then there's the second type," continued Kido who was amused by young McGlynn's tactics. "They meditate in the Zen style and read books. They live a life of discipline when eating, exercising, thinking. They regard the prison as a university in which to study and improve themselves. They learn to accept philosophically both the catastrophes in the world and their own fate. Their fate is to be true to themselves and their comrades and to face adversity calmly—and even death. Tojo-san is that type."

"What type are you?" urged Will.

Kido smiled. "Not the first certainly. And not quite the second. I'm a pragmatist."

"Would you say your first thoughts are for the Emperor, and for yourself second?"

Kido didn't let on he knew he was being baited. "The Allies declared at Potsdam that they did not intend the Japanese to be enslaved as a race or destroyed as a nation. Why then do the British, the Australians, and the Russians still want to arrest His Majesty as a war criminal? The vast majority of Japanese regard him as the embodiment of Japan. And if he were brought to trial it would destroy the nation."

"Don't worry. Neither MacArthur nor Truman would allow it."

"Don't underrate the Australians. Sir William Webb hasn't given up."

Will got down to business. "Tojo," he said, "has been telling me that he did his very best to negotiate a peace with America. He claims he had abandoned his role as Minister of War and was acting as a civilian, a mirror to the Emperor's wishes."

"That was quite evident. All you have to do is examine the liaison conferences. Prime Minister Tojo's military colleagues were not at all pleased with his efforts and I understand they even called him a traitor."

"But you were not at those liaison meetings," said Will as if questioning a hostile witness in court. Only the Big Four of the Cabinet—the Prime Minister, Foreign Minister, War Minister, and Navy Minister—met with the army and navy chiefs and vice chiefs.

"Of course not. But all records of those meetings as well as those of the imperial conferences were made available to me, Major McGlynn."

"I will have to take your word and that of Tojo since I've never seen any of these records."

"If you are implying that they have been destroyed you don't understand Japanese bureaucracy. You may be sure someone has put these records in a safe place. Perhaps you can find them in the library at the Diet." He closed his notebook. "Is that all, Major? I am supposed to be preparing for tomorrow's session at Ichigaya." His face was expressionless. "Perhaps the next time we meet, you might be interested in hearing the efforts of those of us who were secretly working for peace *during* the war. I have already told your father about the attempt of the young army radicals to take over the Imperial Palace, and how His Majesty defied precedent a second time to personally bring an end to the war."

"Thank you," said Will bowing politely.

At dinner that evening he told his father of his meeting. "The Marquis assured me that someone had surely preserved all records of the Liaison and Imperial Conferences. Do you think it's possible?"

McGlynn only shrugged his shoulders in answer. Through friends he already had copies of most of these documents but he had given his promise not to reveal them until all the war crimes trials were over and enough time had elapsed for Westerners to judge the documents with some objectivity. Only then would he himself publish his book *On the Road to Pearl Harbor.*

3.

Kido's prophecy that Sir William Webb had not yet given up hope of bringing the Emperor to trial came true at Ichigaya the following day when the son of Prime Minister Inukai revealed that the Emperor had told his father that the Manchurian Incident should be stopped and negotiations with China initiated to reach an amicable solution.

195

He also said the Emperor had advised his father that a condition should not prevail in which politics in Japan were controlled *only* by the army. His voice shaking with emotion, young Inukai declared that his father—assassinated in 1932 for his anti-militaristic policies— would have "staked his life" to carry out the Emperor's wish.

For the first time in the trial Sir William Webb put a direct question to a witness. "I would like to hear more about the Emperor in relation to the Manchurian Incident," he said, pointing out a contradiction in Inukai's evidence of the previous day. Maggie and the other reporters came alive for they all knew that Webb and other Australians would dearly love to bring the Emperor to trial.

The day before, young Inukai had declared that the Emperor had not issued an Imperial Rescript ordering the withdrawal of troops from Manchuria, but today the prime minister's son was stating that the Emperor had strongly wanted peace.

Tojo was leaning forward with intense interest. In a recent interview he had voiced his extreme relief over Keenan's statement in Washington that the Emperor should not be tried.

"It is the feeling of the Japanese people," began Inukai, "that one should avoid mentioning the name of the Emperor in an argument." But he said he would now do so "to clarify certain phases" in Japanese history. He then launched into a lengthy explanation which failed to disclose exactly what lay behind the Emperor's refusal to issue an Imperial Rescript.

Impatiently Webb stopped the testimony, declaring that only a fraction of it bore on the Emperor, and called another witness. His irritability was causing concern to the defense, as most of his abrasive remarks were directed at them. His attitude, in their opinion, was not consistent with the standards commonly respected in U.S. courts. Attorneys were expected to observe high principles of ethical conduct and courtesy toward the court, and the court was expected to do likewise. During the preceding weeks Webb's arrogance would have been considered in America to be a violation of judicial ethics. "There is no need to shout!" he interrupted one young counsel whose voice had never approached the volume of Keenan's. A little later he told the same man, a captain who objected to a document being offered in evidence, "I cannot allow you to continue indefinitely on these lines." And when the captain, always courteous, said, "May it please the

Tribunal—" Webb exclaimed peremptorily, "I refuse to hear you further."

Webb interrupted one defense counsel with, "This is utterly useless cross-examination." A colleague became so frustrated with Webb's refusal to bring certain witnesses to court for the defense that he blurted out, "So far the way I have been watching this proceeding, and as evidenced by this application now to date, there has been a gradual breakdown of the few things that are necessary to give these defendants a fair trial. There will not be many left, if any, in another week from now. Gradually these applications are getting so they are nailing us to the mast. You cannot defend a client like that. Lastly I might state that *personally* morale is getting pretty low. I mean, I wonder why I am here if I cannot represent my client and get what I think are a few of the things necessary to give him a fair trial."

Other American defense counsel joined the general protest that they were not being given a fair chance. "We have not one single spare lawyer," said one. "We do not have enough to go around, and no overall proposition. We cannot work like the prosecution. Where you can send one or two men into the courtroom and have fifteen or twenty upstairs digging out these things for you, it is incumbent upon us to be here to defend our clients."

They simply had to have more time and more facilities in order to do their job. They had requested access to the Kido diary, which the prosecution had been examining for several months and would use in evidence, only to be told by Webb, "No, you cannot have those books. You know you can't have them." Eventually he promised they would be given every facility to inspect them, but "others may be entitled to precede you." And when Dr. Kiyose persisted that the diary, which had many undated passages, should be submitted to the Language Section of the Tribunal for necessary corrections Webb said, "There is no need to interrupt these proceedings to ask for something you are already entitled to."

"I am not impeding this trial," said Kiyose. "I am trying to help it out."

"You are impeding it when you make unnecessary requests."

A little later an American colleague called it "highly irregular" to use as evidence conversation with a dead man. "Oh, that doesn't make any difference," said Webb. "It is going to be difficult to check

197

conversations with a man who is dead. Nevertheless, the evidence is admissible for our purposes. The objection is overruled."

Webb's testiness extended beyond the courtroom. He roundly criticized the Nippon *Times* for erroneous remarks about himself in an article. "Reference," he said, "is also made to the fact that I do most of the talking in this court. Any one of my colleagues could be as outspoken as the paper says I am if he sat at this microphone and spoke for the eleven of us, but as President that is my function. You will notice I am the only judge before whom there is a microphone. If the other judges wanted to say anything, they would have the greatest difficulty in making themselves understood without a microphone." His ten "able and charming" colleagues he said were giving him every support. "There is not a question of any importance that comes before us on which I do not get the maximum of assistance from each of them."

"There is also reference to my attitude toward defense counsel more particularly. It is said I speak with some asperity and the qualification is made that I do so naturally. Whether that is a compliment or not, I cannot say; but I can assure you that sometimes terseness is mistaken for asperity. As an Australian I think probably I am a bit terse."

Perhaps the president's most acerbic attack was launched against Furness, who had conducted himself in his usual gentlemanly manner. But when he politely pointed out to Webb that the prosecution's charge of aggressive warfare in the indictment was arguable, Webb exploded. "You are very impertinent! You know that I did not pronounce any judgment." It was, he said, a mere warning to counsel as to what their duty was. "Your observations are gratuitous and we will deal with you if necessary."

A few minutes later Furness brought up another arguable point. "The decision stands," said Webb with a glare. "I am not going to debate it with you, Major Furness."

Furness tried to continue, but was again interrupted. "You cannot debate it. I won't allow you to say another word with respect to that decision."

That evening Webb went up to Furness in the Imperial Hotel dining room. The grin on the judge's face turned him from the frightening president of the Tribunal to human being. "A friend told me I was very abusive to you in court today, Major Furness," he said. "I hope you forgive me. I'm sincerely sorry. But this damned heat . . ." He went on to complain at length of the almost intolerable conditions in the courtroom. "They keep promising to get the air conditioning installed."

After Furness recounted this episode Chaucy remarked to Will, "Perhaps the old boy is human. Maybe we'll get a decent break every so often now."

Will admitted that he too was disturbed by Webb's attitude toward the defense. "Perhaps in Australia they don't have the same rules of conduct."

"I'm more concerned by his obvious prejudice," said Chaucy. She took out a notebook. "Remember when he interrupted the prosecution to question the son of Prime Minister Inukai? He asked if the purpose of the Imperial Rule Assistance Association—you know, Japan's wartime political party—was, and I'm quoting, 'to prepare the people for an inhuman and alleged war against Great Britain and America, a war which should not have been begun and a war which cannot be defended?' " She made an impolite noise. "Now if that isn't out-and-out blatant prejudgment, I'll eat my law books!"

"You could be right," admitted Will.

Despite the heat, the battle of the defense, waged most aggressively by Americans to the amazement of the Japanese, continued without respite. Both sides, however, were grateful to prosecutor Donihi for providing welcome comic relief during his presentation of a twelve-reel Japanese propaganda film. After numerous difficulties in getting a corrected translation, and frustrating delays in finding the proper apparatus, the first reel of the film was shown, but the security men refused to darken the windows and the picture was so dim Webb could see some sort of picture but wasn't sure what the devil it was. He ordered Security to darken the windows for the next showing. In addition, a cinema expert from Hollywood was hastily flown over. The expert checked the lighting and pronounced all in shape. At last everything was ready for the showing and Donihi asked the projectionist to please commence the picture. Nothing came onto the screen. "Mr. President," apologized Donihi, "it appears the power is not on."

"Can that be obtained immediately?" asked Webb, who was being extremely patient.

"The gentleman has just signaled that the power is on!" said Donihi triumphantly. At last all his labors over the past weeks were coming to fruition. "May we have the overhead lights cut?" he said. The lights went out and at exactly 2:23 P.M. a picture came upon the screen. It was upside down. The Hollywood expert had not known that Japanese films were wound up backward. The press and gallery were delighted.

"If the court would just stand on its combined head," suggested Donihi.

"Mr. Donihi," said Webb with a small smile, "this is no time for levity."

After some whisperings and mutterings, the president said, "I understand, Mr. Donihi, it will take over an hour to make the necessary adjustments in all the reels. Let us do something useful this afternoon. Put on the lights. Restore the lights, please!"

All Tokyo was sweltering in the hottest summer of the twentieth century. The courtroom, its heat raised by Klieg lights, wilted not only the prisoners but the judges. Webb called a recess on July 10. Five days later, the air conditioning finally having been installed, court was called to order. Webb gratefully noted that the temperature was indeed lowered, but it soon became noticeable that the cold air had ceased after the first blast. After half an hour Webb stopped proceedings and had a brief conference with the marshal, who told him the water supply was insufficient to keep the machinery running. Whereupon the exasperated judge at last said something that everyone in the court, including his most severe critics, heartily approved. He adjourned court for an indefinite period.

"You wouldn't believe what a mess we're in!" Chaucy wrote her father. "We're overwhelmed with rumors about Keenan's absence, senseless arguments, and general confusion. The heat here makes us edgy, and the wrangling becomes nerve-racking. I go crazy hearing inept males on both sides coming to stupid conclusions and spending hours over unimportant matters. I can hardly restrain myself from rushing up to put things in order. But apparently it is decreed that no female will corrupt the air. But what's worse are the complacent correspondents who wouldn't know a good story if it bit them. They are for the most part unaware that, despite all the blather and prejudice cluttering the Tribunal, history is being made here in Tokyo. What the reporters can't see is that this legal battle between defense and prosecution is the most important battle being fought in the world. And it is like war—with long, tedious waits of preparation, then bursts of furious action followed by more stretches of preparation and more action. To those of us on the battlefield it is a constant source of excitement, for we professionals know that only through such obstacles can truth finally emerge. What is taking place here is a demonstration of our bumbling, stumbling democracy. These reporters are like those who only get excited to see triples and homers in a ball game. What we have here is a classic pitchers' duel.

"An epochal law drama is unfolding here, Dad. The press people get bored because they don't see what's going on under the surface. They think everything is cut and dried, and that the issues are already decided and we're only going through the motions. They can't see that the stakes are still high and the battle lines are drawn. Yes, the issues are still in grave doubt. Wait until the defense gets its days in court! As someone once said, 'You ain't seen nothin' yet!' And I'm going to have something to say about things even if I never say a word in public."

Equally sanguine about her defense of Shogo Toda, she outlined the particulars of his indictment. "I've seen him twice and although he still shows little interest, you can bet I'll build a fire under him. We've been told the prosecutor is going to delay for a long time, so I'm putting in most of my time on the Tojo defense. With all my complaints, Dad, you can see I'd rather be here than anywhere in the world because I'm beginning to get into focus the prospectus of all the trials. Yokohama and Tokyo are really tied together. And the trials are only a part of the Occupation, which itself is only a part of the mess we call Asia." She added a short postscript on Will's activities but neglected to mention her increasing interest in his brother.

4.

Chaucy and Mark had been seeing each other regularly, and celebrated a holiday weekend by driving to a mountain resort in his battered pink jeep, its body gaily painted with flowers and the fringe of its top decorated with colorful tassels. He promised they would need a light blanket that night and quickly added that he had reserved separate rooms. The first half of the trip seemed to belie the promise of coolness, for they were bathed with sweat as they headed southwest over dirt roads, but when they reached Sagami Bay and stopped for lunch with Floss at the orphanage, there was a slight breeze. Continuing west they soon glimpsed in the distance one of the great wonders of Japan, Mount Fuji. The closer they came, the more magnificent it grew. Before long they had reached the mountains and Chaucy was amazed at their height and ruggedness; they were so well covered with trees and vegetation that she already felt cool. They followed a winding gravel road through a valley and then up the steep sides of a mountain. Fortunately there was almost no traffic for it made Chaucy dizzy to look down the open side of the winding road into the depths below. They passed through several villages. In one she was shocked to see a country woman relieving herself in the ditch, but Mark wasn't even embarrassed. "It's their way," he said. Finally they reached a village, Miyanoshita. After climbing another long steep hill they could see the entrance of a high, rambling hotel.

"This is the Fujiya. I don't think there's anything else in the world like it."

She was awed as they entered the hotel and started up a wide stairway flanked by rails resembling red dragons. At last they climbed to the main section of the hotel. After unpacking in adjoining rooms, Mark showed her around. Never had Chaucy seen such gracious luxury. There was an indoor swimming pool, game rooms, and mineral baths. Best of all was the service—prompt, gracious, and friendly, but not familiar.

After the rigors and tensions of the trial she could relax for the first time. Everything they did was leisurely. The long Western dinner was delicious and although they had talked little on the trip, she now felt free to ask a question that had been bothering her for several weeks. "Do you think I could use your father as a witness? Not only his books, which explain what led up to Pearl Harbor, but on the stand."

He thought a moment and then said, "I don't see why not. Of course, it's touchy since he's an adviser to MacArthur."

She couldn't help saying, "So the general is really running the trials backstage, just as Furness feared."

"I don't think so," said Mark amiably. "Will told me that MacArthur promised to let Keenan handle the prosecution his own way." He wondered why she had just smiled. "I was just thinking of your father on the witness stand with me asking him about his conversations with

FDR. Would executive privilege apply to these talks, since your father was not a government official? It would certainly give Webb some trouble," she added with some glee. She then complained of the glaring Klieg lights. "They obscure as much as they illuminate. Like most technology they also falsify." There were times when a totally honest witness looked like a crook under that glare, and vice versa.

"There's too much glare in here too," said Mark and turned off the lights. He kissed her. As always she responded. Then he put his hand on her knee. As always she gently removed the errant hand. "I thought you liked me," he said.

"I do. Very much." She kissed him. She knew she was falling in love, and didn't know how to handle it. The last thing she needed at this time in her career was sexual involvement.

Mark had never met anyone like her. It was obvious she liked him and wanted to be kissed. He was sure she wanted to go further but something was holding her back. It was frustrating but he knew he had to be patient.

5.

The war crimes trial not only troubled and perplexed Maggie but made her distressed and depressed. She found it difficult to feel empathy with the cold forms of law, analyzing and putting into neat legal categories the carnage, the bestiality, the bloodshed she had witnessed on the battlefield, and particularly the death of her lover on an unimportant little island near Okinawa. Here were the black-robed judges; the enormous indictment with its fifty-five counts; the twenty-eight Japanese defendants, puny putative masters of enormous evil; the numerous counsel for prosecution and defense; the motions, the objections, the rulings, the rhetorical flourishes of counsel, their curious amenities, their acerbic exchanges, the whole panoply of jurisprudence involved in rehashing a horror that was now history. Tragedy would now repose in the impersonal pages of a stenographic transcript saved for historical archives. The court might be powerless to stifle the groans of the dying, to make whole the maimed and the disfigured, to mend even one broken heart or restore even one lost life. However, the pompous techniques of the law would now fix responsibility and do a postmortem on the corpse of War.

Yet Maggie was supposed to write an account of this effort from time to time and to probe for the basic issues amid the welter of documents, arguments, motions, objections, and rulings. She had to overcome an enormous sense of the futility of the process—colored, of course, by her own personal sorrow. She could understand Will's sense of crusade in an effort to mete out justice to those who were responsible for the horrors he had witnessed. She would try to understand Chaucy's determination as a lawyer to see to it that an abstract concept of "due process" was observed in dealing even with a conquered enemy. She had less patience with her father's more academic interest in the accurate recording of history.

One notion, however, glowed like a light in the shadows. A journalist had his or her own vocation. Somehow she must not let that vocation become submerged in personal tragedy. Why not probe with Will and Chaucy the basic legal issues in the trial, and in their exchange of views find the kind of enlightenment which would give any reader some insight into the basic significance of the trial? She dreaded writing just a chronicle of occasional colorful incidents and personal eccentricities which might enliven a tedious account of testimony, particularly when the testimony came in painful and protracted translated questions and answers.

On the night Chaucy returned from her short holiday, Maggie cornered both Chaucy and Will in a quiet recess of the Foreign Correspondents Club. She asked for their help. "I don't want to hear formal legal arguments and listen to you two debate." She was basically trying to understand what the law was about. Will and Chaucy were both anxious to be helpful and to be noncombative. They sensed that Maggie was making a heroic effort to be a detached reporter of this effort to allocate blame for a cosmic tragedy that had shattered her own life.

"Maggie," said Chaucy, "it would help if you told us the main points you find hard to understand."

Maggie explained that there were aspects of the charges against the Japanese leaders which she felt she understood—cruel mistreatment of prisoners of war, barbaric conduct to people in occupied territory. It was the elaborate charge of crimes against peace and the related conspiracy charges that seemed to her abstruse. She felt the need to better understand the meaning of these charges, as well as the defense.

Maggie opened her notebook. "I have some questions. Let me start with the charge of crimes against peace. Japan commenced the war against the United States with the attack on Pearl Harbor, then on the Philippines and the territory of the British and the Dutch. We know who the leaders of the Japanese Government were at that time and who led the army and the navy. Why are eleven judges, a fifty-five count indictment, and a long trial necessary to settle that issue? It seems to me it is undeniable that Japan committed a crime against peace on or about December 7, 1941. Why do lawyers have to spin that simple issue into a long web of litigation with an admixture of conspiracy charges?"

Maggie had touched a nerve of professional pride in both Will and Chaucy with that last question. Both felt anxious somehow to defend what their profession was doing in Tokyo. "The prosecution," began Will patiently, "maintains that the attacks on Pearl Harbor and the Philippines, and on the Dutch and British territories in the Far East in December 1941 were the climax of a conspiracy existing for at least eighteen years to dominate Asia and perhaps the world. Maggie, you must see that responsibility should rest not only on those who pulled the trigger at the last moment, but also upon those who earlier created and forwarded the long-range plan that culminated in the final incident. Let me give you a crude analogy. Six men plan a bank robbery over a period of many months. One of them gets the layout of the bank. Another one gets the getaway car ready. Another furnishes the weapons and the disguises. Only two, however, actually rob the bank. They would all be guilty of conspiracy to rob. They conspired to commit the crime. Participating in the last act does not limit guilt to the two who actually committed the robbery. So the conspiracy charge in this case makes all the participants in the prolonged conspiracy responsible for all the harm done in its course."

Will's comparison of Kido and Tojo to bank robbers raised Chaucy's hackles, but she controlled herself. "Will," she said as calmly as she could, "has given you a simple illustration of the crime of conspiracy as we know it in our own criminal law. However, I am sure he does not mean to confuse the issue here by greatly oversimplifying it. We are not dealing in this case with a bank robbery under local law but with a much more complex problem. A bank robbery is obviously a crime. But an aggressive war under existing international law was never considered to be a crime."

"Hold it!" exclaimed Maggie. "Everyone agrees that aggressive war is a crime! And the nation that strikes the first blow—like Pearl Harbor—has committed the crime against peace."

"If it were that simple, Maggie," replied Chaucy, "the status quo once achieved by aggression could never be disturbed by aggression. Suppose a nation like Japan, with millions of people crowded in the territory of a few islands, saw all the surrounding Far Eastern territory occupied by powers far removed from the Orient—the British in Malaya and Singapore, the French in Indochina, the Dutch in the East Indies, the United States in the Philippines. Further assume that her leaders concluded that this foreign domination, achieved in part by past aggression, was actually strangling the Japanese people in any future effort for decent human life. Assume that her leaders determined that territorial expansion through diplomacy was impossible and the only alternative for Japan was to fight or become a servile state in an Orient dominated by European powers. Was aggressive war as a last resort under such a hypothesis a recognized crime under international law prior to 1941? That issue is more complex than burglary."

Will groaned. "Chaucy! You sound like an apologist for Japanese expansion and aggression!"

"Will," said Chaucy with exaggerated calmness, "I am not saying that Japan or her leaders acted under the hypothesis I described. I am merely trying to point out to Maggie that the concept of aggressive war may not have been a crime under existing international law in 1941. It is one thing to say *now* that disturbing the peace by the first overt act of war *ought* to be a crime. The question is, was it a recognized crime at the time of the act or are we now making it a crime? If we are now making it a crime, is it not a species of what lawyers call ex post facto law? That, Maggie, is a law which makes an act criminal for the first time after it has happened. Our Constitution bars such a law."

"May I get in a word or two," said Will. "I concede that Chaucy has correctly described a major issue. I was not trying to put this trial in the same category as a bank robbery. I just wanted you to understand the conspiracy theory and the justice in bringing to judgment those who planned the crime but did not pull the trigger." He turned toward Chaucy. "There's an answer to the issue Maggie raises. The prosecution's position will be that existing treaties and the moral conscience of civilized mankind made aggressive war a crime long before Pearl Harbor."

Will's bank robbery illustration of conspiracy still stirred Maggie's curiosity. "Will you lawyers explain to me just how this conspiracy theory applies to this case? If certain men can be identified as having performed certain awful things, doesn't it make sense to punish them without going through the elaborate process of trying to find who was previously in league with them or who earlier planned the action with them?"

"All I can say, Maggie," said her brother, "is that the solution you propose might speed up a trial but it might very well permit truly guilty persons to escape. The instigators of the long-range plan could elude punishment because they did not actually perform the final warlike acts. And—"

"Maggie!" cut in Chaucy. "You have to keep in mind that the conspiracy issue and the aggressive war issue may be logically separate, but they are linked together in the indictment. The defense will try to separate this notion of conspiracy as a crime. The defense will take the position that the notion of conspiracy in which each alleged conspirator is chargeable with the acts of every other alleged conspirator is not a crime known to international law. It is not a crime known to legal systems other than the British and American systems and even there it is a developing and changing concept. I know in this case defense lawyers think that the conspiracy charge is particularly unfair for these reasons. Japanese cabinets and leadership have changed frequently during the last two decades. The conspiracy theory would enmesh those like Konoye. He resigned as Prime Minister in October of 1941 after his effort to avert war with the United States appeared to have failed. If he had not committed suicide he would now be charged in substance because he was in an earlier cabinet at the time of some other act of aggression done pursuant to the overall alleged plan. The conspiracy charge places these particular defendants in a hideous predicament. If any one or all of them while in government actually tried to resist Japanese aggression and was overruled by his associates in the cabinet, he can defend himself only by attributing guilt to his fellow defendants. This puts a Japanese statesman in a cruel dilemma. Defense lawyers for individual Japanese leaders feel that their clients will remain silent rather than try to get out of guilt in a process that involves putting guilt on others." She stopped but couldn't help adding quickly, "And, my dear Will, this is a feature of the prosecution I find *particularly* unfair!"

Will couldn't help smiling in disagreement. The exploration of issues was now merging on argument. Clearly this conspiracy theory was particulary offensive to Chaucy. He suspected that Chaucy's Boston law firm had had bitter experience with the "dragnet" effect of conspiracy charges in cases in which Chaucy had personally participated. He also knew that some of his own colleagues believed that the conspiracy theory would not have much appeal to judges who were not familiar with the common-law doctrine of conspiracy and that lawyers who knew the law of conspiracy dreaded the experience of a joint trial of several alleged conspirators with everyone's individual counsel anxious to extricate his own client even if it exposed another defendant. Will decided to try to move on to other phases of the trial.

Maggie unintentionally assisted that effort by asking what was the point of motions to dismiss? What legal use did they serve? Why did counsel make them at the beginning of the case and submit elaborate arguments to support such motions? Will was afraid he was going to sound somewhat pedantic but he decided to try an explanation, expecting that now he and Chaucy were on somewhat mutual ground and if his explanations were confusing or inadequate she could help him.

"Maggie," he said, "in any case, especially a major case, there arise what are pure questions of law as distinguished from proof of facts. For instance, was aggression a crime under international law prior to Pearl Harbor? That's a purely legal question. Who committed the acts said to constitute the aggression? That's a question of evidence and of proof. So, with conspiracy, whether the crime of conspiracy as British and American lawyers know it was or was not a crime under international law again is a purely legal question. Whether certain people were involved in a conspiracy is a question of proof. Motions to dismiss are generally directed to those issues which raise questions of law and which can be decided without any, or with very little, factual evidence."

He turned to Chaucy with a grin. "Counselor, what other issues do you think are involved in this case that present what might be called questions of law as distinguished from matters for evidence?"

His grin was disarming and Chaucy thought how stimulating it was to discuss something out of court with an agreeable adversary. "I think," she said, "that the jurisdiction of the tribunal to try a 'crime against peace' is pretty much a purely legal question. The Japanese surrendered under the so-called Potsdam Declaration, which provided for the punishment of 'war criminals.' The defendants claim that 'war criminals' as used in that instrument of surrender is a term applicable only to those who have committed so-called conventional war crimes such as mistreatment of prisoners or inhuman and barbarous acts to civilians. Therefore defense claims that the tribunal has no jurisdiction to deal with crimes against peace, which is a different and much broader category than conventional war crimes."

"Are there any other purely legal issues?" asked Will. The two were now so involved they forgot Maggie was there. "Don't you call the bias of the tribunal predominantly a legal issue? Representatives of the victors in the war are deciding whether or not the war against them was aggressive. The injured party is in effect deciding the issue of injury. In the case of the Russian-appointed judge, the problem is particularly acute. Japan never attacked Russia. Japan had a nonaggression pact with Russia. Russia declared war on Japan at the last moment, yet here is a Russian jurist sitting in judgment on whether Japan committed an act of aggression."

Both lawyers suddenly realized their "client" was bewildered. "Maggie," said Chaucy, "we are trying to point out that the so-called motions to dismiss are generally directed to the kinds of legal issues we've just described. In this case the court has taken them under advisement and is proceeding with the evidence. So the trial is now directed to whether or not the defendants actually did the particular acts alleged in each of the counts of the indictment and, if so, which defendant did which act or acts."

Maggie sighed. "Clearly that is going to be a long process and it's going to cover some eighteen years. I don't mean to be stubborn, but I still wonder: If the events of December 7 and immediately thereafter can't be made the subject matter of this trial, wouldn't it be worth letting some earlier instigators escape if the final actors were identified and punished?"

"Can't you see," said Will, "that really is a policy decision which has been made on a much higher level than by counsel like Chaucy or me? I suppose this method of proceeding follows the technique of the Nuremberg indictment."

"There may be another consideration also, Maggie," said Chaucy, "in going back so far into history. The prosecution could fear that isolating the Pearl Harbor attack in the light of our oil embargo and inept diplomatic maneuvers might cloud the issue of whether or not Japan was goaded into attacking. However, that could take us into a long controversy and a lot of speculation. Whether or not your speedy solution was or was not a good one is probably an academic question now. As Will points out, the policy decision was made to follow the long conspiracy route and that is the direction the case is taking and will take."

Maggie closed her notebook. "Tell me, how do you both feel about it now as lawyers at this stage in your careers? Was it worthwhile coming over here and taking on these assignments?"

"I'm glad I did it," said Chaucy. "It *is* progress for civilization to set up a process that gives a defeated enemy a chance to give its version of crucial events with the assistance of counsel."

"I agree," said Will. "This whole trial may seem a ponderous piece of heavy legal machinery, but you have to bear in mind that it was not so many centuries ago that disputes between individuals were settled by what was called trial by battle or trial by ordeal. Indeed, trial by battle was only abolished in England in the last century. Out of trial by battle and trial by ordeal we evolved the jury system. Originally jurors were supposed to be bystanders and witnesses; now they must be disinterested persons considering only evidence in the courtroom. So, it's a slow process, this evolution of the forms of justice. As Chaucy says, cumbersome as this process may be, and with all its problems, it certainly is better than the summary execution of the defeated leaders."

Maggie nodded. She was grateful to them both. They had given her a lot to think about and helpful background, but she could not resist one final question. "Do you suppose the victors in a war could ever be tried for a crime against humanity?"

Will and Chaucy were silent.

"I was thinking," said Maggie, "of Nagasaki and Hiroshima."

PART THREE

Chapter Twelve

1.

Tokyo, July 26, 1946.

When the Tribunal at the War Ministry Building reopened after the long recess the spectators were greeted by a cool breeze from the air-conditioning system. Even the defendants were uplifted by the welcome relief from the oppressive heat. As the assemblage luxuriated in the new comfort, the prosecution case on the Nanking atrocities unfolded with grim efficiency. Will and his colleagues had judiciously selected and thoroughly prepared their witnesses to the pillage, murder, and rape committed by Japanese soldiers.

Today Professor McGlynn sat in the Japanese half of the balcony with Mariko despite disapproving glances from both Japanese and Westerners. He was oblivious, completely enrapt by the appalling court drama which, he was convinced, had all been stage-managed by his son. Mariko, like the other Japanese, was mesmerized as the accounts revealed the ghastly Japanese crimes. During the war she had read of atrocities committed by the Americans and British but had not believed that such crimes were an enemy monopoly. She had felt sure that Japanese soldiers must also have committed their share of crimes. But this was the first time she had heard in gruesome and convincing detail of what had been done by her countrymen.

During the noon recess she and McGlynn discussed the testimony with an American friend from their office who was convinced that such inhuman atrocities were peculiar only to the Nazis, fascists, and Japanese. "I believe everything we've heard is true," said Chaucy, "but don't you think these horrifying things were done under the abnormal conditions of war?"

The American, a middle-aged civilian who had voted four times for

213

Roosevelt, bristled. "Why is it then that there weren't any such atrocities committed by us?"

McGlynn nodded soberly and with a straight face said, "Of course, we all know that such inhumane actions can be laid to political systems which completely disregard all human rights."

"I agree," said the civilian, not perceiving the professor's sarcasm. "Those of us brought up under a democracy could never do what was done in Nanking."

Restraining her annoyance, Mariko observed that she knew many Japanese who would not have participated in the murders at Nanking. "Don't you think there must be another reason for atrocities?"

She brought her displeasure home despite McGlynn's derision of their colleague. She insisted on returning to Ichigaya the next day, and listened possessed as a Chinese doctor described the barbarous executions in Nanking. "Anyone in the streets was shot," he related without emotion. A philanthropic society, of which he was vice-chairman, alone buried over 40,000 bodies. He revealed how women from twelve to fifty years of age were dragged out of houses by the hundreds and raped. The courtroom was revolted to hear his cool eyewitness account of the raping of a woman in a bathroom, and of the time he entered a house where eleven were killed; three of these women were raped and then "desecrated on a table" which was still running with blood. These horrors were confirmed by an American surgeon, who told of the mass execution of a large group who were taken to the banks of the Yangtze River, shot, and pushed into the running water.

As the case continued, Will deftly turned aside objections from the defense, and in rebuttals to cross-examinations solidified the prosecution's case. At the close of the last session Will was congratulated by counsel from both sides. Never had his father been so proud of him. Will himself insisted he was only one of a team. "His only fault," wrote Chaucy to her father, "if it is a fault, is too much modesty. It is obvious he led the prosecution and his appearances were models of brevity, logic, and persuasion." What she didn't write was that she herself could see no possible defense to the indictments. And for the first time she could understand Will's condemnation of a military system which had permitted such things. She was convinced that everything he had revealed was the truth, and her faith in the innocence of some of the defendants was shaken.

Mariko too was so shaken she began to fear that aggressiveness had been inherent in the entire Japanese pre-war system. McGlynn told her she was being ridiculous, but she still feared that the values she had revered were false. "I was convinced today," she said, "of the nonsense of the Japanese army's boast that their soldiers were the model of honor and discipline the world over." She would not listen to McGlynn's protests. "Your own son," she said, "has proved beyond any doubt that the terrible massacre did take place."

"I agree, but they must still debate the responsibility of those in the docket. Don't jump to conclusions yet."

From his desk Will noticed the two in close conference, and wondered whether his father was as serious about the Japanese woman as Maggie feared. He himself thought it was ridiculous to imagine the professor getting seriously involved at his age.

The press was filled with horror at Will's disclosures. "The defendants," wrote one correspondent, "began their fight for life June 3 with hard faces twisted into rigid-jawed scowls which the Japanese for centuries practiced as a mark of defiance." But now they had become sleek and assured: "Civilian suits, sprinkled among the plain uniforms, are clean and pressed. Beards and flowing mustaches have been trimmed. Their scowls and stubborn silence have faded. They chat with their attorney, scribble notes, and join in the infrequent laughter rippling through the courtroom." It seemed almost as though the defendants had become spectators instead of prisoners facing death. Foreign Minister Shigemitsu, for example, appeared to show no interest at all in the Nanking testimony. "He sits staring toward his feet with the solemnity of a man contemplating a great gambling loss." But in fact Shigemitsu, like Kido, was in despair. "One wants to plug one's ears," he wrote in his diary, "so horrifying are the accounts. Has the spirit of Japan gone to rot?"

Although Chaucy was convinced beyond doubt that the Nanking atrocities had been committed, she could not forget the professor's explanation of the cruel behavior of Japanese soldiers in foreign lands or his warning that American soldiers might possibly react the same way out of fear and a sense of superiority. She remembered his comment that atrocity was international and, after analyzing her conclusions, wrote her father, "Do you recall lecturing me one day that occasionally in a controversial case a moment of revelation appears which suddenly brings together the whole defense? And that this illumination is sometimes provided by the prosecution? Well, I think this has happened in the last few days. Will has shed so much light on the whole subject of atrocities that it has made me reexamine my concept of defense for both Tojo and Shogo. I'm really excited, Dad. This could be that moment of revelation you told me about."

During the Nanking evidence she and Will had gotten into the habit of spending the recesses together at the cafeteria, and over coffee she had wormed out of him what it was like to be a prisoner of war. She had to know, she said, so she could properly defend Shogo. Reluctantly, at first, he told of the miseries suffered at O'Donnell and Cabanatuan, then finally revealed that what had bothered him most was his own weakness. He confessed how he had sneaked into the food line of another barracks for an extra dinner. "All I could think of was my gnawing gut." He also told of the time a Japanese guard cut off a piece of meat from a hindquarter of beef and waved it around to tempt a group of prisoners. Then he threw it into their midst and Will had grabbed it. "While I was slicing off a large piece with a jacknife the other prisoners swarmed over me like vultures. I shouted, 'Back off!' and threatened them with my knife. I cut off a couple of pounds and then watched in disgust as the others pounced on the rest of the meat, shouting and cursing. And I hid my meat under my shirt and sneaked off to my shack, disgusted with myself."

She wanted to do something to show she understood, but she could only feel sympathetic.

"Some of us didn't turn into animals—a few priests and a few men like Bliss, who helped save my sanity." He spilled out other stories of his own selfishness, forgetting the unselfish things he had done. For in his mind all the unselfish things were only done to atone for the things that could never be forgiven.

She was so understanding that he began to see himself in a less critical light, and could even relate some of the comic moments of prison life. He finally felt so much at ease that he asked if she would like to see a new segment of life in Japan. She readily accepted, and a few days later they drove to a restaurant midway between Tokyo and Yokohama, standing apparently unharmed in the midst of rubble. They sat on a low bench of beautifully polished cypress to take off their shoes and slide into oversized slippers. Then they were escorted by a constantly bowing little man along a shining, slippery wooden corridor. Chaucy was having trouble with her slippers until she noted how Will slid his along the floor like skis. They were brought to a

private room, its floor covered with tatami which Chaucy found pleasant to her stockinged feet. Girls in colorful kimonos helped them sit
before a table. Chaucy noticed how easily Will sat with his long legs
crossed under him. She did her best to do the same but it was too
painful.

"Just put your legs under the table," he suggested and said something in Japanese to a girl who helped Chaucy into a backrest. She was
surprised to find the sake warm, but forced herself to gulp it down. By
the third drink she realized it *should* be warm and everything began
to look better until hors d'oeuvres were served. The varieties of raw
fish were formidable but she bravely ate something which was not too
bad until she learned it was octopus.

When they were alone she asked if the heavily made-up girl with
the chalked face who knelt beside him and kept filling his sake cup
was a geisha. She was. "I thought she was only . . . you know . . ."

"A prostitute?" He shook his head. "That's what Americans usually
think. These young women have been highly trained to be pleasing to
customers, especially men. But they are entertainers. Some of course
have liaisons with men they like, but not as prostitutes."

A much older geisha with a more subdued kimono shuffled in,
exclaiming with delight, "Magreen-san!" She hovered over him, pouring him sake and feeding him tidbits.

"We have been greatly honored," said Will. "This is Katsutaro. She
is sort of mother to the young ones. Dad brought me here before I
went to Harvard."

"I didn't know there were still geisha in Tokyo," said Chaucy.

"A few of us surviving," said Katsutaro with a wide grin. "I one of
last. We all dying out and are graciously preserved by mighty ones for
the entertainment of *gaijin-san*. Like puppets and Kabuki. And then
they ship us to the museum." She grinned again.

"There'll always be geisha," said Will.

"In old times we breathed easy in the shade. Now we are in glare of
day. Terribly awkward. But it's a different world. People now very
bold and use words like *avec, kiss, erotic*. They have 'romance-seats' in
the movie theaters! Pretty soon no Japanese can understand anything." She asked what state in America Chaucy came from.

"Massachusetts."

Katsutaro tried in vain to say "Massachusetts" to the delight of a giggling young geisha who also tried. Then the old geisha, who had been observing Chaucy closely, said something in Japanese.

"You have a beautiful complexion," Will translated. "Like that of a court lady."

The slight annoyance Chaucy had felt while Katsutaro was fussing over Will disappeared and the two women smiled at each other. A waitress first served two kinds of clear soup, one containing sprigs of bright green vegetables, the other containing the front half of a fish, fried oysters on toothpicks, two balls of sweetish bean paste, a small square of green jelly, and other appetizers. The waitress then began cooking sukiyaki in a saucepan over a gas burner in the middle of the table. After putting a piece of fat in the pan she began laying in slices of beef and onion. Then she poured in a little water, some soy sauce and sake, and a sprinkle of sugar. Since it was a special occasion, she added long green onions, tofu, konnyaku (a gelatinous root vegetable), bamboo sprouts, and then more onions and beef.

Chaucy had never tasted anything so delicious and she loved everything, including mysterious items like konnyaku. Seeing she was having trouble with chopsticks, Katsutaro gave her a short lesson. "Keep bottom one steady and use top one like finger."

During the sukiyaki, which Will said should be pronounced without the "u", the geishas had disappeared, but once the table was cleared they returned, pushing back sliding panels to reveal another room. Katsutaro sat on the side playing a samisen, a large banjolike instrument with three strings stretched over catskin. At first it sounded to Chaucy like a congress of angry cats but as she observed Will's absorption in the music, she began to appreciate it. Against two gold screens at the end of the room, two girls began dancing with slow, stylized movements. They reminded Chaucy of wind-up dolls, but she gradually found the measured movements entrancing.

Then the dancing grew livelier as the girls performed "The Miner's Dance" and a folk dance, "Tokyo Ondo." At the end of this they enveigled Will and Chaucy into joining them in another folk dance, "Sakura Ondo."

On the way home the warm air was pleasantly balmy. Seeing Will in the company of Japanese had made her realize that what she had thought was diffidence and almost indifference in him was only a mask. As a boy he had spent so many years in Japan that he must have unconsciously developed an inner reserve. With the Japanese he was in his element.

At this moment Will was thinking that Chaucy had the sort of beauty that didn't depend on perfect features. Her chin was too firm for ideal beauty and perhaps her turned-up nose was a bit small, but once you got used to these irregularities they seemed an asset. Perhaps the irregularities were what made her beautiful to him. Nothing was more pallid than a girl with perfect features. He thought of pulling the car to the side of the road and kissing her but vetoed the idea. It wouldn't be fair to Mark. Besides, his interest in her was only momentary. For some reason he was still in no mood for involvement with a woman.

She knew he wanted to kiss her and rather liked it that he couldn't bring himself to do so. As the door closed she was amazed to realize that she found his very awkwardness attractive. How was it possible to be attracted to two completely different men at the same time? A nice girl wouldn't be. Not that she had ever wanted to be a nice girl. It was just surprising to realize she knew so little about herself. Perhaps it was only natural since until recently sex had played a minor part in her life. She wished she could confide in somebody sympathetic but the only sympathetic ears she could think of belonged to Maggie and the professor, and how could she talk to them about Will and Mark?

2.

The following day McGlynn roused Colonel Mulrooney from his usual long morning nap on the couch he had ingeniously hidden behind a bookcase. "We're turning in our report on land reform," said the professor.

"*Our* report," muttered Mulrooney drowsily. "I don't even understand it."

"Well, you did a nice job of typing it," said McGlynn. "Besides, Whitney is liable to be very critical and if I'm to be eaten out I expect you to share the blame. And if he likes it he may recommend you for promotion. It's an insult to me to be subservient to a mere lieutenant colonel."

Whitney greeted them affably and started to read the report.

"General, I can sum it up," said McGlynn. "We commend the

chief's desire to end sharecropping and turn over a good portion of the land to the farmers but suggest caution in carrying out the policy since it could upset farm economy. The colonel and I are afraid that postwar inflation is going to result in very high land prices and the landlords will be forced to sell their remaining lands at ridiculously low prices. And this will amount to the outright confiscation of lands such as is perpetrated by Communist countries."

It was difficult to tell from Whitney's silence what he thought.

"Mulrooney and I both conclude that only part of the agrarian problem will be solved by land reform," said McGlynn. "Of course, we could be wrong. Just wanted to point out a few things. We also have a request. We have some ideas on China that might be helpful." He extended several typewritten pages. "Perhaps General MacArthur could spare a few minutes to discuss our suggestions."

"Are you trying to crucify me?" muttered Mulrooney as they returned to their cubicle. "Did you see the look on old Whit's face when you said the nasty word 'China'?"

But McGlynn, having noticed it was past ten o'clock, excused himself and hurried toward the elevator. He was already ten minutes late for his coffee break in the cafeteria. Mariko was sitting at their usual table at one end of the room, smiling serenely despite his tardiness. Feeling a rush of affection, he said something that was as unexpected to himself as to her. "Don't you think it's time we got married?"

She stared at him a moment, then said in a small voice, "I would like very much to marry you . . ."

"But what?"

"Have you considered the reaction of your children?"

"What does that have to do with it?" he said impatiently. "Of course I've thought about it. Mark will be delighted and offer to be best man. Will will think it over for a day and then announce it would be for the best. Floss will be so pleased she'll cry. And Maggie will call me an old fool. But what they think is really not important."

"In my case . . ." she started, and stopped.

He knew Taro, the little pest, would be a problem. "You may think I dislike your son," he said. "I just dislike his surly attitude and I can even understand it. The boy is idealistic, bright, and rebellious. Naturally he's a Communist like so many others who are disillusioned. That's not only understandable but commendable." He reached for her hand but she withdrew it. "Naturally he'll resent our marriage—

but think of the assets. He'll be able to go to a good college in America. He'll eventually get to see that I'm not one of these obnoxious Yankee carpetbaggers."

She had drawn herself into a tight ball but his last words made her relax and the tears that welled in her eyes were stemmed. "Oh, Frank," she said.

"Does that mean you'll marry me?"

"Yes," she said in a small voice. "In good time. Please be patient."

"Then we're engaged."

She looked around cautiously. "Well, yes. But don't tell anyone. Not yet."

There were other reasons for her hesitation. Frank would tell her almost nothing of his first wife as if it were none of her business, and whenever she tried to warn him about Mulrooney he would ignore her or make fun of her fear that Floss might be hurt. Mariko also wondered why he hadn't introduced her to his children. Was he afraid they wouldn't approve of her? If so, it should be brought out into the open. But what concerned her most was Taro. Frank had done his best to be friends with him—and she knew how difficult that was to such a proud man—but Taro was not only still antagonistic to him but was beginning to treat her almost like a stranger.

"Can I see you tonight?" he asked.

She nodded. "Taro won't be home." Then she giggled and looked like a girl. "Imagine being proposed to during a coffee break!"

"Not like in books," he admitted.

"More romantic than in books," she whispered.

McGlynn returned to his cubicle in a state of euphoria. His whole life had changed. His love for Mariko had not only brought him a resurgence of life but had given him more tolerance toward others. He was much more interested and involved in his children's problems and successes. Never had he felt so close, for instance, to Mark. Previously he had looked upon Mark's love affairs with a jaundiced eye. Now he had grown so fond of Chaucy that he was delighted to see she had fallen in love with him. And for the first time McGlynn hoped that Mark was genuinely serious. Chaucy would make a very good wife— and a very good daughter-in-law.

"What the devil are you so pleased about?" asked Mulrooney. "Snap out of it. Whitney wants us to see him for a few minutes."

On the short trip down the hall McGlynn hastily gathered his thoughts. MacArthur had to be convinced that his China policy would lead to disaster throughout Asia.

In the outer office an aide said the general was unexpectedly tied up for a few minutes. This was a welcome respite and gave McGlynn time to review the deteriorating situation in China. Truman had sent General Marshall to mediate the differences between the Communists and the Nationalists. But McGlynn had known from the beginning that a workable agreement between the Reds and Chiang Kai-shek could never be developed. A full-scale civil war would surely soon erupt. Japan's abrupt capitulation had caught Chiang Kai-shek and his aides by surprise; they had assumed the Japanese would be worn down gradually. Only token American forces had been landed in China after the surrender, and what no one in China had foreseen as possible had suddenly become reality: the armed forces of the Kuomintang and the Reds confronted each other with neither of the two great world powers present in force to restrain them. Chiang was not prepared for civil war, according to McGlynn's information from China, for his troops were of poor fighting quality and their morale was low. Most of his soldiers were peasants, shanghaied into service and treated brutally; and they in turn treated the people with brutality.

True, Mao had a much smaller force, even less well equipped, but most of his men were volunteers forged into a hard-core unit by guerrilla warfare and the conviction that each one was fighting for his own piece of land and the freedom of China. Mao called it the People's Liberation Army and it was, in fact, the only large army in China's long history that had not preyed upon civilians. By combining communism and nationalism in his revolutionary movement, Mao was already gaining wide popular support. Mao had talked to McGlynn about this after the Long March; he would leave the urban struggle to others like Chou En-lai and first build a peasant revolutionary army in isolated areas with headquarters in the remote north central area around Yenan. Since the so-called truce with Chiang in 1936, the two had been waging independent wars against Japan while battling each other along the unmarked borders of their zones of operation, even as each one continued "dreaming his own dreams while sleeping in the same bed."

"The general will see you now," said the aide and opened the door to the inner sanctum. Until now MacArthur had greeted McGlynn warmly. Today he looked up sternly from his desk and motioned him to a chair. "I've been reading this." He held up the two pages earlier submitted to Whitney. "You advise me to prepare for the collapse of Chiang within a year."

"Yes, sir."

"And you intimate that any U.S. aid sent to Chiang will go down the rathole."

"Yes, sir."

"You also insinuate that General Willoughby's warning that the Chinese Communists and Moscow are working hand in glove to over-run all Asia is nonsense."

Restraining his resentment, McGlynn calmly told of his own conversations with Chou En-lai after the Long March. He had predicted inevitable conflict with Stalin, who was insisting that the Chinese model their revolution on that of the Bolsheviks.

The mention of Chou aroused MacArthur. "That liar!" Only a few days earlier Chou had emphatically told newsmen in Shanghai that he had no intention at all of attacking in the direction of Nanking and Shanghai. Yet Chiang Kai-shek had just informed MacArthur of the recent arrival of 20,000 Red troops in Shantung Province and the concentration of 10,000 others to the east.

McGlynn was about to point out how many miles it was from Shanghai to Shantung, but fortunately thought better of it. He did make the mistake of observing that Chou feared an all-out war between the United States and the Soviet Union whereas the Nationalists were counting on this conflict to solve the civil war.

"I wonder where you hear such things?" said MacArthur impatiently. "I know for certain that Chou recently called together a group of Westerners in Nanking and informed them he was sick and tired of having the Chinese Communist Party referred to as just a group of agrarian reformers. 'We are Communists and Marxists,' he said, 'with all that means now, and for the future.'"

"You're correct, sir. But Chou, and Mao too, are not tools of Moscow."

"Professor, I have great respect for you, but you've been led down the garden path by men like Chou. So have those liberals in Washington who sent General Marshall over here to force Chiang into a coalition with the Chinese Reds. Our diplomats and their New Deal advisers were so upset by the tales of corruption in high places among the Nationalists that they began denying Chiang full support. And if that continues, it will surely mean turning over China to the Reds."

As McGlynn left the room he cursed his own inept remarks which had so irritated the general that he could not be persuaded to see that neither Willoughby nor Marshall was right. McGlynn agreed that Marshall's dream of uniting the Nationalist and Communist armies would inevitably end in a nightmare. But only trouble lay ahead for the United States, and particularly for those two Marine divisions trying to bring peace in North China.

What also concerned McGlynn were the four million Japanese still in China. More than half were civilians who had lived there most of their lives. Repatriation would be a major operation requiring the most careful coordination. Caught in the midst of a bloody civil war which would eventually be won by the Communists, how many would get home alive? The period of the white man's domination of Asia, dealt such a blow by the Japanese conquest of Singapore, had already come to an end. And the U.S. officials, as usual, were making the wrong choices for the wrong reasons, and would wind up backing the wrong horse for what they considered to be the right reasons!

Central China, August 1946.

It was a sultry month. Although the fighting was spasmodic, the political struggle had intensified. The Nationalists bombed and strafed Yenan with American P-47's and a B-24 Liberator. This resulted in bitter charges from Mao concerning Chiang's insincerity and the duplicity of American policy. The situation was exacerbated when Communist guerrillas ambushed U.S. Marines. The guerrillas claimed that bored Marines had been out hunting for Reds in jeeps "just for the hell of it."

Chiang Kai-shek countered by issuing a message on the first anniversary of Japan's surrender, purportedly intended for the Chinese people but obviously aimed at public opinion in America. Chiang put most of the blame for China's chaos on Mao, who had not lived up to agreements. Chiang's own armies were being demobilized and he had already removed wartime restrictions on civil liberties. But he didn't reveal that he still had two million men under his command as well as the best equipment of his long military career.

In central China Akira Toda had long since transferred his staff and

Japanese workers from the steel mill and ore mine to the relative safety of the company town on the Yangtze River. Built by the Japanese, it had a Japanese name, Shinsho—New District. Although Toda had been ordered by a Japanese staff officer to burn all papers and formulas that could be of any help to the enemy, he had carefully wrapped up this material and placed it in his safe. He could not bring himself to destroy valuable scientific data accumulated over years; such a loss could hold up production for a decade. After turning over this material intact to Nationalist officers, Toda and his men were treated as honored guests. Guards were placed outside the large Japanese compound, but only as protection from wandering Communist guerrillas.

It was so hot that sparrows fell lifeless to the ground. The local joke was: "You must go to India to escape the heat." But despite the debilitating weather and general depression, Toda was determined to return his fifteen hundred men to Japan in good health and with high morale. Other Japanese business enterprises in the area had allowed their employees to go to seed, but Toda kept his men from drink and women by organizing a baseball league and sumo wrestling matches. He also required them to attend classes in literature, history, painting, and the tea ceremony. The men were encouraged to put on amateur shows and concerts. His own favorite recreation was golf. A Chinese officer brought him a set of clubs belonging to Chiang Kai-shek's son and a four-hole course was improvised in the fields outside the walls. Almost every day he played with three American engineers.

On the first anniversary of surrender a Nationalist officer arrived with a promise from Chiang himself, that in several months they would be taken by boat down the Yangtze to Shanghai. Throughout the war years Toda had devoted all his energy to the company and his country. Soon, at last, Toda could return to his family which desperately needed him. His oldest son was dead, murdered in prison; his middle son was in Sugamo Prison awaiting trial; and his youngest son, Ko, was still missing in action.

3.

Tokyo, August 15, 1946.

That afternoon a small wooden box arrived at the Toda home, supposedly from the Philippines. Emi and Sumiko knew without being told what it was, for more than a million such boxes had been delivered to other parents containing the "remains" of their sons missing in the South Pacific. Emi was frozen. She could not speak. Sumiko did not want to believe Ko was dead. They were both motionless, numb. Emi thought of Ko as a baby, as a boy, as a budding artist. Sumiko suddenly burst into tears. She rushed to her mother and they clung to each other, both sobbing. Reluctantly, tentatively, they opened the box and brought out a piece of paper. On it, written in two Chinese characters: "Heroic" and "Spirit." This was all that was left of dear Ko, thought Sumiko.

"He couldn't be dead," said Emi stubbornly. "I know he is alive. I can not believe he would make a foolish banzai charge. He would somehow live."

Indeed, he had run, and now he was approaching Japan aboard an obsolete Japanese cruiser, battered and rusty and loaded with ragged, exhausted survivors of the Philippines. He had escaped with three others in a banca from Negros to a tiny island. There they had hidden for five months until it was safe to surrender. While waiting in a concentration camp for a ship home, he had met his old corporal, Kamiko, the schoolteacher, who had been captured on Negros.

They had not been interviewed, only asked for name, rank, and home address. Ko had given the correct information, but Kamiko was now Sergeant Yokohara.

"I didn't want to get my family in trouble because of my surrender," he explained.

At last they had been loaded onto the cruiser. Some of the men carried equipment and souvenirs, but Kamiko and Ko only had sacks of American K and C rations which they had hoarded. All the prisoners wore American uniforms with a large PW on the back.

On the long trip north they talked for hours of the comrades who had accompanied them to Negros. Probably all were dead, even that natural survivor, Ohno, who had wanted to eat Ko's best friend, Maeda, rather than starve. Ko had saved his friend from Ohno but found himself the next day muttering rhythmically under his breath as they marched, "I-want-to-eat-Maeda. I-want-to-eat-Maeda." Poor, weak Maeda had been swept away while trying to ford a river swirling from heavy rains. For an hour Ko had searched in vain and that was how he had become separated from Kamiko and the others. But now he was nearing home.

The next morning through the heavy mist they could see the vague outlines of the homeland. But no one cheered. The men stood for an hour on the decks like cattle waiting patiently, apathetically. At last they were herded aboard barges without regard to rank. Few spoke as they approached land.

The prisoners were so tense that Kamiko remarked, "You'd think we were going to land on an enemy island."

Once ashore, American soldiers inspected their belongings for weapons or contraband. The guards burst out laughing to see the horde of canned food brought by Ko and Kamiko, but the other prisoners were envious. All were formed into a long line and ordered to loosen their uniforms while a Japanese nurse squirted them with DDT. Some covered their noses with rags, but most did nothing. The only man who objected was a colonel who resented being in the same line as enlisted men. A guard ripped off his insignia and threw them into a can already half filled with other badges of rank.

A Japanese officer from the Demobilization Bureau cautioned them to give their true names to an elderly American captain who would interview them; otherwise they would not get their Certificate of Repatriation which had to be presented to their town office. "If you answer questions honestly," said the Japanese officer, "you will not be punished by the Americans."

Both Kamiko and Ko did so, and, after giving them certificates, free train tickets home, and 250 yen in back pay, the American captain explained at great length that they were now repatriated. "There will be no punishment, no prison," he said. There was no response. "You are civilians and free to live your own lives as you wish." No one moved. "Dismissed!" The men milled around not knowing what to do. They looked at each other perplexed, waiting for an order. But the captain only walked away.

There were no relatives to meet any of them; no messages.

"Let's go," said Kamiko, and headed toward town, dragging his heavy bag. Ko followed, but the others were still bewildered. They were so used to taking orders, Ko realized, that they were at a complete loss.

The mist had lifted and now they could see Mount Fuji. "What have they done to it?" said Kamiko. "It's a different shape." Even the nearby hills looked strange. They used to be green and now were black and somehow disordered.

"Maybe it's not Fujisan?" Ko asked a young man, who looked at him as if he were crazy.

"Of course it's Fujisan," said the young man, staring at them as if they were lepers.

"He thinks we surrendered," said Kamiko. "I was unconscious when they found me, but I guess I surrendered." He looked again at the mountain. "Maybe there's something wrong with my eyes."

"Maybe you never saw it from this angle before."

"Maybe they bombed it."

The railroad station was crowded with repatriated soldiers. As Ko lined up to get another free train ticket, Kamiko pulled him aside.

"May I ask a great favor of you?" He was embarrassed.

"What?"

"Would you come home with me?" He didn't even know if his parents, his brother, and two sisters were alive. "If you could only be with me. I don't know what they will say. You know."

Ko knew. All the men crowding on the platform had the same problem. Would their parents receive them? Surrender was a disgrace and they would be shunned as cowards by the villagers. Most of the faces on that platform were expressionless, but in their eyes Ko could see the common fear.

Ko agreed, and they both boarded the next train for Tokyo. Its locomotive was small and it panted as if about to collapse. The outside of the cars was drab from being abandoned in a country siding. The broken windows had been replaced by wooden planks. Inside the air was stale from hundreds of bodies pressing together. Both young men had to stand, and within an hour Ko would have toppled over if he hadn't been kept erect by the crowd. But there was no pushing and shoving, no outbursts or anger or annoyance. It was like a cattle car and they were the cattle. It was not until they approached Yokohama that they saw widespread damage.

"My God!" said Ko.

Kamiko only nodded, fearful that his family had not survived. Finally, after three hours of bumping and rocking along patched-up tracks, they reached Tokyo. Here they had to fight their way through another mob to change trains. "One consolation," said Ko. "We're not the only shabby ones." The women looked drab, the men dejected. They fought their way onto the next train heading north and got off after an hour.

"Look!" said Kamiko in surprise. He pointed at a scroungy brown dog. "I thought there was no food." That a dog could survive the soup pot was proof things were not so bad here.

They trudged through the streets, their cans of rations getting heavier with each step. After half an hour Kamiko stopped in front of a house. He put down the sack and just stared. A woman stared back from a second-story window and disappeared.

"My sister-in-law," he said.

She came outside and stopped. She said nothing but tears flowed down her cheeks. He looked around for others. He finally asked what had happened to his family. She stammered that the parents were living on a paddy in the next village, otherwise the field would be taken away from them. A messenger was sent and in several hours the mother and father appeared, looking dazed. Kamiko was shocked to see they were painfully thin, and their clothing was ragged.

"How did it happen?" asked the father.

"I thought you were killed like all the other soldiers on Leyte . . ." his mother cried.

"I thought you might be alive since you speak English." His father said.

Kamiko could not hold back his own tears.

His two sisters and brothers, also in tatters, arrived. They too asked how he could possibly have survived. The welcome was so warm that he turned to Ko and said, "I am now Kamiko, not Sergeant Yokohara." He went into the kitchen to wash his face and noticed that there were a few fresh vegetables. There was a big onion, red beans, sweet potatoes, and a little rice. Even so, he realized how privileged he had been in the army, well fed and well clothed.

The family was delighted to get all the rations, and a mixed banquet was served. It was the first time in years Kamiko had tasted bean curd. Ko whispered to Kamiko, "In the jungle I dreamed of tofu. Now it tastes funny." But he pretended it was delicious.

That night Ko was wakened by moans and groans. In the next cot Kamiko was writhing. Ko awakened him. "I was being chased," he said.

"By G.I.'s?"

"Yes. It was the battle in Leyte on top of the ridge. I shouldn't have run away."

"But you led the charge up the hill, you fool!"

"Yes, but then I led the charge back down the hill. No one had ever heard the word 'retreat' before."

"You didn't seem very guilty when we got over to Negros."

"No, that was like a game. I should have been killed on Leyte and that would have been the end of Corporal Kamiko. So on Negros I was another person. I wanted to test my ability to survive."

"That probably kept us both alive."

"But now that I am back and again Corporal Kamiko, I feel guilty."

The next morning Kamiko wrote with white chalk on the bedroom wall, "I shall never get married." Ko did not ask what that meant. He would wait for Kamiko to tell him.

After breakfast the people next door called. Their son had died on the ridge in Leyte and Kamiko forced himself to tell about the battle. Kamiko had only seen the body but he told how heroically their son had fought. It was the truth, thought Ko. Everybody on that ridge was a hero.

Since Kamiko's company came from that area, other parents came to ask questions about their missing sons. Ko could see it was painful for Kamiko's parents to hear story after story. They too must feel guilty. His mother never said anything but it was obvious that she suffered most of all.

The next day as Ko was leaving, Kamiko said, "I will never get married. I must live only for my family and the bereaved families. I must dedicate the rest of my life to them."

Ko knew he would keep his word. Until then he himself had thought only of his own future. But as the train rattled back toward Tokyo, his sole worry was his family. Were they safe? Was his father still in China? Of them all he worried most about Shogo, his middle brother, whom he had idolized as a boy. He had always been so strong and determined. But once Ko had entered Tokyo University he realized Shogo was a flawed hero who worshipped a false god. Yet even though he grew to detest everything Shogo believed in, Ko secretly admired him. Could he possibly have survived?

It was dark and pouring rain by the time he reached Tokyo, and although it was still early September, coming from the sweltering heat of the Philippines Ko felt chilled. As he pushed his way through the crowded station, he noticed everyone else seemed cold too. People shuffled around, mute and shivering, their faces like masks of despair. Most awful to see were the wounded soldiers sitting on the floor with their legs folded, holding out their caps. He came upon a man with no legs who grinned up at him. "Hey *senyu* [comrade]," he said, "welcome home!"

His face was so merry that tears came to Ko's eyes. He dug into a pocket and drew out the money Kamiko had forced on him so he could take a taxi home and not expose that demeaning PW on his back to the damned civilians. He dropped the bills into the cap.

"*Ganbareyo*, comrade!"

He heard someone say it was warmer below and allowed himself to be pushed into the human stream heading down to the lower level. Here men, women, and children were camped out on straw and newspaper beds. The place stank of human filth and the rancid odor of several oil lamps. A ragged man soaked to the skin tried to push in but was thrown back by a big, bearded fellow. "This is our roped area!" he growled. "You got to pay privilege money for a place."

The soaked man pleaded that he and his wife and child were in a bad way and they didn't have a sen. A woman huddled in the corner with a baby said, "Let them in free tonight, Yoshio." Others on the floor were moved with pity and the three newcomers gratefully sidled into the area.

"What's going on?" asked Ko, and was told that those who had been burned out in the bombings had first claim to their place on the floor, and the repatriates who followed had to pay privilege money to the boss, the bearded fellow who ran the place like a dictator. He also protected them from intruders and thieves. By now the privilege money had jumped to a thousand yen.

Ko noticed that the newcomers were as welcome as if they had paid. "Burned out or repatriate?" asked the woman with the baby.

"Repatriates from Manchuria," said the man and broke into hacking coughs which he tried to stifle. His wife, looking dazed, handed him a filthy cloth, then drew a skinny little boy to her breast for warmth. As they settled on a tattered mat, the man explained they'd had a nice little business in Manchuria for twenty years and all they had left was in their two bundles. The old-timers listened intently as the man told of their terrible trek south; it had taken them almost a year to reach Shanghai. Ko was fascinated by the rich detail—it was like a show. But even the warmth of humanity could not stop his teeth from chattering and he realized he had to keep on the move.

It was much colder outside but at least it had stopped raining. He trudged toward home. In the dark the piles of rubble and wreckage were terrifying. How could this be Tokyo? He was hardened to the sight of torn-up towns and fields of battle, but to see his own city in ruins! A few buildings stood solitary, with great gaps in between as if some ruthless giant had ripped out the others. Everything seemed desolate, lost, engulfed in misery. This was what defeat in war had done to Japan. Ko felt confused, apathetic. The war had not only wiped out human lives but deprived the survivors of the old, comfortable ways.

A jeep narrowly missed him and came to a screeching halt. "Want a lift, buddy?" called a friendly voice.

"Are you allowed to carry a Japanese?" asked Ko.

"Nope, but hop in. The hell with it."

Ko tossed his heavy bag in the rear and settled back. What luxury! he thought as they bounced over the pockmarked street.

The G.I., a corporal named Larry, after complaining about the new regulation forcing everyone to drive on the wrong side of the road, wanted to hear everything about Ko's experiences on Leyte and Negros. Larry had only fought at Okinawa and his Purple Heart had come from a stray round. The moon had come out and as they drove through a devasted area which seemed to extend for miles, Ko had a strange feeling of exaltation. The very vastness of destruction was a good omen. Now they were all equals. They all had to start from scratch. And these Americans were not so bad. At last he understood what Kamiko had meant when he said he must now devote his life to others. Never had he seen such sights. While he was at the university his only desire was to go to Paris and become a painter. He had always felt superior to the common people whose dreary lives had bored him, but now he felt he must somehow help people like those huddled on the floor at the station.

As they neared Azabu his heart leaped to see his own rambling home intact. In the moonlight he could see that the garden had been transformed into a vegetable patch. He knocked at the outer entrance as if he were a guest. If he just walked in it would be too much of a shock. A girl he had never seen before eyed him suspiciously.

"I am Ko."

She screamed, for she had seen a ghost, and scuttled back into the house. Emi appeared, standing in worn slippers, her face almost white. She stared at him as if he were a vision. She couldn't believe what she saw. Then she impulsively hugged him.

Sumiko came out. She too stared in disbelief, then burst into tears. She didn't touch him but hugged her mother, and then the three clung together a minute in stunned joy. Emi disengaged herself and said, "*Yoku kaette kite kureta*—Thank god, you made it home! I couldn't believe you were dead." She explained about the "ashes" they had received.

Sumiko wanted to know how he had escaped alive but Emi said, "First you want a bath. I'll get it ready."

It was exactly what he wanted. After he had luxuriated a long time in the hot water, he came out and briefly explained how he had survived. Emi wanted to feed him but he didn't want to take their food and swore he had eaten a big meal at a friend's. But she insisted he at least have some leftover beans and tea. In an atmosphere of relief and happiness they talked for hours about the family and his own fantastic adventures.

As he was dropping off to sleep he muttered, inspired by Kamiko, "I shall devote my life to my family and the people."

4.

For the past month Maggie had been touring the four major islands of Japan to get material for a series of articles on the accomplishments and failures of the first year of occupation. She had visited the main cities, the towns, the fishing villages, the farm communities. Everywhere, but particularly in the urban areas, she found that hunger was worse than in the first days after the surrender. Prices for food on the black market were still rising. Allotted rice rations were becoming smaller and housewives often had to wait days for the rice dealer to hang out his sign that a new supply had arrived. Within minutes a long line would form.

Supplies of miso and cooking oil were even more unpredictable and soy sauce was now so weak that one could easily see through a bottle held up to the sky. No longer were there vegetables planted in the firebreaks. They had been picked or looted during the night. The last of the dried sweet potatoes were being ground into powder to make them edible.

Throughout the country men, women, and children spent most of the day scrounging and preparing enough food to keep them from starvation. Yet nowhere did Maggie find apathy. Somehow people managed to buy newspapers and devour details of the social revolution sweeping the country.

Maggie was especially intrigued by what was going on in the schools where new books provided by SCAP were expounding freedom, liberty, and democracy.

"The *Tenno*'s power is gone," she heard one woman teacher assure her ten-year-old students. "No longer must we bow to the Emperor. We are now free and can live our own lives. Democracy is based on your own willpower, on yourself." But when one of the boys began to argue she said, "You are too young to have an opinion."

In Kyoto Maggie visited the famous rock garden of Ryoanji Temple, designed by a noted Zen landscape artist. To her dismay the attendants openly begged for cigarettes and offered souvenirs for sale at black-market prices.

She spent three days in Hiroshima. The largest of the surviving buildings, a department store now housing a variety of establishments, was crowded with shabby customers, many queueing up for two American movies, *Casablanca* and *Babes on Broadway*. In an interview with the mayor she learned that food was still the major problem. A typhoon and flood had ruined the crops of the surrounding area, and supplies from outside were sporadic. "Our people daydream of American generosity," he said, "to make up for what they did." But he assured her that there was no hatred of Americans because of the atom bomb. "We now know we started the war at Pearl Harbor." In a voice unmarked by emotion he explained that of the 320,000 inhabitants, only 6,000 were left in the city one week after the bomb. Now the population was back to 170,000. "But most of the people still live out in the villages and only come back here to see where their homes once stood."

She walked through the desolate streets and the few people she found were friendly. She was impressed and pleased that none of these asked for cigarettes or money. One boy was leading a girl whose face was disfigured with horrible keloid scars. He explained that she was his sister who had trouble seeing. "I was lucky. I was under the rubble."

"What do you think of Americans?"

He pondered, then said, "I like them. They are very kind, even the soldiers."

At the half-wrecked Red Cross hospital Maggie learned that only ten victims of the atom bomb remained in the wards. "But we get several dozen a day complaining of a strange fatigue," said a doctor. "Can I do anything for them? No." What concerned him most was that many of the *hibakusha*, those exposed to radiation, were unable to get free treatment because their records were in the hands of the American Atomic Energy Commission. He was also dismayed that MacArthur had prohibited dissemination of all reports on the ghastly effects of the Nagasaki and Hiroshima bombings. Maggie made a note to put this in her lead article even if it annoyed SCAP. And she would also point out that recently another American bomb had been tested at Bikini Atoll.

As she was leaving the hospital she met Jun Kato who was also doing an article. They exchanged notes on Hiroshima. "It's not as bad as I thought," she said. She had been much more horrified by what she had seen at Nagasaki two weeks after the surrender. "I think the early reports about Hiroshima were exaggerated."

"You can't mean it!"

"Look around. Has atomic radiation sterilized the soil? Look over there. Weeds and plants are coming up through the ashes." She pointed to green leaves on several scrawny trees. She told about her interview with survivors and their lack of hatred.

"Not the ones I talked to," he said. "They all act like martyrs and think we all should feel sorry for them. The first thing they do is show you their scars and complain about everything. I just got through seeing some relatives. I brought them some food, but they complained it was not enough." He explained that the majority of Japanese immigrants to Hawaii came from Hiroshima. "When the kids see any Nisei in uniform they shout insults."

The next day she boarded the train for Kyushu. She could have ridden in the comfortable car reserved for Westerners but pushed her way into a jammed Japanese car. A middle-aged woman offered to share her seat but Maggie refused. A few minutes later a pink-cheeked G.I. wormed his way through the crowd and the woman again offered her seat. The young American grinned sheepishly and refused. The woman smiled at Maggie. "Like my boy," she said slowly in English. When Maggie replied in Japanese the woman said her son had died in China. She nodded toward the G.I. "His mother must miss him like I missed my son." She folded her hands neatly in her lap and smiled like a benign Buddha.

After a tour of Nagasaki with friends of Mark's she returned to Tokyo with a mélange of impressions. How in a few articles could she possibly accurately assess the staggering task MacArthur had faced in disarming an enemy force, rebuilding its cities, feeding the starving, curing the diseased, and carrying out the great experiment of bringing democracy to an alien people? There were many achievements, and many wise and magnanimous policies had been instituted. Much land had been turned over to the people. Women could now vote and hold responsible offices. They could even control their own money. Young people over twenty-one could marry without the consent of parents or older brothers. Young girls could not be sold by their parents as prostitutes or to factories; and the health of the people had been improved by inoculations and sanitary regulations.

There were many failures and blunders since the Occupation had been hastily manned and equipped. Hunger was pervasive while prostitution and the black market still flourished. Some of the Westerners were inefficient and arrogant but many more had already convinced the Japanese that this was the most magnanimous occupation in history and there was already an absence of bitterness among most Japanese over the widespread destruction. *"Shikata ga nai,"* they would say. "It can't be helped." Many were acknowledging that it was a good thing Japan had been defeated. "If we had won, we would now be under the heels of our own troops."

Her generally upbeat report on the first year ended with a vivid account of her recent trip to a Tokyo poorhouse. It was a six-building compound on the outskirts of the city. She called it "The House of the

Dead," for derelicts were brought here from the streets to spend their last days. Scores died daily, to be replaced before morning in order to sustain the capacity at fourteen hundred paupers. To tend them there were only seventy Japanese girls, a few male attendants, and four Japanese doctors. Maggie interviewed several of the nuns from the Franciscan Missionaries of Mary who had come to help.

"There is a special odor in this house," one told her. "It is a combination of death, disease, and toilets without running water which are cleaned out once a day by the fertilizer collector."

Maggie watched as the nun knelt beside a half-naked gray-skinned old man. "He will die soon, I think," she said in English and then began whispering in Japanese to the man. A minute later he breathed his last.

The man next to him was staring at the ceiling with wide-open glazed eyes. "He breathes, but I'm afraid he'll die soon too."

A doctor joined them. His eyes were troubled. "They are dying of starvation," he said in Japanese. "Some of them can't even eat the little bit we can give them. We do what we can but it is very little. Only the nuns bring them hope."

As the nun escorted Maggie to the door she said, "The poor of the Orient are truly the lost creatures of God."

Maggie finished her article with a quotation from MacArthur to the War Department which a junior officer had smuggled to her: "Starvation breeds mass unrest, disorder, violence. Give me bread or bullets." After final corrections she turned over the copy to a typist. Then she wrote a note to her publisher suggesting that she do major articles on the most pressing problems in Japan: the black market, prostitution, and the starvation which was passing unnoticed in America since the Japanese, stoic by nature and training, were not complaining.

At MacArthur's request McGlynn was also assessing the first year. By now, he concluded, the great majority of Japanese enthusiastically accepted the new shogun and his political doctrine. This was regarded by many Americans as a triumph of U.S. strategy, but was in fact a mere alteration of the outward form of authority. It did not change the people's loyalty and obedience to Japan and Japanese ways. They had shifted obedience from the old regime to the new out of necessity and a natural Japanese inclination to please. But, thank God, they were still Japanese. Only the other day one of McGlynn's old students had told him, "We are sincerely grateful for our new freedom and our new liberty—even though they are rationed by General MacArthur." And as for the "remarkable success" in democratization, that was due largely to the Japanese, who had been brought up to obey and who, moreover, before the war had enjoyed a number of reforms that even his colleagues would describe as democratic. The miracle was that anything had been achieved after such a bitter conflict fought relentlessly with a racial hatred on both sides. There had been no clean hands in a savage war that need not have been waged. Racial and cultural prejudices still lay just below the surface; that was why it was so difficult for McGlynn to see why the Japanese had been docile, even friendly and cooperative, in their response to the occupation. His closest Japanese friends themselves were puzzled by such conduct. One had tried to explain away the matter with a facile reference to the inscrutable Oriental mind.

Some Americans suspected that the crafty Japanese were only trying to lull the victors into a false sense of security, but this could not explain the spontaneous conduct of the vast majority. Some felt the people were only reacting to the admonition of their Emperor to endure the unendurable, while others attributed docility to the ingrained respect for authority or to the theory that the Japanese were susceptible to new ideas since they were basically imitators. More sophisticated observers argued that the Japanese had been forced to adapt themselves to a series of despotic rulers and had learned how to survive by bowing to authority—but by bowing without breaking they would be ready to spring back to the old ways whenever pressure was relaxed.

The professor discussed these theories with Chaucy during one of their sessions, but he concluded that the surprising simultaneous mass reaction to such a new and complex situation could only have come about for a number of apparently unrelated reasons. First, their world had almost completely collapsed with their cities in ruin, their economy depressed, their manpower depleted and spread over Asia and the southern islands. Although many of their leaders had entered the war with trepidation, the mass of people had been accustomed only to victory. For centuries their islands had never been successfully invaded. Then came incredible defeat in Saipan and the resultant firebombings of the homeland, resulting in such horrible losses in life and property that surrender came as a relief. Now demoralized, disillusioned, and nearly paralyzed, they were called upon to face an army of barbaric invaders. Trained to face situations covered by prescribed rules of conduct, they were hopelessly lost. They had no universal ethic to fall back on as had Westerners. That was another reason so many of the Japanese soldiers committed atrocities overseas that would be unthinkable at home.

"It would have taken very little," McGlynn told Chaucy, "to have turned the Japanese violently against the 'Advancing Army.' What if the battle-worn G.I.'s and Marines had raped and pillaged? What if the Emperor had been imprisoned?" It had taken only a little kindness on the part of the victors to turn the vanquished toward wholehearted cooperation. And once the Japanese were on this path, realizing that the old rules were gone they had need of the security of a new set of rules. And so they had turned eagerly to the new shogun, MacArthur, who readily provided for them another way of life that would rescue them from their uncertainty and desperation.

Moreover, America had influenced Japan before 1941 more than any other country, and was regarded generally as the model of progress, enlightenment, and success despite the bitterness of the war. Perhaps, he concluded, acceptance of the occupation was solidified by the warmly emotional nature which lay under the surface of their rigid formal behavior. Expecting harshness, rape, and cruelty, they were overwhelmed by the natural friendliness and generosity of the first G.I.'s and Marines, and responded with grateful docility. And the policies pronounced by SCAP were for the most part benevolent and sound. The great majority of Japanese had philosophically endured the many mistakes made in carrying out the master plan, for they regarded MacArthur as the personification of the occupation and he was still uncritically adored.

"You have to think backward, young lady, if you want to think like a Japanese. In fact, you also have to think upside down and inside out. Empty your mind of Western logic and then you may be able to see that the winds of change are rattling the entire social fabric of Japan, much more so than even in the monumental upheaval created by Hirohito's grandfather, the great Meiji. The winds of the new democracy are sweeping over every Japanese island, often bringing with it a distorted meaning of the term. 'Blondie' is already the most popular Japanese comic strip. Nine million radios are now featuring soap operas, quiz programs, and American songs. In Nagasaki one military government officer recently ordered all the schoolchildren to learn square dancing. Elopements have become a fad since the occupation authorities denounced arranged marriages as feudalistic." Japanese justices of the Supreme Court now even instructed to discard their traditional red robes and wear the black of the West; Tokyo policemen had to use the big nightstick of the New York City force. Confused as to what democracy really was, Japanese women in one city had recently organized an American-style box social at which one man was elected the most democratic male in the city. And in Nagoya an official in one of the new trade unions had confided to McGlynn, "Democracy means my wife has as much right to sleep with a stranger as I do."

The professor pushed back his chair. "You have just had the privilege of listening to a preview of my report to the general. Now I must figure out the recommendations I'm supposed to make." She left and he began doodling on a yellow pad. With all its errors of judgment, its false starts and mistakes, remarkable progress had been made in a single year, and McGlynn finally decided to advise MacArthur that the democratization of Japan was not a spontaneous evolutionary process nor an inflexible one imposed from the outside. It must come from the objectives and plans of the Japanese themselves, not from reforms imposed by the occupation.

McGlynn crumpled what he had just written and in frustration tossed the page into the wastebasket. He saw beyond the democratization of Japan and the sufferings and hunger that stalked the land. All that would end in a few years. What really concerned him was the fate of Asia. Somehow he must make MacArthur see that the civil war raging in China would inevitably be won by the Communists, and that this would not necessarily endanger the security of the United States. The general must be convinced that Mao's brand of communism was not at all like that of the Soviet Union, and that in time it could even be a bulwark against the Soviet drive for world domination.

Chapter Thirteen

1.

Tokyo, October 1946.

As the prosecution case continued, life at Sugamo grew more tense not only for the Class A prisoners but for those being tried at Yokohama. The smallest incident assumed great importance—a rainy day that prevented exercise, or a sudden move to another section. Even events that had nothing to do with the prisoners were discussed with grave seriousness. Could war break out between America and the Soviet Union? What will happen with Korea divided in two? The curious thing, wrote Shogo in his diary, was that although they were being tried by the Americans, the prisoners were all anti-Russian rather than anti-American.

When Japanese workmen started making holes in their cells there was consternation. "What's going on?" Tojo asked an M.P. who replied that pipes were being installed for heat.

"If they're going to all that trouble," complained a man in the cell across the corridor, "they must be going to keep us here forever."

"No," said another man who considered himself an expert on all things American. "They never do anything slipshod. Even if they're only going to use heat for one season, they still do a thorough job."

By now the prison officials had allowed their charges so many liberties that many were convinced the United States was truly a democratic and civilized country. They had even been allowed to celebrate *Kigen-setsu*, the anniversary of the divine founding of Japan. And so there was celebration and song throughout Sugamo with shouts of "Banzai!" and the singing of "Kimigayo," the national anthem.

But the suicide of Goering from poison concealed on his body, following his death sentence at Nuremberg, resulted in stricter regulations. Watches and fountain pens were confiscated. Exercise in the spacious garden was restricted to a narrow area surrounded by barbed wire. The number of guards was increased and the treatment became harsher. Before the defendants left for court their glasses and false teeth were removed and, to their humiliation, they were stripped and forced to get on all fours in the freezing cold for a rectal examination. They had to stand in line naked—generals, admirals, high-ranking diplomats, former prime ministers, privates, sergeants. The humble and the mighty had to endure being inspected clinically by ordinary American soldiers.

"They make me so embarrassed by even peeping into my anus!" one general told Tojo. It was nothing to be ashamed of, replied Tojo. To have someone peek in there in search of something would give anyone a funny feeling, he said. But once you got over the humiliation, it did have its comic side.

"What a grand sight," joked an admiral, "to see a line of us stooping, our hands on the floor with a line of M.P.'s behind, spreading our buttocks. What if one of us released gas by accident? That would be a joke—to us, but not to the poor M.P.'s behind." Someone with a sardonic bent suggested that they all fart in concert as a mass protest, but sober heads prevailed.

Some of the defendants said disparaging things about Goering, who had caused all this humiliation, but Tojo wrote his widow a letter of condolence. "One must admire Goering," he confided to Kido. "He was the only German that stood up like a man to the Allied prosecutors."

Few of the lawyers at the War Ministry feared that the outcome of the Nuremberg trial would have any bearing on their own proceedings. Their concern was focused on the Russian phase of the prosecution case now about to get under way. Both sides were prepared for a bitter contest. Would the Soviets, piqued at the high-handed actions of Whitney at the Allied Council meetings, attempt to retaliate by making a public show of strength at Ichigaya? It was common knowledge that the Soviets had collected a mountain of evidence proving that Japan had attempted to invade the U.S.S.R. long before Pearl Harbor. If the Soviets attempted to overwhelm the American defense attorneys, would Judge Webb back the Russians because he was still upset by the American-inspired refusal to indict the Emperor? And how would Chief Prosecutor Keenan react if the American defenders aggressively opposed the Russians?

There was animated interest throughout the foreign community. American relations with the huge Russian delegation in Tokyo were already badly strained. There were well over four hundred members in the Soviet mission, more than the personnel of all the other Allied missions. The excessive number was explained as necessitated by requiring translators for both Japanese and English, but the Westerners feared the Soviets had set up a military headquarters with qualified specialists in logistics and intelligence.

About half of the Russians lived in a hotel next door to the Foreign Correspondents Club, and Maggie, among other journalists, could see through uncurtained windows that raucous parties went on every night. Their singing alone drowned out any traffic noises. Perhaps, she concluded, this was a devious Soviet plot to persuade the other Allies that their large staff was not busy at sinister tasks. But what about the more than two hundred others who lived at the closely guarded Soviet Embassy or in secluded private homes?

The growing coolness between the Americans and Soviets at the official level was not usually reflected in personal relations. At their embassy the Russians were jovial hosts and when they attended affairs outside their compound they were usually the life of the party. At one affair hosted by Keenan at the Dai Ichi Hotel a tipsy American defense counsel, an Irishman, fell out of the second-story window onto a pile of trash; whereupon an equally tipsy Russian shouted, "If an American can do that, so can I," and jumped out the window. He missed the Irishman, who had received only abrasions and bruises, and broke his own leg.

One Greek-American on friendly terms with the Russians was the combative Marine Aristides Lazarus. He had been chosen to lead the defense for the Russian phase when the man originally assigned to the task had confessed he didn't know where to begin. For some time Lazarus had been suspicious of Russian attempts to establish personal relationships. Once a Russian prosecutor stopped him in the hall to congratulate him on his performance in court, and then asked how he, a distinguished lawyer and a U.S. Marine officer, could defend a criminal who had been his enemy.

Lazarus had replied that his client, Field Marshal Hata, was no longer an enemy. "We are here to prosecute these people for crimes against humanity. To give them a fair trial we must also give them the best possible defense."

The Soviet prosecutor reminded Lazarus of Porky the Pig. He was short, stocky, and husky with extremely white skin. He shook his head incredulously. "It is so different in our country. If the State indicts you, you are guilty. But I don't understand how you, a Marine . . ." He shook his head again. "Who are you? You are not ordinary. How can you bring yourself to defend an enemy so strenuously?" The Russian smiled and continued, "I admire your bold challenges of General MacArthur's authority on certain matters and President Truman's right to give MacArthur such authority. You are an unusual man." Twice more, after sessions, the prosecutor congratulated Lazarus, again marveling that a Marine could challenge his own superiors.

The Russian prosecutor's strange actions puzzled Lazarus, for it was rumored that any Russian caught privately talking with Americans was punished. It soon became obvious that the Soviets were attempting to induce him to betray his country when an attractive young Russian interpreter, a recent replacement for an older, gray-haired woman, stopped him in the hall. "I must congratulate you, Lieutenant Lazarus. You were marvelous in court today." She went on and on, then said suggestively, "We will meet again."

After several similar encounters, Lazarus asked where the interpreter had acquired such an excellent American accent. "Oh, we who will operate in America are taught by instructors who speak American English," she said, then suddenly turned red, put a hand over her mouth and excused herself. The next time their paths crossed, she was her usual calm, inviting self, and Lazarus never let on that he understood the Russian game.

McGlynn was among those in the crowded balcony when the Russian phase began. Chaucy had told him it would be a show to remember because Lazarus would be assisted by Furness and Blakeney, whose clients were involved in the indictment. The three would make a formidable team: a Marine who had been weaned on tempestuous, theatrical cases, a perfect gentleman from Harvard who was adept at calming troubled waters, and a handsome Nebraskan with the confident air of an actor.

The section reserved for prominent visitors was also jammed. The trial started grimly with the Russians ponderously bringing forth document after document showing the dastardly actions of the Japanese in two bloody border incidents, and charging that the Japanese military had urged that their main attack in 1941 be launched against Manchuria, not to the south for oil.

First Furness would politely pick holes in the Russian charges and then Blakeney would change the pace with a rapier rejoinder. Despite their bravura performance, it appeared that the judges were being swayed by the very weight of the Soviet evidence, which included a proposed treaty of peace the Russians had in vain urged the Japanese to sign.

It was then that Lazarus spontaneously decided to take a chance by presenting evidence of his own even though this was the prosecution's turn to present their arguments. Before the Russians realized what he was doing he read word for word three treaties signed by the Russians with Latvia, Lithuania, and Estonia, treaties identical with the one Japan had refused to sign. And then, to the consternation of the Russians, he asked the court to enter those treaties into the record. Will hastily penned a note suggesting Keenan protest on the grounds that this evidence, according to Anglo-Saxon law, could not be entered during the prosecution's case. But before the note could be read, Lazarus caused another shock by asking the court to take judicial notice that despite those three treaties, Latvia, Lithuania, and Estonia were now wiped off the map and made part of the U.S.S.R.

The Soviets objected strenuously, and Webb called a recess to consider the matter in private session. The Court returned to announce that the treaties could be put into the record, thus taking judicial notice of the fate of Latvia, Lithuania, and Estonia.

The humiliated Russians were furious with Lazarus. In the corridor he again met the Russian interpreter. This time she put her nose in the air and hurried by. That night Radio Vladivostok, in its usual Japanese-language newscast, attacked Lazarus. "He daily disgraces the Marine Corps uniform before the IMTFE by attacking the Allies and acting as an agent of the U.S. State Department to bring about the revival of militarism in Japan."

There were no more invitations to the Russian Embassy nor did Lazarus ever again meet the attractive Russian interpreter. If the Russians still had any dim hope of using him, it soon ended when he caused another hubbub by heaping more scorn on the Russian claim to be a peace-loving nation. He pointed at the Soviet judge. "That man should be seated where General Tojo is and General Tojo should be up there sitting in judgment on him."

Webb pounded the gavel as the lights glared and the movie cameras ground away. "Mr. Lazarus, you will retract that statement and apologize or you will be disbarred from further practice before the International Tribunal."

As Lazarus started to argue, his newly arrived wife was saying to herself, "Please, dear God, tell Artie to shut up! Tell him he'll regret it."

"I withdraw my remarks if the Tribunal finds them objectionable," said Lazarus. "I withdraw them completely." But he did not apologize to the Russians. As he turned to wink at Hata, he noted Tojo was smiling.

Since Tojo was not directly concerned with this phase of the trial, Chaucy was spending most of her time preparing the defense of Shogo Toda. Never had she felt so alive or so apprehensive. Never before had another person dominated her utmost privacy—her thoughts. Even while trying to develop a reasonable defense for the intransigent Shogo she would imagine herself drifting into the arms of Mark. It was exhilarating but somewhat humiliating to be enthralled by someone with whom she apparently shared so little.

To settle down, she took off one afternoon to learn about the tea ceremony. A stenographer working for the defense had invited her to attend a lesson given by her mother. By now Chaucy could speak some Japanese and she enjoyed traveling alone on subways, trains, and buses. She had been in this country for only eight months yet already she had revised all of her original concepts. She had arrived believing that Japan was a gangster nation and must be kept in a sort of reform school for reeducation and reformation. As long as the criminals obeyed, and accepted their fate, they would be treated well. And when their aggressive natures had been tamed, they would be allowed to join the civilized nations.

She now realized this would mean not only the destruction of a traditional civilization but slavery for the entire nation. How could you punish those few who had caused war and committed atrocities without punishing millions of innocent citizens? To make them suffer was contrary to everything America stood for.

Fortunately things weren't working out as planned. Many Americans who had come to administer stern justice had begun to like the Japanese and appreciate their good qualities. Most Americans had arrived never having known a Japanese and they soon saw the propaganda built up during the war for what it was. Americans, warmhearted by nature, were affected by the sights of destruction, the hunger and the poverty. They had begun to see the rubble as evidence of human disaster, not as justified punishment.

Even now, when the wind blew in Tokyo the air was full of dust and litter, much of it contributed by the Americans. In former days any debris in the street had been collected and made useful. Now there was so much that it kept piling up and was whipped about by speeding American trucks and jeeps.

At last, after boarding a wrong train, Chaucy reached the home of the Japanese stenographer who had invited her to the tea ceremony. It was a surprisingly large house; though there were few furnishings and no heat, it had obviously been an abode of wealth. The stenographer, Kimiko Shimura, was relieved to see her. "The others are here," she said and led her into a tatami mat room where three American women, all wives of army officers, were sitting uncomfortably, Japanese style.

Mrs. Shimura, a stout but graceful woman wearing kimono, bowed and in excellent English asked her to sit down "as comfortably as possible." There were two beautiful scrolls, several cloisonné vases, and other objects that were obviously precious remnants of the past. The room was almost comfortable, for an open fire burned in a *konro* (brazier) on which stood an iron kettle filled with boiling water.

The room, Mrs. Shimura explained, was purposely small to make everyone feel intimate and harmonious. "As you sit with sleeves brushing against those on either side, you can best understand the other guests' expressions and feelings." The smallness also made them pay closer attention to the various decorations in the room as well as the flowers and utensils. "Everything has been carefully arranged, such as the boiling kettle. Now listen to the soft music of the water." She nodded toward four little girls sitting as still as statues. One, at this signal, walked to the *konro*, sat down and, taking a silk wrapping cloth called a *fukusa* from her kimono, lifted the bowl of tea. She gracefully rose and presented it to Chaucy. As the little girls in turn brought tea to the army wives, Mrs. Shimura explained that the children were studying the tea ritual.

"Now you will all take a sip like this." She sipped daintily then turned the bowl around and drank the remainder in two and a half sips. The army wives had difficulty drinking the tea because it was very bitter. This kind of tea, explained the teacher, was very expensive and not ordinarily drunk. She went on to talk for half an hour on the meaning of the tea ceremony. "The aim of *chanoyu,* the tea ceremony, is to bring people together harmoniously with no artificial barriers. This can only be done in a small room in modesty, otherwise all delicacy is lost and you will not learn the beauty and harmony of nature."

She explained that *chanoyu* was really not a ceremony. "A more proper name would be 'the cult of tea.'" Begun in the sixteenth century when the country was racked with war, it helped relieve people of worries by giving them rest and tranquillity. "In the tea room all are equal. There is no rank and even the wealthiest host waits in humility upon his lowliest guest." Talk of business or politics was forbidden. So was gossip. "Here we speak only of the beauty of nature and arts and common topics in an intimate and congenial atmosphere of complete harmony."

Afterward, Chaucy noticed that the other ladies paid Mrs. Shimura but Kimiko said her mother considered her a guest. On the way to the subway Kimiko said, "I am so happy that we lost to the Americans rather than those Russians! What I like about you is that you work and play so well. And you are clean—not like some of the other *gaijin.* You are intelligent, clever, and frank. And though you quickly get angry—like some of those Irish lawyers—you forget quickly. It is a pleasure to work for you."

Chaucy noticed a passing frown. "Then what is the matter with us?"

"Please excuse me, Miss Snow, and what I am going to say does not apply to you, of course. But so many of your men have a boisterous abandonment of manners. And the American women have beautiful hair and legs. But they seem distant, like the army ladies today. They are such proud beings, so condescending that we feel we are obliged to stay at a respectable distance." When Chaucy didn't reply, she said with concern, "Not you, of course. I hope you are not offended."

"Not at all, Kimiko. I think I know what you mean. But I believe if you knew those army wives as well as you do me, you would see they really are not at all proud. They seem so to you but you must realize that they have come here knowing nothing about the Japanese and your customs."

"You are so right, Miss Snow, and I humbly apologize." They walked silently a moment and then she added, "But I still feel obliged to stay at a respectable distance from the madame colonels, and madame generals and madame judges."

As they approached the station, Chaucy stopped. "The other day I heard the American secretary in our office asking what you thought of the G.I.'s and you said the American G.I. was the best in the world. I want to know what's *wrong* with him."

Kimiko thought a moment, then said timidly, "American soldier is always eating and chewing gum. That's impolite."

2.

Despite the passionate interest of those being tried and those who were trying them at the International Tribunal, the Japanese public was taking little interest in what was going on at Ichigaya Heights. What concerned them far more were the hordes of cocky, brash American youngsters replacing the battle-hardened veteran soldiers and Marines who had now returned home. The people had been terrified by the first Americans to land but soon found them a convincing link to democracy. These men were proud of having won the war but did not act like conquerors.

Many of the new soldiers, however, seemed to look upon occupation duty as freedom from all restraint, and swaggered as if *they* were the ones who had won the war. Many had forgotten any manners they had learned at home and not only bullied Japanese men but looked upon Japanese women as their property. Some beat up men and boys for the pleasure of it. Occasionally brothels would be set afire when tipsy soldiers were not allowed to enter; and gangs would descend like wolves on market stalls, grabbing souvenirs, pushing over counters, and slugging any Japanese who protested.

The matter became so serious that General Eichelberger, commander of the Eighth Army, felt obliged to write a strong letter to all subordinate commanders condemning these "disgusting actions" and criminal acts. Such behavior, he said, was endangering the entire occupation.

The situation was not as bad at Yokosuka where Captain Decker insisted on humane treatment of all Japanese. He made it plain to Billy J. and the Marine provost marshal that sailors arriving for shore leave as well as all personnel on the base were to toe the line, and any offenses—by enlisted man or officer—would be dealt with summarily.

The burden of carrying out this edict fell hardest on those like Mark who had to keep order in the city. Every night his patrol was filled with drunken revelry, brawls between sailors and Marines, black marketing, and occasionally beatings. But as yet there had been no murders and only one rape.

On the night the Russian phase ended, trouble started at the head of Honcho Alley when The Beast stopped his jeep to run after a Japanese who had snatched a sailor's cap. The Beast caught the man and slammed him in the face. Mark shouted to him to lay off. The Japanese stood, hands at his side, laughing. The Beast hit him again but the man kept laughing. By this time Tullio had run up to stop The Beast who shook him off.

"The harder I punch the bastard the harder he laughs!" complained The Beast. "He won't even take a poke at me."

"Maybe he's just showing he's a man—like you," said Mark. "If he hits you, his family will suffer."

"Maybe I should hit him harder."

"Maybe," said Mark who handed the Japanese a handkerchief for his bleeding nose. The Japanese was still laughing. "C'mon, let's go."

"Am I losing my punch?"

Mark saw he was genuinely worried. "You once told me the hardest to floor was a short guy built like a fire hydrant."

"Well, he sure is a fire hydrant." Mollified, The Beast shook his head. "Jesus! The pisser just laughed!"

They inspected a number of bars and a dance hall, reprimanding several sailors who were looking for a fight but backed off at sight of The Beast in an ugly mood. They continued to North Station where the Japanese police force, set up by Decker and Billy J.'s predecessor, had its headquarters. A young woman, face bleeding and swollen, was sitting in a corner. The Japanese police inspector explained that she had been attacked by two sailors. His men were now with the M.P.'s who were apprehending them. Mark drew up a chair and asked the woman in Japanese to tell him exactly what had happened. Two men had broken into their little house. One was stocky and had the face of a gorilla, the other was tall and nice-looking.

"Why did they beat you?"

The gorilla had pushed her on the floor and was trying to tear off her kimono.

"Were you alone?"

"No. My husband and his friend—they had just returned from the Philippines . . ."

"Didn't they try to stop the sailors?"

"Oh, yes. My husband ran out the door followed by his friend. I knew he was going to get the police."

There was a hubbub at the door and the police and M.P.'s herded in two sailors. The first, stocky and low-browed, was stumbling and singing. The Beast seized him and banged him against the wall. "Shut up, creepo." He turned to Mark. "He's just putting on an act, Captain."

The other man, who looked to Mark as if he had recently graduated from an Ivy League college, was composed. "What's all the fuss about?" he said in a soft voice.

"Did they both beat you?" Mark asked the woman.

"No, sir."

"Which one did it?"

To Mark's amazement she pointed at the Ivy Leaguer. He was not at all concerned. "She had a little knife," he said quietly, "and she was trying to stab Buzz."

Mark translated the accusation. The woman said if she had one she would not dared have used it. "Did you find a knife?" Mark asked the policemen. They shook their heads.

"My father is Congressman Allen of Rhode Island. Are you going to believe these Japs?"

Mark ignored him and asked the woman to repeat for the record everything that had happened. While she told how they had ripped off most of her clothes and were spreading her legs the apelike sailor began crying, but Allen remained confident and even insolent. "I imagine she's concocted a real sob story."

But the three police corroborated the story. Allen, they testified, had his pants off and was about to mount her when they arrived.

"Take these men to the brig," Mark told The Beast. "You men will be formally interrogated by the provost marshal tomorrow morning.

At that time you can tell him your side of the story. If you are court-martialed a defense counsel will be provided you for your trial."

The police inspector was quietly translating all this to the woman.

"Wait until my father hears about this," snarled Allen. "He'll have your ass! We were only having a bit of fun with a damn whore. And besides no damage was done."

The woman rose to protest. "Sir, it's all done and over. How will it help me and my family if they are tried and put in jail? It will only bring shame on me if there is a trial."

"We must do it to prevent this happening to other women," said Mark.

"What punishment will they get?"

"Perhaps five years in prison. Maybe less, since there was no actual rape."

"But they are both so young and it would be so terrible for their families."

He explained that Captain Decker, General Eichelberger, and General MacArthur all demanded severe punishment in such cases. That was democracy.

"I do not know what that means. We had a war and those boys are sailors. Maybe some of their comrades were killed. Couldn't that be some justification?" He shook his head. "If they have to be tried, please write down that I do not want them to be punished."

The sergeant of the guard interrupted. "The main gate is calling, Captain McGlynn."

It was the sentry at the Fleet Landing Gate. "Sir, I have an unusual problem that is very delicate. Would you please come over to handle it?"

In ten minutes Mark and Tullio were at the Fleet Landing security office adjoining the gate. A fleet chaplain with Navy lieutenant's insignia rose with some difficulty from a chair. He looked like Santa Claus in his raincoat, and Mark guessed the unusual problem was black marketing. "Lieutenant, would you please come with me to the back room?" he said. When they were alone Mark asked him to remove his raincoat. Sheepishly the chaplain complied. Strapped to his chest and stomach and around his legs were cartons of cigarettes. "Please remove the cartons." As he did so Mark asked, "Why, Lieutenant?"

"Everybody else is doing it," said the chaplain. "Why not me?"

"This has to appear in the officer of the day's log," said Tullio as they headed for a final inspection of Honcho Alley, joined by The Beast. "It will go to the provost marshal's office and then to Colonel Sullivan. And by noon tomorrow the word will be spread all over the base. Do Protestants bust a minister?"

Their final stop was the Club Espoir, a posh bar for officers that had just opened. The young woman who ran it was supposed to be a first-rate singer and piano player. It was on the third floor of a dilapidated building. They could hear a woman singing "Smoke Gets in Your Eyes." Unlike other bars, it was not gaudily decorated but done simply, with taste. Mark could see scrolls that looked as if they were originals. The song ended and there was loud applause. Then a four-piece orchestra started playing dance music. Mark peered in and saw half a dozen officers dancing with girls in kimono. He wondered how long this place would last with such overhead. A young woman in an elegant kimono approached as if they were friends. She was obviously the owner.

"Mark, don't you remember me?" She looked vaguely familiar. "Fumiko Kano. We had the house next to you at Karuizawa one summer."

He gaped. Could this be the skinny, gawky girl who was always begging him to play tennis with her? Her father had been some sort of industrialist. While they sat at the bar she told how she had been married in 1943, but her husband went down with his carrier in 1944. Her name was now Matsutani. Both her father and father-in-law, the Baron Matsutani, had been purged. "There was only enough money left to start this place."

"I love it," said Mark. "If there's ever anything I can do, let me know."

When the music stopped, loud voices were heard in argument. A big navy commander was drunkenly berating a flustered waitress.

"What's the matter, Commander Bradford?" asked Mark who didn't enjoy dealing with someone who outranked him and was a lot bigger.

"This is a damned clip joint!" he said thickly. "Look at the bill they just gave me!"

Two other navy officers joined in the complaints.

"Let's go into the manager's office and settle this quietly," said Mark, and tried to escort him.

"Take your damned hand off me, McGlynn!" The commander

jerked himself free. Mark never had liked the former All-American halfback, a hero to a small group of officers who disliked the Japanese. "Get moving, sir, or I'll place you under arrest." Tullio and The Beast, who had stayed discreetly in the background, pushed forward and it was obvious the latter was eager to cool off an officer in the line of duty.

In a little office Bradford complained that girls had cadged drinks from him and then had gone off and danced with other officers. Besides, the drinks were watered and cost too damned much.

Fumiko took the check and tore it up. "You will not be welcome in here again."

"I'll come in whenever I please. This is just a damned whorehouse."

"Commander," said Mark, "I'd advise you to stay away from here. Mrs. Matsutani, if this officer causes you any trouble, report it to me."

Bradford, sobered by anger, glared at Mark and then stormed out, muttering to his cronies, "God-damned Jap lovers!"

Chapter Fourteen

1.

Tokyo, November 1946.

The prosecution was now in its final and most important phase, the events leading up to Pearl Harbor. Though few correspondents realized it, the crux of the matter was revealed with the appearance of Joseph Ballantine, the State Department's leading Far East expert in that crucial period. He claimed, to McGlynn's amazement, that the Japanese had *not* been sincerely negotiating for peace and were to blame for the deteriorating relations between America and Japan during the months before Pearl Harbor. The professor could not understand why Ballantine, who'd always been sympathetic to Japan, was now supporting the pre-war anti-Japanese sentiments of former Secretary of State Hull. In those tense days McGlynn had warned President Roosevelt that Hull and others in the State Department were being blinded by personal dislike for all Japanese and were leading the country into a war that need not be fought.

The chief counsel for defense was Major Blakeney, who had so ably and courageously shocked the court by naming those Americans personally involved in the dropping of the two atomic bombs. Again, like a consummate actor the handsome Nebraskan began his cross-examination of Ballantine with questions so incisive that the State Department official was continually on the defensive. An electric tension was felt in the big room as Blakeney's searching interrogation uncovered that Roosevelt's freezing of Japanese assets in July 1941 was exactly what the Japanese had claimed it was, an economic encirclement of their country by the ABCD (American, British, Chinese and Dutch) powers.

But this was only the beginning. Blakeney then launched a relentless attack on the State Department's inept handling of Japan's final

255

proposal for peace on November 20, 1941, a proposal which included an offer to withdraw in stages from China. Was it or was it not, he asked, given proper consideration by the State Department?

"Of course it was," said the harried Ballantine. "We studied it very carefully."

"Did it seem to offer to the State Department any possibility for settlement of the current issue?"

"It did not," retorted Ballantine sharply.

Were the Japanese insincere? The answer was a quibble: the proposal gave Japan just what they were seeking. "If there was something we could have done that would have been practically possible—bring Japan into line and bring support to a more peaceful course—we would have been very glad to consider what could have been done."

Blakeney caught Ballantine off guard by suddenly asking if Secretary Hull had not met privately with the ambassadors of Great Britain and China to discuss the situation. The disconcerted Ballantine admitted the meetings had taken place. Did the Department of State consider presenting a modus vivendi, a temporary settlement of its own, to Japan?" asked Blakeney.

"Yes."

McGlynn leaned forward. At last they had reached the nub of the matter. He would never forget the day Roosevelt had summoned him for advice on a possible answer to this Japanese proposal. Roosevelt had been so intrigued by the proposal that he had already written out his own proposed answer. He showed it to McGlynn. It was a reasonable offer to resume economic relations with Japan and immediately send oil and rice. In return Japan would send no more troops to Manchuria, Indochina, or any place south. Japan would also agree not to invoke the Tripartite Pact even if the United States got into the European war.

"Do you think the Japs will buy it?" Roosevelt had asked, and McGlynn had emphatically replied, "Yes, sir."

McGlynn was now waiting to hear Blakeney repeat, word for word, FDR's counterproposal, and he felt a chill up his back when Blakeney asked, "Was it felt in the State Department that a modus vivendi plan could be drawn up which might be acceptable to Japan?" McGlynn could see that the major was leading Ballantine into a trap.

"No," said Ballantine. "We tried the best we could do, but we felt all along the modus vivendi was very short of what Japan had been asking." The prospects were extremely unlikely, he insisted, but he did admit that three drafts were made and that the final one was shown to the Chinese Ambassador and British Ambassador for comment.

But wasn't it ever presented to the Japanese? persisted Blakeney. No. "Then would it be correct to say that it was not presented finally to the Japanese because of the opposition of the Chinese as expressed by the Chinese Ambassador?"

"That was one important factor in the situation."

And so instead of sending off a conciliatory answer that even Hull had admitted had a one-in-three chance of being accepted, a reply was dispatched to the Japanese that was even harsher than the American proposal submitted earlier in June. The Japanese took it as an insult and felt obliged to set the course for war.

By the end of the cross-examination, the harried Ballantine looked exhausted and distraught. The defense counselors felt like cheering at Blakeney's brilliant performance. Chaucy had never seen a witness manipulated so adroitly. Once the defense reached its main room, the major was showered with compliments. The Japanese lawyers and stenographers were astounded. The Japanese were even more astonished when prosecution lawyers poured in to add their congratulations. What curious people these Americans were!

It was still light when Will walked outside to think over what had taken place that afternoon. From the hill of the War Ministry he gazed down at the ruins of what had been one of the best residential sections of Tokyo, an area where there had been lovely ornamental gardens which now were checkered patches of wheat and potatoes. Here and there, like lonely sentinels, stood tall chimneys, the only remnants of modern homes. In the distance rose what appeared to be minarets but were actually the tops of apartment houses in the downtown area. What had happened to the old Tokyo? There was nothing in sight that was Japanese. And where were the trees that had once graced this section? The only relic was the skeleton of the famous camphor tree in the utterly destroyed Shinto shrine of the War-God. When he was a boy Will had been fascinated by the tree's glossy greenery which had housed hundreds of nesting birds. Now it stood with its charred limbs stretching out like beseeching arms. For five hundred years it had

257

been the most sacred tree of Edo. Was this also the end of everything from the past?

At dinner with Will and his father, Chaucy was baffled to find the professor unenthusiastic about the day's session. He could not see why Blakeney had not revealed Roosevelt's enthusiasm over the original Japanese proposal and then read out for the record the proposed modus vivendi word for word. Was it possible that FDR's hand-written note had not been made available to the defense? Could it have also been suppressed at the Pearl Harbor inquiry in Washington? And could he use this material in his new book? He was tempted to tell both Chaucy and Will about Roosevelt's note, but decided it was privileged information. And what good would it do now to set off a scandal and so infuriate MacArthur that his own influence with SCAP would go down the drain?

He was concerned, moreover, about the deteriorating situation in Asia and intended asking MacArthur for permission to go to Korea so he could find out what was really going on there. He feared that Korea could be the tinderbox that could set all the continent ablaze. The problem had started during a private talk between Roosevelt and Stalin at the Yalta conference in 1945. The two had agreed to set up a four-power trusteeship under the Russians, the Nationalist Chinese, the British, and the Americans. Roosevelt thought that Korea would not be ready for full self-government for at least twenty or thirty years. The two men made no plans for zones of ground operations or for occupation. Nor did they even discuss making the 38th parallel a dividing line in Korea. Upon the capitulation of Japan it was only agreed that all Japanese troops above the 38th parallel would surrender to the Soviets and those south of that parallel would surrender to the American Army. During that operation the Russians would allow no traffic across that line without their express permission, thus arbitrarily treating it as a permanent dividing line. And so the infamous barrier of the 38th parallel, like Topsy, just growed.

The source of the problem, so old friends in Korea wrote McGlynn, was Syngman Rhee, head of the South Korean Government. A wily old man, he wanted independence for Korea only to turn it into a feudal land with himself as ruler. He opposed land reform, social and civil liberties, and had already set up a corrupt political machine with a brutal police force that worked with terrorist gangs. To gain control of all Korea, McGlynn was informed, Rhee was willing to take grave risks that could set off a war with North Korea, now run by a Moscow-trained Communist. Such a conflict would inevitably involve Red China.

A friend in northern Korea had written that in contrast to the reformist and at times radical direction of the occupation policy in Japan, the Americans had revived the old corrupt Korean bureaucracy as well as the occupied Japanese police system. They had also set up a national defense for southern Korea along with a separate southern administration. All this had been done by the Americans unilaterally, and appeared to be aimed at impeding the peoples' demand for political, economic, and social changes.

But this, according to McGlynn's friend, was not happening in northern Korea where the same popular call for social revolution was heard. At first there had been violence but by now the Russians had retreated into the background, letting the Moscow-trained nationalists carry the burden of revolution. Already, to the Soviets' dismay, these ardent nationalists, veterans of the long underground battle with the Japanese, had bridled at Soviet control and were taking over control of northern Korea.

It was an exciting prospect and McGlynn longed to see what was going on. But after their recent acrimonious meeting on China, the professor doubted there was much chance the general would approve the visit. Instead McGlynn asked Whitney almost casually if he could take off for a week or so to visit friends in Korea, and suggested he go with a group of correspondents that were leaving early in November.

"Why not?" said Whitney, who felt that McGlynn deserved a little vacation, and to the professor's amazement MacArthur approved.

A week later MacArthur surprised Maggie McGlynn by requesting her presence. Since she had not seen him for several months, she wondered whether he had taken exception to something she had written. Lately he had become very sensitive, claiming that such papers as the *Christian Science Monitor*, the Chicago *Sun*, *P.M.*, and the *Daily Worker* were not only slanted but "approached quackery and dishonesty." Some correspondents were on his bad list for "associating with the wrong kind of Japanese" or simply "being critical of the Occupation." One reporter who claimed the general was using hair dye had been scratched from those eligible for dependents' housing, and another became persona non grata for referring to him as The Chief; yet when *Fortune* magazine published an uncomplimentary article he merely canceled his subscription. Several lines had been deleted from Maggie's own assessment of the first year of Occupation; perhaps he objected to her stark stories of starvation and deprivation.

He rose lightly from his chair to greet her and his smile was so wide she wondered what she had done right. "I have a suggestion you may like," he said waving her to a seat on the couch. "I presume your father has told you he's going to Korea with a group of correspondents."

"Yes, sir."

"Why don't you go along?"

Her publisher had already suggested she take an extensive tour there. "When do we leave?" said Maggie. "You're very thoughtful."

As she went down in the elevator her initial resentment at being pushed into anything was replaced by the excited anticipation of getting to see a country she knew very little about. It would also be fun going with her father, who had always liked the Koreans even though most of his Japanese friends did not. She started toward the Imperial Hotel grill where she was to meet Chaucy and Will for dinner. The more she thought of the trip to Korea, the better she liked it. It would give her a chance to get closer to her father, who still treated her like an undergraduate. She neared the old Takarazuka Theater, the former home of the so-called Girls' Opera, a company that produced modern revues with no male performers, in contrast to the classical Kabuki Theater where all parts were taken by men. The outside had been repaired and the interior refurbished at great cost to the Japanese Government. Renamed the Ernie Pyle Theater, it was a mecca for U.S. servicemen who could see live USO shows and the latest movies free of charge.

As Maggie glanced at the large sign, "Ernie Pyle," a spasm of tears flowed down her cheeks. Her heart thumped. What she had kept locked inside her for more than a year burst apart. It was as if she had just learned for the first time that MacDowell, the only man she had ever loved, had been hit with the same burst of fire that killed Ernie.

Chaucy, also bound for the grill, saw her standing across the street as if frozen. Though they had become fast friends, Chaucy still didn't know what made Maggie tick—what made her at times hard and even arrogant. No one had told her that Maggie had lost her lover on a tiny, unimportant island off Okinawa. Dodging jeeps and trucks, Chaucy hurried to her side. "My God, Maggie, what's wrong?"

Maggie, unaware that a crowd was gathering, clutched Chaucy. "He's dead," she said.

Chaucy was struck with terror. Please, God, not Mark! "Who's dead?"

"Mac," she mumbled. She looked around. "For Christ's sake, get me out of here."

Chaucy herded her into the Imperial and up to her room. Maggie fled to the bathroom and Chaucy could hear water running in the sink. At last she emerged looking haggard. "I'm so goddamned embarrassed," she said and started weeping, this time angrily.

Chaucy comforted her as if she were a child. They sat together on a sofa without speaking for half an hour. Then Maggie began talking of MacDowell—how dull he had first seemed, how he had kept two drunken Marines from attacking a black sailor on Guam, threatening to shoot them. "Mac was pointing his finger at them and then he told me he forgot he didn't have his side arms." She told how Mac had stopped Heavy Hand Hank from mauling her at the Guam Officers' Club by calmly dumping a pailful of ice and water over his head and saying, "I'm sorry, sir. I spilled my drink." They both laughed but Maggie's laughter was near hysteria. She went again to the bathroom, bathed her face, and came out looking composed.

"Let's get the hell out of here," she said. She was again the hardboiled reporter, but for the first time Chaucy felt she knew the real Maggie.

2.

Enroute to Korea, December 1946.

Maggie and McGlynn left for Korea a week later in a battered transport plane. The professor was as excited as a kid bound for his first day at college. He seemed ten years younger. He wanted to talk about his hope of finding something in Korea that might set MacArthur straight, but Maggie preferred to think, and pretended she was sleeping. She was no longer embarrassed that Chaucy had seen her go to pieces. Thank God it was Chaucy who found her bawling like a baby, and not someone in the family. The droning of the engines finally lulled her to sleep and the next she knew someone was announcing they were coming in for a landing. Several staff cars were waiting for the correspondents. The one ferrying the McGlynns and two others threatened to break down at any minute on the wide dirt road leading to Seoul. On both sides McGlynn could see only poverty: bare yards, shabbily dressed men carrying loads of straw on their backs, and equally shabby women balancing huge bundles on their heads.

Above they could hear American planes swooping down in a mock attack. "Psychological warfare," said their driver, an army lieutenant. "That's the only way to show those gooks we won't stand for any monkey business."

They were put up in the large rundown Chosun Hotel, a billet for field-grade officers that reminded McGlynn of a combination small-town Midwestern hotel, an army barracks, and a Korean roadside inn. Maggie complained of the eternal, potent smell of *kimchi*, but her father liked it. There were many varieties, he said. A common one was a mixture of fish, onions, garlic, and red pepper. "It's the only thing that keeps the Koreans from freezing in the winter." The other correspondents were also complaining that the bellhops and maids only smiled when addressed, since they didn't understand a word of English. McGlynn, happy to exercise his rusty Korean, did his best to help them.

Maggie sought out two locally based correspondents for dinner partners. They spoke of bloody riots in the Seoul area. The cause, they agreed, was not the leftists but economic distress and hatred for the tough Korean police. "This place is the capital of intrigue, beatings, and general screw-up," explained one of the correspondents. When the first Americans had marched into Korea they were met with cheers and signs such as USA ARMY WELCOME HURRAH and AMERI-CANS-KOREANS FRIENDS IN CHRIST. "Our men thought they were being hailed as conquerors. The Koreans were greeting them as liberators."

"In a week both sides were disillusioned," said the second correspondent. "Our people, generals as well as privates, had no concept of the history or character of the Korean people." They only were convinced that the people were high-strung, hot-tempered, proud and sensitive. The Korean men refused to make way for jeeps and the women couldn't be bought for a few Hershey bars.

They talked of the 38th parallel, the boundary between North and South, which had been arbitrarily set up at Potsdam. "And so when the Japs surrendered, all their troops north were rounded up by the Russians and we got those in the south." As a result Korea was now the only place in Asia where U.S. and Russian troops faced each other. "This place is going to be the cockpit of Asia and who the hell in the States gives a damn? *You* tell 'em, Maggie. Maybe they'll believe you."

"And Japan will be the staging area for the next anti-Soviet operation," said his colleague. "Tell 'em, Maggie, before we all go to hell in a basket!"

An interview next day with Syngman Rhee left both McGlynns with a feeling of despair. "The old boy looked like a mummy," said Maggie.

"Don't let his appearance fool you. He's a very sharp character. You thought he was half asleep but he was surveying us through those slits of eyelids." Rhee had spent the hour attacking the Communists, the U.S. commander, General Hodge, and the corruption of his troops in Korea. "Rhee could be a dangerous man. For years he's been a legend and a symbol in Korea; and he's mastered the complexities of Korean politics. No one else here can play that game so ruthlessly and successfully."

Late that night the McGlynns made a walking tour of Seoul. The well-lit streets were jammed even though the shops were closed. Maggie was furious to see so many drunken G.I.'s. They came upon one who had seized a Korean. "I'll show you, you goddamned gook!"

"Take it easy, soldier," said Maggie, good-natured but authorative.

The G.I. turned angrily but two of his comrades pulled him away. Such incidents, they learned at the hotel, were common; that was one reason the people had grown to resent the Americans. Many, they learned, were openly complaining that the Japanese conquerors had been preferable.

"I'm glad you took over back there," said McGlynn. "I'd have botched it." Praise from him was rare and Maggie was pleased.

After a dozen interviews set up by Army public relations with American and Korean officials, the professor declared it was now time to see some of his own friends. From an English-speaking Korean editor named Kim he learned that those he wanted to see were all underground.

"Why?" said McGlynn. "They're not Communists. Just left of center."

They're still either underground or in jail. Come back tomorrow."

They did, and, after a circuitous ride by taxi to shake off anyone following, they reached the meeting place, a street corner in the center of the shopping district. Kim scuttled into the front seat and said without turning around, "Don't act nervous."

Maggie had to repress a giggle, for no one could have looked more suspicious than the furtive Kim. After a number of stops with Kim darting in and out of buildings for information, they drove into the country. The two Koreans they were to interview were hiding in a mountain village. After an hour it was obvious no one was following and they drove up a narrow lane to a rundown house. They walked through a yard littered with jars large enough to hide a man.

"What are they for?" asked Maggie.

"Kimchi," said her father. "The winter supply." He opened a low, handsomely carved door. "We must step over the door sill."

"Why?"

"Superstition. Each house has its own household god. The threshold is the god's neck and He'll be angry if we step on him and will then bring great misfortune upon the household." In Japan, he added, it was also bad manners to step on any threshold.

They were greeted by two old men who were so excited to see McGlynn they could hardly speak.

"The one on the left," explained McGlynn, "is Hu Sic, a professional revolutionary, and the other is Li Woon Hun, a labor leader. Both are good friends of mine."

Hu broke in with a remark punctuated by a deep bow to Maggie.

"He congratulates me on having such a young, pretty wife and hopes we have many children." He didn't explain it was his daughter for fear of offending Hu who was already launching into an excited harangue. "He studied in Chiang Kai-shek's Whampoa Military Academy and during the war was in the Korean underground in Manchuria and North Korea," translated McGlynn. "He served three jail terms for anti-Japanese activities and then, when released after the war, was forced to go underground in South Korea. He says Rhee is as bad as the Japanese. And the American officials here close their eyes to Rhee's fascist methods. Rhee's own terrorist group, the Great Korea Young Men's Association, is the worst of all and works closely with the police."

There were no chairs and all sat on the floor. Chilled by the autumn air, Maggie was delighted to feel warmth rising from the floor. "An old Korean invention," said her father and later explained that the hot smoke from the kitchen stove ran under the floors of the house and then escaped up a chimney. The floor, made of stone slabs cemented together so no smoke could leak into the room, was covered with thick oiled paper.

The labor leader was now talking. "Mr. Li," said McGlynn, "insists he is not a Communist, and says Rhee's labor association is utterly corrupt. It allows factory owners and the military government to force workers to become members. Last month's strikes were caused by low wages and short rice rations."

Without warning there was a crash and the door caved in. A heavy-set policeman entered brandishing a bayoneted rifle. Behind were four hard-faced young men, all armed, in dingy civilian suits. Behind was another young man in a flashy business suit. He pointed his pistol at Kim, informing him he was under arrest for subversive activities.

"Who the hell are you?" asked McGlynn angrily.

The young man politely bowed and brought out identification showing he was a detective in the Korean National Police.

"Do you have a warrant?" asked Maggie, angrily pushing the pistol aside. She was furious because they had carelessly stepped on the door sill, bringing bad luck to the house as well as tracking in mud.

"Oh, yes," he said but explained he had left it at the police station. He suggested the two Americans leave at once. They would be taken to the Chosun Hotel in a police car.

"We'll wait here until you get the warrant," she said. "What about these two men?" she indicated Hu and Li.

The detective laughed. "Those old men are harmless." He said something in Korean and the two, heads bowed, left. "I told them to go home and be good boys." He instructed another plainclothesman to get the warrant and for the next fifteen minutes he joked with Kim, every so often clapping him on the back. But then he abruptly got to his feet, shouting that the two Americans were interfering with justice. "Who are you and what are you doing here?"

"I'm McGlynn of the Fredericks Chain."

"And I'm Professor Frank McGlynn, special adviser to General MacArthur, sent here on orders to investigate charges of police brutality."

The detective paled and without comment told them to follow him to a police car. Once in the yard McGlynn asked one of the four young toughs if he also was a detective. "No," he said proudly. "I'm a member of the Great Korea Young Men's Association. We help the police catch leftists." A comrade shouted to him to shut up.

After an hour's wait at the central police station an American major arrived. He introduced himself as Halliburton, the chief of the police division of the military government for Seoul. "General Hodge ordered me to investigate this incident," he said affably, and remarked that only a few months ago he'd been an investment banker in Minneapolis. "Have you lived in the Orient before?" he asked McGlynn.

"Mostly in China and Japan."

"Then you understand that the police over here never heard of democracy and believe in force."

"What concerns me," said McGlynn, "is using a private terrorist gang to make this arrest." But Halliburton had never heard of the Great Korea Young Men's Association. He asked the chief of police who claimed he'd never heard of it either. "You must be mistaken, sir," said the chief of police. "Since you don't speak Korean."

After McGlynn answered him in Korean, Halliburton said, "Chief, if this is true your detective is in real trouble." He turned to McGlynn. "Couldn't you have made a mistake?"

"No. One of them told me he was in the Young Men's Association."

The arresting detective angrily jabbed a finger at McGlynn. "He interfered when I was making an arrest, sir. He even ordered me out of the room!"

"No," said Kim. "He never said any such thing."

"How can you believe a man who arranged this secret meeting with Communists?"

"Mr. Kim was following my instructions," said McGlynn. "And since I have been instructed by General MacArthur to investigate conditions over here, he was following the Supreme Commander's orders. I insist on seeing General Hodge without delay."

"No need to go that far," said Halliburton who was used to handling rich clients at his bank in Minneapolis. "This has been an unfortunate mix-up and I don't see why we can't settle everything right here and now. Just among us."

The police chief was agreeable.

"Does that mean that charges against Mr. Kim are dropped?" asked McGlynn.

Halliburton looked hopefully at the police chief who, after a brief hesitation, nodded.

"Now let me take you back to your hotel, Dr. McGlynn," said Halliburton, rubbing his hands as if he had closed a big loan. "And we can all have a couple of drinks."

"Mr. Kim too?"

"Of course."

Once they were alone, Maggie said, "Glad you took over today, Daddy. I'd have botched it."

3.

That night in Tokyo counselors for both prosecution and defense along with a few friends, were gathering at a famous restaurant, Gajoen, a very large Japanese-styled building in Meguro which was used for banquets as well as serving small parties of people who came for the famed Chinese cuisine. The party was a farewell for half a dozen men leaving for the United States. Donihi was bound for Germany to help prosecute some of the post-Nuremberg trials and three others could not afford to stay any longer. Furness and Lazarus had solved the money question by becoming civilians, thereby boosting their salaries.

The judges were also getting impatient. They had been assured the trial would surely end in September, but the defense wouldn't even start their case for several months and they would probably take even longer than the prosecution.

Chaucy had just learned that Judge Pal had already requested his government to replace him since he had many important matters back home. "If he leaves," she told Will as they approached the restaurant, "it'll be tough on the defense. He's the only one with any extensive experience in international law."

"Don't worry. The word is that his government recently telegraphed him to stay on, extending his assignment for another six months."

"How did you find out?"

"MacArthur told Keenan whose secretary told my secretary who told me."

They found the parking area jammed with cars and jeeps. And

inside there were at least a hundred people sitting on the floor of the main room before foot-high tables. They found places at a table with two prosecutors and two defense counsel. Sake was flowing freely and the newcomers were greeted boisterously. A prosecution lawyer sitting next to Chaucy said he was leaving as soon as their case wound up. "Let me tell you, pretty lady," he whispered loudly, "you can't quote me, but I think the defensh hash not had its full day in court."

"I'll drink to that," she said. "Too bad you won't be around to see the blood flow when we present our side." She helped herself to various dishes of shrimp, fish, chicken, and unknown tidbits, all of which she ate with relish.

In the middle of dinner, a prosecution lawyer stood up to give a ten-minute description of a session at Ichigaya in the style of a fight announcer. Chaucy thought he was funnier than any of the professional comics who had come to Japan. Next was a tongue-in-cheek oration by Furness praising the prosecution for their gentlemanly conduct and no one laughed louder than his opponents at his good-natured parody of Keenan at the rostrum.

The main speaker was Dr. Somei Uzawa, chief Japanese defense counsel, the former head of Meiji University. He was dead serious but when he said, "The Japanese have always been a peace-loving nation," there was raucous laughter from a tipsy prosecutor who was silenced by a colleague. Except for that moment the evening was free of unpleasant partisanship. After dinner, the wife of Mark Gayn, the correspondent, asked the geisha to do "Tokyo Ondo," her favorite song and dance. The girls inveigled most of the men to their feet. A rhumba-like line was formed and there was unrestrained dancing which soon degenerated into an orgy of giggling girls being hugged by enthusiastic counselors egged on by cheering bystanders.

"Let's get out of here," said Will.

4.

Maggie and McGlynn were staying at Kimpo Air Base near Seoul, their escort a Nisei lieutenant named Nara who was explaining that the mission of his intelligence unit was to search out spies and saboteurs coming across the 38th parallel, and also interrogate Japanese repatriates to gather information about North Korean airfields.

The next morning Lieutenant Nara drove them in a jeep along the parallel. There was one jeep behind and another ahead. Maggie noticed that both drivers kept carbines on the seat beside them, and the officers in the rear wore automatics in shoulder holsters. The road, little more than an oxcart lane, was so rough that the McGlynns bounced up and down while yellow dust from the front jeep almost choked them. Every time they stopped at a village, children would swarm over the jeep fingering their clothing and tugging at their buttons. Nara would shout at them in Japanese, but the only way he could clear them away was to gun the motor.

The road grew worse and there were no houses, only desolation. Ahead a G.I. was pointing a submachine gun at the first jeep. After a cursory check, he waved the convoy on.

"This is U.S. Outpost No. 7," said Nara as they drew up to several Quonset huts.

Maggie went up to a G.I. squatting in the sun like a Korean. "Pretty grim out here, eh?"

He gave her a sour smile. "I wouldn't want to live here. This is worse than Arkansas. Nothin' to do out here but stare off there." He pointed at a hill. "See them Russkies up there? They squat there and I squat here and we both wonder what in hell is gonna happen." He grinned. "One day I got so bored I waved. And one had the guts to wave back. Probably got shot. No one ever waved again." He waggled an arm but there was no reply.

"God damn it to hell, Hulse." A captain came loping toward them. "I told you not to do that." He looked at Maggie as if he had never before seen a girl. "Excuse the language, miss. We're getting cabin fever out here."

They drove on several hundred yards to a wooden barrier across the road. Nearby was a sentry box where a Russian soldier stood shivering. He wore only thin trousers and a thin shirt. He stared at them.

Lieutenant Nara said they would have to wait until a Russian guide appeared. After an hour of peering into the bleakness Maggie finally heard the rattle of a truck. The vehicle, a Studebaker probably sent years back to Murmansk, came to a screeching halt and two young officers bounded out. One came forward briskly, saluted the four American officers and tried talking in Russian, then German. The Americans answered in English and French. One of the Americans had come from Latvia when he was a baby. He said something in Latvian and the Russian replied eagerly. The American turned to the McGlynns. "He says America is an interesting country and has many races and nationalities." By now everybody was smiling but the conversation soon petered out and the Russian said, "Let's move," in Latvian. The sentry raised the gate.

Both McGlynns felt a thrill at finally traveling in Soviet territory. Near an airfield, Red Army troops watched them curiously. Maggie noticed they all smiled. In a group of rundown buildings she could see Russian women hanging out laundry and children playing in the barren courtyard. Just down the road they passed under a large wooden arch decorated with red flags and large portraits of Stalin and Kim Il Sung, the leader of North Korea.

"This is Kaesong," said Nara. "One of the biggest cities in North Korea." Almost every lamp post, fence, and building was covered with slogans and decorations proclaiming the glory of the hammer and sickle. The main streets were jammed with people marketing. To McGlynn's surprise there were few police and only an occasional Russian soldier escorting his wife. Children ran along shouting, "Americansky!" Several held out fingers in the V for Victory sign of World War Two. But Maggie noticed one Korean sticking out a single little finger.

"That's the Korean sign of contempt," explained her father. "Maybe they got it from Marco Polo when he passed through."

An hour later they reached the end of their tour of the Soviet zone, arriving at U.S. Outpost No. 4. After washing off most of the grime, they ate in the mess hall tent. Their host, a pink-cheeked captain, was the military governor of the county, so lonely that he kept talking without restraint. He told of the junks smuggling people and goods from the north; of a patriotic youth association being set up by his interpreter; of food and prices; of how they had to break up a riot in a nearby town recently; of how—

A corporal tapped him on the shoulder. "Sir, could I speak to you for a second?" The captain blushed as he followed the corporal to a Quonset hut. Someone explained that the corporal was with Military Intelligence and Maggie felt so sorry for their informant when he came meekly back that she didn't ask any more questions.

Two days later the McGlynns were on another battered C-54. The bucket seats had no cushions and they huddled together for warmth.

"Learn anything?" asked McGlynn as they headed across the relatively narrow channel separating Korea from Japan.

"I now see why they eat so much *kimchi,*" she said. "In fact, I'm getting to like it."

"Do you think our rule in Korea is better than Japan's was?"

"Not by a damned sight," she said angrily. "Now the Koreans have two masters, not one. Their economy appears to be miserable—perhaps because their country has been artificially split in two. They have been divided against each other." Instead of liberating them the Americans and Russians had turned the Koreans into mercenary troops. "Our liberation certainly can't be called humanitarian. Nor does it even seem to be sensible power politics."

McGlynn was pleased but said nothing until the mountains of Japan hove into sight. "I imagine," he said, "we'll both catch hell from the general."

"For the hassle over Hu and Li?"

"Among other things."

"Well, he can kiss my ass."

Never had he felt so close to her and he thought this might be a good time to talk frankly about her shield of hardness, and the coarseness of her speech—which fortunately never crept into her articles. But all he said was, "We'll both probably be called in." The first one to see MacArthur should make queries on Hu and Li. "I didn't believe for a minute that the detective was going to let them go. They're probably in prison and about to be executed."

Her face was like stone. "I don't give a damn if the Chief throws me out of the country." Her features softened. "But I'd hate to leave with things in such a mess for Floss and the Todas."

"I came to Japan under protest, but I'd rather not go back yet either. There's too much to be done."

As the plane approached the west coast of Japan he began talking of his deep concern over Asia. "I'm really not a scholar where this continent is concerned. It's much more personal. Many years ago I found I was more at home in China, Korea, and Japan than in New England." He grinned in memory. "What a young fool I was in those days. A real Innocent Abroad! I was impressed by almost everything I saw and everyone I met. I blundered my way about, learning to speak half a dozen languages colloquially and finding new friends in the most unlikely places."

271

Never had Maggie found him so open. Without reserve he told funny anecdotes of the ridiculous things that had happened because of his naïveté during his adventures throughout Asia. He was acid about colonial rule in Hongkong, Singapore, and China. He laughed at the follies of a fabulous Chinese warlord he stayed with several months, and became choked in memory of the kindness from peasants who would share their meager meals with him. He made life in the East seem grotesque, bizarre and ludicrous. Yet he was never sarcastic or condescending toward the people, and moved Maggie with tales of their heroism and selflessness. "I finally became convinced that the Asians were right to look upon Europeans and Americans as barbarians, and that the Western way of life was a folly." He gazed over the Japan Sea and his face became serious. "Over here life is often led so that a sensible man can see it has a genuine sense of reality."

Maggie was touched. It was as if he had briefly lifted a curtain to reveal beyond a world rich in color and significance. Her father was not the aloof, cool, self-contained man he pretended to be. And the past few weeks had completely changed their relationship. She always had known that she and Will were the professor's favorites, and secretly it had pleased her. But now she was no longer his dear little girl. They were equals. She decided to bring up a subject that had concerned her for a long time. "When are we going to meet Mariko?" she said bluntly.

It was the first time she had ever seen him startled and at a complete loss for words. "Are you under the impression we don't know about her? My God, Daddy, everybody in Tokyo has known about it for months."

He looked at her sheepishly, and smiled weakly.

The plane was starting its descent.

"I guess you all think I'm a damned fool," he finally said.

"At first I thought so," she admitted. "Mark agreed with me and Will wasn't quite sure. But Floss knew Mariko and thought you were lucky."

He sighed as if in relief. "I never met anyone like her. How about Christmas dinner with us at the Imperial?"

Maggie leaned over and kissed his cheek.

The wheels screeched on the tarmac, and McGlynn peered eagerly out the window. The first thing Maggie saw was the tall figure of Will pushing through the crowd. Everyone seemed to have the same look of relieved anxiety. As Floss hugged her father and Will kissed Maggie, she saw in the background Mariko Tajima, whose face brightened on glimpsing the professor.

With some embarrassment, McGlynn introduced Mariko to Will and Maggie, then shook hands with Mariko formally. But on the tedious drive to Tokyo Maggie noticed her father and Mariko getting as close to each other as possible. Just like high school kids on their first date at the movies! It was funny but Maggie felt a catch in her throat. It was obvious that he had found what he had sorely needed for many years.

The Christmas party at the Imperial Hotel started uneasily when Mariko apologized for Taro's absence, but soon Mariko began to fit into the festive family which treated her as if she were already one of them. By the end of the evening, during much of which she and McGlynn held hands under the table, Mariko finally felt as if she belonged. He was chiding himself for not realizing that most of life's problems are solved simply, and hoped that the last obstacle to their marriage—Taro's antagonism—would also be overcome before he lost his mind.

There were no messages from MacArthur until two days after Christmas. Finally one came for Maggie. She found the general more formal than usual. "I understand you and your father had some problems. General Hodge was quite concerned."

Maggie told what had happened and before he could make any comment insisted on a report regarding Hu and Li. "Both are in their eighties. They're highly regarded in Korea by conservatives as well as leftists."

Apparently taken aback, the general asked what she thought should be done with them.

"Let them go home and keep writing their pamphlets which no one reads. They are no threat to us." She saw he was actually listening. "You may not approve of everything I write in my article on Korea but please read it yourself. Then you can send me home."

"You McGlynns seem born for trouble." His face became stern but she could see a ghost of a smile. "I guess," he said, "there's nothing more to tell you—except Happy New Year!"

PART FOUR

Chapter Fifteen

1.

Tokyo-Yokohama, January 3, 1947.

With the prosecution case winding down at the Tokyo Tribunal Chaucy was spending so much time on the Tojo defense that she was seized with panic to hear that Shogo Toda's case was scheduled to be tried in Yokohama in two weeks. She had been led to believe that the prosecution would not be ready until late summer, and there were bound to be long recesses before then at Ichigaya. So she was just now formulating her defense of Shogo. In the past few months she had visited him four times. Although he still refused to speak against Tsuji he did talk at length about the fanatic colonel whose hatred of whites had led to numerous atrocities during the war. Shogo told about the exciting days in 1941 during the planning of the invasion of Malaya, when Tsuji had driven his staff relentlessly. "He would seldom sleep, and ate only when I shoved food in front of him. He felt that the fate of Japan rested on his shoulders. One night about a month or so before Pearl Harbor I found him in a trance. He said without looking at me, 'I abandon all wordly passions, even life and death. I must concentrate on victory.' I can still see him, his shaven head shining with sweat. 'We will win!' he chanted. 'We will win!'"

She was such a sympathetic listener that Shogo told her how one day Tsuji, in a fit of moral indignation, had burned down a geisha house filled with fellow officers who had to escape naked, and how dedicated he was to saving not only Japan but Asia in those early days and to prove his own sincerity and devotion lived in a filthy little room behind a stable. The headquarters officers were all rotten, Tsuji told Shogo. "They were only working for their medals. Every night they went to parties and played with geishas. Since the China Incident, all the military had gone bad. They hated me because I knew all this and spoke out."

Chaucy said she had heard from Major Senda, a colleague of Tsuji's who now lived in Tokyo, that he had done more than speak out. "Senda told me Tsuji turned over one fellow staff officer to the Kempeitai for 'corruption' and that man then committed suicide."

"The man was corrupt!" said Shogo heatedly; then, after a long pause, he added, "If I should save my life by saying a word against Tsuji-san, I would be dishonored." The moment of heat was over and he lapsed into his usual philosophical calm. "What will happen is going to happen."

In another long interview he responded factually to information relevant to the indictments against him. He told of the exciting days of the Malaya invasion and of the secret night talks Tsuji had held with carefully selected young officers. In the light of a small campfire Tsuji would relate the long history of Western depredations in Asia—of the arrogance of the British, Dutch, and Portuguese.

"During these meetings," asked Chaucy, "didn't he also preach that natives who helped the British should be punished?"

"Did you get that from Major Senda too?"

"Yes. And he's going to testify to it at your trial. He was at one of those evening meetings, and he also was a witness to the murder of five thousand Chinese after the battle of Singapore."

Shogo shook his head. "Senda was always jealous of Tsuji-san," he said. "I'm sure I would have known if this had happened." He had convinced himself that the Singapore murders were Allied propaganda, but when she asked him about the charge that Tsuji had ordered the execution in 1944 of several captured Allied airmen in Burma, he refused to comment. Witnesses had told him at the time of those murders and of the horrifying incident that followed when Tsuji forced a selected cadre of young officers to eat the Allied airmen's livers. This, according to Tsuji, would raise the morale of the dispirited survivors of the disastrous Imphal campaign in India. For some time Shogo had feared his revered leader was going mad. This cannibalism had so sickened him that he had arranged to be transferred to Tokyo where he joined the idealistic military group which briefly seized the Palace grounds in an unsuccessful attempt to prevent the Emperor from surrendering.

"I was caught short," Chaucy wrote her father. "And it was all my own fault. I should have suspected Hanging Harry—that's what we call the character prosecuting Shogo. He let it be known it would take another six months before he was ready to try the case." She explained there were four specifications of the charges against Shogo: involvement in the Chinese murders in Singapore, atrocities committed during the Bataan Death March, the murders in Burma, and the murder of Chief Justice Santos in the Philippines. "My best lead is on the Santos murder. Will recently learned that General Okamura, the Japanese commander in Mindanao, was being tried in Manila for the Santos murder. Will managed to get a transcript of his testimony. The general claims that he is taking the rap for a death order which Tsuji secretly arranged. Okamura claims he fought the order since it was an outrageous betrayal of Bushido, but was forced to execute the Chief Justice by a direct order from 14th Army." In court Okamura testified how he had stormed up to Manila to confront General Ito who had written the order. "I told Ito," said Okamura, "that he had done a shameful thing and I had trusted him as my classmate. He excused himself by saying that Imperial Headquarters had insisted on the execution of Santos. I asked whom he meant by Imperial Headquarters and he said Tsuji." Okamura then testified that the whole thing could be cleared up by a Japanese colonel named Iwata who could put the blame on one person alone, Tsuji. Unfortunately Iwata could not be located since he had been transferred to China. "I know this doesn't sound like much, but Will—he's been a great help lately—thinks it could lead to something. Anyway, it's about the only thing left. If I had more time I think I could peel Shogo down like an artichoke."

She added a hasty postscript. "Remember when you told me that a lawyer caught up in a tough murder case is like a man just fallen in love? His involvement is total. All he can think about day and night is his case. The lawyer and the lover, you said, share a strange and exhilarating experience. In this dratted case, Dad, it looks as if I'm falling in love."

Professor McGlynn had promised to advise her on Shogo's defense. But he told her he'd just had time to glance through the evidence. "I've worked out a pretty good defense for you," he said. "But it will take a month's research to pull it together."

"What is it?"

"Get a retrial and I'll tell you." He shook a finger at her as if she were a dull student. "You have only one chance. Get Shogo to tell the truth about Tsuji. You've tried reason and logic but that can't work on a man who cut off one of his little fingers when he was a young cadet, then sent it to the Emperor in a jar of alcohol, along with the little fingers of eight other young radicals. Those nine fools wanted to be tried in place of the assassins of Prime Minister Inukai. They all were convinced that assassination was the only answer to the corruption of political leaders. Such misplaced idealism has been common in Japanese history. The assassin was often a more sympathetic figure than the victim. Wasn't there some lack of virtue in a man who let himself be killed, and wasn't an assassin who murdered for lofty purposes merely defending the common people against tyranny?"

"Where's the lofty purpose in killing prisoners of war on the Death March?"

"Right you are! And don't forget that Shogo was brought up as a Christian. Although Will still has his doubts about him, I am positive Shogo knew nothing of Tsuji's crimes. But since Shogo comes from a family with a samurai background he feels obligated to practice Bushido, the samurai code of loyalty to the master, valuing honor above life. I know this doesn't make any sense to Westerners. The classic case of such loyalty is that of the forty-seven *ronin*. Those samurai warriors avenged the honor and death of their lord by brutally murdering his enemies. Then they all committed hara-kiri to maintain their own honor. I think Shogo didn't know of his master's atrocities until they were transferred to Burma in 1944. Shogo is still too confused and depressed by guilt to realize Tsuji is not a true samurai. Other disciples of Tsuji must already have been disillusioned. Find them! Then I'm sure Shogo also will come around."

"I haven't given up hope yet. I'm flying tomorrow to Manila to interrogate General Okamura. It might lead to something substantial. In any case it's better than doing nothing."

The following day Chaucy's plane approached Clark Field. "See," said a young army lieutenant sitting next to her. He pointed at a cone-shaped mountain. "Arayat! The gooks think that's where Noah's ark landed. We'll be on the ground in a minute."

Even though it was late afternoon the hot air of the Philippines was like a blast from a furnace as Chaucy climbed down to the tarmac. This was her first taste of the subtropics and she had imagined she would be engulfed by exotic scenes once they left the expansive airfield. But there was little tropical splendor on the bus trip to Manila, merely stretches of rolling cane fields with some mountains on the right. They passed through a cluster of elevated nipa huts. There was a peculiar pungent odor. A middle-aged Filipino next to her said, "The smell of the barrio. You'll get used to it, miss."

The next afternoon she finally was admitted to General Okamura's cell. He was incensed that he was being tried unjustly, but finally got around to telling her about Colonel Iwata. Some time after Santos's execution General Manuel Roxas, former Speaker of the Philippine House of Representatives, was also captured in Mindanao. A message came from Manila ordering the local commander to execute Roxas "secretly and immediately." As in the Santos case, the order was authorized in the name of General Homma. "This also was instigated by Tsuji," said Okamura. "Colonel Iwata was ordered to carry out the execution. As he was driving Roxas and another high-ranking captive —a governor—toward the execution grounds, the governor begged for his life and grew so hysterical that Roxas patted his shoulder and said, 'Look at the sampaguita.' He pointed at clusters of delicate white blossoms, the national flower of the Philippines, and said, 'Aren't they beautiful?' "

Iwata thought no samurai could have acted more nobly and decided to save Roxas no matter what the consequences. He persuaded his commanding officer that Roxas should be saved so he could help restore law and order, and then flew up to Manila to see Homma himself, who not only countermanded the order of execution but promised to report the matter to the Emperor.

"Is this the same Roxas who is now the President?"

"The same."

The next morning, through the efforts of a helpful official at the U.S. Embassy, Chaucy was granted an interview with President Roxas at Malacañan Palace. She asked if he knew Iwata had saved his life. Roxas did, and revealed that upon learning Iwata was a prisoner in China awaiting trial as a war criminal he had written a personal letter to Chiang Kai-shek requesting amnesty for Iwata. "I was informed he was released and should be back in Japan shortly."

Since Chaucy's plane would not leave for five hours, she accepted an invitation from Mateo Domingo, who had shared with Will the hell of the Death March and Camp O'Donnell, to visit those sites. They drove along the entire march with Domingo relating in gruesome detail what had happened along the way: the brutal bayoneting of an exhausted American captain who fell to the ground; the cold-blooded murder of a sympathetic Filipino who had handed him a leafful of rice.

Then he took her north to the Capas railroad station. "This is where we got off the freight train and started walking to Camp O'Donnell." On that trip, he said, half a dozen prisoners in his tiny boxcar had suffocated, too weak to make a final groan.

They headed down a dusty road toward the mountains. It was stiflingly hot but after six miles Chaucy felt a slight breeze as they reached the top of a rise. Down below she could make out a jumble of buildings in the midst of a vast rolling plain covered with tall cogon-grass. The few straggly trees only made the vista more desolate.

As they neared a high barbed-wire fence and wooden sentry towers, Domingo told how the camp commandant, Captain Tsuneyoshi, had strutted up to a platform, his sword clanking, and begun shouting at the assembled prisoners: "You are our enemies! Be grateful to the great Imperial Japanese Army for saving your miserable lives! Forget America!" He had then shouted arrogantly, "Anglo-American imperialism is dead! And if you get near the barbed-wire fence a sentry will shoot you dead!"

Chaucy was appalled by the pitiful rundown buildings that had housed thousands of prisoners. They must have lived like animals. Domingo told her about Zero Ward where the dying were abandoned. He and Will had once helped put a corpse on a wooden shutter for the trip to the mass grave. The procession of death had moved through the front gate and off to the burying ground where buzzards were eating bodies which had recently floated to the surface because of rainfall.

"Let's get out of here," said Chaucy.

2.

Before Chaucy could find Iwata, Shogo's trial began in the same courtroom where the other Camp 13 defendants had been tried. Chaucy knew that with a client who would do little to defend himself there was almost no chance of an acquittal. Then she would seek a retrial and hope she could find Iwata and other new evidence in the meantime. Sounding more optimistic than she felt, she remarked to Lieutenant Browne, who had been assigned to work with her, that since there were only four members of the Commission it should work in their favor. "We'll have fewer to convince."

Browne was more realistic. "So will the prosecution."

Watching them intently on the other side of the barrier were Will, the Toda family, and their friends. Will was attempting to explain the court procedures to Emi while Sumiko's eyes seemed fixed on the impressive but empty judge's bench.

A door on the right opened and in walked Shogo escorted by an M.P. Shogo stopped, turned toward his family and smiled reassuringly. And when the M.P. gently nudged him he apologized in Japanese and moved to his place.

Chaucy was hurriedly giving last-minute directions to Browne who had done little research and would be used primarily to keep all the affidavits and other papers in order. Then as the president and four members took their places, everyone rose and the trial started. The chief prosecutor, "Hanging Harry," was a portly lieutenant colonel named Chestnutt who had left a prestigious law firm in Chicago to serve his country in a legal capacity in the Pacific. Persuaded by Keenan to stay in Tokyo and help prosecute the top war criminals, he had proved to be one of the ablest counsel at Ichigaya. Since the notorious Colonel Tsuji was connected with this case, he had agreed to prosecute. He had a deep base voice which, together with a completely assured manner, made every word—so Chaucy declared—seem to have come directly from God. He and Chaucy had been at odds from their first meeting at the Tokyo Tribunal, since the colonel was one of those who resolutely believed that all the Jap defendants were evil.

His opening statement was short, clear, and impressive. "The prosecution will prove beyond doubt that the defendant Toda . . ." he pointed a finger at Shogo, "was the closest aide, confidant and accomplice of probably the most vicious war criminal in the annals of civilized war, Masanobu Tsuji. We will prove their close relationship from days before Pearl Harbor when together they planned the insidious surprise attack on Malaya, and of their instigation, after the conquest of Singapore, of the cold-blooded murder of more than five thousand innocent Chinese civilians in Singapore. This would be the first step toward their mad goal not only to wipe out all white men in Asia but to punish those Asians who had collaborated with the Caucasians. The trail of blood led to the heinous Death March in Bataan and ended in Burma with the murder of captured American airmen." He promised to give details of this trek of horror and prove that Tsuji's fanaticism was shared by Shogo who willingly helped him carry out such unspeakable atrocities.

Chaucy objected to equating Shogo with Tsuji and said there was not any hard proof that Shogo had participated in, or even observed, any of the alleged atrocities. She offered statements from three of General Yamashita's staff officers describing Shogo as an honorable officer who was only doing his duty. All three testified that he had shown none of Tsuji's fanaticism and, in fact, was a restraining influence on the flamboyant Tsuji.

Chestnutt, as was his right, called Shogo to the stand to testify on the first affidavit. "Is it true that during the battle for Malaya you would organize secret meetings of young key officers to listen to Tsuji's plans for the future of Asia?"

"*Hai,*" said Shogo, refusing to say "Yes" in English.

"What did Tsuji tell them?"

Shogo replied in Japanese that Tsuji spoke of his great dream of making Asia one great brotherhood, an Asia for the Asians. And that could be accomplished only by driving all Westerners out of the continent by force.

Chestnutt approached Shogo. "Force? You mean killing?"

"In battle, yes, sir."

"Didn't he talk of punishing those Asians who collaborated with the Westerners?"

"No, sir. He said they had to learn to be men and drive out those foreigners who had taken over much of Asia."

"We have five statements from young Japanese officers who attended those—pep talks. They all say he wanted to execute those Asians who collaborated with the enemy."

"I never heard him say that."

"Are we to believe this defendant or the sworn statements of five other Japanese officers?" He turned on Shogo. "You admired him, didn't you?"

"All those who served with him revered him. He was the God of Operations, the hope of Asia."

"I understand he once burned down a geisha house filled with fellow officers."

"I never saw that. He was a young officer then. I heard about it."

"You admit it's true?"

"I only said I heard it. They said it was because he was disgusted with the corruptness of those in the geisha house."

"Do you approve of what he did?"

"I do not approve or disapprove. I am not a judge. But I can understand his indignation."

Late in the afternoon Chaucy claimed that all the evidence against Shogo was circumstantial and his guilt was only the guilt by association. Chaucy and Will had no chance to talk in private as they accompanied the Todas to the railroad station.

During the long, uneasy wait, an elderly Japanese man was pushed off the crowded platform onto the tracks. The old man lay stunned. In the distance the rumble of an oncoming train could be heard. While the Japanese crowd watched, Will leaped down, seized the old man by the shoulders and tried in vain to heft him up. A big Marine jumped down, grabbed the man's legs and together they flung the man to the platform. A G.I. grabbed Will's right hand and yanked him to safety with seconds to spare.

Sumiko Toda was watching, mouth agape. Americans! No wonder they had won the war!

As their taxi headed back to the hotel near the courthouse neither Will nor Chaucy said a thing. She was still in shock and he at last realized how close a call it had been.

"That was a wonderful thing you just did."

He grinned sheepishly. "I was about to bug out when that Marine jumped down. *He* was wonderful."

Chaucy spent the night at the hotel while Will found a room at a nearby BOQ. Soon after the lunch recess on the second day, the Singapore phase was finished and Chestnutt introduced another pile of affidavits from American and Filipino soldiers claiming they had seen Shogo with Tsuji during the Death March. With information gleaned from Will she was able to discredit most of the affidavits.

The Todas, who had arrived in a state of depression, left encouraged. But Will knew that little had been accomplished. "I hope they don't get too hopeful," he told Chaucy. "The worst is yet to come."

It came on the third day—after damning affidavits on the murder of

Justice Santos—when Major Ohno, on Tsuji's staff in Burma, related how seven captured American fliers had been brought to Tsuji's headquarters. He ordered Ohno to kill them and then remove their livers. When he refused, Tsuji ordered Ohno to consider himself under house arrest.

"He told me to send in Lieutenant Toda," testified Ohno. "I watched Toda enter the office and then went to my room." The next morning he heard that the seven men had been executed and the livers fed to a group of young officers.

"Did you go into Tsuji's room as Mr. Ohno says?" Chestnutt asked Toda.

"Yes, sir."

"And what did he tell you?"

"He ordered me to take a small patrol and investigate the site where the American plane had crashed. I did so."

"Can anyone on that patrol corroborate your . . . story?"

Chaucy replied they had failed to find any of those on the patrol. Three were known dead, the fourth missing in action.

"Very convenient, defendant Toda." Chestnutt lowered his booming voice in a confidential manner. "Perhaps you can tell us something about this liver-eating business."

"What do you mean, Mr. Counsel?"

"I mean exactly what I said. Did you hear about the eating of livers out there in Burma?"

"Yes. We all did."

"Did you believe it?" For the first time at the trial Shogo was flustered. He knew it was true but out of guilt for having shut his eyes to the earlier atrocities committed by his idol, he was still determined never to say a word against Tsuji. "What's the matter? Why don't you answer?"

"I am not a judge."

"That's not answering the question. Did you believe Tsuji did this ghastly thing?"

He could not lie because he had sworn to tell the truth. So he said, "I am not a judge."

"Mr. President, will you please instruct the witness to answer yes or no?"

The president, a colonel with medals and ribbons indicating he had spent much time in battle, repeated the question.

Chaucy looked imploringly at Shogo.

"I cannot answer," he said.

Chestnutt then called as the prosecution's next witness, a Japanese war correspondent named Tomita. "Do you know the defendant?"

"By sight only. I know he was one of Colonel Tsuji's assistants. I saw them together in Rabaul in 1942 just before they left for Guadalcanal."

"Will you describe what you saw?"

"Colonel Tsuji was holding a press conference. That officer—" Tomita pointed at Shogo—"was standing near me while the colonel was telling us about the battle going on at Guadalcanal. He shouted, '*Oi*, you newsmen! You know the expression *gashin-shotan?*' We all did, of course, since our leaders had called upon the people to face years of *gashin-shotan.*"

"What does that mean?"

"It means 'to sleep on kindling and lick liver.' We all knew it meant to endure a life of hardship and austerity to win the war."

"Is that what Tsuji meant?"

"Oh, no. He held up something which looked like a lump of black sugar. 'This is the enemy's liver!' shouted Tsuji. 'I lick it every day.' And then he licked it."

"And during all this the defendant was near you and listening?"

"Yes, sir."

Shogo was called back to the stand.

"Defendant," said Chestnutt accusingly, "was this newsman telling the truth?"

"Yes, sir."

"And you heard every word this Tsuji said?"

"Yes, sir."

"And you saw him lick the liver?"

"Yes, sir."

"That's all," said Chestnutt and looked at Shogo as if to add, "and that's enough."

The president asked if Chaucy wanted to question Shogo. She was about to say yes but decided her client would only make things worse.

The next morning it was the overconfident Chestnutt who made the mistake. After Chaucy had given a long and persuasive recital of the intense strains all men of battle underwent whether they were American or Japanese, Chestnutt became sarcastic.

"I would like to congratulate my colleague on her eloquence," he said, irked that the members of the Commission, all of whom had served in battle, had been impressed. "One would almost think the defense counsel was a Japanese. But then, of course, you're defending the worst of them in Tokyo."

Chaucy never thought of objecting but the president did. In the gravelly voice that had reamed many a subordinate, he said, "Major Chestnutt, those of us who fought the Japanese respected their devotion to duty. And it is also my understanding that the American defense counsel at the International Tribunal are only doing their duty. Miss Snow is due an apology."

"I apologize to you, sir. I intended no insult."

"I didn't mean apologize to me. To Miss Snow."

So piqued by the mistake he had made, Chestnutt made another. "I thought I did."

"Don't bandy words with me, Major. Apologize directly to Miss Snow."

"I apologize, Miss Snow."

The next day, January 16, both defense and prosecution finished their cases at noon.

"How long does the prosecution desire for its arguments, opening and closing?" asked the law member.

"I think one hour is sufficient," said Chestnutt.

Chaucy said she would need only about an hour and a half. "We can finish it all in the afternoon."

The president called a recess until 13:30.

Although Will still was not sure of Shogo's innocence, he was doing his best to keep up Chaucy's spirits. At lunch with the Todas at the nearby restaurant there was little talk since it was obvious Chaucy wanted to compose herself. When they returned to the courtroom the president announced that the commission, upon completion of the arguments, would retire to consider its decision. "The Commission proposes to announce its decision in open court at ten hundred hours, Friday, 17 January 1947, providing a decision has been reached."

"If it pleases the Commission," said Chestnutt opening his argument, "before I discuss the law and facts of this case, I would like to express to the Commission the appreciation of the prosecution for the manner in which the Commission has cooperated with and assisted the prosecution in presenting this case for trial." It had been difficult, he said, for both prosecution and defense to present their evidence in a manner that was proper and legal since this case was so unusual. He listed the major points made by the prosecution, pointing out the inadequacy of the defense evidence. After almost an hour of elaboration on the facts, he said, "It would appear to me that I could go on at great length, but you have heard the evidence, and there is no question but that the prosecution has shown beyond a reasonable doubt that this accused is guilty upon every one of the specifications. In determining the penalty to be imposed upon this accused, let us not forget that he has committed such atrocious crimes that only the penalty of death is appropriate. In closing let me conclude with a joint statement made by Roosevelt, Churchill, and Stalin on the twelfth of November, 1943. They were speaking of the war criminals: 'Most assuredly the three Allied Powers will pursue them to the uttermost ends of the earth, and will deliver them to their accuser in order that justice may be done.' "

Chaucy slowly rose. "The issue now before this Commission is whether the weight of all the evidence which has been submitted by both the prosecution and the defense has carried the burden of proof, which is upon the prosecution, of establishing the accused as the man who committed the charges against him." The position of the defense was that it did not, and Chaucy proceeded to point out where the prosecution had failed. "There has been no definite proof that the defendant ever planned or participated in any of the crimes he is alleged to have committed. It has only proved that he was a subordinate of the man who did commit these crimes. The prosecution wants to hang him for the deeds of his superior officer, a fanatic who defied his superior officers for years, and his subordinate was no more able to stop him from his mad plans than it is possible for a boy to stop a charging bull."

After a profound silence in the courtroom, Chestnutt rose and briefly claimed the prosecution had proved beyond any reasonable doubt that the defendant was guilty of all charges and it would be a grave injustice if he didn't finish his life at the end of a rope.

The Commission adjourned at 1600 hours.

The next morning the president called the Commission to order. "The court interpreter will interpret to the accused as I make announcement of the decision." He cleared his throat. "Shogo Toda, the

Commission in closed session, and upon secret written ballots, two thirds of the members present, finds you: of specification 1 of the Charge: Guilty." This was for involvement in the Chinese murders in Singapore. He was also found guilty of specifications 2, 3, and 4— atrocities committed during the Death March, the murder of Chief Justice Santos, and the murders in Burma.

There was stillness throughout the room.

"The Commission," said the president solemnly, "sentences you to be hanged by the neck until dead."

There was not a sound from the Toda family, but Chaucy could feel their grief. A note was passed to her from Shogo. She stood up and in a shaky voice said, "Mr. President, the accused has an unusual request."

"Yes?"

"He wishes to say a few last words."

"This *is* most unusual. But this has been an unusual case. Shogo Toda, you may proceed."

"Mr. President," said Shogo in English, "I would like to thank the Commission for giving me an honorable trial."

The sincere thanks of the Todas for all she had done were bitter to Chaucy. She had failed and there was no excuse.

McGlynn put an arm around her shoulder. "It was inevitable, my dear," he said. "What you must now do is get a retrial, and then I'll show you how to bring young Shogo to his senses."

She hugged him. Holding back tears, she clenched her jaw. "You can be damned sure I'll get that retrial!"

Chapter Sixteen

1.

Tokyo-Yokohama, January 21, 1947.

"We must not give up hope!" This exhortation from Chaucy the day after the trial had a greater effect on the Toda family than on herself. But she hid her concern as she explained that every Class B case was automatically sent to the Review Branch of the Eighth Army which would diligently examine the transcript and the exhibits.

"We are hoping to find enough fresh evidence that will enable us to get a new trial. So far we have located one promising lead but nothing solid enough, I'm afraid, to convince the Eighth Army judge advocate to give us a new trial. But there is still hope! You are allowed to send letters to either MacArthur or General Eichelberger, Commander of the Eighth Army, or both, petitioning clemency. I suggest you urge your friends to send hundreds of petitions."

Chaucy said this even though she had no faith at all in the efficacy of letters from family and friends who were already convinced the accused could never have committed a wrong. But it would keep them busy. The Todas knew all about the petitions after the famous case of the renowned Japanese doctor who was charged with murdering an American patient. More than forty thousand letters, some containing the signatures of hundreds, had engulfed the two generals—all to no avail.

While the Todas took to their task with vigor and faith in God's mercy, Will and Chaucy pored over the transcript looking for possible flaws in the prosecution. Nothing could be found that could conclusively prove the sentence was excessive. Shogo had damned himself by his own silence.

While Chaucy and Will were checking records in an attempt to find Iwata, the Todas were industriously gathering petitions, many from prominent friends. All testified to Shogo's fine background and his good records in school. Christian ministers testified that he was gentle and sincere by nature and could never have committed such violent crimes. Examples of his character from the age of six were listed. Many pointed to his unblemished military record and asserted that if anything wrong had been done it was by the infamous Colonel Tsuji. Many told of the fine family he came from, of their service to people in distress, of their contributions to the public welfare. Even Sumiko's high grades in school were mentioned, as well as her winning of the prestigious English Composition Contest. The amount and quality of the petitions were impressive but Chaucy felt obliged to warn the family that the only realistic hope would be for a new trial. Never had she faced a more difficult task, and she blamed herself for not having prepared the defense properly. But the family thanked her for all she was doing. This only made her feel more guilty. While brooding in her room that night—it was the second day of February—she was startled by an exciting knocking at the door. It was Will. "I found him!" he said excitedly.

"Iwata?" She felt gooseflesh.

"Yes! He's living in Meguro!" This was a section of Tokyo. "He's willing to see us tomorrow night."

In her joy Chaucy hugged Will. What a wonderful friend he had turned out to be! How could she ever have thought he was narrow-minded and stuffy? In the morning she phoned Mark that she couldn't spend the evening with him. She and Will had to go to Meguro. This was the third date she'd broken in the past few weeks and he was piqued. "Whose girl are you anyway?" He meant it to sound like a joke but she knew he was upset. And this riled her.

"I'm my own girl," she said.

He quickly apologized and both of them tried in vain to make little of the matter. As she hung up she wondered why he was acting so damned jealous. Will was just a very good friend who was helping her out of a mess.

Iwata was living with relatives. His wife and child had died in one of the firebombings. He was a tall thin man who looked more like a monk than an army officer. Having recently arrived from China he was still shocked at finding his homeland in ruins.

"What can I do to help?" he said and told in detail how he had saved Roxas. "When I went up to Manila to see General Homma he was out of the office. His chief of staff could not believe General Homma ever ordered such an execution. They started an investigation and learned that two staff officers had stamped the orders with Homma's name."

"Why?" asked Chaucy.

"Because of Tsuji, of course."

"How can you be sure?"

"One of the guilty staff officers, General Hagashi, rushed at me and tried to hit me. He shouted, 'Tsuji-kun will see that you get paid for this!' A few months later I got to meet Tsuji when he was sent to Mindanao with two aides to help plan the coming attack on New Guinea."

"Was one of the aides Captain Toda?" asked Chaucy.

"One was a major, the other a young captain. His name could have been Toda. I was interested in him because I heard he was a Christian. I'm a Catholic, you know."

"That must be Shogo," said Will and described him.

"When I heard he also was a Christian I invited him to my quarters for a cold drink while Tsuji-kun and the major were conferring with General Futami."

"Did this captain tell you about his family?" asked Chaucy.

"I believe he did mention that his father was in China running an ore mine."

"That *was* Shogo Toda!" she said. "What did he have to do with the orders to execute Roxas?"

"He was just an innocent fool! While we were having our cold drink I told him how Tsuji had tried to get Roxas executed and was probably going after Roxas again since he was still in prison. I told Toda, 'Do what you can. As a Christian.' He said he was no longer a Christian and what I'd just said was treasonous. Colonel Tsuji could never do anything so dishonorable. I could see he really believed that and thought I was for sure a dead man. He called me a stupid fool. But the strange thing was, he never reported me."

"Will you testify to this in court?"

"Of course." As Will and Chaucy rose to leave he said, "Would you like to hear how I ran into Tsuji in Nanking recently?"

Chaucy pulled out her notebook.

"While I was getting my release papers at the generalissimo's head-quarters, I saw him walking out of a conference room followed by two Japanese intelligence officers I knew. They told me that after the surrender Tsuji had fled Bangkok in the saffron robes of a Buddhist priest and had just written a long paper for Chiang on how World War Three was going to start and how it would be carried out. They said he was depressed because he'd just gotten a letter from his wife saying that most of his old comrades were cursing him as a coward for letting others pay for the crimes he had committed. She told him, 'Please die in such a manner that the children will not be ashamed of you.'"

In the morning Chaucy read her notes of the Iwata meeting to Shogo. He bowed his head when he heard that many of Tsuji's colleagues now considered him a coward for escaping as a Buddhist priest and allowing innocent men like Okamura to be sentenced for his crimes. Shogo now realized he'd been hiding the truth from himself. It was like a curtain rising before him. For years his life had revolved around his idol. Now it was all so obvious: Tsuji had *never* acted like a true samurai!

"Do you want to be hanged for a man like that?" said Chaucy. "I know we can get you a new trial with our new evidence. But we will certainly lose it again unless you tell all the truth."

He raised his head. Tears were slowly rolling down his cheeks. He brushed them away angrily. His jaw stiffened. "I will," he said.

She shook his hand. "Now we have a chance."

As she was leaving he said, "Will you tell Major McGlynn that I *was* the one who picked him up on the Death March?"

2.

The new trial began a week later in the same room where Shogo had been convicted. The president was Colonel Pearson, who had presided at the Camp 13 trial. Will was pleased at this but Chaucy groaned. "That condescending relic of the Old South! He called me Miss Chaucy as if I were someone out of *Gone With the Wind.*"

The Chief Prosecutor was again "Hanging Harry," Lieutenant Colonel Chestnutt. Again his opening statement, delivered in his deep booming voice, was short and impressive, ending with the assurance that the defense's new material would prove flimsy. Moreover, he himself would offer some new evidence, so convincing that he had no doubts the first judgment would be upheld.

Chaucy's first witness, to the surprise of Chestnutt, was Will. He told how Shogo had saved his life on the Bataan Death March.

"Why wasn't this evidence presented during the first trial?" asked the prosecutor.

"At the time I was not sure this was not a hallucination," said Will. "And Captain Toda would not confirm he was the man who saved me."

"And now he does say he was the one?"

"Yes, sir."

"How convenient!" said Chestnutt sarcastically. "And what is the defendant's explanation for this miraculous change of heart?"

"It would have appeared like boasting," said Toda in Japanese, adding that during the first trial he felt compelled to say nothing harmful to his former commanding officer.

"How interesting. And now you are ready to tell all?"

"Yes, sir."

"In that case, Mr. President," said Chestnutt, "I object! He is changing his testimony!"

"This is not a civil court," said the president calmly. "We are much more lenient. Our major objective is to find the truth, and to administer justice. You may proceed, Miss Snow."

"Mr. President," said Chaucy, "I would now like to present further proof that my client did indeed save Major McGlynn." Father Thomas O'Malley, a Maryknoll priest presently stationed in northern Honshu, took the stand. He testified that on the third or fourth day of the Death March a Japanese officer brought an unconscious American officer into a rest area in San Fernando. "He refused to leave until I promised to take care of the American."

"Who was the American officer, Father?" asked Chaucy.

"Major McGlynn."

"And who was the Japanese officer?"

"I believe he is that man." He pointed to Shogo.

"You only believe!" cut in Chestnutt. "Must we continue with this?"

"Would you please let Miss Snow present her own case?" said Colonel Pearson.

"Thank you, Colonel," said Chaucy, pleased she was no longer Miss Chaucy. "Mr. President, would you allow me to question my client at this time?"

"As you know, Miss Snow," said Colonel Pearson, "we run things more liberally than up in Tokyo. We want the facts so please proceed."

"Mr. Toda, do you recognize Father O'Malley?" He did. "Will you please tell the court what you told Father O'Malley that day?"

"I object—" started Chestnutt.

"Not yet," said the president calmly.

Shogo spoke in English. "I told him to take care of Major McGlynn —I think he was a captain then. The father then asked me why a Japanese officer was treating an enemy like this. And I said, 'Because I know him from childhood, and I was brought up as a Christian.'"

"Now I'm sure he's the man!" exclaimed Father O'Malley. "I'll never forget those words."

"I object!" Chestnutt's face was red. "This is getting out of hand, Mr. President!"

"Mr. Prosecutor, please bear with the ways of a country boy from Georgia."

Maggie punched her father in the ribs. "There's one for our side!" she whispered, and then grinned at the Todas who were not quite sure what was going on.

In the afternoon Iwata took the stand. After he told of saving Roxas, Chaucy presented a statement of confirmation from President Roxas. Iwata then told how he had later met Toda. "I heard that Tsuji-kun was going to try again to execute Roxas and begged Captain Toda to do what he could. I had been told he was a Christian. He could not believe his commander could do anything so dishonorable and called me a traitor. I expected to be arrested but he never reported me."

During the cross-examination Chestnutt belittled the story. "Mr. President, how can anyone take this muddled story seriously? What does it prove except that Toda so revered his chief that he covered up the whole matter? If he had turned in Iwata that would have opened up a can of worms. My esteemed colleague, Miss Snow, has gone to great pains to prove that Tsuji had to connive secretly to carry out his grisly murders. That was why his trusted confederate, Toda, did not turn in Iwata. I welcome Iwata's revelations. They support the prosecution's charge that Toda was a willing tool of the infamous Tsuji."

After the adjournment, Chaucy assured the Toda family that there was a good chance Shogo would be acquitted. "You all look as if we were losing. When you go back into court tomorrow I want you all to look confident. You've got to keep up Shogo's spirits." But when she was alone with Will she admitted that Chestnutt had made an impression on several of the judges. "I think it's going to be decided tomorrow when Chestnutt introduces his new evidence. I found out that he has two Korean laborers who claim they saw Shogo cut out the livers of the Allied airmen. They're either lying or mistaken and we have to prove one or the other."

The courthouse was jammed an hour before the trial was to resume. Only two Japanese correspondents and Maggie had covered the first day but word had gone out that there was an even more dramatic charge to come—Cannibalism!—and the foreign press corps was out in force. As the judges took their places a dozen flash bulbs went off. There was another series of flashes as court was called to order.

"We are very pleased to find so many ladies and gentlemen of the Fourth Estate here today," said the president affably. "It is very rare that we outdraw the Big Show up in Tokyo. But I must ask you photographers to restrain your enthusiasm until a recess. We're not used to such excitement. The popping of bulbs is distracting to those of us trying this difficult case."

Like an actor playing to a full house, the pudgy Chestnutt slowly and effectively took center stage. A flash bulb exploded.

"Another such incident," said Pearson crisply, "and I shall clear the court of the press!"

Chestnutt surveyed the judges and then said ominously, "The most horrendous of all the unspeakable crimes committed by that arch criminal Colonel Masanobu Tsuji and his cohorts was the cold-blooded murder of seven captured Allied aviators in Burma in 1944." He paused. "Followed by the"—he again paused as if having difficulty to proceed—"by the cutting out of the livers of our brave airmen and eating them!" He shuddered. "Cannibalism in the twentieth century!" He turned and pointed at Shogo. "And we are going to prove conclusively that the defendant Toda was not merely a witness of these events but actively participated—I say *participated*—in those acts." He again turned toward Shogo. "This man has been described by the defense as a noble, self-sacrificing man. Yes, so noble was this pleasant fellow that he not only could eat human liver but boast about it. I now call my first witness."

A small, wiry middle-aged Korean, Muk Hun, was sworn in. His dark eyes glistened. In fluent English he testified that even though he had graduated from college, the Japanese Army had sent him in a labor force to Burma.

"Were you present when the Allied airmen were executed?"

"Yes, sir. As I remember there were about ten of them. An officer, a captain, ordered soldiers to bayonet them."

"Who was that officer?" asked Chestnutt.

His face transformed by hatred, Muk pointed at Shogo.

"Was there any mutilation of the bodies?"

"Yes, sir. This officer"—he again pointed at Shogo—"knelt and slit open the belly of one of the airmen. He cut out his liver. I heard him say, 'This makes good medicine.' Then he ordered the soldiers to cut out the other livers. One of the soldiers vomited and Toda-san laughed and said eating human liver made it possible to make love to a prostitute ten times in one night. Later we heard that the great officer named Tsuji fed these livers to young officers to restore their confidence after the great defeats at Imphal. But I didn't see that."

The second Korean, Kim Woon Heung, could speak no English. He was large, heavyset with a low forehead. Through an interpreter he confirmed everything Muk had said. Chaucy noticed that he kept looking anxiously toward Muk as if for encouragement. She guessed he was under Muk's influence and would be the more vulnerable to attack. In cross-examination she asked him if he was absolutely sure Shogo was the officer who had ordered the murders. He grunted in the affirmative but turned away from her piercing gaze. "How can you be sure?"

Kim began to sweat profusely and twitch restlessly. "Because I see him cut out the liver. I know his face and see he was a captain. You think I forget a man doing something like that?"

Chaucy was sure he was lying but decided to let him stew in his own juice. He would either get more nervous or think he was out of danger; and then she would suddenly attack him again. Instead she asked Shogo to take the stand. As he walked forward Chaucy noticed that Chestnutt was grinning confidently as if to throw her off.

"Colonel Chestnutt," she said calmly, "made a great point at the first trial of the defendant's reluctance to say anything that might involve his former commander, Colonel Tsuji. My esteemed opponent will then be pleased to know that Mr. Toda is now willing to talk freely."

Making no noise, Chestnutt slowly, sarcastically clapped his hands.

"This is not a play, Mr. Chief Prosecutor," said the president. "We are not amused."

"I apologize, Mr. President."

"Continue with the witness."

"Mr. Toda, do you recall being asked by the prosecutor if you *believed* about the eating of livers out there in Burma? And you refused to answer, only saying that you were not a judge? And when the president ordered you to answer you said you could not answer?"

"Yes."

"Will you answer now?"

"Yes. I knew the livers were eaten by some of our young officers."

"And do you know who ordered the execution of the captured Allied airmen and the cutting out of the livers?"

"Yes. It was Colonel Tsuji."

There was a stir in the courtroom but was instantly stilled by several raps of the president's gavel.

"Let me ask you this. Do you now believe Tsuji secretly ordered the massacre of five thousand innocent Chinese after the battle of Singapore?"

"Yes."

"And that he was responsible for the death of Chief Justice Santos?"

"Yes."

"And that he was the one principally responsible for the atrocities committed on the Bataan Death March?"

Shogo was pale. His throat was so dry he could not speak. The president noticed this and ordered the clerk to give him a glass of water. After a swallow Shogo cleared his throat and said hoarsely, "Yes."

"And now let me ask why you refused to say such things at the first trial."

"At that time," he said hoarsely, "I was not sure about the Death March or the Santos case. Since then from the information given me by Colonel Iwata and two other former comrades of Colonel Tsuji I have been forced to face the truth."

"That's enough for me," said Chestnutt, returning to his seat with a smug smirk.

"But you did know the truth about the Burma murders?" asked Chaucy in redirect.

"I did. And that was why I arranged to get transferred to Tokyo."

Chestnutt was so upset he pushed back his chair and with difficulty got to his feet. "I object, Mr. President."

"Why? I see nothing to object about."

"It is my right to cross-examine the witness!"

"The Court is not going to deny you that right, Colonel. Please be patient and let defense counsel finish." He nodded to Chaucy.

"Mr. Toda, if you knew about the liver incident before, why didn't you speak out?"

Shogo was sweating. "I felt it was not proper to give testimony against my superior officer. I felt it was not right. I . . . I thought Colonel Tsuji had gone mad in Burma. Yes, I had suspicions of this when he ate the liver in front of the newsmen just before we went into Guadalcanal. But I couldn't believe he was really serious. Then at Burma I knew what he had become."

For fifteen minutes Chestnutt sarcastically attacked Shogo's story. "How can any sensible, fair-minded person believe such a fantastic tale?" he concluded and sat down so energetically the president said in a kindly manner, "Please spare our furniture, Mr. Prosecutor. It's all we have."

The other judges laughed and this set off the entire room. Pearson lightly tapped his gavel. "All right. That will be enough. I asked for it." The mood had suddenly become light after the gruesome details of Burma, and Chaucy noticed that the two Korean witnesses were smiling and nudging each other. Chaucy quickly asked for permission to recall Muk. "I understand that you got your law degree at Tokyo University, and consider yourself an expert on the Japanese Army."

"That is true," said Muk.

"Is there any penalty for cannibalism in the Japanese Army?"

Muk pondered a moment. "I'm not sure but I don't think so. I never saw any reference to this in a law book. I doubt it was even considered a possibility." He was so confident he crossed his legs and leaned back insolently. "Do you have regulations about cannibalism in the American Army? Is that sort of thing common in your army?"

Chaucy wanted to punch him. "In our country cannibalism is universally regarded as repugnant, beyond the pale."

"Obviously the Japanese are different," said Muk, reveling in the spotlight. He acted so sure of himself that big Kim grinned, thinking this was the end of their ordeal. Noticing this, Chaucy immediately recalled Kim who stumbled to the stand, a look of dismay on his face.

"Now, Kim, I ask you for the last time, why are you so confident you know Toda was the guilty Japanese officer?"

"I told you before," he stammered. "Because I saw him as close as you."

"And that is why you testified you were absolutely sure that Toda was the man?" She saw Kim look hopefully toward Muk.

"Yes, I'm absolutely certain."

"Does 'absolutely' mean the same in Korean?" she asked the interpreter.

Chestnutt started to object but changed his mind.

"Yes," said the interpreter.

"Mr. Kim, do you know what 'perjury' means?"

"Objection!" exclaimed Chestnutt.

"Objection denied."

The interpreter spoke to Kim then said, "Yes, he knows."

"Mr. Kim, do you know the penalty of perjury in this court?"

"I object! This is an open threat!"

"Objection denied."

Sweat was pouring down Kim's brutish face.

"Mr. Kim, I repeat. Do you know the penalty for perjury?" The interpreter said he did. "And Mr. Kim, you know the definition of 'absolutely?'" Kim was wiping his low brow with a dirty handkerchief.

"He does," said the interpreter.

"Mr. Kim, I am not accusing you of lying, only asking if you really believe *beyond any shadow of doubt* that Mr. Toda is the officer you saw rip out the liver? *Beyond any shadow of doubt!*"

Kim's eyelids fluttered as he stammered a few words.

"What is the answer?" Chaucy asked the interpreter.

"He says that he is *almost* sure."

"Almost true," said Chaucy and recalled Muk.

This time Muk did not cockily cross his legs. He leaned forward clasping his hands tightly as if afraid they would betray something.

"Mr. Muk, I now ask you the same question. Are you sure beyond a shadow of doubt that the defendant is the guilty man?"

"Well, I . . ." he started.

"Come now, Mr. Muk, I asked a simple question and I am sure the court is as anxious as I am to hear what you have to say."

"Miss Snow is badgering the witness," complained Chestnutt even though he knew his objection would be denied.

"Answer the question," the president ordered Kim.

"I would have to say that I also am almost sure."

"I'm finished with the two witnesses," said Chaucy. Suddenly she felt drained of all energy and she walked back to her seat on rubbery legs.

Chestnutt had no more to say and after a long recess for lunch, Chestnutt opened his argument. By this time he had recovered his poise and he discussed the law and facts of the case expertly and persuasively. He made the most of the overwhelming mass of evidence used in the original trial, and then pointed out the inconsistencies in the Iwata testimony and the contradictions between Shogo's original testimony and that of the second trial. "Now," he said, "we hear the defendant declare he has seen the light. That Tsuji was not the hero he revered but a villain among villains. Now he disassociates himself from the man he previously praised to the skies. Which Toda can we believe? Or can we, indeed, believe in either Toda? The law requires only that we stick to the facts."

Chaucy was washed out, but she realized Chestnutt had done well and she must concentrate. As she went forward she noticed Will in the first row of spectators make a movement apparently to get her attention. He looked supremely confident, and she felt a sudden flow of energy.

"I also ask the Commission to stick to the facts," she began. "And what are they, for the most part, but implications and guilt by association? In the past two days the defense has tried to go beyond the facts into the character of the defendant. We have shown a man who dared show humanity to an enemy prisoner on the Bataan Death March. We have shown a man who had great respect, even reverence, for a commander he and other idealistic young Japanese officers regarded as their God of Operations. Unfortunately Mr. Toda had so much respect and reverence that he could not believe for many months the rumors and conjectures that Colonel Tsuji was also committing atrocious acts on the enemy. He refused to believe Colonel Iwata's charge that Tsuji had connived in the death of Justice Santos and the attempted execution of General Roxas. Yet even so he would not turn in a report on Iwata that would have meant death to Iwata. We have shown, I believe, that Shogo Toda was a noble man if a naïve one."

Chaucy then charged that the prosecution had a faulty concept of the chain of responsibility in the Japanese Army and that a huge bulk of the so-called documentation would have been thrown out of any civilian court. "I realize this is a military court but so is the Tribunal in Tokyo on which I am proud to be serving for the defense. Let me remind you of the noble words spoken by the chief prosecutor, Joseph Keenan, at the beginning of that trial. The war criminals, he said, were going to be given a fair trial according to the principles of American justice. It is too early now to say if that trial is a fair one or a trial that is only purveying victor's justice. Time only will tell." As Chaucy wiped her forehead, she could see that both the president and the law member were displeased.

"May it please the Commission," she continued, "to indulge me for a few more minutes. The trials here in Yokohama are just as important for the future of justice as the more widely publicized one in Tokyo. I ask you to look upon the defendant, Shogo Toda, not as an enemy but as a human being. This trial in particular should *not* be remembered as one of vengeance against a man who happened to admire many qualities of the actual perpetrator. Nor is he being tried by neutral judges. It's like a man being tried rightly or wrongly for rape, and finding the girl's father is the judge."

Chestnutt fumed and the law member indignantly rose to protest, but Colonel Pearson signaled him to desist. "Are we going to hang Shogo Toda only on affidavits and statements?" continued Chaucy. "The Japanese people are not on trial, the Japanese Army is not on trial, Colonel Tsuji is not on trial. This accused is on trial for crimes he did not commit. Has he really been proven guilty? I don't ask mercy for him. I ask only for justice. And I say, as Mr. Justice Jackson, the Chief Prosecutor at Nuremberg, is quoted as saying, 'We must never forget that the record on which we judge these defendants today is the record on which history will judge us tomorrow. To pass these defendants a poisoned chalice is to put it to our own lips as well.' There were no clean hands on either side in the savage war between America and Japan. Both sides were guilty of racism and cultural prejudice which still lie just below the surface." She paused, exhausted.

"If it has been proven that Toda was guilty, he should be punished firmly. But was he? That, gentlemen, is your decision. If you hang a man on affidavits and statements alone, it will be on your conscience. Thank you."

After a profound silence in the courtroom, Chestnutt rose and briefly claimed that the prosecution had proved beyond any reasonable doubt that the defendant was guilty of all charges and it would be a grave miscarriage of justice if he didn't hang. "We have been asked to believe the unbelievable!" he concluded. "To believe in the miraculous seeing-of-the-light by this despicable defendant. In all my experience in court I have never heard such a preposterous story!"

"The Commission," said the president, "will announce its decision in open court at ten hundred hours, Thursday February 13, 1947, provided a decision has been reached." He banged his gavel. "This Commission is adjourned."

Emi Toda was thrilled by Chaucy's summation, certain it meant freedom for her son. But Ko was worried. "It can go either way," Chaucy told them.

"Is there anything we can do?" said Ko.

"Pray."

In the morning Colonel Pearson called the Commission to order at exactly ten o'clock. "Shogo Toda," he said, reading from a paper, "this Commission in closed session, and upon secret written ballets, two thirds of the members being present, finds you: Of specification 1 of the charge: Not Guilty . . ."

Chaucy held her breath. This meant he was freed of charges on the Singapore murders. That was expected. The next charge would be the Death March.

The president cleared his throat. "Of specification 2 of the charge: Not Guilty . . ."

Now would come the charge on the execution of Justice Santos.

"Of specification 3 of the charge: Not Guilty."

Finally would come the charge in grave doubt—Burma.

"Of specification 4 of the charge: Not Guilty."

Flash bulbs exploded and reporters rushed up to interview Chaucy and Shogo. The Todas were stunned with happiness, hardly able to believe it was at last over.

Chaucy felt a surge of exaltation. Like Prometheus she had stolen fire from the gods. All the agony and frustration were gone. This was payment in full. She had become the successful rebel who had gone against the grain, against the blind laws of legal truisms. Now she knew why her father could never retire. Photographers were taking pictures of Colonel Chestnutt approaching Chaucy. She wondered if he was going to cry foul or be sarcastic. But he held out his plump hand. "Good work," he said with a crooked smile. "Guess you were just warming up for Ichigaya."

"No," she said simply. "Just trying to save an innocent man." Neither she nor Chestnutt, she concluded, would ever understand the other, but she appreciated his generous gesture. He had paid her the ultimate compliment: he had accepted her as an equal.

The Todas, with deep bows, profusely thanked Chaucy. She invited them to a celebration at the Imperial Hotel but Emi apologetically declined. The McGlynns and Chaucy celebrated until midnight, when the professor and Will excused themselves.

Mark and Chaucy had a last drink in her room. "My usual limit is one drink," she said. "But I don't feel a thing!" She was still glowing from her triumph.

What a lovely sight! thought Mark, and kissed her.

Her pent-up feelings for Mark burst, and she made no protest when he led her to the bed.

It was light when she wakened. She turned over to find Mark beside her. His face was as untroubled as a child's and she kissed his cheek. His eyes remained shut but he smiled and she felt a surge of affection that was as amazing as the fact that she felt no guilt or shame or even embarrassment for being in bed with a man. It all seemed natural.

Then she realized he was grinning at her. "Good morning, counselor," he said and kissed her lightly.

Here was a new situation and she didn't quite know what to do. Then to her own surprise she found herself saying, "It was wonderful."

He kissed her again, this time fervently, and the wonder of the previous night was repeated.

When Will arrived at Ichigaya that morning he found a message from the prosecutor of the Camp 13 Trial in Washington of Lieutenant Colonel Harry Abbot. The heart of his defense of Major Watanabe was affidavits from fifteen American POW's who were testifying against Abbot for collaboration with Billy the Kid. The prosecutor of that case had assured Will that Abbot would surely be found guilty. Will opened the envelope and read the contents. He paled.

"What's the matter?" asked a colleague.

"The son of a bitch was acquitted!" Down the drain went his best evidence to free Major Watanabe.

Although Will and Chaucy were on opposite sides in Tokyo, he had been unofficially helping her in Yokohama. That afternoon, to reciprocate, she went over every possible defense of Watanabe with him. "There's not a dog's chance," he said. But Chaucy remembered her father telling her, "If you can't win in court, win out of it. Try the Old Boys' network." Major Watanabe's wife and children had been killed in an air raid. But his in-laws, the Takamis, had shown keen interest in his trial. Chaucy persuaded Will to visit the Takami home. They went together.

Although half destroyed, it had obviously been the residence of influential people. Mrs. Takami was tall and stately. She had already been informed of the results of the Abbot trial but showed no distress.

"There is still hope—if your husband will help," said Will.

"He will do anything."

"Major Watanabe told me your husband was a major general during the war."

"Yes. He was on the general staff."

"Has he ever met General MacArthur?"

"I don't know. Why don't you ask him?"

General Takami—a tall, urbane man who wore civilian clothes like a uniform—entered the room. He was eager to do anything he could for his son-in-law. "He was really not cut out for the army, but I know no more honorable man. He could not have committed the atrocities he was charged with."

Will explained the necessity for a new approach. "Have you met General MacArthur?"

"No, unfortunately."

"How about General Eichelberger?"

"We became friendly after the first World War." Chaucy felt goose pimples. "He was with the American Expeditionary Forces in Siberia. We were both lieutenants and we've kept in touch throughout the years."

"Would you be willing to come to Yokohama and speak to General Eichelberger about your son-in-law?"

"Of course. But first I must know more about the case."

Will had prepared the major points of the trial and after studying them Takami thought a moment. "I can see you have complete faith in his integrity."

"I can assure you he did more for the prisoners than any Japanese officer I ever met." said Will. "But he could not control Billy the Kid and his goons." He told how Watanabe had saved his life at the risk of his own.

"My son-in-law is fortunate to have your help."

"He is not fortunate until we get him acquitted, sir."

Takami stood up. "Let me study these papers."

"We don't have much time, sir."

"Then I'd be grateful if you would set up an appointment for next week."

Despite his busy schedule, General Eichelberger readily agreed to see his old friend from the Russo-Japanese War. General Takami entered Eichelberger's office with a briefcase of documents and they were closeted together for an hour. Chaucy and Will were waiting outside the office, she apparently at complete ease and he nervously trying to read a magazine, but getting up every few minutes to stretch his legs. He was convinced that this kind of approach was not only useless but somewhat demeaning, while she was not nearly as confident as she let on. At last the door opened. Eichelberger was escorting his old friend into the anteroom, arm around his shoulder. Will could not read any message on Takami's face which was as composed as a Buddhist priest's. Eichelberger shook hands with both Will and Chaucy, and thanked them for their services at the trials both in Tokyo and Yokohama.

Not until they were outside did Takami say a word or show any emotion. Then he grasped Will's hand. "How can the Takami and Watanabe families ever thank you enough! My son-in-law will be forever in your debt."

"Did General Eichelberger reduce the sentence?" asked Will.

"No," said the general. He paused to control his emotions. "My son-in-law was acquitted."

Chapter Seventeen

1.

Tokyo, January 1947.

Newcomers to Tokyo arriving at night during the first weeks of the new year could see little physical war damage, and some of them at first glance assumed that earlier reports had been grossly exaggerated. The Japanese had rebuilt so industriously that there were few remaining signs of destruction. Many of the streets had been given American names such as Avenue B or Sycamore Street, but some of the main arteries had two names such as "12th Street—Hashimoto Avenue." And still to be treasured were incongruous Japanese shop signs: "Curious Antics" (Curios and Antiques), "Pearls, Curios and Fresh Fish," "Off Limits—Venereal Disease—Welcome Foreign Traders." There was "Curb Service for Shrimps," "Forgive and Forget, Swan Radio Company," and "Doctor of Births and Skin."

Tokyo, like the phoenix, was rising from her ashes, and in the light of day the ashes *were* clearly visible to the newcomers. Tons of refuse from the 740,000 buildings destroyed in air raids still lined the bomb-pocked streets, and the city in sunlight remained a monument to war. The newly arrived, stunned by such sights, were informed that city engineers were making elaborate plans for a modern metropolis. The new Tokyo, according to its chief planning engineer, would be one of the wonders of the world with glass-fronted buildings arranged in symmetrical patterns to admit light and fresh air, wide tree-lined streets, elevated sidewalks, and canals spanned by double-deck pedestrian bridges. "The city will have," he said, "seaside, hillside, and riverside resorts and ten Coney Islands."

Not waiting for the future, the Japanese union leaders were already imitating America by planning a general strike in late January. Under Communist leadership, the workers aimed to drive out the government of Prime Minister Yoshida and ultimately establish a "people's government" and revolution. Indirectly MacArthur recommended that the strike be called off; but the unions, emboldened by his acceptance of individual strikes in the past, refused.

Seven hours before the walkout, MacArthur issued a statement that such a strike would paralyze the nation and he would not "permit the use of so deadly a social weapon." A bill was introduced in the Diet to ban strikes by public employees, and the Communist newspaper, *Akahata,* was censored. There was no walkout.

The aborted strike had come at a time of severe food shortage and no sooner had MacArthur been condemned by American liberals for strikebreaking than he confused such critics by his humanity. He diverted to the Japanese large quantities of army food stockpiled in the Pacific. This angered economy-minded conservatives in the United States Congress who demanded an explanation. He replied that he had done so to prevent starvation, "and starvation breeds mass unrest, disorder and violence. Worse still, it renders a people easy prey to any ideology, however evil, which bears with it life-sustaining food." He also pointed out that under the responsibilities of victory the Japanese were now Allied prisoners. "As a consequence of ill treatment, including starvation, of Allied prisoners in Japanese hands, we have tried and executed many Japanese officers upon proof of responsibility. Yet can we justify such punitive action if we ourselves in reversed circumstance, but with hostilities at end, fail to provide food to sustain life among those Japanese people over whom we now stand guard within the narrow confines of their home islands?"

He further confounded his liberal critics during a visit that month to the Japanese Correspondents Club. He walked in unannounced at noon, sat down, and proclaimed he was ready to talk for the record. Taken aback, the newsmen fumbled for paper and pencils. To their amazement he said the Occupation had already accomplished the task of demobilizing the Japanese and bringing political reform. "The time is now approaching when we must talk peace with Japan."

"When?" asked someone.

"I will say as soon as possible. Prolonging this Occupation will only create a 'colonial' psychology. Within a few years Occupation personnel will begin to act like carpetbaggers. The Japanese are already getting restive."

Still another side of the general was shown late that afternoon when he was returning to his headquarters. As his car slowed down, he observed Aristides Lazarus on the sidewalk carrying a large bag of groceries in his right arm while holding his wife's arm with the other. Since civilian lawyers were paid more than those in the service, and as a civilian Lazarus could bring his wife to Japan, he had resigned his Marine commission. But he still wore his Marine uniform without insignia. A Marine at heart, he tried to salute and ended by bowing. Seeing his consternation MacArthur soberly saluted, then winked roguishly at Mary Lazarus.

"Artie," she said, "if that man ever runs for President, I'm voting for him."

Roger Baldwin, the founder of the American Civil Liberties Union and one of America's outstanding liberals, was another convert. After several long interviews with MacArthur, he returned to the U.S. with the zeal of a missionary. The general was engaged in a crusade for democracy, he wrote. "I know little of the general's past in relation to his understanding of democracy, but I do not hesitate to say that today he is one of the few men I have met in public life with an almost missionary spirit of promoting it. On every point we discussed I found him at once sensitive to the highest concepts of our democratic ideals. That covers not only political and social democracy but economic too —the issues of trade union rights, monopolies, or special privilige in any form."

Professor McGlynn did not share the euphoria felt in many Allied offices. He had just been informed by Maggie, returned from a junket around the country, that the food crisis was worse despite MacArthur's efforts. Many people were starving, she said, particularly in the large cities. The situation was so bad, she wrote in one article, that there were numerous unlawful claims in the emergency relief program. "In Tokyo alone investigators found 100,000 'ghosts' on the relief rolls. Multitudes were drawing rations for deceased relatives or Koreans and Chinese who had long since left the country. In Hyogo Prefecture during a three-month period, 2,571,028 days' rations were drawn by such 'ghosts.' The shocking thing to those Westerners who knew the old Japan was this un-Japanese disrespect for the law. What drove them to it was starvation. And that is the responsibility of their captors. For what is Japan today but a benign prison camp?"

Maggie's editor deleted the last two sentences but cut nothing out of companion articles on what she considered two of the most adverse products of occupation: prostitution and the black market. She described the historic Yoshiwara gay section—now, after firebombing, a rambling complex of shacks and stalls. In graphic detail she described its suburban competition, the vast *joro* house on the highway between Tokyo and Chiba. It looked like a large factory dormitory. Nicknamed "Willow Run" by the G.I.'s, it housed three thousand girls. Hundreds of cars and motorcycles were parked along the highway despite large signs lit up by spotlights reading "OFF LIMITS V.D."

But the professionals were only a part of the 15,000 *shogi,* the polite name for prostitutes, in the greater Tokyo area. The amateur competition caused numerous fights, particularly in Hibiya Park. The amateurs included college graduates, opera singers, ex-geishas, working girls without jobs and made-up, prettily kimonoed men.

Maggie told of the twenty-two girl employees fired for visiting rooms at night in a posh officers' billet in the Peers Club. The girls protested that they had only come to teach Japanese but the club manager reported the sounds he heard behind locked doors were not language lessons. Maggie wrote of another raid by M.P.'s at the Nomura Hotel, which housed 350 Allied civilian employees. They routed out more than a hundred girls who had set up housekeeping in the dormitories and another homeless hundred who were bunking in the lobby. Immorality, she discovered, was rampant on all levels. Little brothers would "lend" their sisters in exchange for candy bars, and some fathers thought a carton of cigarettes was a fair price for one night with a daughter. Then there was the fourteen-year-old pimp who not only had three teenage girls working for him but guided Americans to a special *shiro-kuro,* blue show, to see three pretty girls and Kobayashi, the "Number One Penis of Japan," demonstrate forty-eight Japanese positions.

She concluded with the sad story of a high school girl from a good family who plied her trade in the shadows of Ueno Station's railroad viaducts. She and others tried to keep their pride by sleeping in the park rather than in dingy rooms where other girls let a man stay all night. This girl never solicited anybody. She merely waited until a nice man made advances, and sometimes she would go for two days without a customer. "What can a girl do these days to earn a living?" she told Maggie. "No matter how often you round up the angels of the dark, even should the sands on the beach disappear you will find us here again. It makes me sad, for I am still young. But there is no use being despondent. For me there is a special wind that blows." She put on a brave smile and said goodbye. "I'd better regain my humor and start off for business under the girder bridge."

These articles were followed by a major one condemning the growing black market which was also corruptive but on a much larger scale. Operators, Maggie revealed, had spread from the street stalls to train aisles as speculators crowded onto cars equipped with rolls of hundred-yen notes and knapsacks loaded with illegal vegetables. These black marketeers would travel far out into the country to buy food cheap and sell it in the city at exorbitant prices. Shrewd farmers had caught on and were also bringing their wares to town. All of the city's railroad stations were jammed with people transporting loads of illegal food to the capital.

Many were part-time black marketeers. One man told Maggie that his salary as a clerk of 500 yen a month could not support his family, so he would take sick leave once a week and make a thousand yen a day. Other workers who commuted could more than double their salaries by bringing in a sack of country food for a quick sale at Ueno Station.

In her interviews with Japanese government officials she was told—off the record—that they had given up their futile attempts to end the black market but saw hope in the trend toward more successful crops. That would surely bring down food prices. These same officials also complained—again off the record—that the big-time profiteers were the Koreans and Chinese, since they had been given special privileges as neutrals. The Americans were not as well organized but were willing to dabble in buying or selling dollars. And almost every American, it seemed, thought there was no harm in making money from cigarettes, soap, or PX goods.

The victims of the black market were the Japanese people, who had been forced to sell their possessions to get enough food to supplement inadequate rations. The allotted rice rations, for instance, were getting smaller. And people still had to wait for days before the dealer hung out the sign announcing that some rice had arrived at last. And when this happened the queue would form so quickly that those living far from the store would have to wait hours, often to no avail. Even more unpredictable were the supplies of miso, cooking oil, and soy sauce. What did become available was often of poor quality, and sweet potatoes were spotted with rot.

She ended her article with the pathetic tale of her father's close friend, Judge Miyagi. Calling him Mr. Sato, she wrote that he was too honorable to buy anything on the black market, although he criticized none of his fellow men for doing so. He had grown thinner and thinner, his voice becoming so weak he could barely make himself understood by old friends. His stomach finally distended, to his shame, and the time at last came when he could not even eat the legal food prepared by his housekeeper. "He faded away," the housekeeper told Maggie.

All of Maggie's articles had pleased McGlynn but none more than the last. This one expressed his own indignation and sensibility to the sufferings of the Japanese. Mariko shared his feelings and her open admiration brought her closer to Maggie. The only subject about which Mariko and the professor disagreed was Mulrooney. McGlynn still felt she was taking the major's black-market operations too seriously. Wasn't he only doing what the majority of Americans in Tokyo were doing?

Nor was the problem of Taro any nearer a solution. It was getting increasingly difficult for McGlynn to hold his temper. He had done his best to be friendly to the boy, who was obviously bright and energetic, but instead of improving, Taro was becoming even more arrogant and insolent, and McGlynn feared he was falling under the influence of those radicals who were tired of obeying their leader's demand for a "lovable Communist Party."

2.

At the International Military Tribunal in Tokyo, the case for the prosecution finally ended at 4:10 P.M. on January 24. In the nine months the trial had lasted, more than four million words had been recorded. The prosecution had reduced to sworn testimony almost two decades of Far Eastern history, much previously published only as rumor by contemporary authors hampered by censorship.

One hundred and two witnesses had appeared in person. Another 1,200 witnesses had presented affidavits, and extracts from 1,100 documents were read. This great mass of testimony revealed only two secrets: first, that early in 1941 the Japanese had perfected shallow-running torpedoes necessary to cripple American battleships in Pearl Harbor; second, that four months beforehand, the Japanese Navy had rehearsed the attack under physical conditions simulating those at Pearl Harbor.

Three days later, on January 27, the defense in the person of David Smith, former Prime Minister Hirota's attorney, requested a mistrial on behalf of eleven defendants. Webb and Smith, a dedicated Mormon, had already clashed, and President Webb quite reasonably exclaimed, "I have never known of such a motion until now," and peremptorily refused their request. Generally a mistrial was declared because of some improper conduct such as jury tampering or disclosed bias.

Unabashed, Smith challenged the authority of MacArthur to create the Tribunal. After a response from Webb which Smith found not to the point, he asked for the opportunity to say something in reply.

"Be as brief as I was, Mr. Smith."

This irritated Smith. "If necessary," he retorted, "we intend to go to the federal courts in Washington and raise these matters all over again!"

"It is a matter of sheer indifference to us whether you go to the federal court in Washington or the federal court in Sidney or the federal court in Ottawa or the federal court in Moscow or any other court!"

The two men were like two dogs competing over territorial rights and Chaucy was apprehensive when Smith again challenged the authority of MacArthur to create the Tribunal. Webb bristled. "This," he said, "is not the floor of Congress or the floor of the Senate of the United States or any other parliament!"

It was no surprise when, after lengthy wrangling, both of Smith's motions were denied and Will afterward complained of the waste of two days on matters that should have been settled quickly and without rancor. Chaucy disagreed. "In a month it will be our turn. And during these last two days we've shown we're going to put up a tough fight and won't let Webb get away with anything. There's no doubt he's prejudiced and we're going to make it evident to judges like Pal. We must convince our clients that their American counsel are going to fight for them all down the line."

The length of the trial was concerning everyone. But some problems had already been solved. With the air-conditioning system in order there would be no need for long adjournments in the summer. And by now the translators and the interpreters both had gained valuable experience. The greatest difficulty for both groups was still the fundamental differences between the Japanese and English languages. In the former, exactness of expression was purposely avoided. A Japanese would say, for instance, "I arrived at the meeting *around* thirty-two minutes and forty-five seconds past three o'clock." The language was so subjective that a reader had to put himself in the shoes of the writer to follow his words. Perhaps the greatest difficulty was the weakness in the syntax of modifiers. There were no relative conjunctives and only slippery connectives, forcing the reader to puzzle out the proper positions in thought sequence. Often the reader felt as if he were being led blindfolded through a maze, and the translator found it necessary to think and express the same thoughts and ideas on two completely different planes of language psychology and construction.

There were additional technical difficulties. In Japanese there was no singular, no plural, no masculine, no feminine. Perhaps most puzzling to the Japanese was the English use of articles, which didn't exist for them. Another problem was the mixture of Chinese characters with Japanese letters in an unsystematic manner. Each character could be pronounced in more than a dozen ways and the trial had already been slowed by the difficulty of transcribing names and places into Roman letters.

The interpreters had an even more exacting and harrowing task. They had to strain to catch every word, and a cough or rustling of papers picked up by the sensitive microphones would often blur the reception. Some speakers talked in long, involved sentences, others with the rapidity of machine-gun fire. Webb was the easiest to follow. He spoke clearly, slowly, and in short sentences. Yet even he baffled interpreters by using so many legal phrases in Latin.

There were only nine interpreters, all Japanese. Most had American or English university education as well as Japanese government service and a background in journalism. This was a modest staff compared to three teams of twelve members each at Nuremberg. Those in Tokyo worked in teams of two with a monitor who controlled a red light to prevent any speaker from talking too long. Often in heated arguments, such as those between Webb and Smith, the red light would be ignored.

Another continual headache was the impossibility of determining whether a Japanese sentence was a statement or a question until the very end, since that was where the verb was placed. Unless the interpreter had a very retentive memory, he would botch the sentence and the proceedings would come to a halt.

Chaucy was deeply perturbed. She felt some of the rights of the defendants were being violated, including the appointment of defense counsel only *after* the prosecution had had the freedom to interrogate those under arrest. This, she complained to Will, put together the case against the defendants before they were advised of their rights. Such liberal views were not shared by some of her own colleagues, and she was pleased when Will, a prosecutor, agreed with her. Their relationship, starting in outright animosity, had grown from friendship and admiration into affection.

At the same time there were important concerns which she didn't feel free to discuss with Will. For example, since Japan surrendered on the basis of Potsdam, did the Allied Powers in substance violate the terms of the surrender document in the breadth of the Charter? Chaucy's colleagues on defense were so busy with their individual cases that she had not felt it was the time to bring up such matters for the common defense. Perhaps during the adjournment of three weeks for preparation of the defense counteroffensive she could get together with Kiyose, Blakeney, Lazarus and a few others.

Will also felt isolated from his colleagues. He was concerned by the prosecution's linkage of the military and civilians, as well as by Webb's peremptory treatment of defense counsel. Although he could not discuss such matters with Chaucy, he could not hide his concern. She tried to help him with general hints. "Eventually this mass of evidence is going to let one of us see and understand the case. It may be you and it may be me. Once a lawyer really understands the case, half the battle is over."

A few nights later the Japanese defense counsel invited their American colleagues to a dinner attended by Prince Takamatsu. During the long meal Kiyose and other Japanese rose to thank the Americans for their help. Chaucy, sitting near Smith, noticed that he ate and drank nothing. Finally a Japanese asked if the food was unpalatable.

How could he eat a bite, Smith replied, when millions of Japanese were starving? Then, after expressing optimism about the chances of the defense despite the political flavor of the trial, Smith complained loudly enough to be heard at the next table that in his opinion most of the prosecutors and all of the judges, including Webb, were second-rate.

Chaucy wrote her father what she had overheard. "I'm afraid poor Smith is heading for real trouble with Webb. Several of us have tried to cool him off but he is genuinely incensed at Webb's outspoken partiality. And Smith does have a valid point. So far the Australian seems to be running a one-man show. Webb appears to be the only member of the Tribunal who has anything to say in court. I can't recall any of the other judges saying a damned thing. It's clear to all of us, of course, that Pal of India, who has openly bowed several times to the prisoners in the dock, is sympathetic. And both Röling, the Dutchman, and Bernard, the Frenchman, do give off some objectivity. Everyone *is* convinced that the scowling Russian and the Filipino are going to say, 'Off with their heads!' But the rest of the judges just sit like statues. The Chinese, naturally, is inscrutable, and one can only guess what the American—little General Cramer, a very pleasant chap—is thinking. He has already been nicknamed the Dormouse for nodding off into dreamland. Webb makes a show of consulting with his fellow judges but why has he been the only one so far to speak out? I don't like it. Will doesn't talk about this but I know he also is concerned. He is showing a real grasp of this complex trial and I can now see why you were so anxious to get him into the firm. Belated congratulations."

3.

By general agreement Tojo's chief counsel, dauntless little Kiyose, was selected to make the opening address for the defense. Primarily prepared by Kiyose himself, his speech forthrightly declared that the war had been provoked by the Allies and was therefore a matter of self-defense.

Chaucy had argued that the civilian defendants, like former Prime Minister Hirota, might protest that there was no good war and no bad peace. But Kiyose was adamant, and when he was about to start reading his opening address on February 24, Chaucy was not at all surprised that there were several protests. Hirota, for one, refused to put his name to the address on the grounds that even a war in self-defense was unjustified, and that he himself was responsible for having failed to prevent hostilities with China. Shigemitsu, who had lost a leg in Shanghai, and three others also would not approve of the statement in its entirety.

After a recess during which Kiyose made a few corrections and deletions, Webb ordered him to read his statement. The defense, began Kiyose, would disprove each and every charge of criminality against the accused. Japan moreover invoked the right of self-defense in attacking Pearl Harbor since she was deprived of her "inalienable right to live" once America had applied economic sanctions against her. Kiyose claimed that the strike on Pearl Harbor was no surprise to America since she knew, "by conjecture," that an attack was imminent. For two days Kiyose, whose remarks were still not fully supported by all the defendants, presented the case for the defense.

He was eloquent and his arguments ably presented, but Chaucy feared that the dissension among the defendants was having an adverse effect on the judges. A few days later came another damaging blow to the defense when what she had feared became reality. Smith openly defied Webb during the examination of a witness by another defense counsel. To the astonishment of Chaucy he began berating Webb for "undue interference" with the witness, a Japanese newsman.

Webb, his face purpling, leaned across the bench. Pointing a finger at Smith he exclaimed loudly, "You will use respectful terms here, Mr. Smith! You will not speak of undue interference by the Tribunal. You will withdraw that or you will leave the court as counsel. And you will apologize."

Smith looked directly at Webb. "I would like to explain to the Tribunal. I have been trying cases for twenty years and using that language—"

Webb broke in. "You will withdraw that offensive expression 'undue interference by the Tribunal.' I will not listen to another word from you until you do!"

Smith refused to back down.

Webb's face was crimson. "I ask you again to withdraw the offensive expression 'undue interference by the Tribunal.'"

"Well," said Smith coolly, "I decline to do that, your honor."

"The court will recess to consider the position. We will recess for fifteen minutes."

During the recess Chaucy and the other defense counsel were trying to get Smith's attention. They all admired him for his spirit, but while some of them agreed that Webb was being vindictive, the fate of his own client was at stake. Smith was too busy making notes to listen to advice.

"Mr. Smith," said Webb when the trial resumed, "the Tribunal has decided to exclude Mr. Smith from all further proceedings before it until such time as full withdrawal of the remarks which the Tribunal considers offensive and apology for making them is tendered to the Tribunal by him."

Smith drew himself up with dignity. "May I say to your honor, most respectfully, I have no intention of changing my position and see no reason to change it." He collected a batch of documents, put them under an arm, and stalked out of the courtroom.

The expulsion of Smith was unsettling to the defense. It seemed obvious they would have trouble pressing their clients' causes forward with Webb so touchy. Moreover they needed more time to shore up their united case. And so Blakeney, speaking on behalf of the entire defense panel, told Webb that the defense urgently needed a week's recess to organize a complete case.

"Your application is received with profound regret and apprehension," said Webb, concerned about any further delay in a trial which had already taken almost a year.

Blakeney assured him that if the recess were granted the defense could continue without interruption until June, but then cautioned that this was a speculation and not a commitment. The defense, if necessary, could continue for another week but, he warned, a breakdown was inevitable.

Both Webb and the prosecution were distressed. After arguing against it the chief prosecutor said, "If there is a breakdown we feel that we cannot oppose the application for a recess. I am certain that we all—Tribunal, prosecution, and defense—view with alarm the length of the trial and the time consumed in the presentation of the case."

By the time court reconvened, Lady Webb had arrived from Australia. "I hope she soothes the savage breast," Chaucy remarked to Will, but he felt the president had been so severely stung by the obstinacy of Smith that the tension would grow even worse. In early April Webb became so annoyed with lengthy Japanese testimony that he threatened to completely revise procedure for examining witnesses if long, drawn-out answers were not cut down. He would, he warned, delete unnecessary testimony without hearing argument.

Later Will, cornered by an American reporter, explained that Japanese witnesses were by nature long-winded because of the profuse nature of their language. "How can a Japanese change his manner of speech overnight?" A Japanese was not intentionally avoiding direct answers. "It is only his trend of thought." He liked to bring out lengthy details to get to the heart of the matter.

Will tried to get away from the reporter but he followed tenaciously. "It's true," Will said, "that 'yes' and 'no' have equivalents in Japanese but they are seldom used by Japanese witnesses in court." Admittedly their language was cluttered with long-winded phrases that often skirted fact. "But they are not lying, only trying to consider all four sides of a question. Now, please excuse me."

A few days later another American defense counsel, Captain Brooks, protested that his client was not allowed to explain himself fully during cross-examination.

Webb's face flushed. "We are not going to allow this Court to be used for propaganda purposes!"

Brooks denied the charge.

"We are here to conduct a fair trial," exclaimed Webb, "and we are not going to be browbeaten by American counsel or any other counsel!"

Brooks apologized and the dispute ended. But the following week came an even livelier conflict. This time Webb's ire was directed at Lazarus, who had already tried his patience during the Russian phase of the prosecution case. The ex-Marine brought forth a vigorous objection from the prosecution by stating, "It will be shown that Japan had reasons to fear and in fact did fear that the spread of communism in China and then in Japan would mean Japan's destruction. The clinching evidence in support of Japan's rightful fear of the spread of communism is President Truman's address to the United States Congress last month on that subject and the desperate measures recommended to stop its spread."

Webb, angrier than the prosecution, rejected those two sentences and refused to listen to Lazarus's explanation of what they intended to prove. But Lazarus, like Smith, would not be silenced. The defense had had no opportunity to answer prosecution's objections, he said. "We will show," Lazarus continued despite Webb's obvious annoyance, "that a reasonable and proper fear of the spread of world communism existed during the Manchurian occupation, and we will introduce evidence showing that the Japanese Government was dominated by the fear of Russian aggression. President Truman said in his recent address exactly what these people said at that time, and therefore we want to introduce that statement."

Webb interrupted. "American counsel will not indulge in the tolerance of this court to engage in what might be termed enemy propaganda," he said and immediately recessed the court.

Once they returned, Lazarus demanded a definition of "enemy propaganda." "We never expected that the remarks of the President of the United States to the United States Congress would be called in this court enemy propaganda."

"That is utter nonsense that you are putting forth now! You are persistent in using the President's remarks as an attack on an Allied Power in a situation which is wholly different from the matters now before the court." All of Lazarus's previous barbed remarks came to Webb's mind. "We had earlier permitted you to attack the great United States of America where your attack revolved around issues now before the International Tribunal. We did not stop your attack on Great Britain, where it was relevant, but you appear to take great delight in insulting our Allied countries. That is how it appears to me. I am not going to take back a thing I said." He cold-eyed Lazarus. "Throughout all of this I remain a British judge and I will always be mindful of any gratuitous insults either to my country or to any Allied country represented on this court."

Chaucy hoped Lazarus would back off and not make the same mistake Smith had. To her relief—and that of Mary Lazarus who was saying to herself, "For God's sake, Artie, keep your mouth shut!"—the ex-Marine calmly replied that he took no delight in presenting an unfriendly aspect toward any ally, and he never thought of gratuitously insulting an ally. "I never forget that they fought on our side and that because of these Russian fighters I am today allowed to speak in this courtroom. I never forget that. As attorneys appointed by the

United States and requested by the Tribunal, we have a high duty to perform and we must present all evidence that is available."

There was no need, said the mollified Webb, of presenting the two offending sentences. "It looks bad. We accept your explanation and the incident is closed."

Chapter Eighteen

1.

Tokyo, June 1947.

The heat of early summer at Sugamo was made bearable by the cool breeze from the air conditioners. During the exercise periods the prisoners could walk freely and play Japanese checkers in the shade of the trees. They devoured the newspapers they were allowed to read, and the principal conversation was about the growing antagonism between America and Russia and the return of Keenan from still another trip to Washington. At a press conference he had revealed how authorities in charge of the Occupation had instructed him to complete the trial "as soon as compatible with a fair and just hearing."

Now that the defense case was under way, supervision at Sugamo was stricter. Cells were ransacked, tatami mats overturned. All shoelaces and belts were confiscated and families could only send in books. Before leaving for Ichigaya, and again after returning, all the accused were searched from navel to anus. There had been so many attempted suicides lately that lights in the cells were kept on all night. If anyone covered his face with a blanket he was awakened. Glass was also removed from the windows facing the corridor and replaced b wire netting.

The defendants had become so bored with prison life that th looked forward to the hearings. Though the windows of their were papered over, there were now so many rips in the paper they could catch glimpses of the passing scene. They were a lowed to converse en route without restrictions. Once in th room at the War Ministry, they were given American cigaret were occasionally allowed unguarded visits with their counse ily members. By now they regarded Colonel Kenworthy, the charge of the M.P. detachment, as a friend. He was strict b ous, and so considerate that the defendants now respectfully bowed their heads to him every morning.

On one cloudy June day they talked during exercise about a major general in the cell across from Tojo's who had started babbling incoherently. "Poor fellow," observed Tojo to Kido, and explained that the prosecutor had recently cross-examined this man at Ichigaya about his responsibility for atrocities committed by subordinates in Burma. "They pinned a piece of red paper on his cell," said Tojo. This meant he was a possible suicide. It was miserable, remarked Tojo, to see men who were brave on the battlefield go to pieces in prison. "I saw the most unusual thing at the last exercise period," he said. "There was Dr. Anami staring at a bunch of ants going in and out of a hole. He suddenly unbuttoned his fly and pissed on the anthill. I asked why he did such a mean thing and he said, 'Those ants have been dragging insects into their hole, and the insects are still writhing in death agony. I never saw anything so cruel. I had to show those ants how I felt about it.'"

"Isn't he the doctor on trial in Yokohama for poisoning fifty Allied prisoners?"

"That's the one."

During a break at Ichigaya, Will and Chaucy were mulling over the limitations of the Tribunal. "The Dickens character was right," she said. "The law is an ass."

"Maybe it's an ass but it's the difference between a barroom brawl and a debate. You can't measure justice with calipers."

"Well, it's certainly elastic in its rigidity. Our mutual friend Webb is a prime example of that. He's like the referee in a bloody heavyweight fight. Despite all the big words, we're running a criminal trial and that makes it deadly partisan—not a reasoned, scientific, polite contest of words and ideas." What most bothered her, she said, hoping to get Will to confide in her, were the conflicting interests of the Allies. "We Americans resent the positions taken by the British and the Dutch who assume that their interests in the Far East are entitled to be inviolate in perpetuity. How did they acquire these interests?"

"It all seemed clear-cut a year ago," said Will.

"I know exactly what you mean. In Massachusetts our courts understand the rigid burdens of defense in a conspiracy case. How many of us on defense have even tried a criminal conspiracy case in the United

States? I know *I* never have and I've had more experience in court than most of the others. And your Mr. Keenan. Maybe he hits the bottle too much, but he's been very cute in adapting the conspiracy theory to this case." She grimaced. "We're in for a real fight! And I'm beginning to get those 'preparation of the case' jitters!"

In recent weeks she had been seeking advice from Will's father on the Pearl Harbor phase of the defense. McGlynn had agreed to help if she promised not to quote him on his sources. They had several long sessions in her room at the Imperial Hotel going over the completed rough draft of his book, *On the Road to Pearl Harbor.* She promised not to use the names of any of the Japanese he had interviewed concerning the Liaison and Imperial Conferences. Nor would she reveal how much valuable material on these conferences had not been turned over to the defense. In fact, it was probable that even the prosecution didn't have access to documents he had uncovered through old friends. What was most valuable to her was his assessment of men like Tojo and Kido. Chaucy was shocked to learn, for instance, that when Tojo was unexpectedly made Prime Minister he had gone to Yasukuni Shrine and pledged he would henceforth think as a civilian, not as a soldier. He would scrupulously follow the wishes of the Emperor. That certainly explained the antagonism of some military men to Tojo that she had seen at Sugamo.

McGlynn told her it was clear from his new material, particularly the detailed notes on the Liaison and Imperial Conferences, that the Japanese had been negotiating with America honestly—if ineptly. And his conclusion was that the war had come about through mistakes made by both sides. There were no heroes or villains on either side. Roosevelt, with all his shortcomings, was a man of broad vision and humanity. The Emperor was a man of honor and peace. Tojo and the other militarists, caught up in a medieval system, were driven to aggression out of dedication to their country. Nor were Stimson and Hull the rascals pictured by many conservatives.

That, he concluded, was why he found the Tokyo trial so distasteful. "Yet it has to be. Imagine the shrieks of the people back home if we don't hang Tojo and a few others! In his own land Tojo is now a villain and few have pity for him. But in a hundred years I bet he'll be regarded with tolerance even in Tokyo. I'm looking forward to seeing him take the stand in his own defense. That should be a show to remember!"

Chaucy asked if he would be a witness for the defense.

"No. It would involve my special relationship with President Roosevelt."

"But were you a paid official at the time you were advising him?"

"Not even travel pay."

"I think executive privilege may only apply to conversations with a government official." Her eyes lit up. "You could refute the notion that there was a coherent, persistent conspiracy by the Japanese!"

"What about Will being on the prosecution?"

"I think he already has some doubts of his own. But in any case he'd be the last one to oppose your appearance." She could see a look of rascality on his face as if he savored the thought of upsetting so many apple carts.

But he shook his head. "I couldn't do it." Although MacArthur had no love for FDR, dead or alive, such testimony at the Tribunal could endanger SCAP if things went awry. And that would endanger McGlynn's own relationship with the Supreme Commander; furthermore, he had to stay in MacArthur's good graces and try to edge him toward a more pragmatic view of Red China. Only that could ease matters in Korea, the probable flashpoint of calamity in Asia.

2.

During recesses at Ichigaya, McGlynn would stand outside in the welcome green shade of the huge cryptomeria tree. He was now an almost daily visitor despite warnings from Colonel Mulrooney that his absence from the office was unfavorably noted by General Whitney. But the professor couldn't resist being on hand to see history made; besides, Webb's persistent clashes with both the feisty defense and the stubborn prosecution never failed to entertain him. They often reminded him of Shakespeare's blend of low comedy and high tragedy.

Colonel Rufus Bratton was called as a defense witness by Blakeney. Before the war "Togo" Bratton had served three terms in Japan and McGlynn knew him well. He was a heavyset, burly man with the face of a friendly bulldog. This fooled many of his colleagues into thinking he was not very bright. But he was scholar as well as soldier, and had not only studied Japanese history and customs but could both write and speak the language.

In the months before Pearl Harbor, Bratton had been chief of the Far Eastern Section of Army Intelligence. A colonel then, he had the same rank now, and McGlynn wondered what had happened to his career. At the moment he was deputy chief of counter-intelligence for MacArthur.

Blakeney asked him to examine defense document 2094 and state whether it was his affidavit.

"It is."

"Are the contents true and correct?"

"They are."

Immediately the obstinate prosecutor objected that the matters contained therein were immaterial and irrelevant to any issue in the case. "The fact that the United States might have correctly anticipated what was likely to occur is certainly no justification for the aggressive acts of these accused."

The professor leaned forward eagerly. Could they finally be revealing solid evidence of Roosevelt's foreknowledge of Pearl Harbor? And of why General Marshall had been so out of touch with events during the crucial last hours before the bombs fell?

"I feel," said Blakeney in his low-key but dramatic manner, "that this evidence can be established as relevant on several grounds. In my judgment it raises squarely one of the fundamental questions for decision by the Tribunal." In the middle of his argument, recess for lunch was called. McGlynn hurried from the balcony and reached Bratton just as he was being escorted out of the room. "Togo!"

The ruddy Bratton smiled broadly. "Frank! What are you doing here?"

"The same as you, working for SCAP. And we're both so unimportant we haven't met."

Bratton said he had been brought over after his testimony in 1946 at the Pearl Harbor congressional inquiry. They agreed to meet at the Dai Ichi Hotel for dinner.

During the afternoon session Blakeney continued his argument. "The testimony of Colonel Bratton will additionally provide evidence for the Tribunal on the point of whether the Japanese Embassy in Washington was given ample time by the Foreign Ministry for preparation and distribution of the final message. His testimony is clear that the message came in ample time to the War Department—that in fact the entirety of it, as well as the instruction when to deliver it, was in

327

the hands of the War Department four hours before the time set for delivery."

The majority of the court overruled the prosecution's objection and Bratton's affidavit was admitted; furthermore, the colonel testified that he had intercepted orders from Tokyo on December 3 to the Japanese Embassy to destroy codes and documents. "I sent one of my officers to the embassy and he reported that they were burning their papers in the backyard." He informed his chief first and then General Gerow, chief of the War Plans Division. "We both agreed that it meant at the least a break in diplomatic relations, and probably war."

After briefly relating his actions in Washington the night of December 6 and the morning of the 7th, Bratton was released, to the disappointment of McGlynn, without cross-examination.

During dinner Bratton was uneasy. But later in McGlynn's room, fortified by a tall drink, he spilled out a lengthy story of why he had never been promoted. "In the fall of 1941 we intercepted a message from Tokyo to Honolulu in the consular code." It was addressed to the consul general but was meant for a Japanese spy in Honolulu who was posing as a minor official. It instructed him to report about vessels in Pearl Harbor and divided its waters into five sub-areas.

He was to record all warships and carriers at anchor, tied up at wharves, buoys, and docks. "Both Colonel Sadtler—he was senior intelligence officer of S.I.S.—and I thought it important that it should be sent on to Pearl Harbor. But the brass said no and later both Sadtler and I had to pay for it. In my first report of what happened on the night of December 6 it was obvious I'd given both my chief and General Marshall sufficient warning that they should have been sleeping in their offices instead of remaining comfortable at home. I knew right away it probably meant the end of all chance of promotion." He finished his drink and poured himself another. "That's not all. In 1943 I was ordered to write a study on Japanese preparations for war from 1935 to Pearl Harbor. A friend of mine, Colonel Ivan Yeaton—you've probably met him, a Far East expert—looked over my shoulder while I was checking the study, which had been corrected. When Yeaton saw marginal notes and many lined-out words and phrases he said, 'Who dun it?' And I said, 'The Old Man himself.' Marshall had edited out all the parts damaging to himself and left the rest too vague to be considered as cause for immediate alarm over Japanese intentions. Ivan begged me, for my own protection, to photostat the entire volume and keep the evidence in a safe place. I did." He got up and paced the room. "You remember that because of the stink, they had to have Pearl Harbor investigations on both Army and Navy activities just before D-Day. I testified right after Marshall who said he had never seen the Japanese message on the night of December 6. I told the truth—that I left a copy of the message on Marshall's desk about 10:30 P.M. I was asked if I'd delivered the message personally. 'No,' I said, 'I very seldom delivered anything to him in person. I gave it to his secretary in a locked bag.' And you know who that secretary was? Colonel Bedell Smith! Who soon became a three-star general. I might as well have signed my own death warrant."

"Don't you think you're exaggerating . . . ?"

The bulldog face was anguished. "I wish I were." He took a long drink then gathered himself together again. "They shipped me off to Europe like they did 'Betty' Stark, Chief of Naval Operations, so we couldn't talk. I took Ivan's advice and brought copies of my report to Germany. After we took Berlin I was moved there as Chief of Intelligence of the district; and I put the papers in the office safe. Even so I felt I had nothing to worry about. Then that July I was on the Autobahn on the way to British Sector headquarters and this British car overtook me and flagged me down. Out stepped this Yank colonel. Said he was Clausen and had been selected by Stimson to make further inquiries into Pearl Harbor. When he asked me to go to Paris with him to get some important papers he'd left there, I knew I was in trouble. I went to a good friend, Bill Heimlich, head of Combat Intelligence, Fifteenth Army. I said I had to go with Clausen to Paris and—well, that I was afraid I'd never return. I told him what I've just told you and took my copies of the Marshall report out of the safe. I showed him the deletions of whole paragraphs with the initials G.C.M. on the side. If I didn't return, I asked him to hand-deliver the papers to my family." Bratton suddenly excused himself and went to the bathroom. It sounded to McGlynn, over the sound of a toilet flushing, as if Togo were vomiting. He came out a few minutes later, deathly pale.

"Are you going to use this?"

McGlynn explained he was writing a book on the subject. "But you can take my word I won't use anything that's not in the record."

"Do you think I can have another drink?"

McGlynn poured him a whiskey heavily watered.

"This fellow Clausen was as cocky as a four-star general, but he didn't pressure me in Paris. Just said that both Generals Smith and Gerow denied any knowledge at all of the message left on their desks on the night of December 6. We were at the Hotel Prince of Wales. He showed me some of the affidavits he had collected in his travels to the Pacific and Europe. When I saw those of Smith and Gerow refuting my testimony I knew they had me." He was silent a moment. "I didn't have the guts to hang tough, so I dictated an affidavit refuting myself." He bowed his head. "I said it represented a better recollection of those events than when I testified at the Army Pearl Harbor Board . . . I think the exact last words were, 'and is made after having my memory refreshed in several ways and respects.'" He struggled to his feet and again started to pace. "Don't get me wrong. Clausen didn't bully me. Hell, I outweighed him by more than fifty pounds. He was just doing his job. He made no threats and we parted with no hard words. I went back to Berlin, got my papers from Heimlich, and then waited for the other shoe to drop. It came when I was called to Washington last year to testify before the Joint Congressional Committee investigating Pearl Harbor. I'll never forget that day. I've never heard a shot fired in anger but I guess I felt like someone just ordered me to capture a machine-gun nest. When I walked into that room, passing all those unfriendly faces, I had under my arm an envelope filled with the photostats I'd brought from Berlin." He told how an associate general counsel began grilling him as if he'd committed a murder. "'Why had I changed my testimony in Paris?' he kept asking. I confess, Frank, I was really scared. I said something like, 'On this my memory begins to go bad on me. I can't say positively if I made any deliveries to those officers that night.' I said that after reading the affidavits of Smith and Gerow I was convinced I was wrong because they were men of honesty and integrity, and if they said I hadn't delivered the pouches to them that night, my memory must have been at fault." His face sagged. "I was ashamed of what I said the minute I opened my mouth. I remembered the brave words I'd said to Bill Heimlich when I left Berlin, 'I'm going to blow the roof off that inquiry!'" He went to the bathroom again and McGlynn could hear the water faucet. He came out wiping his face with a towel.

"The next day," he said, "it was Colonel Sadtler's turn to face the firing squad. At the Army Board he had testified that on December 5, 1941, he had told both Bedell Smith and Gerow that the 'Winds' execute message had come in. You know about that message, don't you Frank?" This was the controversial message from Tokyo to the Japanese Embassy in Washington which meant a break with America. Most of those who had previously testified they had seen the message later changed their testimony. "Well, Sadtler told the Army Board that he asked Smith and Gerow to authorize him to send a war warning to Hawaii but they refused. And the same thing that happened to me happened to Sadtler. Months later Clausen showed him affidavits from Smith and Gerow denying Sadtler's story. Gerow also denied ever seeing the 'Winds' message. Like me Sadtler then changed his testimony. But unlike me, he had the guts to tell the Joint Congressional Committee that he *had* told Gerow about the 'Winds' message and he had told Bedell Smith that the 'Winds' message was in, and that he *had* talked about it with Gerow. But Smith told him he didn't care to discuss the matter further. No need to add that he is still a colonel just as he was back in 1941 and just as I was." He struggled to his feet. "I've been talking too damned much. Maybe you think I should bring this up over at the Tribunal. No way! I'm indebted to MacArthur who's given me a good post, and if I blew off it could embarrass him." He put on his cap and started unsteadily for the door. "I've got a pretty good thing here and I'm keeping my mouth shut until I retire." He opened the door. "Thanks for letting me spill this all over you. I'm glad I got it off my chest."

McGlynn felt exhausted. What Bratton had told him would be dynamite in Chaucy's hands, but he had promised Bratton he'd keep quiet for the moment. Moreover, when the story did come out he wanted it to be in his book.

McGlynn was kept awake that night with thoughts of his new history. He'd have to confirm the Bratton story with Sadtler, Heimlich, and Yeaton. This, together with the official notes he'd found on the Japanese Liaison and Imperial Conferences in 1941, could set the record straight. Then his mind turned to Mariko. The situation with Taro was growing worse, and the strain was obviously telling on Mariko. And the more he kept assuring her that it would all work out if only they were patient, the more his own words lacked conviction. Moreover, he and Mariko were also still at odds over Colonel Mulrooney. Last night she had reiterated her warnings. The latest rumor, she said, was that the colonel had been involved with the enlisted men in their office who had been sent back to the States for dealing in black-market dollars. McGlynn himself suspected the rascal, and was tempted to speak about it to Mulrooney since he and his daughter still spent most of their weekends at Floss's orphanage—and perhaps Mariko was right in suspecting that Floss was falling for him. But the professor was reluctant to interfere in other people's business. So he assured himself, though it should have been obvious that the main reason he didn't speak up was reluctance to offend a friend.

At the Imperial Hotel, Chaucy was writing to her father for advice on the coming defense of Tojo which would be the climax—the obligatory scene—of this historic trial. "Both Will and I are getting enmeshed personally in these complex proceedings. We're on opposite sides but there is no real conflict. I'm not sure we should be doing this, but I can assure you my first and only concern is my client."

As she sealed the letter she wondered why she still hadn't written a word about Mark. Was she ashamed to admit she had fallen in love with a Marine? She knew her father had been hoping she'd settle down and start a family before she reached thirty. And it didn't take a mind reader to guess that he hoped Will would be the one. She was extremely fond of him—but only as a brother.

It was obvious that her father would be deeply concerned that she was having an affair, and that not a word of marriage had yet been mentioned either by her or Mark. Recently she had felt that he was about to ask her, and she had been relieved when he hadn't. For years she had put sex in the background. Her career was everything. But for the past months she had continually longed to be with Mark, even while feeling guilty that she was giving so much time and thought to him. Before meeting him she'd convinced herself that love was merely a disease like the mumps—once you got over it you were immune. Instead she was becoming more and more immersed. Never had she dreamed she could become so obsessed by another human being.

At Yokosuka Mark was awake in bed, thinking about Chaucy. Never had he felt so dependent on a woman. He had been on the point of asking her to marry him the last time they met. Yet something stopped him. Perhaps it was because she acted so damned superior about being a lawyer—as if just *anyone* could be a Marine! He was very proud of what she was doing, so why couldn't she be proud of his work?

3.

On the morning of August 30 all the unindicted Class A prisoners were escorted to the yard. While they were wondering why they alone had been brought outside an M.P. captain said, "Those whose names are read will return at once to their cells."

The prisoners stiffened. Were they to be indicted? Then the M.P. captain smiled. No, it meant release! Fifteen names were read out. As they left the yard, the lucky ones called out words of hope to those left behind.

On September 5, there was a stir of excitement throughout the courtroom when David Smith, the ardent Mormon who had refused to apologize to Webb and stormed out of the court, approached the lectern.

There was a hush.

"If your honors please," said Smith, "I would like to say most respectfully that Mr. Hirota has been without assistance of American counsel since March 5."

"A preliminary statement is required from you, Mr. Smith," said Webb.

"I should like to recall briefly my statement on March 5 before the Court rendered the decision and to repeat this statement as a purely preliminary matter."

"In a few words you could state the position as it should be," said Webb curtly.

"All I have to say, your honor, is that I profoundly regret the occasion which gave rise to the misunderstanding. I have since learned that certain language we use in American courts, while considered orthodox there, has a special significance in Australia."

"The entire Tribunal took that action, Mr. Smith," said Webb stiffly, "and the Australian member is only one member of the Tribunal."

It seemed to both Will and Chaucy that Smith was valiantly controlling himself. "Well, the important thing, your honor, is that Mr. Hirota shall have the benefit of counsel during his individual defense, whether it is me or some other counsel, and as I have stated to the Tribunal, I profoundly regret the occasion. I have also previously explained to your honor that I had no intention of offering any offense to the court, and this Tribunal is the first Tribunal I have ever been before, many times in twenty years, that has ever suggested that my attitude has been offensive."

Webb's next words were cold. "I think, Mr. Smith, although we are most anxious to hear you, you should make this application again on Monday morning, when we hope to have the *whole* Tribunal present."

Smith struggled with his temper. He was being forced to return and make another apology. "If your honor please, if I may be permitted to say this: I understand it was not necessary for me to repeat the formula which the court prescribed on March 5, and if I appeared at the lectern and expressed *profound* regret on this occasion that it would be sufficient to remedy the matter." Chaucy prayed he would stop and accept the humiliation, but he could not. "I do not intend to come back Monday morning, and—"

Webb interrupted sternly. "What you propose to say now to eight members I hope you will say to eleven members on Monday morning, if it is what I anticipate and hope it will be."

Smith was bitter. "Your honor, I am sorry to announce my withdrawal as counsel and ask your honor to see that Mr. Hirota has the assistance of an American counsel. I think the Court—"

"There is no need for you to say any more," said Webb, and ordered the testimony to continue.

It was sad watching Smith make his final exit. He had fought hard for his client, thought Chaucy, but could not humiliate himself further —as she or Will certainly would have done. Chaucy also felt sorry for Webb who seemed troubled by the ruckus. His temper was so frayed that the next day he again flared up, at another defense counsel who asked that "the truth and facts come out here right in front of the witness box and right in this courtroom."

At this Webb leveled a finger at the counsel. "Your conduct is most disorderly. You are not behaving like a lawyer today!" A little later the perturbed Webb assailed another defense counsel who charged that a prosecution objection was an insult to the U.S. Government.

"You cannot be allowed to proceed this way!" exclaimed Webb, who apparently took the charge personally. "The United States Government is prosecuting your client! We are not going to permit you to make an attack on this court!"

PART FOUR

As the trial continued down the alphabet toward the most important defendants, the battle between defense and prosecution grew even sharper. Webb was like a lion tamer in his attempt to keep some order among the tendentious Americans.

Whenever Mariko was able to attend she was constantly amazed to see American lawyers fighting each other so energetically. What a dramatic demonstration of democracy! She was even more amazed to learn from McGlynn that after one particularly aggressive session, the counsel on both sides enjoyed coffee together as if nothing untoward had happened.

At last it was the turn of Marquis Kido, the Emperor's chief adviser, one of the key characters in the trial, to defend himself. On the eve of his appearance McGlynn visited him at Sugamo. Was there anything he could do? he asked. But Kido needed nothing.

He assured McGlynn he had confidence in his senior defense counsel, Logan, who came from a prestigious New York City law firm. His specialty was admiralty law, but he was an experienced trial lawyer skilled in litigation. Kido's son, still in law school, was also important to his father's defense. He could explain and clarify to Logan, who knew little about Japan, the background of his father's diary. For months lawyers defending the military men had been urging Kido to make certain changes in the diary which they felt put their clients in the wrong light. But Kido had refused to delete anything in defense of the Emperor, nor would he even say anything that might possibly reflect on His Majesty.

McGlynn knew all this from previous talks with Kido. What concerned the professor was the probable two-pronged attack on the Privy Seal: one from the prosecution and the other from indignant fellow defendants who still despised him for turning over his private diary to the prosecution.

Kido did his best to reassure his old friend without revealing the details of his lawyers' strategy. His son and Logan had prepared a voluminous affidavit for the defense on the assumption that Arthur Comyns-Carr, the formidable chief British prosecutor, would be the cross-examiner.

Because Comyns-Carr had already demonstrated his great skill, it was a stunning surprise to McGlynn on the first day of cross-examination when Keenan strutted forward to take the Briton's place. Why the sudden change? Couldn't Keenan resist taking center stage at one of the most important phases of the trial?

From the beginning Will writhed to see Keenan's brow-beating questions adroitly turned aside by Logan. At one point Logan objected when Keenan introduced new evidence against a previous defendant in the form of a statement reported in the Japan *Times*. Kido flatly denied any knowledge of the statement but Keenan still insisted on introducing the newspaper as evidence. Unfair tactics! charged Logan. "It will make this case go on forever!" This wrangle forced a half-hour recess and took the steam out of Keenan's attack.

If Kido had an easy time on the stand that day because of Keenan's blunders, the Privy Seal's relief ended on the trip back to Sugamo. One general pointed at him. "There is no lying swine like this one!" he shouted. "We don't get angry when people say bad things about us soldiers. But what kind of a swine is this who shamelessly admits he connived for peace during the war?" A colonel joined in the attack. "Ordinarily a scoundrel like this would be choked to death. Too bad we can't do that now!" Kido ignored his tormentors by burying his head in a newspaper.

A few days later Judge Webb set off a storm of protest from the defense when he announced that he was leaving in a few days for the November sittings of the High Court of Australia. The defense cried foul. It was the right of the defendants to have the president of the Tribunal present at all times! If he couldn't remain throughout the proceedings then the defendants shouldn't have to stay in court either. If Webb left, it would be a reflection upon the dignity of the court and the importance of both the proceedings and the loyalty of the Supreme Commander! The argument raged on with a defense counsel finally exclaiming that Webb should either adjourn the court until his return or resign and request MacArthur to name a new president. "Either that or dismiss the case so we can all go back to our countries!"

But the harassed Webb would not bow. He set off for Australia leaving behind him a defense enheartened by their united show of defiance to the chief justice.

Webb did return in December just before the crucial appearance of Foreign Minister Shigenori Togo, who had stoutly opposed the military during the critical pre-Pearl Harbor Liaison Conferences. Many Americans confused Togo with Tojo because of the similarity of their names. To Japanese this was a mystery since "Togo" was pronounced approximately "Tohngo." In Japanese the sound of *g*, except when the first letter of a word, was somewhat similar to *ng*.

Togo was detested as heartily as Kido. Thoughtful, straightforward, he talked in a heavy, measured Kyushu accent that was harsh to Tokyo ears. An experienced and competent career diplomat, he had a rare understanding of European ways which disturbed his own family who were scandalized when he married a German. He was something of a puzzle to many of his colleagues, for unlike most diplomats and most Japanese, he said what he meant with a bluntness that was mistaken for rudeness. During the trying negotiations with America he had done his best to bring peace, and in doing so was a constant irritant to the military—but not to Tojo who had "become a civilian" once he was selected as prime minister.

In his direct testimony Shigenori Togo told of his opposition to militarism and how he had worked with others in the Foreign Ministry for settlements with China and later with America. During the war, he testified, he had disagreed with Prime Minister Tojo regarding the Greater Southeast Asia Ministry and was finally asked to resign. "But I refused, saying it was the premier and the other supporters of the plan, not I, who should reconsider the matter." But when his plan for compromise was turned down, he voluntarily resigned "out of a desire not to cause annoyance to the Emperor by further complicating the matter."

Foreign Minister Togo then testified that Admiral Nagano had revealed there was to be an attack on Pearl Harbor. And after that another admiral, Ito, had requested that the negotiations be left unterminated.

"And did these conversations take place at a Liaison Conference?" asked the American defense lawyer, Brannon, who represented Admiral Shimada.

"Of course, yes."

"Mr. Togo," said Brannon, "Admiral Shimada came before this Tribunal and said these words: 'Not long before his death Admiral Nagano and I were told of this contention and we jointly questioned every one of the accused who attended the Liaison Conferences, including General Tojo, Suzuki, Kaya, Hoshino, Oka, and Muto.' None of them, Mr. Togo, remembered such a thing occuring."

McGlynn was taking notes frantically. He had seen detailed notes of the Liaison Conferences and he knew Togo was right. But the minor official who had shown them to him had made him promise never to use the material until after his death.

"Are you prepared to say that these men are actually lying now?" asked Brannon.

"Well, I do not have much confidence in the memory of these men," said Togo in his ponderous way. "Why? Oh, I have a number of examples or illustrations and I give you one of them. I entered Sugamo Prison in May of last year. I entered the prison later than the others because of sickness. At the time I entered the prison the men whose names you have just mentioned had all forgotten the fact that an Imperial Conference had been held on the fifth of November, 1941. And it was only after I told them of this fact that these men for the first time recalled it in their minds. In view of the fact that they are so forgetful of such a highly important conference, it is possible that they would forget some other things that are unfavorable to them."

Will could see Admiral Shimada leaning over to poke another admiral, then furiously write something. It was a note to his Japanese counsel: "Let me take the stand again." Other defendants were also showing emotion.

Brannon asked Togo to elaborate but not to quote the words of Nagano since he was dead. This brought Keenan to his feet. "Mr. President, we respectfully object to the restriction of this witness's answer. This accused's counsel has asked for it and he ought to receive the full truth under oath as this witness purports to see it at this time. The question invites a broad answer."

"It is often said, Mr. President," retorted Brannon, "that where death has sealed the lips of one person the law has sealed the lips of another, but I will withdraw that restriction and allow him to proceed with the answer."

Togo now revealed that the preceding May, after lunch at Ichigaya, Shimada had proposed a talk with Nagano and himself. "At that time Shimada expressed the desire that I not say anything about the fact that the Navy desired to carry out the surprise attack."

Will saw Shimada about to rise from his seat but someone restrained him. Chaucy wrote a note to Kiyose suggesting they have an emergency meeting of all the defense.

During all this Togo doggedly continued his testimony. "Nagano also made something of a threat, saying that if I made such a remark, it would not be worth my while. He then told me, 'Even if I might have said so, the Foreign Minister need not have adopted my proposition,' to which I explained to Nagano that the situation was not so. At Sugamo Prison, about ten days before the death of Admiral Nagano he remarked to me that he was going to bear the full responsibility for the surprise attack on Pearl Harbor." Togo paused. "There were other occasions, outside of these conversations at Sugamo Prison, in which the Navy side requested me not to speak of the Navy's desire for conducting a surprise attack."

"Do I understand you now to say that Admiral Shimada and Admiral Nagano confessed privately to you that they wanted an attack on the United States without notice, but they wanted to tell a different story before this Tribunal? Is that the effect of it?"

"Well, the conversations which took place among us did not put any restrictions as to where they would not want me . . . that is, where they desired that I would not speak of the matter, but I should think that the Tribunal was included."

Brannon took a new tack. "Did you ever advise members of the Liaison Conference, as Foreign Minister at that time, that hostilities commenced by Japan one hour after giving notice would be in compliance with international law?"

"I advised the members to take the customary procedure, but there was no opportunity to discuss such a question as just suggested by you."

After lunch Brannon asked Foreign Minister Togo if he thought the Americans would be informed of the attack at least an hour before it came. "Legally speaking," he replied, "it is a very clear fact that a one-minute notice would be sufficient. However, from the standpoint of international good faith, and to be in accord with the spirit of treaties, I thought it would be proper to avoid surprise—to avoid a surprise attack." A one-hour allowance would be sufficient warning. "Admiral Nagano at first entertained a different opinion from mine but afterward he agreed to sending the notification prior to the opening of hostilities." Nagano had then suggested that the notification, being such an important one, should be hand-delivered to Secretary of State Hull.

"And I charge, Mr. Togo," challenged Brannon, "that it is highly inconsistent for you to say that Admiral Nagano was this precise about international law one time and a few days before had wanted to ignore it entirely. Does that seem consistent to you now?"

"I do not think there is any inconsistency at all. Delivering the note to Hull was not a question of international law. It was only a matter of taking careful steps. Admiral Nagano first advocated a surprise attack as an operational necessity to obtain the maximum success in the attack. And so I do not see any room for inconsistency there."

On the bus ride to prison, Shimada lunged at Togo who sat stolidly. The admiral had to be restrained by force but his curses lasted throughout most of the trip.

McGlynn was so excited by Togo's testimony that he spent the next day poring over his new raw material. Recalling Kido's complaints about gross mistranslations of his diary by the Americans, the professor now carefully went over the message from Foreign Minister Togo in November 1941 to his ambassador in Washington. It was a long cable containing two offers of peace to the United States: Proposals A and B. This cable had been intercepted by U.S. Intelligence, then decoded, translated, and rushed to Secretary of States Hull.

McGlynn was shocked to find a number of mistranslations of Togo's instructions to Ambassador Nomura. One read in Japanese:

THE SITUATION BOTH WITHIN AND OUTSIDE THE COUNTRY IS EXTREMELY PRESSING AND WE CANNOT AFFORD ANY PROCRASTINATION. OUT OF THE SINCERE INTENTION TO MAINTAIN PEACEFUL RELATIONS WITH THE UNITED STATES THE IMPERIAL GOVERNMENT CONTINUES THE NEGOTIATIONS AFTER THOROUGH DELIBERATIONS. THE PRESENT NEGOTIATIONS ARE OUR FINAL EFFORT . . .

This responsible declaration was changed by American translators into an irresponsible one, and McGlynn angrily underlined the most provocative phrases:

CONDITIONS BOTH WITHIN AND WITHOUT OUR EMPIRE ARE SO TENSE THAT <u>NO LONGER IS PROCRASTINATION POSSIBLE</u>, YET IN OUR SINCERITY TO MAINTAIN PACIFIC RELATIONS BETWEEN THE EMPIRE OF JAPAN AND THE UNITED STATES OF AMERICA, <u>WE HAVE DECIDED AS A RESULT OF THESE DELIBERATIONS, TO GAMBLE ONCE MORE ON THE CONTINUANCE OF THE PARLEYS, BUT THIS IS OUR LAST EFFORT.</u>

The American translation of instructions then stated that unless these proposals succeeded, relations between the two nations would be broken off.

. . . IN FACT, WE GAMBLED THE FATE OF OUR LAND ON THE THROW OF THIS DIE.

Togo's actual words to the Japanese Embassy in Washington had been:

. . . AND THE SECURITY OF THE EMPIRE DEPENDS ON IT.

And where Hull then read in English

. . . THIS TIME WE ARE SHOWING THE LIMIT OF OUR FRIEND-SHIP: THIS TIME WE ARE MAKING OUR LAST POSSIBLE BARGAIN, AND I HOPE THAT WE CAN THUS SETTLE ALL OUR TROUBLES WITH THE UNITED STATES PEACEABLY.

Togo had really instructed Nomura:

NOW THAT WE MAKE THE UTMOST CONCESSION IN THE SPIRIT OF COMPLETE FRIENDLINESS FOR THE SAKE OF PEACEFUL SOLU-TION, WE HOPE EARNESTLY THAT THE UNITED STATES WILL, ON ENTERING THE FINAL STAGE OF THE NEGOTIATIONS, RECON-SIDER THE MATTER AND APPROACH THIS CRISIS IN A PROPER SPIRIT WITH A VIEW TO PRESERVING JAPANESE-AMERICAN RELA-TIONS.

The more McGlynn read the more he was astounded that American historians had concluded that only minor mistranslations in this cru-cial message had been made. Minor! The professor read half a dozen further gross distortions in the Togo message. He banged a fist on the desk. To a man like Hull, already convinced that the Japanese were sneaky as a race, these mistranslations were proof positive of Japan's deceitful intentions. Yet it wasn't entirely Hull's fault, conceded Mc-Glynn. It was a series of colossal blunders by the translators. McGlynn could hardly believe what he saw in front of him. The American translators had misled Hull into suspecting that the Japanese were purposely attempting to avoid committing themselves to any formal agreement. Why? Was it a conspiracy? But his long experience in the hurly-burly of official Washington before and during the war per-suaded him it was far more likely American incompetence in transla-tion of a most difficult and complex language, probably combined with the translator's desire to pass on a version that would conform to the common convictions of higher-ups. No, it could not have been a conspiracy by underlings; rather, it had been human error in high places. He felt that thrill of discovery when a historian manages to dig

up raw material shedding dramatic light on an accepted thesis! It only
briefly occurred to him to pass on these revelations to Chaucy for the
defense of both Tojo and Togo. First, he must honor his promise of
silence to the Japanese informant who had shown him the Liaison and
Imperial Conference notes, and second, he had much research still to
do before the full facts could be published.

PART FIVE

Chapter Nineteen

1.

Tokyo, December 1947.

Early the next morning McGlynn went to Will's quarters. He was concerned by his son's agitation during Foreign Minister Togo's interrogation. Apparently Will was confused about the course of the trial, and it was time he learned more of the facts before the defense of General Tojo began.

Will was surprised to see his father. "What's wrong, Dad?"

"I wanted to clear up a few things before you went to Ichigaya." He sat down heavily. "I've been trying to put you straight for months, and I'm afraid I've only added to your confusion. There's something you should know." He told Will about Bratton's revelations.

With a lawyer's caution Will took the startling tale with a grain of salt. "Do you really believe it?"

"Yes. But you can't use any of this in court. I promised Bratton I'd hold the story until I could check it out."

"It sounds pretty farfetched."

"I just wanted you to know for your own protection." He handed him a thick sheaf of papers. "I thought you might be skeptical so I brought along some excerpts from my new book."

"I'll read this when I get some free time." He was already putting on his overcoat. "I've got to get over to Ichigaya."

"Promise me one thing, son."

"What?"

"Read this before General Tojo takes the stand."

"I will, I will," he said flinging the papers on his desk and starting for the door.

2.

On Christmas night Chaucy and her associates were making last-minute preparations for Tojo's defense since it was estimated that the Togo defense would end the next morning. The New York *Times* had already revealed that Emperor Hirohito had recently displayed concern lest the testimony of Tojo raise the question of Imperial responsibility for the war. Despite Kido's testimony there was a growing demand in the Western world for the Emperor to abdicate, since it seemed obvious that His Majesty had been well aware of the steps leading to Pearl Harbor.

Tojo, reported the *Times* correspondent, was possibly in an even better position than Kido to uncover Hirohito's actual role. Moreover, in the eyes of the world Tojo was the supreme warlord, the Hitler of Japan. For this reason Palace emissaries had quietly investigated Tojo's latest views on the Emperor, and presumably what they learned had set Hirohito's mind at rest. "General Tojo," wrote the *Times* correspondent, "still believes the Emperor is divine, despite Hirohito's own disclaimer of his 'godhood' in his radio address at New Year's, 1946. In his cell at Sugamo he still draws his spindly body to attention whenever the Emperor's name is mentioned."

Chaucy was confident that Tojo would defend His Majesty at his own expense. His defense team had rewritten a lengthy affidavit four times, each new version based on the numerous notes Tojo had made during the preceding 344 courtroom days of the trial. Every time Tojo's own name had been mentioned—about twelve hundred times, Chaucy estimated—he had passed a note to his lawyers advising them what questions to ask in the cross-examination of witnesses. These notes, along with his diaries and notebooks, had been translated by his senior Japanese counsel, Kiyose, whose English had been corrected by Blewett. It was, Chaucy wrote her father, a meticulous and honest record of four years of the Japanese political scene: the shift toward militarism from July 1940, when Tojo became a cabinet minister until the dissolution of his own cabinet in July 1944. The following day the senior American counsel, Blewett, would begin reading the 64,000-word document.

Will was having difficulty getting to sleep that night. His doubts

346

about the Pearl Harbor phase, raised by the Togo interrogation, had been heightened by his father's private revelation about Colonels Bratton and Sadtler. And the excerpts from his father's new book had unsettled him. What impressed Will most was the professor's even-handed approach to the negotiations which had led to Pearl Harbor. Hull's insistence on the immediate liberation of China might very well have forced the Tojo government into a war that even the militarists hoped to avoid—a war they were not even in a position to wage. The American diplomats in 1941 had made the mistake of doing what the prosecution at Ichigaya was presently doing, equating Japan with Nazi Germany, and so had maneuvered their nation into two completely different wars, one in Europe against Hitler and one in the Far East, unfortunately linked with the aspirations of all Asians for freedom from the white man's bondage.

Despite Will's early resistance to his father's thesis, it made more and more sense the longer he considered it. He had to admit the new findings were presented quite objectively; the professor had found no villains on either side. The Japanese militarists, he concluded, had been caught up in a medieval system and were primarily driven by dedication to their country. They wanted power for Nippon, not for themselves. And if that was true, why should Tojo be hanged?

Neither could Chaucy get to sleep that night—even though the team had a sound defense of Tojo—as sound, at least, as it was possible to make with the available material. In her last meeting with Tojo he had shown eagerness to take the stand. He realized it was his fate to be hanged but he wanted to tell his story, which the team had put together in a 318-page affidavit. His mission, he told Chaucy, was to take the main responsibility for starting the war, and above all to protect the Emperor.

What would happen in the next few days would make history no matter what happened, and she felt a thrill to be part of it, even as a silent participant. In her father's latest letter he had urged her not to be despondent about the shortcomings of the legal system. "The law," he wrote, "is one of the last citadels of vacillating conservatism in a muddled world." So far the defense had been spirited, but unfortunately the varying points of view of the defendants weakened the combined defense. The rancor displayed during Togo's testimony, for instance, was going to have its effect on General Tojo's defense. All the counsel working for Tojo were convinced he had done his utmost to prevent war, but the documentary evidence could not be found. They faced a tremendous task, and Chaucy argued that it should be left up to Tojo himself. He was a fighter.

Early the next morning Tojo could hear voices reading the Kannon Sutra and Lotus Sutra. He was as calm as he had been the day before, when someone asked him during the exercise period what there was to smile about. "My future is decided," he had jokingly replied.

As Tojo left his cell that morning, an enlisted man being tried at Yokohama called out, *"Gambatte kudasai!* [Stand firm!]" Tojo turned with the suggestion of a smile, then strode away as if to chair a conference.

There was already a large crowd milling outside the War Ministry as the prisoners' bus arrived. McGlynn was standing with Mariko in the line for balcony seats. It was the largest turnout since the first days of the trial, for this was what everyone had been waiting for.

Inside, even the everyday movements of those connected with preparations seemed vital. Clerks carrying papers and workmen making last adjustments on the sound system moved about with self-importance. At last the prisoners arrived, the judges took their seats, and there was polite silence as everyone listened patiently to the last moments of the Togo case.

At last it did end. George Francis Blewett, who had come to have great regard and respect for his client, said, "Mr. President, we are now ready to open the individual defense case of former Premier Tojo. If the Tribunal please, a brief opening statement will be read by Dr. Kiyose, Japanese counsel for the defendant."

Kiyose said he would outline the representations of the defendant. Brief it was not, but the audience listened quietly if impatiently. Tojo was either glancing up at the ceiling or eyeing intently the big courtroom clock. Finally about two hours later Kiyose finished. Will saw Tojo break into a broad smile. Usually he came to court in faded military garb, but today he wore a brand-new greenish uniform. Where did he get it? wondered Will. He blew his nose vigorously, rose and strode twenty paces to the witness stand accompanied by an M.P. as photographers' bulbs flashed and newsreel cameras ground. While being sworn in, he carefully removed his glasses and stamped his 318-page affidavit with the Japanese characters of his name, his personal seal, affirming that the document was his. He affixed his fingerprints and then, when asked his name and the authenticity of this document, said crisply, "*So-desu* (That is right)." Noticing he had a string tied around the middle finger of his right hand, Chaucy wondered what he had forgotten. He saw her and smiled slightly, then calmly took a seat in the witness box. He folded his hands as Blewett began to read the affidavit stating that the Allies had maneuvered Japan into firing the first shot of the war "in self-defense" to preserve the "national existence." Tojo absolved the Emperor of all fault and accepted full responsibility for launching the war, while denying any intention of making Pearl Harbor a sneak attack. He regretted the delay of the warning message which was supposed to have been handed to Secretary of State Hull at least an hour before the first bomb fell. Losing the war, he concluded, was his only crime.

During the reading Tojo sat quietly, earphones on his head, listening intently. Maggie noticed that occasionally he would sip water and at times seemed to be studying the United Nations flags lined up behind the eleven judges. She never noted any nervousness even when he occasionally glanced toward the other defendants, some of whom had attacked him at Sugamo for waging the war. Several times she caught him staring up at the ceiling as if containing himself until he could get up and defend himself.

But by the time court was adjourned until the following Monday only a dent had been made in the lengthy deposition. Even so, McGlynn was surprised to hear the excited comments of the Japanese in the balcony as they filed out. The man they had reviled was now speaking sense with *seishin* (spirit). One had to admire him for standing up to the Tribunal like a man!

"What do you think the Japanese papers will say?" McGlynn asked Mariko and was surprised when she said, "Much the same thing." He protested that yesterday these had been the people who ridiculed Tojo.

She pressed his arm affectionately. "You know so much about us— *most* of the time!"

On Monday morning Blewett walked up to the stand to continue. Just then McGlynn recognized Mrs. Tojo, dressed in a black silk ceremonial kimono, taking a seat in the second row. Tojo in the witness box noticed her and when he stared at her she burst into convulsive sobs. She tried to bow, then covered her face with a handkerchief.

Chaucy could see her client peering up at the balcony, his face impassive. Then he turned to face the judges as Blewett read on and on.

Mariko nudged McGlynn. "The daughter," she whispered and with a slight move of the head nodded to the other side of the balcony. There was sixteen-year-old Kimie, Tojo's fourth daughter, dressed in an orange Western-style dress. Even at a distance McGlynn could see her eyes were red. She and her mother had chosen separate seats, he guessed, to avoid attention. Her father was lolling back in his chair as if nonchalant while his wife's shoulders continued to shake as she kept her face partially covered with the handkerchief.

On the way home to Mariko's after the session, McGlynn told of a call he'd received from Maggie late the night before. SCAP was irate at the Japanese press for revealing that most young Japanese and a great many servicemen agreed with Tojo's view of the attack on Pearl Harbor as "self-defense." It was common, reported one daily, to hear people who had booed at newsreel pictures of Tojo during the early days of the trial now saying, "It took Tojo to say it!" He had suddenly become a hero among those who secretly felt Japan had been forced into the war.

Several editorials and editorially slanted stories, according to Maggie, were suppressed by the censors. But MacArthur himself apparently hadn't been too troubled, remarking, "How can we expect the Japanese to be anti-Japanese?"

The next day, December 30, Blewett finally finished reading the affidavit and the long-awaited moment arrived for the cross-examination of Tojo. Today McGlynn was in the press section with his daughter since he wanted to see how the foreign correspondents reacted to the high drama that was sure to follow.

He was shocked to learn, however, that John Fihelly, who had conducted the numerous Tojo pre-trial interrogations, would not cross-examine even though he had been preparing himself for this moment since 1946. Just as he had done with Kido, Joseph Keenan suddenly decided to ask the first questions. "The damned fool wants to be the star of the show," said Maggie. "Look at him over there pumping himself up."

But before Keenan could take center stage, attorneys for Tojo's fellow defendants began leveling hard questions at the general. "Do you know of any instance whatsoever," asked Kido's counsel, "where

Marquis Kido acted or gave any advice contrary to the Emperor's wishes for peace?"

"Insofar as I know," said Tojo, "there was no such instance whatsoever. And I further wish to add that there is no Japanese subject who would go against the will of His Majesty, particularly among high officials of the Japanese Government or of Japan."

The answer visibly unnerved Keenan who frantically scribbled a message to himself as Webb observed with relish, "Well, you know the implications of that reply!" Keenan was so pale Will brought him a glass of water. "The stupid bastard," muttered Keenan. Unwittingly Tojo had placed a weapon in the hands of those like Webb who wanted to bring the Emperor to trial. Fortunately for Keenan other questions from the defense continued for half an hour and by the time Webb asked the chief prosecutor to proceed with the cross-examination Keenan had recovered his composure.

His face was ruddy as he came forward to ask permission for Fihelly to relieve him if the cross-examination continued too long. But Webb refused to allow more than one prosecutor to cross-examine. "A majority of the court is against you, Mr. Chief of Counsel. You will not have the assistance of Mr. Fihelly." Maggie whispered to her father, "You can bet he won't turn over the whole thing to Fihelly."

Keenan was ruffled. "I shall, of course, proceed and complete the cross-examination myself under those *peculiar* circumstances." Maggie jabbed her father in the ribs.

Keenan turned away from Webb and pointedly ignored Tojo. Then he abruptly turned and stared at the general. Tojo—it was his sixty-fourth birthday—calmly returned the look. It was as if he were amused, thought Chaucy, who felt her client had already won the first round. Will was praying that Keenan would stop acting as if he were trying a Chicago gangster.

Keenan stared distastefully at Tojo. "Accused Tojo," he said, "I shall not address you as general because of course, you know there is no longer any Japanese army."

McGlynn could feel how this attempt to demean Tojo had suddenly generated sympathy for him in the big room. The general sat erectly, proudly, his chin high, his eyes steady. The American correspondent next to McGlynn muttered, "Arrogant bastard!" But the professor was as impressed with Tojo's poise as the Japanese spectators in the balcony.

"I want to ask you," continued Keenan with cold disdain, "if this affidavit—or testimony or argument, as it may be called—that you have given from the witness stand or through your counsel at the lectern for the preceding three or four days, has been intended for the purpose of convincing this court of your innocence or has been intended to be a continuation of imperialistic, militaristic propaganda directed to the people of Japan!"

Keenan thought he had struck the first blow, but it proved to be a mistake in tactics. He had unwittingly gained sympathy for the witness even among some Westerners. He continued browbeating by charging that the entire affidavit was an insult to the intelligence of this Tribunal.

Webb put him down. "I have not yet heard any member of the court suggest that the purpose of the witness is to insult the Tribunal."

Despite the rebuke, Keenan spent the remaining minutes of the session badgering the witness, once urging him to talk straight and not make a speech, and several times disdainfully calling him *"Mr. Tojo."*

3.

Upon resumption of the trial the following week, Keenan abruptly interrupted himself and asked Tojo, "You have told us that the Emperor on repeated occasions made known to you that he was a man of peace and did not want war, is that correct?"

But Tojo was not taken by surprise. "War was decided on in *my* cabinet."

"Was that the *will* of Emperor Hirohito, that war should be instituted?"

"It might have been against his will, but it is a fact that because of my advice and because of the advice given by the High Command the Emperor consented, though reluctantly, to the war." After the interpreter made a slight correction in the translation, Tojo continued. "The Emperor's love for and desire for peace remained the same right up to the very moment when hostilities commenced, and even during the war his feelings remained the same."

Will noticed Tojo glance up at Webb with some triumph. If Webb was aware of this, he ignored it.

PART FIVE

Later, as those in the balcony were filing out, McGlynn heard two elderly Japanese excitedly commenting on Tojo's remarks about the Emperor. "It's like Kabuki!" one exulted. "The samurai defending the *daimyo!* (lord)"

"What a great day for Nippon!"

A young woman who had lost her husband in China was just as enthusiastic. "He is *Boku-no-Tojo* [My Tojo] again," she remarked to a middle-aged man, referring to a song popular in the early days of the war.

Her escort, who looked to McGlynn like an office worker, agreed. "We must admit he made great mistakes during the war but I really believe he is an honest man. He isn't afraid to tell all those *gaijin* exactly what he thinks. He's *Boku-no-Tojo* all right!" Two students were arguing. One criticized Tojo for waging war. "What the hell do you expect a soldier to do?" asked his companion. "A general is supposed to fight."

Reports of the trial in America were picturing Tojo as arrogant, contemptuous, vague, and seedy. He was reported as "gesticulating wildly," "barking defiance," and testifying "with the cold assurance of a conquering samurai." While admitting that these descriptions were somewhat accurate, McGlynn felt that such descriptions were based primarily on the court interpreter's version of what Tojo was saying. To someone bilingual it was obvious that there was often a breakdown in communications. By the time one of Keenan's questions was translated, Tojo had to think how he should answer and hesitated, giving the impression of vagueness. The professor sympathized with both Tojo and Keenan, laboring under great difficulties.

By the third day of cross-examination the chief prosecutor seemed exhausted whereas his opponent was sharper than ever. By now most of the Americans in the balcony had become irritated with Tojo and McGlynn heard the word "insolence" again and again.

"You, Tojo, had made up your mind on the policy of attacking the United States in war unless the United States desisted in sending supplies to China, had you not?" Phrased as a question, it was more of a charge.

Smiling slightly, Tojo replied quietly, "I never dreamed of it." But the translation came out as insolence, and Chaucy knew he had smiled because the question was referring to the summer of 1940 when Tojo first became War Minister.

Later he admitted that in November 1941 Foreign Minister Togo had sent to America proposals A and B, asking the United States to abandon aid to China. "Was Togo carrying out your instructions or was he disobeying them?"

"It was not against my will."

"You take responsibility."

"Of course," said Tojo and glowered at Keenan as if he were an imbecile. For the past week Tojo had been taking complete responsibility for starting the war. And Chaucy knew by the look on his face that he wondered why the chief prosecutor was going over the same old ground.

It was apparent to Will that Keenan was struggling. He should have been relieved by Fihelly but Webb had prevented that. And by now Fihelly, dismayed and frustrated, had returned to the United States. Sweating profusely, Keenan handed to Tojo a copy of the famous note Hull had sent back to Japan in reply to the last Japanese proposals. It had been far more harsh than the American proposal made five months earlier and the Japanese had taken it as an insult. "Are you familiar with it?" he asked.

Tojo carefully examined the document, and then said with deep emotion, "I shall never forget it as long as I live." The entire cabinet, he explained, had been stunned by its uncompromising, impossible terms.

Will flinched to see the pain on Tojo's face. It seemed to reflect the horrors of war and the surrender of his beloved land. The Hull note *had been* tantamount to an ultimatum and *had been* the result of American impatience and indignation.

Keenan then made much of Tojo's having declared in his affidavit that the Hull note had literally been thrown in their faces. Wasn't the document, Keenan charged, handed by Secretary Hull to Nomura and Kurusu in a very dignified fashion? "Is not that true?"

"In form, yes."

"And it was . . ."

"In content there was no spirit of concession whatsoever," said Tojo sadly.

"We will come to that in a moment," said Keenan aggressively. "As a matter of fact it was handed to your ambassadors at a time when they were receiving the utmost courtesy in the United States, being privileged to see the Secretary of State and even the President of the United States almost at their will. Do you admit that?"

"That is a fact, and it has nothing to do with the contents of this document."

Will winced. It was a good point and Keenan seemed flustered. "But I suppose you know," he said as if in rebuttal, "that the President of the United States is the highest authority of that Republic?"

Again Chaucy saw the little scornful smile on Tojo's face. "I know it in the sense that I know that the Emperor of Japan is the highest authority in Japan."

There was a light burst of laughter from a Japanese in the balcony before being restrained by a friend.

"Well, there is this difference: the people of the United States choose their President every four years by direct voice. That is not true in Japan, or was not true in Japan at the time we are talking of. Was there that difference?"

Webb had been uncommonly patient, but he couldn't endure any more of this. "What is the relevance of this, Mr. Chief of Counsel?"

Being too bullheaded to take advantage of the interruption, Keenan dug himself deeper into a hole. "The relevance of it, Mr. President," he retorted, "is this: With this witness I am attempting to show that he was dealing with authorities of direct responsibility whereas the representatives of the United States were dealing with those of ambiguous responsibility."

Webb's face was now as red as Keenan's. "But that, at all events, is your submission," he said, believing this would stop Keenan's garrulity.

"But, Mr. President," persisted Keenan, "if it is offensive in any way to take a few minutes in this courtroom in this historic trial to let the people here know the authority of the President of the United States Government, I shall not press my point. I shall go immediately to something else on a further indication from the court."

Webb leaned across the bench and loudly exclaimed, "Please, go immediately to something else!"

According to the *Life* correspondent who was near Chaucy, Keenan "sneered" as he said, "I believe the court means that it would like to have me do so; it is not a command."

"It is the acceptance of an invitation by you," snapped Webb. He had had enough. "We don't want to hear any more questions of that type."

Keenan began berating Tojo for declaring that the Hull note ignored the way America and Britain were exercising strong military, economic, and political pressure on Japan. "I am not interested, at the moment," he exclaimed, "in your insolent remarks about the representatives of the United States of America."

Chaucy feared Tojo might be roused by the word "insolent" but he never lost his composure during the four days he was on the stand. The sedulous notes he had taken during the long trial had prepared him for unexpected questions; he was never at a loss for an answer nor, unlike Keenan, did he ever lose his temper. He even had moments of humor which appealed to Westerners as well as his countrymen. Once Keenan struggled to get Tojo to admit that Japanese institutions were now far more efficient under the Occupation. "Having been imprisoned by the Allies in Sugamo Prison for two years," he replied good-naturedly, "I am in no position to comment." Even Webb was amused.

As Keenan grew weaker, Tojo gained in strength. When Keenan asked, "Do you agree that wars are crimes against the people?" he quickly replied, "I don't agree that war is a crime. I do agree that wars have an unfortunate effect on the people—the same for the victors as for the vanquished."

Keenan's frustrations only encouraged Tojo to sharper retorts, branding some of the cross-examiner's questions as "preposterous" or "absurd." He even used subtle shades of Japanese slang such as, "But, of course, you wouldn't understand that," or "You're way off the mark." And once, after being halted while explaining that in order to understand military reports it was necessary to know the psychology of the battlefield, he added disdainfully, "I wouldn't attempt to explain psychology to you, Mr. Keenan."

Such courtroom demeanor irritated some Japanese. "I can't bear the haughty way he lolls back in his chair and plants his right hand on the table," an elderly Japanese remarked to McGlynn. "It reminds me of his gestures in the Diet in the old days."

But some Americans, such as the correspondent from *Newsweek*, realized Tojo's stock had risen dramatically in Japan. Another Western observer declared that the general had developed from "Tojo the Idiot" to "Tojo the Teacher." First he had been reviled and ridiculed for bungling his suicide, but he had ended by gaining sympathy and admiration as "an anti-democratic martyr."

At last the ordeal for Keenan approached its end, and he asked his final question. Tojo, seated erect, extended his right hand onto the desk and threw out his chest. "I feel," he said in a ringing voice, "that I committed no wrong. I feel I did what was right and true."

"So, if you should be acquitted by this court," said Keenan, "you would feel free to go with your associates, whoever they might be, and do the same thing again. Is that your position?"

As Tojo was considering his answer Blewett objected and this was sustained by Sir William Webb.

"Then I have no more questions," said the spent Chief Counsel.

4.

When Will heard Tojo's final words, "I feel I did what was right and true," his doubts and confusions came to an end. It was as if something had mechanically clarified his muddled mind. Everything became resolved. He believed Tojo. And the defense had not even had its full day in court. At first it came as a shock, then an odd feeling of relief washed over Will. He felt a strange invigoration, as though he had broken out of a thick fog into clear daylight. The strong light hurt his eyes but his head was clear.

That night he told Chaucy. It did not surprise her, for she had been sure he would never allow his previous prejudices to cloud his ultimate conclusions.

The next morning Keenan gave his staff a pep talk on the importance of their summation and the lengthy final arguments that would follow. The work had already been done. Almost everything was on paper, but there were some changes now that the prosecution had received the best shots of the defense. The great majority of the prosecution lawyers still had perfect faith in their case and went to work energetically. But one middle-aged counsel confessed to Will he had some doubts after listening to the defense. "What if they, and not us, had had the atomic bomb? What if they had dropped the bomb on San Francisco and New York? We'd have had tons of affidavits and eyewitnesses. We'd have called it the greatest atrocity of mankind. I bet we even would have put the Emperor on trial. When Blakeney argued in this way in the first days of the trial I thought it was only effective rhetoric. Since then I have visited Nagasaki and Hiroshima and talked to some of the survivors. Doesn't seem irrelevant any longer, Will."

Will said nothing. "We have justified our use of the bomb," continued the middle-aged counsel. "How can we now prosecute the Japanese for waging war?"

Another member of their team joined them. He too had a few reservations. "I can't see equating Tojo with Hitler. The Japanese are nothing like the Nazis. I think the defense can claim it's a case of guilt by association. Can you imagine if Hitler had taken the stand at Nuremberg and said the things Tojo did? It would have been too ridiculous to take seriously. But Tojo said some things that made sense even to me. Oh, hell, let's get back to work and wind up this farrago so we can go home."

As for Keenan, he was so exhausted that he turned over cross-examination of the final witness, General Umezu, to the redoubtable Comyns-Carr. Keenan then went off to recuperate at a luxurious Japanese villa near Atami, sixty-four miles south of Tokyo, the guest of two former prime ministers.

During the exercise period at Sugamo, Kido found Tojo quite willing to talk. "My physical condition is good," he said, "but my mind is tired because I had to keep my wits about me all the time I was on the stand." He was relieved, he said, that it was all over. "The war crimes trial may serve as a warning against inhuman acts in future wars, but I doubt if this trial will prevent war itself." Above they could hear the angry roar of two American jet fighters engaged in a mock dogfight. "Look," he said. "They're training for the Third World War. Did you know what Prosecutor Jackson said before the Tribunal in Nuremberg? 'This trial will be meaningful only if conducted on the premise that America and the Soviet Union would never go to war. If not, then this trial will be meaningless.'" Tojo again pointed to the sky. "The two war allies, America and the Soviet Union, are getting ready to go at each other." His eyes were sharp, his cheeks glowing. "Do you mean to tell me, while that noise is going on up there, that justice is being meted out at Ichigaya by sending me to the gallows? It's a hollow mockery."

5.

It was ironical that Keenan began reading the prosecution's summation of the entire trial on the morning of February 11, 1948, the former national holiday (now banned by MacArthur) celebrating the founding of Japan in 660 B.C. "To borrow a phrase from an ancient system of law," he began, "we have reached 'the closing of the gates.' For the better part of two years we have been engaged in the preparation and presentation of the evidence in this case. There remains now the summation and the judgment of this court. This is indeed a very long period for any criminal trial; but there are many reasons and ample justification therefore.

"The matters under inquiry here are not at all of the nature of those with which our domestic tribunals have been concerned in criminal proceedings. For here we are examining events of the greatest historical importance vitally affecting the affairs of the world occuring over a period of fourteen years." He then likened the defendants to outlaws deliberately embarked on aggressive war. "No one of them had consideration for the dignity of the human being. The revolting slaughter of millions of their neighbors was largely brought about by the domination and utter subjugation of their own people. This they accomplished by free employment of any method that suited their purpose —superstition or brute force or a combination of both." He called Tojo "the leader of those irresponsible militarists," and then expressed surprise that even such a malevolent character as he "would have the brazenness to contend that Japan really sought peace." For their crimes he demanded the "sternest punishment known to the law."

At dinner with Chaucy and the professor, Will told about his dilemma. He was now convinced that Tojo had done his utmost to prevent war, and that there was no proof he had been guilty of committing atrocities. Wouldn't it be best if he just withdrew from the case?

Chaucy was shocked. "How could you do such a thing?" It would be letting down her father who had invested such hopes in Will.

The professor laid a restraining hand on hers. "Will," he said quietly, "we all know there have been inequities in this tribunal. But it was the best tribunal that could have taken place so soon after the war. The worst Nazis had to be executed, and now the American people want Tojo and some of his henchmen to hang." Will started to protest. "I know it's not fair but it's going to be for the good of Japan."

"How can you be so cynical?"

"Do you think it makes a damned bit of difference if you quit this case? Do you think it will help Tojo if you run to the newspapers and reveal what you and I know? It would only cause a stink. And the last one to want that is Tojo himself. He knows he has to die because he's the symbol of everything America hates in Japan. And most Japanese have come to hate him. Let him die his way—like a man."

Will bowed his head.

"Why don't you ask Keenan for advice?" said his father.

At first Chaucy thought Professor McGlynn was being sarcastic but then she considered the proposal. "It'll give you a chance to consider your options," she said.

Will was reluctant but Chaucy insisted that he see Keenan in the morning. "I heard a rumor he wants to get back to his home in Ohio so he can run for Congress."

He found the chief prosecutor packing his bags. In an expansive mood, he was amused when Will asked if he really was going to run for Congress. "Why not?" he said. "Didn't you know that lawyers make the best politicians? Is this just a good-bye call or did you have something on your mind?" They sat down and haltingly Will explained that he had become disillusioned by certain aspects of the prosecution's case. Keenan showed no surprise. "I know you've been bothered about Kido. I know how you feel. I have my own misgivings about Shigemitsu."

"It's more than Kido. I'm even having doubts about Tojo."

Keenan was astounded. "The hell you say!"

As Will explained in more detail, Keenan listened without comment, his brow furrowed. When Will stopped there was silence. Finally Keenan said, "This is more serious than I imagined, son." He leaned over and patted Will on the knee. "This wouldn't be the first time this ever happened. Every lawyer occasionally has doubts about his case but it's never wise just to drop out. We often have to make adjustments. You know . . . the important thing is to keep your mouth shut. You haven't told anyone, have you?"

Will admitted he had told his father and Chaucy, adding that both of them had recommended getting advice from the chief prosecutor.

"For God's sake, don't say anything to that sister of yours. Let's keep this to ourselves." He planned to leave for America the next day and let the other prosecutors work for a change. The closing arguments of the defense and the final summation by the prosecution were all matter-of-fact affairs. All Will had to do was appear in court and make no comments to the press. "Just promise me one thing, McGlynn. Keep your mouth shut and your mind open." He led Will to the door, and patted him paternally on the back. "Get some sack time. You look terrible."

Most of the prosecution's rebuttal was the introduction of excerpts from the memoirs of Prince Saionji, the nation's most honored elder statesman. This detailed the political history of Japan from 1930 until the Prince's death in late 1940. It appeared to corroborate the prosecution in many cases, but McGlynn had known the wise old *genro*, as the remnants of the Meiji oligarchy were called, and he told Chaucy that many of the excerpts were out of context. And so, without the benefit of Keenan, the prosecution completed its presentation on March 2.

Without delay the defense began its closing arguments, with Kiyose and his assistants preparing 253 pages on behalf of their client. Chaucy finally made her appearance in court. As she walked forward there was a stir in the balcony. It was inconceivable to many of the Japanese that a woman should be allowed to take such a prominent role.

"May it please the Tribunal," said a fellow defense counsel, "I now have the pleasure of presenting to the Tribunal my colleague Miss Snow, a practicing attorney from the State of Massachusetts, who has not yet appeared before the Tribunal. She will continue the summation in the case of General—I beg your pardon," he bowed toward the prosecution table, "*Mr.* Tojo."

"Miss Snow," said the president affably.

"May it please the court," she began, and for almost an hour held center stage with Will leaning forward devouring every word. How poised she was, he thought. How cogent. Not a word wasted. She moved easily, completely at home, the very model of a seasoned counsel.

Webb smiled. "That was a very clear presentation, Miss Snow," he said.

"Thank you," she said. Although her knees felt wobbly and she was sure she looked terrible, she appeared to be cool and confident. She had never before been nervous in court and she hoped her jitters had gone unnoticed.

It was not until mid-April that the final word for the defense was spoken. Then, in a short but eloquent final argument, the prosecution retorted that those on trial were not automatons nor playthings of fate but the brains of an empire. "These were not the hoodlums who were the powerful part of the group which stood before the Tribunal in Nuremberg, dregs of a criminal environment thoroughly schooled in the ways of crime and knowing no other methods but those of crime. These men were supposed to be the elite of the nation, the honest and trusted to whom the fate of the nation had been confidently entrusted."

The Japanese in the balcony were surprised to hear their leaders, lately branded by Keenan as malevolent outlaws, now described in such terms.

"These men knew the difference between good and evil." They had made their choice for evil. "With full knowledge they voluntarily elected to follow the path of war, bringing death and injury to millions of human beings and destruction and hate wherever their forces went." And for this choice they now stood before the Tribunal awaiting judgment. "They made their choice for aggression and for war and they made it freely and voluntarily. For this choice they must bear the guilt."

And now the last word had indeed been spoken on that sixteenth day of April, almost exactly two years after it all had begun. As the spectators slowly, contemplatively, filed out of the balcony, McGlynn could sense a feeling of relief. Now it was up to the judges, yet there was little doubt that almost all the accused would be either hanged or given long prison terms. But would this trial even begin to answer the question of national guilt?

The long-drawn-out trauma had ended and McGlynn, though merely an onlooker, felt as if a large weight had been lifted from his shoulders. He could imagine how those involved—the defendants, the judges, the counsel for both prosecution and defense—must feel. There had been many mistakes committed by all concerned, yet much had been done that reflected honor on that ramshackle contraption known as democracy.

There had been rare drama and days of tedium, but McGlynn felt the cast of characters for this historic event could not be matched for human interest. A playwright could not have created two more stageworthy characters than Webb and Keenan. The Australian had been argumentative, touchy and arbitrary, but never arrogant. He had apologized several times for his demeanor and then repeated the offense. Keenan, flamboyant and a victim of alcohol, had been both brilliant and flawed. Yet he had often shown humanity and understanding.

It was raining as the accused prisoners boarded their bus. Little was said on the trip back to Sugamo Prison. After entering the main gate the bus proceeded to a different building entrance. There were mutters of conjecture. M.P.'s escorted them to a room where they were ordered to strip and then bend over for the degrading rectal inspection. After being forced to submit to X rays, they were taken to the dental surgery for an oral inspection. When it was discovered that they harbored no poison or other instrument of suicide, they were given plain uniforms marked on the back with a large P, the usual uniform of the Class B and C defendants who had already been found guilty.

They were brought to Block 1. The first floor was empty but they were led to the second floor and put in solitary cells. The concrete building, long in disuse, was dusty and cold. But they were given a treat—a good Western-style dinner, including meat and fruit, served to them by the American officer in charge of the kitchen. From now until the day of sentencing they were to eat the same meals as those given to the American guards. A comrade called out to Tojo, "This is a good omen. No?"

"No," he said but didn't add that it must be because the Americans feared a Japanese cook might manage to smuggle poison into their food. How ridiculous, he thought. Who but a coward would take this escape from fate? It was not that he longed for the end. No. He needed every day of respite to compose himself for that final moment. He still felt he had done no wrong, but he wished to examine what he had done so he could face death with a clean slate. He wrote a poem:

OCCUPATION

> Whether life is long or short,
> Whether we succeed or fail,
> Is in accordance with the will of Heaven.

It would be months before the Tribunal would be able to reach a verdict.

Chapter Twenty

1.

Washington, D.C., March 3, 1948.

Meanwhile President Truman was convinced that the Cold War was coming to a climax. "We made agreement on China, Korea, and other places, none of which has Russia kept," he wrote his daughter. "So now we are faced with exactly the same situation with which Britain and France were faced in 1938–39 with Hitler." All totalitarian states were alike. "Things look black. We've offered control and disarmament through the United States, giving up our most powerful weapon for the world to control. The Soviets won't agree. They're upsetting things in Korea, China, in Persia, and in the Near East. A decision will have to be made. I am going to make it . . . We may have to fight for it." He hoped the course he took would end in peace. "I went to Potsdam with the kindliest feelings towards Russia—in a year and a half they cured me of it. Lots of love, Dad."

Several months earlier Truman had sent a message to Congress proposing a European Recovery Program, the Marshall Plan. Once this began to function, Truman contended that it would prevent Russia from communizing the countries of Western Europe by exploiting their economic miseries. And when, three weeks after his letter to Margaret, the Soviet Union announced that the Russians would check all U.S. personnel passing through their zone to East Berlin, the President was sure his fears were justified. Soon would come a blockade which would trap all Western forces and Berliners inside East Berlin with only a month's supply of food and fuel.

And so both Truman and the Pentagon agreed upon a new policy for occupied Japan. Now the talk in Washington was of transforming the former enemy into "a bulwark of democracy," and "the workshop of the Far East." They would turn the former enemy into an ally.

The makers of policy in Washington also realized that their plan of uniting Mao and Chiang Kai-shek was hopeless, and that the Reds were winning the civil war in China. American forces had already left Peiping in despair. The liberal Kuomintang newspaper, *Ta Kung Pao*, which had openly criticized the ruthless greed and corruption of its own party, published its epitaph: "The Americans came with the great hope of stopping China's civil war; they go disillusioned. We wish here to thank our American friends and to hate our own stupidity."

American aid, as McGlynn had long ago warned MacArthur, had done little to help Chiang, for it marked him as a tool of white imperialist forces, a puppet of the West. And that was one reason why many Chinese who were unsympathetic to communism felt China's only hope was the People's Liberation Army. The Kuomintang forces under Chiang had turned into a mere paper dragon. McGlynn's best source in Yenan had just informed him that Mao was finally convinced it was time to turn away from guerrilla warfare and mount large-unit offensives in two provinces. When the professor sent MacArthur a memorandum that the end was near for Chiang Kai-shek, the general returned the document with a curt comment: "I doubt it!"

2.

Central China, April 1948.

The situation was so desperate by early April that Akira Toda got word from the Nationalists that his Japanese work force—the last Japanese civilian contingent in the area—would be transported in a few days from Shinsho, the company town on the banks of the Yangtze, down the river to Shanghai. Toda passed the word to prepare secretly, fearing that some Chinese civilians might attack them. Each person could take as much as he could carry, and there was much packing, unpacking, discarding, replacing. On the eve of departure one couple with a year-old son decided to leave behind all their precious mementos and take only food and diapers. Rice was cooked late that night, for they were to leave in the dark.

Toda led the long silent procession to the Yangtze at two in the morning. The continuous noise of the river drowned out all other sounds and they boarded their ship without trouble. It was already filled, and sailors had to forcibly make way for the newcomers. Soon came the rattle of firearms. Bandits! There was near panic aboard but the captain called out it was only guards shooting at would-be looters.

At last the overcrowded ship started down the Yangtze in the light of a full moon. A good omen, someone said. But an old woman replied that it was the worst possible omen. Toda was urging a large dark cloud to hurry up and cover the revealing moon. Rifle shots grew louder and they could see figures on the bank. Someone cried out in pain. A hit! Just then the cloud touched the edge of the moon and slowly began to cover it. There were more shots, other cries of distress. At last it was dark, and they were out of range.

Three days later the ship sprang a leak just as they were approaching a large city. The captain, a friend of Toda's, told him the ship could not be repaired for weeks and advised him to take his group at once to the railroad yards. If they were lucky they could board a freight train before the other passengers found out they were on their own. It was dusk by the time the large Japanese group, led by the ship's first mate, found a train being loaded with other repatriates. The first mate, a burly man with a booming voice, chased away Chinese about to board the last four flatcars. The Toda group scrambled aboard with the men protectively surrounding the women and children. All managed to squeeze onto the flatcars, the last ones sitting on the edge with their legs dangling over the sides.

Their slow progress towards Shanghai along the desolate wind-swept land was painful and dangerous. It was bitter cold and at every stop Chinese villagers would swarm along the train jabbing home-made spears at the Japanese, demanding money and possessions. After the first attack, Toda placed the strongest men at the edge to fight off the raiders. In the meantime he would rush up to the head of the train and offer the engineer a fountain pen or watch to speed up the taking on of water and fuel. But they eventually arrived in Nanking with most of their possessions intact and few casualties. One man complained that his shoes had been pulled off at the last stop, but Toda persuaded someone with an extra pair to lend them until they reached Japan.

Thanks to Toda's perseverance and good luck, the group finally arrived safely in Shanghai. Toda had always loved this strange, conglomerate metropolis. Unlike other Chinese cities, it had the skyline of a Chicago and was graced by the remnants of the luxurious international settlement. The modern Bund, the main thoroughfare, was a conglomeration of West and East: automobiles, rickshas, pedicabs, jeeps, and bicycles. The streets were crowded with hordes of Chinese, many tattered and exhausted after long treks from the north. There were rich Chinese still buying everything available and poor Chinese trying to make a living selling shoelaces, eggs, pencils, postcards, and U.S. Army surplus goods. The shops were filled with pre-war Swiss watches, fountain pens, jade, junk, leather briefcases, and elixirs of life guaranteed to make an old man young. Everything seemed for sale, including the shop girls and young boys; money was god, if it was U.S. dollars or Chinese silver dollars, but Chinese paper money was worthless.

"You cannot stop speculation in Shanghai any more than you can stop war," Toda told his assistant. "If you dropped an atomic bomb on the Bund today, tomorrow a thousand survivors would crop up selling radioactive calcium powder guaranteed to give you eternal youth." At the same time Toda noticed that the end of extraterritoriality had turned Shanghai itself into a genuinely Chinese city. The *Pax Britannica* was finished when Chinese roads changed from the British system to right-hand drive, a trick which even the Americans couldn't accomplish in Japan. The white man's domination in China, concluded Toda, had come to an end. No successful government could ever again yield to foreign power.

Toda's people had to wait in tents for several days before boarding their repatriation vessel, V-90, a Liberty ship. Few brought aboard much baggage since most of their possessions had been sold for food. But Toda had two footlockers filled with company papers and documents. At the bottom of one were a hundred slender bars of gold given him by the Nationalists as reward for turning over intact the valuable formulas and scientific documents of the mill and mine. This would give him and his staff a new start in Japan.

Toda watched enthralled as the muddy yellow waters of the Yangtze estuary met the deep blue seawater. Those next to him were silent, their minds so crowded with emotion they couldn't speak. For three days the ship, loaded with three thousand passengers, pitched and rolled until they finally reached Hakata on the first day of May. After a long wait they were allowed to disembark. Toda, like the others, felt a thrill to step on home land at last. American M.P.'s systematically went through every piece of baggage. Toda's footlockers stopped the line. He was sprayed with DDT and led into a small office.

"Where did you get all this gold?" asked an officer. After Toda explained, the grim-faced officer told him the gold was confiscated. "Sign this release, please." He was told to report to M.P. headquarters in Tokyo, then allowed to join the others. All were given a thousand yen apiece in new bills and escorted to the train station. Toda fumed. He was being treated like a foreigner in his own country!

After another long wait, a battered train limped into the station. Toda was shocked to find windows and doors broken. The dusty seats were ripped and there was debris all over the floor. Disgusting! What had happened to Japan? As their train passed through station after station, the piles of wreckage told the story of defeat. He felt sick. The worst moment was their arrival in Hiroshima. A loudspeaker on the platform blasted out: "Welcome home, soldiers and repatriates! Welcome home! You probably have heard many conflicting reports about our city. Though little repair has yet been done, we are, as you see, definitely on our road back to recovery." Through a filthy window Toda could see an unimaginable stretch of charred rubble with only a lonely chimney or occasional gutted stone building left like mammoth gravestones. "So we would like to see *you* get back on your feet."

All in the car were shocked; no one spoke a word until they had pulled out of the station. They passed a clean train where American soldiers were sitting on spotless, comfortable seats. But this sight of the military train brought no envious or resentful complaints. The Japanese military had done the same in China. "If we suffer now," Toda told himself, "we have only ourselves to blame."

At each station oncoming passengers ignored protests from the stationmaster that this was a reserved train and, burdened though they were with heavy knapsacks, climbed in through the windows. It was difficult to breathe. Babies cried. Cigarette smoke was stifling. The acrid smell of sweat and fish in shopping bags was overpowering.

At one station an old woman repatriate refused to open her window but those outside screamed so threateningly she reluctantly did so. As the newcomers piled through over her lap they rebuked the old woman. This shocked Toda. What had happened to his people? This was like a strange country. Where was the traditional Japanese modesty and courtesy?

To the distress of Sumiko, who had been romantically dreaming for months of this first meeting with her father, and to the secret relief of her mother, Toda walked calmly into the house as if he had been gone only for the weekend. Although he had returned for short visits several times since leaving home in 1942, he had not seen his family for more than two years. He was a stranger to his daughter. She too was a stranger to him, and even his wife was a completely different woman —so sure of herself, so decisive. Everything had changed, and it was a painful effort to hide his dismay behind a stoic mask. He had paled on entering the house to find it almost barren, and, worst of all, half occupied by Americans. He had even kept his composure the next morning upon reporting at the M.P. station to learn he was under house arrest because of his activities during the war in China. And he managed to keep his temper a week later, after release from restrictions, when he protested confiscation of the thin Chinese gold bars. A rude M.P. captain loudly explained it was done on orders from Mac-Arthur, and Toda was lucky he hadn't been "put in the slammer" for attempting to smuggle in illegal gold.

It took more than a month for Toda to adjust. Only by then had he grown used to the Mulrooneys and regarded their occupancy as a benefit. He found the colonel an amusing and knowledgeable companion who made fun of MacArthur for thinking he knew all about the Japanese, and for his belief that they had the minds of twelve-year-olds and the best way to bring democracy to Japan was to turn them all into Christians. At first the colonel's daughter, Jo, had raised Toda's hackles with her pointed questions: "Why do Japanese men walk ahead of their wives, Mr. Toda?" "Why do Japanese men make such a funny noise drinking soup, Mr. Toda?" Even more embarrassing were her comments about the filth of the streets, and the unsanitary toilet system. But gradually Toda came to welcome seeing the new Japan through Jo's searching eyes. He also became inured to the damage done to his beloved Tokyo and accepted the humiliating hordes of breezy occupation troops. Most of them *were* kind and thoughtful in their haphazard, happy-go-lucky way, and he always had liked Americans. But his visits to old friends were disturbing. Most of them had lost their spirit, and one who had not—Yabe, the former second secretary to Marquis Kido—was extremely thin. And all the talk centered on the marquis who was in prison awaiting his fate.

Toda's greatest pleasure was the almost daily visit with his old friend McGlynn who seemed for some reason to be less caustic than formerly. Together they would sip tea and bemoan the effects of democratization on traditional cultural values. Both agreed that the Americanization of Japan had pitfalls and already many Japanese had become corrupted by the instant liberalization of a society which had survived because of its universal acceptance of proper behavior and formality. What bothered Toda most was the degeneration of Japanese traditional modesty and courtesy. Now everyone seemed to live only for himself.

Hardest of all for him to understand were the young people of Japan. They seemed uninterested in history and knew so little about it they were insensitive to what had been good in the old Japan. They were being taught by the Americans that times had changed, and before long even his own children might look on the gardens and shrines of Kyoto as if they were sightseers, and might find the artificial fountains and geometric paths of a Western-style public park more beautiful than the rock gardens of the Temple of Dragon's Peace.

The customs and character of the Japanese, he observed, were already being changed by poverty. Even though he had been disheartened by what the war had done to his country, he still felt an indescribable peace enfolding him now that he was at last on Japanese soil. He vowed not to sink into depression like so many of his friends but hang on to what he remembered of the old days. Japan had not been a bad country and he felt sorry for the young savages growing up in these days of occupation, ignorant of what had been good in the ways of their ancestors.

During his six years in China he had been forced to rely on himself. If he had remained in Japan during the war he too would probably have been crushed to watch authority crumble and foreigners rule the land. His chief desire was to see his own children strong, but as yet they worried him. His daughter Sumiko still treated him like a stranger and he did not realize that it was because he *was* a stranger. Even before leaving for China he had been away from home so often on business that there was little communication between them. He had been a distant, almost cold figure who only checked her report cards and gave her presents. The only times they had even talked had turned out to be opportunities for lectures. And now he was even more of a stranger, arrived from a strange land.

His son Shogo was even more disturbing. Since release from prison he had taken a job as a loader at the Tokyo railroad yards. Every night he arrived home exhausted and only talked of the unfair treatment of workers by the Japanese National Railways. He talked so radically that his father feared he was mixed up with the Communists.

The child who dismayed Toda least was Ko, who had previously distressed him most by dreaming of becoming an artist and living in Paris. Now the boy worked diligently in the Ginza, sketching Americans to help support the family. Late in May Ko revealed to his father that he had another dream. "When I came back from the Philippines," he said, "I had no idea what I wanted to do. I was just sick of the war." He told of his trip to Kamiko's home and what his friend had written on the wall of his bedroom. "Those words were like a message to me. And when I saw the ruins of Tokyo I had the strangest reaction. Instead of being depressed, I felt—almost inspired. I felt, well, finally we are all equal. Now all of us are starting from scratch. It is going to be a new world." Then in embarrassment he said, "I want to do something for my country. You remember how I longed to live in Paris and be a painter? Now that all seems petty."

At last, after a year of planning, he had decided that his future was in the family silk business. Toda listened in disbelief as Ko told of advice his son had been given by Yamaoka, a friend of Toda's at Nippon Steel. Instead of producing and exporting raw silk, they should get the raw silk from China and turn it into pajamas, shirts, and dresses. It sounded like a crackpot scheme to Toda until his son told how he had learned from Yamaoka that MacArthur was planning to rehabilitate the three key areas of industry: transportation, coal, and steel. Yamaoka had just received secret approval to produce some twelve million tons of steel a year. This meant that by the time the Japanese reached the peak wartime level they would be able to build six or seven new blast furnaces that could produce a thousand tons of pig iron a day. In several years Japan would have more modern blast furnaces than America and Britain combined.

"Don't you see what that means?" said Ko excitedly. "As steel goes, so will go our entire economy." Now was the time to act, he said, and asked his father to arrange a meeting with Toda's uncle who ran the family silk firm.

PART FIVE

Despite Ko's enthusiasm it was with misgiving that Akira Toda took his son to the home of Uncle Isamu who at eighty-nine was still vigorous and hardheaded. The old man's partner, Akira's older brother, had no initiative and was little more than a bookkeeper. They all met in the ruins of Uncle Isamu's mansion which had once been a showplace. One wing had been totally destroyed in the firebombings and the rest of the rambling structure was run-down.

It was a cold day. Rain leaked into several pans placed in the formal tatami room, which smelled of decay. Akira was greeted coolly by the old man who had never forgiven him for refusing to carry on the family business.

Isamu, sitting on the floor, crossed his arms, looked down and grunted. Akira's brother imitated him.

Ko proposed he be allowed to come to work, starting at the bottom. He became so enthusiastic that he forgot traditional courtesy to his elders and began outlining his plans for revolutionizing the system. His father inwardly groaned. All was lost. Uncle Isamu was too wedded to the past.

The old man, offended by the cocky greenhorn, finally spoke slowly but with authority. "For more than one hundred years . . ." he began, and recounted the time-honored glories of the firm, neglecting to add that it now was little more than a shell of the past. "Unfortunately, nephew," he told Akira, "there is no position available to your son. Perhaps in a year . . ."

That evening when Colonel Mulrooney came for his usual chat with the Todas, he noticed that Ko was downcast. The young man told what had happened. Mulrooney tried to cheer him up. "All you need is a little capital and you can start on your own. Remember what you told me last year? You said that if young Japanese could make up their minds to march forward empty-handed, not burdened by anything from the past, it would be the start of new life in Japan. That's why you liked living in Tokyo. It was a mass of ruins. Everything was destroyed so you couldn't rebuild the dead past. You had to build something new and completely different. You've got a great idea. Stick to it." He took Ko's arm. "Let's take a walk."

It was a balmy night in early June. "I wasn't just making conversation when I said that all you needed was a little capital to start on your own. I think I can help you. I've got a deal going on the outside that's making good money. I could use some help—and pay you well."

Ko was wary. "Black market?"

"It's strictly legitimate, believe me."

"What would I have to do?"

"I need someone who can speak both Japanese and English to make some deliveries. In a month you'll make a couple of thousand dollars. No sweat." He lowered his voice. "On the side I'm helping some Japanese businessmen get contracts and permits. If I were a civilian it would be simple, but I have to stay in the background. Practically everyone at the Dai Ichi Building is moonlighting. We just have to be cautious."

Ko knew what his father would say! He was still clinging to the old-fashioned samurai ways. But in today's world you had to be more realistic. As the colonel had once told him, "You've got to play hard ball to get along in modern times." What harm was it to cut a few corners?

3.

Mulrooney would never knowingly have involved Ko in trouble. But he was dealing in "dangerous dollars" not contracts and permits. Having lost most of his savings by playing poker with enlisted men, he desperately needed money to augment the pitifully small college fund for Jo. The easiest and safest way, he learned, was selling U.S. dollars for yen, and then converting the yen back into dollars. In the past few months he had accumulated twenty thousand dollars and would quit once he had thirty thousand. Unfortunately the enlisted man who had been his courier had recently been shipped home and there was no one else in the Dai Ichi Building he could trust. He had briefly considered acting as courier himself, but realized he was too well known. Now he had found someone he could trust and who would profit handsomely at no risk, since Mulrooney had a foolproof method of buying dollars, finding trustworthy buyers, and carrying out the exchanges.

Two days later Ko carried out his first assignment. He was both frightened and excited as he carried a neatly wrapped package into a newly opened bookstore in the Ginza. It was exactly 2 P.M. Self-consciously he searched out the stacks until he found a battered English-language copy of War and Peace. He turned to page 350, feeling like an international spy, and waited. Nothing happened. He looked around nervously. A fat student wearing a brown overcoat and gold-rimmed glasses was supposed to come up and ask how he liked Tolstoy. Half an hour passed. At last a heavy-set young Japanese entered, breathing heavily. Could you call him fat? wondered Ko. He did wear a brown overcoat but no glasses. The young man approached and picked out a book. "Secondhand books cost too much," he said casually. "It's absurd. Here's a trashy novel and they want two hundred yen for it. And if you want a foreign book that's famous it costs a fortune." He peered into Ko's book. "You like Tolstoy?"

Ko didn't know what to do. His heart beat hard. The fellow wasn't wearing glasses.

"Want me to hold that package while you browse?" said the student. He put on a pair of gold-rimmed glasses and peered closer at *War and Peace.*

"If you don't mind," said Ko clearing his dry throat, and handing over the parcel.

The fat student wandered down the aisle and disappeared in the back room. He emerged moments later and handed a package to Ko, who could feel it was heavier than his had been. "Thanks," he said stiffly, and stumbled over the sill as he left the bookstore. Once outside he felt he could breathe normally and within a few minutes he was enjoying himself. How easy it had been! And he was getting fifty dollars for an hour's undemanding work, more than he made in a month by sketching G.I.'s.

Within two weeks, after eight more deliveries, he was no longer nervous. But as the money he earned piled up he suspected that the colonel had lied about the contracts and permits. Ko was nagged by remorse for getting involved in what appeared to be black market dollars. He tried to convince himself that practically everyone in Japan was dealing in the black market every day. How else could people live? These were new times with new situations. But finally he felt so guilty that he decided to have it out with Mulrooney.

The colonel laughed. "I didn't expect you to believe that contract story very long." He treated it like a joke. "We're only getting our share. This is penny ante to what the fat cats at the Dai Ichi Building are pulling off. What's wrong with dealing in money? Nobody gets hurt. We're not cheating the Japanese. They get their money's worth. Who loses? Nobody."

Ko had been consoling himself with similar arguments, but when he heard them spoken aloud they pricked his conscience. He knew what his father would think. "I can't do it anymore," he said.

"I know how you feel. How about one more deal?" Another ten thousand dollars and he'd have enough for Jo's college and then some.

"I really don't think I should."

"I'd appreciate it. Just one more and it's quits." This time he'd make it worthwhile for Ko. He thought of promising him five hundred dollars—no, make it a thousand.

"I'd rather not."

Mulrooney had been sure that if he offered the thousand dollars, Ko would be offended. He shrugged his shoulders. "Okay, forget it," he said good-naturedly.

Ko realized how much the money would mean to Mulrooney and his daughter, and the fact that the colonel didn't apply any more pressure made him feel guilty. "All right," he said reluctantly. "Just one more."

This time the package was heavier. The rendezvous was a restaurant named Misono. As soon as he entered, a slender middle-aged man wearing a red tie left a booth and approached as if he were a friend. "Glad to see you."

It was the right signal, and Ko extended his hand. "Nice seeing you too, Harada-san."

The man's hand was unpleasantly sweaty and Ko had the feeling he was not quite dependable. A girl led them to a private room decorated with hanging scrolls, flower arrangements, and expensive-looking decorations. "Please wait," she said and left.

Harada reached for Ko's package but he was suspicious and hugged it to him. "Where is yours?"

Harada smiled crookedly. "My partner has it. He's waiting at a nearby coffee shop. I'll telephone him." He bowed and left. This was strange and Ko was about to leave with his package when the waitress returned with little cakes and tea. Ko hadn't had lunch and the cakes were tempting. While he was eating one, Harada returned. "He'll be here in a moment."

Half an hour passed and Ko was now angry. "What's going on?" he said.

Just then a tall man with a cavernous face entered with a package. Without a word he passed the package to Harada, who handed it to

Ko. As he was holding out his own package, the *karakami,* the sliding partition, opened with a bang and two large American soldiers wearing combat boots burst in. "CID," said a red-haired captain. "Put up your hands!" Ko could hardly move. "I said put up your hands!" Ko's arms shot up. The man with the cavernous face slowly raised his arms. He was stoic, but the man calling himself Harada was trembling with fear.

The second American, a burly staff sergeant, was tearing open Ko's packages. "Dollars, sir," he said.

"What are you doing with dollars?" asked the captain. Ko was unable to say a word, but the tall Japanese answered aggressively, "We carry dollars for business. And we don't answer any questions except at headquarters."

"Get moving," said the captain, motioning with his pistol.

He herded the three Japanese outside and hailed a taxi. "Get in, all of you," he barked and instructed the driver to head for CID headquarters. "We'll be right behind so don't get any ideas." He hailed another taxi.

As the two cars headed down the narrow street, the tall Japanese swore. "They're fakes! They should be in a jeep!"

At the first corner the second taxi swerved to the right and sped off. Ko seized Harada by the throat. "You bastard! You tricked me!"

"I don't know anything about it! I swear." Harada began to cry. "My three million yen! Everything I had is gone!" He babbled like a baby.

When Ko told Mulrooney what had happened, the colonel said nothing for almost a minute. Then to Ko's amazement he said blandly, "Easy come, easy go." He shrugged his shoulders. "Sorry I got you into this mess. Just keep quiet and there won't be any trouble."

But Ko could not keep quiet. He had to tell the whole story to his father. Toda listened without comment, then said, "When I was young I did a very foolish thing. I found some money in the street and kept it. And I felt so bad I finally told my father. And he told me that he too had done a very foolish thing when he was young." Never had Ko felt so close to his father and he was ashamed for having ridiculed the samurai way of life.

The next day he was back in the Ginza sketching G.I.'s. Late in the afternoon a Japanese police sergeant watched as he worked. "I would like to ask you a few questions," the sergeant said when the G.I. left with his sketch.

Ko tried to hide his fear. "What about?"

"Last night. Would you please come to police headquarters?"

"I haven't done anything," he said, doing his best to act casual.

"I'd appreciate it if you'd come with me."

"I didn't do anything."

"Weren't you robbed by two men pretending to be CID officers?"

"I don't know anything about CID's." Harada, who had wept about his three million yen, must have squealed to the police, hoping to get it back. The fool! "I'm trying to earn a living here," he said. "I don't know anything about robberies."

"One of the men robbed reported to us. And we picked up the two suspects. One was a red-haired captain, the other a big sergeant. They both confessed and we checked out the people at the Misono Restaurant. I'm going to be frank with you. We need your help. The two fake CID's claim we beat them to get the confessions. They'll be tried by the Americans and we need witnesses. You won't get into any trouble, I promise."

Ko knew his father would want him to cooperate. "Well, I guess so," he said reluctantly.

"There's going to be a court-martial next week. The police report will read that you were robbed of yen, not dollars. The Americans are only interested in dollars and we'll forget about the yen. You have my word. Your testimony will prevent other crooked Americans from robbing Japanese."

"I'll do it," said Ko.

As Ko was walking up the stairs to the military courtroom, the red-haired American captain accosted him. "Are you going to testify against me?"

"Let me pass."

The captain seized his arm. "If you do . . . ." he pointed a finger at Ko's forehead as if it were a pistol and made a clicking noise.

Ko was tempted to go down the stairs but instead hurried into the courtroom, and once he found himself in the witness chair he had no qualms. He was going to do what his father would have done in his place. He pointed at the sergeant and then the captain. "They are the ones who robbed me!" he said.

They were sentenced to terms in Leavenworth. Mulrooney's name was never mentioned during the trial, but on June 29 he was transferred to Fort Hood, Texas. His daughter Jo, who had spent many happy weekends at Floss's orphanage, was invited to stay there until Mulrooney could find her a suitable home.

The colonel's abrupt departure caused a multitude of rumors at the office. Only McGlynn knew the truth, which Mulrooney had sheepishly disclosed with apologies. Then it was the professor's turn to apologize to Mariko for his own arrogant stupidity. He borrowed Maggie's car and at dawn next day headed for the orphanage to apologize to Floss. To his amazement and relief she said there was nothing between her and the colonel except friendship.

"How could you possibly think I'd marry him? I always knew he was a rascal, but I'm sorry he got himself into a mess." Her main concern was Jo. "She's a strong girl. She's known about her father for years. You can't help liking Tom, and he can't help being himself. He's got so many friends he always manages to squirm free."

As they strolled along the beach McGlynn spoke of his own problems. Taro was now at Tokyo University, a hotbed of communism, and he'd joined an activist group which demanded force, not talk. "He stays out all night sometimes and then refuses to tell Mariko where he's been. God knows what mischief those fools are up to! Taro treats me like the plague and his mother like a servant. I keep telling her she should marry me and then I could handle him. But she keeps putting me off."

"Don't rush her, Dad. I know how she must feel. Please be patient."

He growled. "I don't have many years for patience." They spoke little on the long walk back to the orphanage. He was mulling over the lack of love in his family. Only Mark was in love and lately he was moody. What had gone wrong in the McGlynn family? wondered the professor. Could it have been his fault? When Clara died he had shut himself off from love and shown damned little to his own children. How little affection he had given to them, particularly to Floss and Mark! He was paying for it now.

As they neared the orphanage Floss cheered him with good news. The artificial arm for Masao that Mark had ordered from America had arrived. He'd been at the Yokosuka Naval Hospital the past week getting it fitted. It had all been arranged by Mark's commander,

Colonel Sullivan. She had just received a call from Mark who was driving Masao home.

After lunch she proudly showed her father the latest improvements at the orphanage. A Marine detail was setting up a new addition with the help of older children while the young ones gaped in wonder. When Mark later drove up in a jeep with Masao there was a wild celebration. Masao proudly demonstrated how he could maneuver his new arm, and struggled to free himself from his mother's embrace.

Mark took his father aside. "Do you have a few minutes?" he asked uneasily.

"Of course."

"If you don't mind I'd like to get your advice."

McGlynn was pleased. He couldn't remember the last time Mark had sought his counsel. "What's the problem?"

"No problem really. It's just . . ." he hesitated. Ordinarily confident, Mark was embarrassed. This disconcerted the professor. Was Mark going to ask him something about sex? My God, he'd only known two women in his entire life, and Mark had that many in a few months.

"You know how much I love Chaucy . . ."

Here it comes! McGlynn averted his eyes.

"Well, I'm sure she loves me too, and, well . . . Damn it, I think we ought to get married."

McGlynn expelled a sigh of relief. "I can't think of a better idea! What's holding you back?"

"Nothing's holding *me* back. Oh hell, Dad, every time I get ready to pop the question, I get the feeling she wants to change the subject."

The professor was at last on firm ground. "How can she change the subject if you never bring it up?"

"That's just it. She doesn't say anything but I get the feeling that she thinks she's too good for me."

"Too good for a McGlynn? That's ridiculous!"

"You know—I'm a Marine and she's a hot-shot lawyer."

"Well for Christ's sake, Mark, speak up—ask her!"

Mark's eyes lit up as if he'd never thought of anything so simple. "Why not? I'll do it! Just as soon as she gets back from the States!" Chaucy was presently in Washington checking the records of the congressional Pearl Harbor inquiry to find material for the Tojo appeal, since it was taken for granted he would be sentenced to death.

"I was beginning to think I was crazy. Thanks." Mark was so relieved, he felt like doing something for his father. "Say, Dad, how about coming to our Fourth of July party at the Officers' Club? You could bring Mariko. She'd love the crowd down here."

McGlynn hesitated. "Do you think it would be all right?"

"Because she's Japanese? Benny Decker wouldn't stand for any crap. My date is going to be Fumiko. You remember the skinny little girl I used to play tennis with? She married a Matsutani."

A week later McGlynn arrived at the Yokosuka Officers' Club party alone. Mariko had refused to come for fear of causing an incident. "She's not feeling very well," he said. Fumiko Matsutani, looking stunning in her best kimono, pretended to believe this. But McGlynn realized she guessed the real reason, and his lame attempt to enlarge on Mariko's supposed illness worsened matters. The mutual embarrassment was interrupted by the arrival of Maggie, who had come in early that afternoon to do a feature story on Decker's rejuvenation of the naval base.

There was a loud burst of laughter from a nearby table where Captain Decker and his effervescent wife, Edwina, were holding court. Benny was telling about a young ensign, a supply officer, who had made a killing selling coffee and sugar on the black market. "He must have had a degree in business administration before he came over here, and was clever enough not to send home big money orders. Instead he took his payments in diamonds."

The McGlynns and Fumiko joined the crowd around the Decker table.

"Well, this young supply officer left here with a big bag of diamonds. But a jeweler in San Diego told him, 'Sonny, you've got some of the best cut glass I've seen in years.'"

There was a burst of laughter.

"You haven't heard anything," said Benny. "Our young genius recently sent me a letter demanding action against the Japanese who had given him glass instead of diamonds!"

The party was already a roaring success and by ten o'clock the newcomers to the base and the guests were drawn into the fellowship generated by the Deckers. Then Mark noticed that Commander Bradford, the man who had made the ugly scene at Fumiko's club, was having a drink with Colonel "Heavy Hand Hank" Evans, Mark's old nemesis, back for another inspection. A few minutes later Evans began cruising the room in search of attractive women. He made the mistake of cutting in on Maggie without recognizing who she was. On that eventful night in Guam the only face that was still clear to him was Mark's. As he had done at Guam, he now laid his heavy hand on her bottom. She whispered into his ear, "How would you like a knee in the crotch?" It was obvious Maggie was capable of doing just that, and the colonel moved in search of easier conquests. While Mark was getting drinks, Evans advanced on Fumiko, who was sitting with McGlynn. As they whirled a bit unsteadily onto the dance floor he began his usual tactics. She tried to pull away but was helpless.

Seeing Fumiko struggling at the far end of the room, Mark hurried to her rescue. "I believe it's my dance, Colonel," he said, fighting his temper. Evans was first startled, then infuriated to see it was McGlynn. "Mind your own damned business, Captain!" He started pulling Fumiko away, but Mark grasped his shoulder.

Evans was about to swing when Commander Bradford interrupted. "Need some help, Colonel?" he said. "This scumbag making trouble?"

By the time a crowd gathered, Billy J. had Heavy Hand under control but Bradford was loudly proclaiming that it was an insult to every woman in the place to have a Jap barroom madam polluting the air even if she did call herself a baroness. What threatened to be a major fracas abruptly ended with a few quiet orders from Captain Decker. Heavy Hand was diplomatically escorted back to the BOQ while Billy J. was persuading Bradford to take his distraught wife home. In ten minutes the party was back on course. But Mark still seethed since it was obvious that some of those present shared Bradford's indignation that a Japanese had been brought to the Officers' Club. His father escorted him outside. Mark was still so angry he didn't even realize he was trembling. "Take it easy, son."

McGlynn put his arm around Mark's shoulder. "What kind of a Navy do we have that breeds such scum? I'm afraid there are going to be some repercussions tomorrow morning. I saw several disapproving faces in there." He chuckled.

"What's so damned funny?"

"Thank God Mariko had the sense to stay in Tokyo!"

Mark remembered Fumiko. "I'd better get back to her," he said and hooked arms with his father as if they were brothers. "C'mon, McGlynn gang, back into the fray!"

Chapter Twenty-one

1.

Yokosuka, July 5, 1948.

There was a new provost marshal at Marine headquarters. Major Matt Patterson, after being seriously wounded at Guadalcanal, had spent seventeen months attending the Japanese language school at Yale. After VJ Day he had expected to be sent to Japan where his long training would be useful. But having graduated from law school in Chapel Hill, he found himself assigned as a judge advocate in the 1st Division legal office in China, in the center of Tientsin. Among his cases was prosecution of a Marine corporal for stealing and selling seven jeeps. Patterson's primary witnesses were Italian nationals awaiting repatriation. They had confessed not only their own implication but that of the local police department. Fascinating as this and similar cases were, Major Patterson was relieved to be transferred from China to Yokosuka Naval Base where not only could he use his Japanese but he could bring over his wife and two small children. That morning he had been welcomed warmly by Colonel Sullivan. While they were chatting, Mark came in. Upon learning he had been raised in Japan and spoke the language fluently, Patterson suggested he become chief investigator, since the current man was about to be rotated back to the States.

"Good idea," said Billy J. but left it up to Mark, who was enthusiastic. This would be far more challenging than patrolling Honcho Alley.

"I don't know if you're familiar with the duties of a provost marshal on this base," said Billy J. Besides handling all crimes committed by naval and Marine personnel, Patterson would deal with those involving the civilian population. "Usually it's petty theft or black marketeering, but it could be something much more serious."

Patterson explained that he had dealt in China with a number of civilian cases ranging from assault to murder, and he was used to dealing with the local police. Sullivan showed him the directive from General Eichelberger calling for more severe action against military offenders. "As yet we haven't had any major cases, but Army court-martial boards in both Yokohama and Kobe have recently imposed very heavy sentences." In Kobe, for example, two men got life sentences for rape. And five others got a total of 147 years' confinement for robbing the Fifth Medical Depot warehouse in Yokohama. Patterson would be covering not only the naval base but the city of Yokosuka and the entire prefect.

In the next two weeks Mark and his assistant, Sergeant Rossi, handled a variety of cases involving Japanese workers on and off the base who were selling American greenbacks and dealing in thievery of PX and commissary supplies; a false alarm which sent twenty M.P.'s to the Enlisted Men's Club to stop a fake riot; theft of several hundred pounds of sugar from the mess hall; and the sinking of the admiral's barge by three drunken sailors.

Mark was beginning to get bored, since all these episodes required little more than surface investigation. But on July 21 a case presented itself which intrigued him from the beginning. Commander Bradford, the former All-America halfback who had caused the disturbance at the officers' club, stormed in complaining that their Japanese maid had stolen four gold medals and his collection of gold coins.

"I want you to throw the book at the little tramp," he said officiously.

"Do you have proof that she was the thief?"

"Of course!" He tossed a Japanese lunch box on Mark's desk. It landed with a thud. Mark opened the box and spilled out coins and medals. "I found it in the kitchen this afternoon."

"How do you know it's the girl's box?"

"I've seen her carrying it and I'll bet that's her name." He pointed to a strip of adhesive tape on which was written a name in Japanese.

"Hiroko Kato," read off Mark. "Is that the maid's name?"

"That's the little lady."

"We'll make inquiries, Commander," said Mark. Bradford started scooping up the coins. "I'm afraid we'll have to keep the evidence."

"What the hell for? These are mine."

Patterson entered. "What's the matter, Commander?" he said in his soft voice.

"This Marine wants to keep my coins!"

Mark explained.

"That's evidence, Commander. Please return them to the lunch box." Bradford reluctantly complied.

Patterson read the address on the tape. "Bring her in, Mark. But don't drive the jeep up to her house. Park it a few blocks away."

"Afraid the neighbors will see she's a thief?" said Bradford.

"She's not a thief until we prove it." said Patterson. "Thank you for bringing this to our attention. We'll keep you informed." After Bradford left, he said, "Unpleasant fellow."

Mark told of the scenes Bradford had made at the Club Espoir and the officers' club. "He's a big hero to some of the cowboys at the Officers' Club who think we're too easy on the Japanese."

It took half an hour to locate the address on a hill south of the city. The house was large and obviously belonged to once well-to-do people. The woman who opened the door was startled to see two men in uniform and when Mark told her in Japanese that he would like to see Miss Kato she wanted to know what had happened. Her niece had come home from work in tears but wouldn't say why. Mark explained that her employer had made a complaint about her and it was necessary to take her to the provost marshal's office for questioning.

The woman was terrified. "What has she done?"

Mark tried to calm her. "There is nothing to be concerned about at this time." He explained he had left his jeep near the bottom of the hill. "We will wait for your niece there."

On the trip to the base Mark tried to calm the frightened Hiroko by saying she would be taken home after a brief interrogation. Once in the office, Mark showed her the lunch box. "Is this yours?"

Hiroko stiffened. *"Hai,"* she said.

"Do you know why you're here?"

She nodded. Commander Bradford, she related, had held up the box and shaken it and said it was full of stolen gold coins. "But I didn't put them there!" Tullio brought in tea and persuaded her to drink some.

"Tell me about yourself," said Mark.

She told how she had spent most of the war on Saipan where her father had run a sugar plantation. She was the only one in the family who had survived. Her aunt, who lived near Hiroshima, was killed in the bombing and so Hiroko had come to Yokosuka to live with another aunt. She'd been working as housekeeper for the Bradfords so she could go to a school for nurses. Telling about herself calmed her, and she reiterated her innocence. She didn't know how the coins had gotten into her lunch box. She begged them to talk with Mrs. Bradford. "She will tell you I'm an honest girl."

After taking her home, Tullio said, "Something stinks." They drove to the officers' quarters. The Bradfords lived in a two-story house surrounded by a garden. Mrs. Bradford could not believe Hiroko could steal anything. "She's such a lovely girl, so neat and hardworking. Not at all like the girl she replaced."

Her husband had entered so quietly they were all startled to hear him say, "What the devil are you two doing here?"

"Asking your wife some questions, Commander." Mark was so unabashed that the commander apologized.

"Sorry I'm so edgy. C'mon in the other room and have a drink." Mark refused, but Bradford insisted on showing Mark and Tullio cups on the mantle as well as pictures of himself with famous people, including a President and several senators.

Mark reported to Patterson that he was not satisfied with Bradford's story, then admitted he could be prejudiced because of their previous arguments. "But it doesn't make sense. The Kato girl wants to become a nurse. She doesn't look like a thief or talk like one."

"I'm afraid your impressions won't carry much weight. I know she's supposed to be innocent until proven guilty. But we're going to have to *prove* she's innocent. Keep digging."

The next day Mark found a Japanese waiting in the office when he returned from lunch. It was Jun Kato, the reporter turned Communist, who was a friend of Maggie's. He explained that Hiroko Kato was not only his second cousin but his fiancée. Hiroko's aunt had telephoned him about the stolen coins. "She couldn't possibly have stolen them!" he exclaimed, and told in detail how she had volunteered to be a nurse during the battle for Saipan. "I interviewed one of her patients for my paper. He told me how she operated on the men, risked her life to get water for them, kept up their spirits by singing. They called her Our Little Nightingale. Do you think a girl like that could be a thief?" He was going to cover the story for his paper and would see she got fair treatment.

"You don't have to threaten us, Mr. Kato. We are still investigating the case and would appreciate it if nothing at all was written until we come to some conclusion."

Patterson joined them. "None of us want to hurt the reputation of Miss Kato. If she's not guilty we hope to keep the matter entirely out of the papers. You can count on us to investigate thoroughly and without prejudice." After Kato left, Patterson said, "There's something about Bradford that doesn't ring true. You and Tullio dig into his record."

Within a week Tullio reported there was talk that Commander Bradford was involved in the black market; his specialty was exchanging dollars or military scrip for yen or yen for dollars. "I think he's using several of his naval ratings in his office to pass the money. He's buddy-buddy with his men. You know, slaps them on the back, acts like a clown around the office. He's a real cutup, but I think he's a mean son of a bitch."

Mark discovered at the Officers' Club that Bradford was fresh with the waitresses and they all tried to avoid his table. "We also checked out Mrs. Bradford," he told Patterson. "Everyone likes her. She is as nice to the Japanese as Bradford is overbearing."

Mark had just learned from Maggie—she was on the post doing her own investigating—of Hiroko's extraordinary exploits on Saipan as a nurse. "With a record like that how could she possibly be a thief?"

Patterson had his own doubts about Bradford. "I've checked his version of when and where he was on the day of the theft," he said, "and it doesn't coincide with his wife's schedule or that of Hiroko. Bring her in again tomorrow morning. I'm going to ask Colonel Sullivan to sit in too."

Hiroko could not sleep that night. She was still too stunned. How could an American officer tell such lies! Scenes of the battle of Saipan kept flashing in her mind's eye. From the safety of Mount Tapotchau she could vividly see the American Marines landing on the western beaches of Saipan. The day before, her town of Garapan had been destroyed by shelling from U.S. ships and she was the only one in her family who had escaped. And so she had resolved to volunteer as a nurse at the main Japanese field hospital on the other side of the island. She was the only female nurse, and when the desperate need arose she steeled herself to operate on patients. As the battle raged she had risked her life by running for water in the daylight, forcing herself to pluck maggots from a patient's hollow eye, and raising the spirits of the men at night by singing songs of home. But once the American troops began closing in she had tried to kill herself with a grenade, only to be saved in spite of herself by Negro G.I.'s.

As she tossed restlessly in bed she recalled the day she finally left Saipan after tedious months of filling out applications. From the deck of the battered Japanese destroyer taking them back home she watched Mount Tapotchau grow smaller, and she once more gave a silent farewell to the middle-aged doctor in charge of the hospital who had died at her feet and to those soldiers on whom she, a novice, had operated. Then she had bade farewell to her dead mother, father, and sister and finally to her beloved brother whose tank had been destroyed at the waterfront on the first day of battle. "Hiroko is going back to Japan," she said to her family. "Alone."

Then she again pictured her sight of the first tiny island of Japan. Her homeland at last! And soon after came the thrilling sight of Mount Fuji, its peak covered with snow; and she remembered the young soldier who had died in her arms, saying one last word, "Fujisan!" Then she had stepped at last on Japanese soil.

And now she was called a thief!

She was in a defiant mood by the time she arrived the next morning at the provost marshal's office, and answered in monosyllables when Major Patterson requested her to go over once again the exact time she left the Bradford's, and how long it took her to get home.

"Did you have any trouble with Commander Bradford before he accused you?" asked Billy J.

She only shook her head.

"Did you know Commander Bradford had a bad reputation with the waitresses at the Officers' Club?" asked Mark. She shook her head. "Aren't you holding back something?" Her eyes teared.

Maggie walked in.

Mark was annoyed. "Maggie, can't you see this is a confidential interrogation?"

Hiroko was trying to control herself but Mark heard her say, *"Uchi no haji!"* (A family disgrace!)

"Major," said Maggie to Patterson, "I think I know what she won't tell you. May I have a few minutes with her?"

Mark protested, but not Billy J. or Patterson. Maggie led the girl to the anteroom. While Mark fumed, the others were silent. At last the two women reappeared. Mark had never seen such an expression of disgust on his sister's face. Finally she spoke. "The son of a bitch raped her!"

2.

Bradford was informed he would be tried by a general court-martial, and by late August Yokosuka Naval Base was divided into three camps. One camp, staunch defenders of the commander, were incensed that the famous football hero could possibly have raped a Jap. This group consisted of those who enjoyed basking in the shadow of his former glory on the gridiron, and the enlisted men in his section who considered him a good Joe because he was jovial, played practical jokes, and wasn't too proud to give out autographs. The second and largest group were those like the Deckers who were devoted to improving relations with the citizens of Yokosuka and deplored Bradford's overt dislike of Japanese. And then there were those who pitied Bradford's wife.

At the enlisted men's club there was lively betting on the outcome of the court-martial. This illegal waging was organized by a sergeant experienced in such dealings. Among his other profits was from ferryboat transportation to a nearby whorehouse.

The main target of the pro-Bradford people was Mark. He was not only an aggressive investigator but still possessed a talent for making enemies. Normally good-natured, he occasionally lost his temper at what he thought was injustice to others, and said exactly what he thought. He had improved greatly in the past few years under Billy J.'s tutelage, but his tongue still wagged when he felt he was right. And never had he been so sure he was right.

With the help of Tullio and The Beast he had interviewed thirty people, Japanese as well as Americans. From the three Japanese carpenters who were working on the front of the Bradford house on the day of the alleged rape, he learned that Bradford had come home that afternoon about four o'clock. In his first official statement Bradford had mentioned nothing of this visit, but when shown the affidavits of the workmen he admitted he had stopped to get some papers. He claimed he hadn't stayed more than ten minutes, and later statements from three enlisted men in his office corroborated his statement. The three workmen were again questioned about the time and there was some discrepancy in their answers.

At the suggestion of Tullio, Mark had already telephoned the provost marshal at Pearl Harbor where Bradford had served for a year. Mark had asked if Bradford had ever had any trouble there. The first reply was that there was no record of anything, but further search would be made. While Major Patterson and the investigators were going over their evidence that morning, a call came from Hawaii. In the files was found a complaint registered by Bradford of a theft of jewelry from their home in Makalapa by their Hawaiian servant. She, in turn, charged he had tried to kiss her and she had run out of the house. "Since the girl liked Mrs. Bradford," explained the provost marshal, "she said nothing and came back to work as if nothing had happened." Mark was making hurried notes, and his excitement was communicated to the others. He could hear the rustling of papers over the phone. Finally the provost marshal said, "There are a few brief reports which only indicate that the jewelry was found behind the bureau. And so there was some suspicion the girl might have brought it back. Anyway the whole matter was dropped and there is no record Bradford was even reprimanded. I'll send you copies of everything we have."

Patterson did not share Mark's enthusiasm. "It could indicate a pattern of behavior, but I don't think it will hold much water. But it won't hurt to introduce it."

Mark slapped his head. "Dummy!" Why didn't I think of finding out if there'd been another girl at the Bradford's *before* Hiroko?" Mark grabbed his cap and was at the door with Tullio at his heels. They found Mrs. Bradford at home. Her eyes were red as if from crying and she reluctantly let them into the living room. Mark noticed a half-filled glass—either Coca-Cola or something stronger. "I'm terribly sorry to disturb you, Mrs. Bradford. We'll only be a minute. Was there another housekeeper before Hiroko?"

With a guilty look, she took a sip of her drink. "Oh, yes. Tomie seemed like such a nice girl at first. But Tomie wasn't very clean and she became quite sloppy. I had to let her go. Hiroko was just the opposite." She pretended to blow her nose but Mark could see she was trying to hide her tears.

In twenty minutes Mark and Tullio were at the home of Tomie

Komura. Her mother, terrified to see two Marines, finally revealed that Tomie had moved to her aunt's home after being fired.

Mark assured her they only wanted to ask Tomie a few questions. "She is not in any trouble at all. Could we please have her address?"

It was a village near Sasebo in Kyushu.

That afternoon Mark was in a navy plane bound for Sasebo Naval Base. The local provost marshal lent him a car and two assistants to get a proper statement. It took an hour to find the little house of Tomie's aunt. The girl was at a neighbor's and a boy was sent to fetch her. She arrived breathless and nervous. Mrs. Bradford was right. Tomie was sloppy, unlike most Japanese girls. But she was pretty.

Mark first assured her she was in no trouble. "We only want to ask you some questions about the time you worked for Commander Bradford and his wife."

She was suspicious and her answers shed little light.

"Did you ever have any real trouble with the Bradfords?"

"What do you mean?"

"You know . . . I don't mean did Mrs. Bradford scold you for anything . . ."

Tomie interrupted. "Oh, she didn't appreciate anything I did. I could never get anything right."

"What about the commander?"

"He was all right. I didn't see much of him."

"He didn't make any trouble for you? You know, criticizing you."

"He was mad one day when I broke a dish and he said he would take it out of my wages."

"Nothing else." She shook her head. Then he told the two men from the provost marshal's office to wait for him in the car. When they were alone he said in Japanese. "I think we can talk more freely with them gone, don't you?"

"They made me nervous. Looking at me like I did something I shouldn't."

He smiled. "Police are always like that," he said. "I'm not a policeman. I just try to find out what happened and try to protect those who are innocent." He could see she was already more relaxed. "I think you can help the girl who took your place, Hiroko Kato." She didn't know any Hiroko Kato. "She's your age and she's engaged to a nice young man who works for a Tokyo newspaper."

Tomie smiled. "I'm getting married too. To the boy whose father owns the big fish market."

"Congratulations. I hope you both are very happy."

She was now so at ease she went out to get tea. As they sipped tea he said, "Poor Hiroko is in bad trouble." He told how Bradford had charged her of thievery. "But we couldn't believe it."

"Japanese girls don't steal."

"Finally she admitted to us what the real trouble was."

"What was it?" She was as eager as if she were listening to a radio show.

"She said he raped her."

She exploded with an epithet he had never heard before.

"Do you think Hiroko lied?"

"He tried the same thing with me!"

Mark felt a chill run up his back.

"I was making the bed and he came up behind me and pushed against me. He laughed and said I needed help. Then he tried to kiss me and I swung at him and accidentally hit him in the eye." She laughed vindictively. "When I came in a few days later he had a big black eye."

"And after you hit him?"

"This made him mad and he pushed me down on the bed."

"Did he rip off your clothes?"

"I never said that!"

"Don't be afraid. Just tell me what happened."

Her eyes were suspicious. "It would be in the newspapers."

"All we want you to do is tell what happened. Think of poor Hiroko."

"I'm thinking of poor me. You get out of here." She called her aunt. "Please, listen . . ."

"What do you think will happen to me if it gets in the newspapers! Yukio wouldn't have me for a wife. You speak Japanese but you don't know anything." Even though Bradford hadn't actually raped her it would ruin her reputation. She started to cry. Her aunt, followed by an old man, entered tentatively.

"There's nothing to worry about," Mark told them. "Would you please leave us alone for a few minutes."

His soft manner was convincing and the aunt and old man disappeared.

"Now, Tomie, I promise you'll be in no trouble." She looked at him suspiciously. "I'm not asking you to come to Yokosuka and testify. I can arrange it so you can give your testimony on paper."

"But they'll still know it's me and it will get in the papers." He explained that his sister was a famous correspondent and would cover the story. "She will see that your name is not mentioned. And Hiroko's young man will cover the story for the Japanese papers."

"You promise I won't get my name in the papers?"

"I promise," he said, wondering how this could be arranged. He told himself he would do his best to keep his promise. But he had to do it for Hiroko—at least he kept telling himself so on the trip back to Yokosuka, as he clutched the detailed statement of the attempted rape signed by Tomie and witnessed by himself and the two Sasebo assistants.

"Maybe we can persuade her to come down and testify in person," said Major Patterson.

"I doubt it," said Mark almost wishing he had been unsuccessful.

"We have enough now to get a general court-martial. But keep working. Try to get something on those two enlisted men Tullio thinks are working the currency scam with Bradford." He patted Mark on the back. "You did a good job."

"Yeah," he said disconsolately.

"Anything wrong?" asked Patterson.

"No, sir."

After studying the Komura girl's statement, Patterson was sure he could convict Bradford and completely clear Hiroko. Then Mark confessed to Patterson and Billy J. that he had promised the girl there would be no publicity if her statement was used in court. Mark could feel Colonel Sullivan's displeasure. "You can't go back on your promise," said Billy J.

"I'd feel better if we didn't use the statement," said Mark. "Don't we have enough without it?"

Patterson shook his head. They discussed other possibilities but none held water.

"I have an idea!" said Patterson, and after he explained it both Mark and Billy J. thought it would work.

The following afternoon Mark was in Kyushu again telling Tomie that his superior, Major Patterson, believed there might be newspaper publicity if her statement was used. "But we've come up with a way to save you any embarrassment at all." Tomie eyed him suspiciously as he brought from his briefcase a sheaf of papers. "This is a shorter version of your original statement. This one ends after Commander Bradford tried to kiss you and you hit him in the eye."

She remained suspicious.

"Don't you see? There's not a word about rape. No one could possibly criticize you for preventing the commander from kissing you. All you have to do is sign it."

"I don't want to sign anything—Yukio will still be mad and won't marry me."

"For defending yourself? He'll be proud of you."

"You don't know Yukio. If it's in the newspapers he'll still feel he has been shamed."

He dreaded to do what was now necessary. "I'm afraid you don't understand the position of the United States Navy." Mention of the Navy and his stern voice brought a look of fear. "If you don't sign this statement, then we'll have to use the original which is in the hands of the provost marshal of Yokosuka Naval Base. And that original gives all the details of the rape."

Tomie burst into tears and her aunt hurried into the room, a look of terror on her face. The girl begged her to leave and said there was nothing at all the matter. She took Mark's pen and scratched her name on the new statement.

"You're doing the right thing, Tomie," he said and put it into his briefcase. "But there's one more thing. Since this statement never mentions the rape, it will be necessary for you to testify in court."

The look of fear returned. "You mean I'd have to say those things in front of people?"

"It will only take a few minutes and no one will think you did anything but the right thing."

Her fear turned to sullenness.

"There is nothing to be embarrassed about. It will be over before you know it. The United States Navy is going to pay all your traveling expenses and you'll be put up at some nice Tokyo hotel. Or if you prefer you can stay with your family in Yokohama."

Her eyes had lit up at the words "Tokyo hotel." "I never was in a nice hotel." She knew about the running water in every room, and the private bathroom, and that some even had showers. "But mother would be so upset. I'll stay with her."

3.

On the morning of September 7, 1948, a Thursday, the general court-martial of Commander James Bradford started in a building near Captain Decker's headquarters. Because of the fame of the defendant, the courtroom was crowded. There had been few trials at the naval base of such a serious nature and none that had generated such controversy. The rich alumni of Bradford's university had raised enough money to bring one of the most famous trial lawyers in America to Japan. He was assisted by two naval officers.

The president of the court-martial was a senior naval captain, and the other eleven members of the court ranged from captain to commander. Major Patterson was judge advocate and handled the prosecution. He was assisted by a Marine captain with legal experience. Mark was not permitted to help, since he had been the investigating officer and would be a witness. Seats had been reserved for thirty Japanese and the remainder were for naval base personnel and their families. The press was represented by Maggie, two other American journalists, and four Japanese reporters, including Jun Kato who looked strained. McGlynn and Will were there.

Major Patterson's wife, Sally, just arrived from America with two small children, sat in the fifth row and could see that Matt, who appeared calm to others, was disturbed. Mark had just arrived to tell him something and she hoped nothing had gone wrong at the last moment. "Tomie wasn't home when I went to pick her up," Mark was telling his chief. "She's already gone back to Kyushu. Her mother said she was practically hysterical. Couldn't face Commander Bradford and his wife."

"Fly up to Sasebo and bring her back," said Patterson calmly. "Otherwise I'm going to have to use her original statement. Tell her how many reporters are here."

A few minutes later the president of the court-martial entered, took his seat, and as his gavel struck the table said, "The court will come to order."

Major Patterson rose. "The prosecution is ready to proceed with the trial in the case of the United States against Commander James Bradford, charged with rape, who is present in court."

After Patterson, the members of the court, and the reporters were sworn, Patterson read the charges and the sole specification. Then a not guilty plea was entered, and Hiroko was called as the first witness for the prosecution. But before questioning her Patterson addressed the court. "The general nature of the charge in this case is rape. The charge was preferred by Miss Hiroko Kato. And to save time I'm going to have her tell you in plain, simple terms exactly what happened on the afternoon of Wednesday, the thirtieth of June, 1948."

Hiroko, looking neat in a modest Western-style dress borrowed from Sally Patterson, came forward tentatively. She looked toward Patterson who asked her in Japanese to tell the court what happened. After taking a deep breath, she glanced again at Patterson who nodded, and began to speak quietly.

The Japanese interpreter asked her to speak louder. "After lunch," she said nervously, "Mrs. Bradford asked me to clean the upstairs. She was going to visit the Kamakura Buddha with some friends and would not be back until six, and since I would leave at five she paid me for the day." No one interrupted her, and she was gaining confidence. "After I finished the bathroom and guest room, I began cleaning the big bedroom where the Bradfords slept. He came in as I was taking off the old sheets for washing."

"Who do you mean by 'he'?" asked Patterson.

"You know, the mister. Commander Bradford. He began to joke. I think he was joking but I couldn't understand his English very well. Anyway he was sort of laughing. I said something polite, I don't remember what, and went back to my work. All of a sudden he grabbed me from behind and pushed against me, and said something like, 'Kissy, kissy!' I was frightened and tried to break away but he pushed me on the bed and turned me over."

"I know this is difficult for you, Hiroko-san. Please continue."

"He . . . he pulled down my panties . . . ." She put a hand to her mouth and began to weep.

The President, a grizzled captain with a weather-worn face, asked if Patterson wanted a short recess but he said, "I think if someone gives her a glass of water she'll be able to continue."

Sally Patterson could feel the wave of pity for the girl, but there were also those whose stony faces indicated they didn't believe a word she said.

Hiroko was ready to continue. In short sentences that seemed wrenched from her, she told how he had roughly spread her legs and slapped her face when she resisted. And when she had screamed he punched her in the stomach. At last she was finished and started to rise from her seat. Patterson signaled her to sit down. "Does the defense desire to cross-examine?"

"Defense does," said Francis X. Flaherty tersely. He walked slowly toward Hiroko like, thought Patterson, a fox edging towards its prey. Flaherty was a small, wiry civilian who oozed confidence and energy. He had defended those accused of murder, kidnapping, treason, and corruption for twenty-five years with astounding success. He had been widely praised for representing prisoners too poor to pay any fee, and even more widely damned for freeing underworld characters.

Hiroko had been prepared by Patterson to expect him to assault her story without mercy.

"Yours is truly a heartrending story, Miss Kato, and no feeling person in this room can fail to have been moved by it." His voice was quiet, almost soothing. "I have a daughter your age and I know how every father would feel if his child were so savagely attacked as you say you were. There is only one little problem, Miss Kato." He approached to within a yard of her, fixing her with his small blue eyes. "The little problem, Miss Kato, is that the defense is going to prove beyond a shadow of doubt"—he suddenly jammed a finger almost in her face—"without a shadow of doubt that you are a liar!"

Patterson was about to protest when the president said sharply, "Mr. Flaherty, will you please back away from the witness. This is not some civilian trial. There will be no further pyrotechnics. This court is only interested in finding out the truth and we shall proceed properly."

Flaherty, not at all disturbed, apologized. "I am through with the witness," he said affably. "For the time being."

One of the Japanese carpenters was called by Patterson as his next witness. He testified that Bradford had entered the house at about four P.M. and came out an hour or so later. After being warned not to communicate with his colleague, the carpenter was dismissed. Then another carpenter was called. He verified the first story. "This," concluded Patterson, "refutes the defendant's claim in his original state-ment to the investigating officer that he had only stayed five or ten minutes."

"I note," said Flaherty, "that my worthy colleague has not called the third carpenter. I wonder why?"

"We submit his statement," said Patterson. "The court will note that while the third man confirms that Commander Bradford did enter the house about four P.M., he was not sure when he left."

Flaherty requested the third workman be brought into court. Patterson assured him he would be on hand the next morning with the other workmen, and then introduced the exhibits from Pearl Harbor showing that in 1945 Bradford had accused their Hawaiian maid of stealing some valuable jewelry, but later dropped the charge after the maid claimed he had tried to kiss her.

"What does Pearl Harbor have to do with this case?" asked Flaherty. "This matter here . . ." he held up his copy of the exhibit, "is not only irrelevant but the material evidence should not ever have been introduced. These papers, some written in pencil, are only ini-tialed."

"They show a pattern of behavior by the accused," said Patterson. "This case began with a complaint by Commander Bradford that Miss Kato stole his gold coins. Our investigators could find no proof at all that she had."

"This specious evidence from Pearl Harbor," persisted Flaherty, "Is not in proper form. It is pure hearsay." It was obvious to Patterson that the members of the court-martial were favorably impressed by Flaherty's argument, and he immediately called to the stand a Japa-nese doctor to testify on the injuries to Hiroko's vulva. This ended the prosecution's case, and court was adjourned.

At dinner Matt told Sally that unless Mark could bring back Tomie Komura, even the introduction of her full statement might not be enough to convince the members of the court.

It took an hour for Mark to persuade Tomie to return to Yokosuka. At first her aunt refused to let him see her, but when he said that he would then have to appeal to the officials at Sasebo Naval Base—the very words "Naval Base" sounded ominous—she practically dragged Tomie from the kitchen. "Do you want to force us to use your entire statement?" he sternly asked the girl.

"But you promised," she protested tearfully. "You said you wouldn't break your word."

"You broke yours by leaving Yokosuka, so I am free to break mine. I'm not going to argue any further. I am sorry all this will be in the newspapers now, but you are responsible." He started toward the door.

"I'll go," she said sullenly.

The wind was bending over the trees by the time they climbed into the jeep.

"Typhoon," said the driver. "No flights tonight or tomorrow."

On the way to Sasebo a tree crashed across the road and it took an hour to make a detour. Once in the provost marshal's office Mark learned more bad news. Rail communications between Kyushu and Honshu were cut and there could be a long delay. Mark phoned Matt at his quarters. They might not get back until late Saturday afternoon. The major told him to do his best and to keep in touch.

Even though Patterson had not raised his voice during the telephone conversation, Sally knew something was wrong. He told her the problem, adding that it would mean juggling a few things to slow down the trial. Earlier he had estimated that the defense would probably end its case in a day and a half. Somehow he had to stall so the case would have to be carried over to Monday.

On Friday morning Flaherty briefly stated the defense case, then surprised everyone by calling as his first witness the third workman. He repeated what he had previously attested in his statement. At the longest, the commander had not been in the house more than twenty minutes.

"Did you notice anything unusual about him when he came out?"

"What do you mean?"

"I mean in his actions or appearance."

"No."

"Did he look as if he had been in a fight? Any scratches on his face, any blood on his uniform . . ."

Patterson objected that he was leading the witness.

"Objection overruled," said the president after consulting with other members.

"In other words he looked just as neat as he had when he walked into the house?"

"Yes, sir."

After Patterson's cross-examination failed to shake the witness, Flaherty, using a large drawing of the house, argued that it would have taken far more than twenty minutes for anyone to have gone to the second floor, engaged in conversation a few minutes, attacked Miss Kato and reappeared looking "as neat as a pin." He then asked the workman if he had heard any screams while Bradford was in the house. The answer was no.

"Did you see Miss Kato leave the house?"

"Yes. A little while after the commander."

"What's a little while?"

"Oh, ten or fifteen minutes."

"Did she act or look unusual?"

"She just walked right past us."

"Was her dress torn? Her face bruised?"

"No, sir."

Flaherty separately recalled the other two workmen. They both insisted Bradford had been upstairs at least forty minutes or so but agreed there was nothing unusual about his appearance when he left. Nor had Miss Kato said anything to them.

"Gentlemen," said Flaherty, "can anything be harder to swallow than the tale concocted by this poor girl? The three workmen all testify they heard no screams and she waltzed out of the house without saying a thing. Can you imagine that any girl who had just been raped would go silently past three of her countrymen? Can you imagine she wouldn't have cried bloody murder?"

Patterson praised his opponent for his ingenious theory. "There are only two things wrong with it. First, a Japanese girl who had been raped would not have said a word to the workmen. She would have been too ashamed. To 'cry bloody murder' would only broadcast her shame and ruin her reputation. Secondly, my worthy opponent makes much of the fact that the three workmen didn't hear screams. Our investigators also had suspicions and so conducted an experiment. Three naval officers who had no connection with this office stood outside exactly where the workmen had stood. Then Miss Kato, myself, and three other naval officers who had no connection with this office went to the bedroom, which is at the back of the house. Miss Kato screamed half a dozen times. The three officers outside could not hear a thing. I can see the defense counsel has doubts. But he neglected to ask the workmen if there could have been anything that prevented them from hearing the very loud screams of Miss Kato." He went to the prosecution desk and picked up a little radio which had a long extension cord. "This radio, Exhibit L, was playing music."

The three workmen confirmed this. "We asked the commander's wife if she minded," said the third workman. "She let us plug it into the hall socket."

"Of course, if the defense protests we have no objection to calling a recess so we can make the same test in front of the members of this court." That would take at least two hours. But Flaherty would not take the bait. He said he would accept the evidence of the first test.

Late in the morning Bradford gave his version of the event in the bedroom. Even Sally Patterson had to admit he looked like the ideal clean-cut American. Well-coached by Flaherty, he spoke convincingly and made no disparaging remarks about Hiroko. Mrs. Bradford's appearance and manner were also convincing. No, Jim had never shown the slightest interest in Hiroko. No husband could have been more thoughtful and kind.

Patterson's mild manner in cross-examination put her off guard. "You never had any trouble with Hiroko-san?"

"Oh, no, she was a very good worker. Not like . . ." she suddenly stopped but couldn't help glancing instinctively toward Flaherty who had warned her never to mention the previous maid.

Flaherty was afraid the prosecution counsel would say, "Not like who?" But Matt pretended to be unobservant since he wanted the appearance of Tomie to come as a surprise.

"You never had any complaints about Hiroko-san?"

"Oh, no. She was very efficient. She came from a very nice family."

"I see. You wouldn't call her a liar?"

"Oh, of course not. She was . . ." She realized she had made a mistake and didn't finish the sentence.

"I agree that anyone who has known Miss Kato any length of time would realize she is honest. Now since you admit freely she would not lie, then you must believe her story."

Mrs. Bradford went pale. Her eyes were wide. She was about to stammer something when Flaherty objected. But before the president could say, "Overruled," Patterson said, "I withdraw the last sentence. The witness is excused."

Flaherty was secretly triumphant, concluding that Patterson, like so many military lawyers who had never tried a case in civil court, didn't have the stomach for the rough and tumble of a criminal case. He himself began a relentless attack on Hiroko's character. He brought forward witnesses who had seen her at the Communist protest rally at the gates of the naval base. Another witness claimed she had attended Communist meetings.

She admitted she had been at the rally.

"Why?"

"Because I believe we should never again have a war." She spoke fervently out of her own experiences as a nurse on Saipan. "Everyone I know is against war and General MacArthur won't allow us to have an army anymore."

"If there is another rally at the base will you attend?"

"Yes, sir."

"And you also have attended Red meetings?"

"Yes, sir. They have some good ideas. They want to help the people."

"So you are a Communist?"

"Oh no, sir. I want to be a nurse."

This brought a laugh which the president quelled even though there was the suggestion of a grin on his own leathery face.

"But you like their ideas?" pressed Flaherty.

"Some of them."

"How about free love? They preach free love."

"Isn't everyone for free love?"

Patterson objected. "She has no idea what you're talking about."

"Explain to her, Mr. Flaherty, what you mean," said the president.

"It means the practice of free choice in sexual relations, without legal marriage or any obligations."

It took some time to put this into Japanese. Hiroko put a hand over her mouth. She laughed nervously. "I never heard of that."

Flaherty quickly changed the subject. "I understand you were the only female nurse for wounded Japanese on Saipan."

"I never saw another woman there, sir."

"So you were surrounded by thousands of men without privacy. That is, you didn't have separate quarters?"

"Separate quarters!" She couldn't believe anyone could be so stupid. "There was no such thing as quarters. We all worked and slept under the stars."

"One girl and a thousand men."

"May it please the court," said Matt Patterson. "This line of questioning is distasteful and unfair. This girl was performing a courageous duty, and you are trying to imply that she was sexually loose."

"Sexually loose?" said Flaherty in mock horror. "Did I ever say sexually loose? Not at all. You are the one who said sexually loose. I would not even dream of using the term sexually loose."

"Mr. Flaherty," rasped the president in a peremptory manner, "will you please cease treating this court like one of your juries in Chicago."

But Patterson could see that the constant use of the phrase could have had some effect on those members who had doubts about Hiroko's behavior.

The rest of the day was spent in the introduction of statements from prominent people, including three senators, a former Vice President of the United States, and a retired Supreme Court justice, testifying to Bradford's character. The latest word from Mark was that he and Tomie were finally on the main island of Honshu but a washed-out bridge was holding them up. He had tried to get motor transportation but there were also washouts on the highways, and he had been advised to stay on the train. The earliest they could arrive in Tokyo, he estimated, was 5 P.M. Saturday.

Trees were also down at Yokosuka, and the roof above the courtroom was leaking when court was called to order on Saturday morning. Matt brought back the Japanese doctor who had examined Hiroko and managed to take until midmorning proving that on the day of the alleged assault Hiroko had come to his office with her girlfriend. "Were the injuries to her vulva from rape?" he asked.

"I believe so," said the elderly witness.

"Can't you be more definite?" said Matt, "rape is a felony and can be described as carnal knowledge of a woman by force and against her will. Force is the—"

"Objection!"

"Overruled!"

"*Force* is the essential element of the crime of rape, and this court must be satisfied beyond a reasonable doubt that Commander Bradford used such force and that Miss Kato either did her utmost to resist or was afraid to resist. Now I ask you again, Doctor. Be more definite. Was this particular rape according to the terms I have just described?"

Matt could see sweat form on Bradford's forehead.

"Based on my previous experience I can state almost positively that the injuries were caused by forcible entry."

"If it wasn't rape, Doctor, then what else could it possibly have been?"

"I can think of no other reason."

In cross-examination Flaherty questioned the doctor's ability to make such conclusions. "You are a practitioner of medicine in a provincial town."

"What better place to gain experience on such cases?" He also testified he could have ended up in a prestigious Tokyo hospital but preferred helping people in his home town.

During a short recess Matt and his assistant ate sandwiches in a little room, trying to devise other ways to delay; for it was apparent that Flaherty was eager to get to the arguments before the lunch break and finish off the case in the afternoon.

"Look what I've got!" exclaimed Tullio, bursting into their waiting room followed by a Japanese wearing a clean but multipatched uniform. A medic—one of the few survivors of Saipan. He had read the morning paper about the slurs against Hiroko as a nurse at Donnay Hospital. He had been with her until the end.

His appearance caused a mild sensation. His recitation of how she learned to operate, how she plucked maggots from a soldier's eye, and how she risked her life to get water kept the listeners spellbound. And when he told how, in the evening, she would sing songs of home and family, tears came to Sally's eyes. "We called her our 'Little Nightingale.' She kept us alive with her courage. Do you think anyone was thinking of her as a woman?" He pointed at Flaherty, who had grilled him. "I don't think that man was ever a soldier, but you others"—he turned toward the members—"you were in battle and you know what I'm talking about."

Patterson had managed to delay until 1:30 P.M., but he realized he could do no more. "May it please the court," he said. "I realize this is time for the prosecution to start argument. I plan to take an hour and the assistant judge advocate needs at least half an hour. Then I may be able to conclude in fifteen or twenty minutes. The prosecution would appreciate it if the court would recess until Monday morning."

"Objection!" exclaimed Flaherty.

"Overruled!" said the president sharply. "I think I speak for almost everyone. This has been an exhausting case and I agree with the prosecution. Some of us would like to get home and stop up the leaks caused by the typhoon. And the rest, I am confident, have other priorities for the weekend."

The other members agreed and court was adjourned.

Mark and Tomie arrived in Tokyo just before 7 P.M. First they ate at a good restaurant, and then he brought her to a modern Japanese hotel. Tomie gaped at its luxury. "After our rough trip you need a long rest," he said. Since the trial had been adjourned until Monday, Patterson had suggested they keep Tomie out of Yokosuka until the last moment. "If it's all right with you we can stay in Tokyo tomorrow night too, and then take the train to Yokosuka early Monday morning."

She needed no further persuasion. She felt as if she were in a dream.

On the taxi ride to the Dai Ichi Hotel where he would bunk on his father's couch Mark reread the last letter he had received from Chaucy. She had complained about the delay in her return from America. While going through the records of the congressional Pearl Harbor inquiry she had been summoned to Boston. Ropes-Gray, she explained, wanted her to consider joining the defense for six Negro boys accused of raping and murdering a white girl. "Our senior partner," she wrote, "thinks the firm should take the case as a public service. As yet there's not a single white witness for the defense and I'm leery about our chances. Even so I've promised to hang around a few more weeks to consider the matter." She made it sound as if she were being held in bondage, but he had a suspicion she was a willing captive. He swore so loudly that the driver almost ran into a pedestrian. "Watch the road!" exclaimed Mark in Japanese, and vowed he was not going to be swayed from his determination to ask Chaucy to marry him the moment she arrived.

Again there was standing room only when the court was called to order on Monday morning. The professor was sitting with Maggie, Will, and Mark. Those at the defense table looked supremely confident after Patterson said, "The prosecution has finished its case . . ." But he paused. "Except for a final witness. She was supposed to appear earlier but was delayed in coming here from Kyushu by the typhoon."

Flaherty leaned toward his client and said something. Bradford shrugged his shoulders indifferently.

"I apologize to the court for this delay, but if there are no objections I would like to call this witness."

A clerk escorted a girl into the room. Mark saw Mrs. Bradford, who sat nearby, give a start and put a hand to her mouth. Bradford wore a sickly smile at the sight of Tomie.

"Your name and residence, Miss Komura?" asked Patterson.

She nervously replied.

"Please speak up, Miss Komura," said the president.

She did and smiled apologetically. When she saw Bradford staring at her she looked toward Patterson in panic. He spoke quietly, reassuring her there was no need to be nervous. "This court only asks that you tell the truth—all the truth."

"Hai!" she exclaimed so loudly that several spectators laughed.

"There will be no further outbursts!" said the president.

"You also worked for the Bradfords?"

"Yes, sir. For three months."

"Did you like working for them?"

"She was a nice lady. A little fussy but she was kind to me."

"Why did you work only three months?"

"She thought I didn't clean in the corners and things like that."

"Did she discharge you?"

Tomie looked about nervously. "There's nothing exceptional in being discharged, Tomie-san," said Matt in Japanese, his fatherly voice reassuring her. "I imagine," he hastily added in English, "that almost everyone in this courtroom has been fired once in his life."

"She came to me one day and said her husband, the commander, was complaining how sloppy the house looked even after I cleaned it."

"I see. So it was the commander who got her to fire you."

Flaherty objected and the president told the judge advocate to rephrase his question.

"Delete the sentence," said Patterson who had made his point. "Did you get along with the commander?"

"I object," said Flaherty. "Whether or not this witness did or did not get along with the defendant has absolutely no bearing on the issue of his guilt or innocence in this case."

"Overruled. The witness may answer."

"Did you get along with the commander?" repeated Patterson.

"Oh, I guess so. Until the day he cornered me in the bedroom."

Flaherty hurried to his feet. "I move to strike that answer! The words 'I guess so' are purely speculation and the balance of the answer is not responsive to the question, is highly prejudicial and should be stricken."

The president struck the answer.

"At any time," continued Patterson, "did you encounter Commander Bradford in the bedroom of the household?"

"I object," exclaimed Flaherty. "May we approach the bench?" He acutely sensed the developing storm and wanted to prevent the prejudice of the testimony from taking place before he had a chance to make his substantive objection. "It would appear to me to be quite clear," said Flaherty, "that the prosecution is about to embark on a description of some other incident between this witness and the commander. I respectfully submit that we are trying only one case here and that any alleged incident involving any other party has no bearing on the guilt or innocence of the defendant as charged in this case. If evidence of this character is admitted, we are embarking upon the trial of another case as to which the defendant has no previous notification of any alleged wrongdoing. We are involved in an entirely separate and collateral issue which is not only remote but highly prejudicial. I have no idea as to what direction the prosecution intends to take, but I think that I must make a timely objection to the possible direction of such evidence."

The president was impressed. "Major Patterson, what is your position with respect to Mr. Flaherty's objection that this evidence is irrelevant and remote and prejudicial?"

"I intend that the court should consider this evidence as probative of a design on the defendant's part to commit the crime charged here. There is a pattern of conduct involved in both incidents: one, a servant girl of another race is the victim; two, the incident takes place in the defendant's household in the absence of his wife; three, the incident takes place when the defendant returns to the household in his wife's absence during normal duty hours; and finally, the incident is followed by an effort to intimidate the victim by causing her discharge from his employment."

The president conferred briefly with the other judges. "We will take this evidence on the issue of design on the part of the defendant to commit the crime alleged, reflected in a pattern of conduct in a kindred incident."

"My objection to this line of testimony," said Flaherty doggedly, "and my continuing exemption should be noted as it proceeds."

After the president noted the objection, Flaherty still persisted. "I recognize the Tribunal has noted my objection and exception to this testimony. I also move that it be stricken from the record."

"Your motion is denied. Your exception noticed and your rights preserved."

Hiding his triumph, Patterson asked Tomie to continue her testimony.

"He grabbed me and tried to kiss me. I tried to get away and my hand accidentally hit him in the eye."

Maggie could see Bradford grow deathly pale. Flaherty was talking to him but he didn't seem to be listening. "The next day when I went back and was fired by Mrs. Bradford I saw he had a big black-and-blue eye."

There was a spontaneous burst of laughter at the picture of an All-American football star getting a black eye from a girl barely five feet tall. As the president called for order, Bradford lowered his head into his arms.

"I suggest we take a short recess," said the president.

When the session resumed Major Patterson said, "The testimony of Miss Komura is not finished, but perhaps defense counsel would like to cross-examine at this time?"

During the recess Flaherty had forced out of his client the entire story. The counsel slowly approached Tomie whose eyes bulged with fear. Then he turned. He had done his best to keep her evidence out, and wisely concluded that cross-examination would involve much more than the big black eye. "I see no reason to subject this young woman to any more stress. The defense rests."

"Do you wish to continue, Major Patterson?"

"I agree with defense counsel, sir. If the court please, I would like to make my opening argument."

Some in the audience felt cheated of further drama, but the majority were relieved that the humiliation of the Bradfords was ended. Matt's summation, Flaherty's rebuttal, and the prosecution's final argument were concise and without rhetoric on either side. Just before noon the president said, "The court will recess at this time. If a decision is reached today, it will reconvene between the hours of fifteen hundred and sixteen hundred. If a decision is not reached by sixteen hundred today the court will then convene at nine-thirty tomorrow morning."

The crowd emptied the room slowly, quietly, as if stunned by the sudden turn of events. Tomie spun away from Mark when he tried to escort her out of the room. Her eyes were red and her voice shook with anger and despair. "Now everyone will know! They will know everything!"

"I'm sorry," said Mark. "I never thought it would be like this."

She pulled free and darted through the crowd followed by Mark.

"What did she say?" Maggie asked Will.

" 'Now everyone will know everything.' And Mark said he was sorry and never thought it would end like this." Will was bitter. "Another trial where no one wins and everyone loses."

Hiroko was surrounded by three Japanese reporters, including Jun Kato and Maggie. Noticing that Hiroko was distraught, Mark said, "The trial isn't over yet. Break it up." He suggested they all have lunch at the nearby restaurant. Hiroko only picked at her food.

"What do you think the sentence will be?" asked Maggie.

"Guilty, of course," said Mark. "The only question is how long. He could even get death."

Hiroko got up from the table and hurried to the ladies' room followed by Maggie. "It's all over, honey," soothed Maggie.

"It's all over but what will become of me?"

"You'll go to Tokyo and become a nurse."

"I haven't worked since the trouble started and don't have enough money."

"How much will you need?" Hiroko gave a figure in yen which translated into approximately five hundred dollars. "You have more than that already."

"I have only a few hundred yen."

"The Fredericks Chain owes you seven hundred dollars for the stories I've been running about you in America." Hiroko looked at Maggie in wonder. "I didn't want to tell you before the deal was okayed by Mr. Fredericks."

When they returned to the table Mark was saying that Tomie wouldn't let him take her back home. "She thinks I lied to her."

"She'll cool off," said his sister. "What came out in court didn't make her look bad."

But he could not be assured. "She says her boyfriend will surely find out everything."

Maggie changed the subject. "I was just telling Hiroko she can leave this crummy town and go to Tokyo and become a nurse." She told about the money the newspaper was going to pay. "Hiroko should get it in a week or so." Maggie nudged Mark, and took him aside before he made a stupid remark. "The poor kid only has a few yen left. How about splitting the seven hundred dollars with me?"

"Tough Girl Reporter Has Heart of Gold," he said, and promised to give her a check for $350 that evening.

"While you're at it, make it for seven hundred, I'll pay you back."

"That's more like my girl."

"You know you can trust me."

He kissed her forehead. "Darling, of course I trust you. To be yourself."

At 3:30 P.M. the members of the court resumed their seats. "Commander James Bradford," said the president, "the court in closed session finds you of the only specification of the charge: Guilty."

Bradford tried to maintain his poise but his jaw fell.

"And again in closed session," continued the president, "and upon secret written ballots, two thirds of the members present at the time the vote was taken, the court sentences you to be confined at hard labor, at such place as naval authority may direct, for thirty years."

Bradford burst into tears and any triumph Matt may have felt disappeared. Mark still felt no pity for the man who had brought such tragedy to innocent girls, but the sight of Bradford's sobbing wife gave him a strange sense of guilt. Besides the unbearable shame, she would lose all privileges as an officer's wife since he was now reduced to the rank of seaman. The long travail was over but Mark felt little satisfaction. Justice had come but not mercy, particularly for the victims. His guilt over Hiroko's humiliation had been somewhat assuaged by the seven hundred dollars, but he knew he could never forgive himself for what had been done to Tomie—in the name of justice.

410

PART SIX

Chapter Twenty-two

1.

Tokyo, October 1948.

It was the time of year for McGlynn's annual report on the Occupation "For SCAP's Eyes Only." A personal note from MacArthur reiterated his desire for an assessment "with no holds barred." McGlynn set about the task with reluctance, for it had been a year of great change —particularly regarding America's political policy toward Japan and the Japanese. The year had also marked the end of the reform era, with the Japanese Diet finally approving bills defining the scope of trade associations, decentralizing the administration of education, and completely overhauling the legal structure. In addition the Japanese were drastically revising their political life along the lines of the new Constitution.

These reforms were augmented by new instructions from Washington to discontinue the dissolution of the *zaibatsu*. Elated, those Japanese family business combines had already changed plans in accordance with Washington's new trend which, inspired by the Cold War, was to make Japan the workshop of Asia. It was now obvious to McGlynn that Japan's economic life would have to be ruled by the *zaibatsu* so detested by all good American liberals. In some ways, he thought, this was the only way to rehabilitate Japan's economy; and yet it could mean a marriage of American capitalism with the *zaibatsu* in the pre-war mold of those international cartels so condemned by all his favorite commentators. The first step in this new concept had been authorization by Congress for pump-priming; America would pump some $150 million into Japan every year for the next four years. Not a bad idea, he thought, but wondered how the American voters would like paying out that much money to a nation not long ago a cruel enemy. Of course, the voters would never know what was going on until it was all over.

In his outline for MacArthur, the professor listed the four main ways America was planning to help a former enemy regain her pre-war industrial power: first, by permitting her to retain industrial plants which the Allies originally intended to seize as reparations; second, by financing the modernization of her plants and securing overseas raw materials and overseas markets; third, by restoring the *zaibatsu;* and last, by limiting some of the new freedoms given to Japanese trade unions. It took five pages to list what he thought were the benefits and dangers of these measures, and he eventually became so frustrated by his inability to make sense of his own assessment that he sent for Mariko.

After scanning his comments on the *zaibatsu,* she said, "All I know came from my husband. He told me the *zaibatsu* firms were *not* the evil genius behind the militarists' program of imperialistic expansion, and that the Americans had been misinformed." In fact, the *zaibatsu* were just the opposite. Their motto, "live and let live, prosper and let prosper," was based, she said, on the premise that Japan needed foreign trade to survive, and that this depended entirely on conciliation and friendship with other nations. "The *zaibatsu* could no more avoid helping the war effort than American industrialists could help supplying Roosevelt with the tools of war."

"I have another question," said the professor. "Tell me frankly what the average Japanese thinks of the Occupation after three years."

She paused a moment and then spoke of the incredible changes since the day her country lay defeated, naked and starving, its cities destroyed. Countless new buildings had already sprung up throughout Japan. The streets were lined with rebuilt shops brimming over with food and commodities. The people were dressed even better than in pre-war days. Black marketeering was almost gone. Morale was returning and the people enjoyed unprecedented freedom of thought and speech even though there was still a long way to go on the road to democracy.

"All Japanese women are grateful to America for at last giving us legal equality with men. And by your example you are teaching our men 'ladies first.' I know some people say the present democracy we have in Japan is prefabricated. But as far as woman's liberation is concerned that is not so. Women here were ready to be liberated and now, believe it or not, they are almost on an equal footing with men in family and social life. That famous modesty and sweet naïveté we Japanese women were formerly praised for is fast disappearing." Postwar Japanese girls had already shown they were even more realistic and aggressive in bargaining than boys. Women also got jobs, and stuck up for their rights with the Americans. "We women of today are more hardheaded than our men. Many of us have become complete mistresses of our circumstances."

This, she explained, was particularly true among the upper classes. Deprived of their money and servants, the men were helpless. Spoiled for generations by privileges, they had become dependent on their resourceful wives. For example, one of her neighbors, a baroness, now ran a successful food shop. "And she won't give her husband spending money unless he works as a clerk. She told me the other day that she was getting tired of such a loafer and was going to divorce him. Can you imagine such a thing happening in Japan?"

McGlynn thought of her own son.

"It's time you learned that a selfish son is not better than a selfish husband," he said. "I've been very patient with you about Taro."

"Please," she said, "not here."

"I also think it's time I talked some sense into Taro. I've tried your way for months and he's only grown worse."

She looked around uneasily. "Please," she said. "Come tonight after dinner. He told me he was staying home to study."

The hours dragged for McGlynn, and the more he thought about Taro, the angrier he grew. It was his own fault. He should have had this showdown with Taro long ago but it was easier to pretend that time and patience would bring the boy to his senses. The professor had recently seen Taro's name on a CID report of the sensational assassination of a prominent socialist. A Tokyo University student, Mikio Omi, had rushed onto the stage at Hibiya Hall where the socialist was making a political speech. Shouting, "Down with all tyrants!" Omi had stabbed the terrified man six times as the audience gaped in horror. An American cameraman had caught all the bloody details for Fox Movietone News, and Maggie had written a dramatic eyewitness account likening the butchery to the Kabuki-style assassinations committed by idealistic young officers in the years before Pearl Harbor. Taro was one of a dozen students rounded up at Hibiya Hall after the

assassination. He and the others had been released after being interrogated, but were being kept under surveillance.

McGlynn found Taro and Mariko sitting at the kitchen table. He
was sullen and she, distressed at the professor's stern face, looked up
appealingly. McGlynn had come determined to speak frankly but
without resorting to the scathing wit he'd so often unleashed on
bumptious students. "I was very distressed," he said quietly in Japanese, "to read that you were picked up after the Omi stabbing."

Mariko put a hand to her mouth in horror.

"I assume he never told you he was questioned by the Japanese
police and released. Don't worry, he's not going to be arrested." He
turned to the boy who showed neither alarm nor shame. "For a long
time I've tried to reason with you. I came tonight hoping to talk some
sense into you. But I can see it's hopeless. You're going to do what you
damned please no matter what pain it causes your mother."

Mariko was crying in spite of attempts to control herself.

"Do you have anything to say for yourself?"

Taro shrugged his shoulders insolently.

"Let me tell you something then, young man. Your mother and I
are going to get married. I hope you accept me as your second father.
I don't . . ." He was unsettled by Mariko's distress and found it difficult to continue. "Your mother and I have our own lives to lead, and
we hope . . ." There was no response from Taro. McGlynn knew that
if he stayed much longer he would only lose his temper. What more
could he say? He left.

For a long time neither mother nor son spoke. Suddenly Taro went
to the cupboard and seized a knife. His face was contorted. "If you see
him again, I'll be another Omi!" He plunged the knife into the table.

The next morning McGlynn summoned Mariko, purportedly for
more advice on his report to MacArthur. Her stoic face told him
something drastic had happened after he'd left last night. "What the
devil's the matter?"

"I can't see you again," she said. Her blunt words were like a punch.
She told him Taro was threatening to leave home.

"My God, how can you take him seriously?"

She fought her tears. "Please don't make it worse for me." Her eyes
were pleading. She hurriedly left.

He was so stunned he did little but stare at his report for almost an hour before he angrily scrawled his name at the bottom. Then, temper aroused, he attached a note summarizing his startling findings on the months preceding Pearl Harbor. He requested a private meeting with the commanding general so they could discuss what should be done, adding that they should also review the worsening events in Asia.

The following day McGlynn received a short memorandum from MacArthur thanking him for his report, but regretting the impossibility of a meeting in the foreseeable future due to the pressure of work. The judges of the International Tribunal, for instance, had finally delivered their judgment, and the Tribunal was scheduled to reconvene shortly.

2.

On the day after Chaucy's return from America, she had dinner with Mark in an intimate Japanese restaurant. They sat in a booth far from the other customers. He listened patiently while she talked at length of the Mississippi case. Despite efforts, no white witnesses had yet been found and she remained reluctant to take on the case. It appeared to Mark that she protested too much.

Finally he said, "What about us?"

"What do you mean?"

"Let's stop pretending. You know I want to marry you."

"I know. I'm sorry."

"Sorry for what? That you won't marry me?"

"I'm sorry I haven't been perfectly honest with you. I've been thinking about the same thing."

"Well—" he said eagerly.

She leaned across the table and took one of his hands. "I do love you, Mark. You're the first man I've ever loved."

He squeezed her hand. "I love you!"

"There's so much to consider . . ." She hesitated.

"Well, how about it?"

"Mark, I'm so tied up right now. The Tribunal reconvenes in a few days. We're sure Tojo will be sentenced to death, and then we'll have only a few weeks to prepare the appeal. Please understand, darling."

"Do you know how long it's been since I last saw you?" he said desperately. "Four and a half months! One hundred and thirty-seven days."

"My God, darling, has it been that long?"

"Three thousand two hundred and eighty-eight hours. I've also got it figured out in minutes and seconds!"

"What are we waiting for?" she said, hurrying into her coat.

On the morning of November 4, the Class A defendants at Sugamo Prison prepared to meet their fate. They breakfasted early and filed into the bus looking unusually spruce, having bathed and shaved the evening before. There were only twenty-two, since three—former Prime Minister Hiranuma, General Umezu, and Ambassador Shiratori—were in the army hospital.

It was a bright, clear day. At Ichigaya the gallery rapidly filled with foreigners without sufficient rank for reserved seats, and Japanese, including women in their kimonos. The corridors of the War Ministry Building were dotted with M.P.'s in shining white helmets, mounting guard over the aisles of the large courtroom. Looking down from the gallery, McGlynn sought out Will in the crowd of attorneys gossiping in the well of the court. He was not at the prosecution table but was talking with Chaucy and Blakeney.

There was a buzz of interest as the prisoners entered and took their accustomed seats. They looked in good health, each having gained an average of ten pounds. At 9:30 A.M. the judges solemnly marched in, wearing black judicial robes, except for the American and Soviet judges in their military uniforms. The room was brilliant under banks of floodlights for the Allied and Japanese photographers.

As President Webb began reading the majority opinion of the Tribunal in his sonorous voice, the prisoners, earphones clamped to their heads, listened attentively. An American correspondent next to Maggie whispered that they looked like a gang of tired old men with little interest in what they heard. He also noted that, contrary to his early beliefs, all Japanese didn't look alike. "Some of those monkeys have round heads and some have long faces." Why, thought Maggie, did they send over such a snotty correspondent? He was amused by General Doihara, and jotted down, "A little fellow with the face of a frightened rabbit." A few chairs away General Minami was "only notable for a long straggly goat beard." In the second row Tojo was impressive in his arrogance—" the very picture of the sneaky, sly Jap warrior." And Shigemitsu reminded another correspondent of a "worried professor in a small college, scribbling notes and rumpling his hair as he listens."

The session proceeded smoothly. Japan, Webb read with feeling, had been found guilty of waging aggressive wars against China and planning similar wars against Russia, the United States, Britain, and other Western powers who opposed Japanese plans to dominate East Asia and the western Pacific area. By late afternoon Webb was still condemning the rulers of Japan for crimes against humanity and violations of the laws of war during 1928 to 1938, and those in the gallery who had expected the drama to conclude on the first day were disappointed. It was obvious it would take another week.

The big news the next day was not the trial but the unexpected victory of Truman over Dewey in the U.S. presidential election. Almost every pundit had projected a landslide for Dewey. In America Truman's resounding triumph was called the biggest election upset in history. The Japanese press called it, "the miracle of 1948." In Paris, United Nations delegates hailed it as a firm mandate to end the wavering American resolve that had plagued the United Nations. But Nanking was in despair. Nationalist Chinese officials feared that they had lost their ally. The Soviets announced they were only mildly surprised; this was just another reactionary victory and would make no difference. But the man in the street from Dublin to Vienna and from Oslo to Rome, according to the United Press, applauded the comeback of the feisty man from the Midwest as a victory over big business.

During the third day Kido was charged with playing a major role in starting the war. But again what happened in the courtroom was overshadowed by another international event. Yingkow, one of Nationalist China's two escape ports from Manchuria, was reported to have been captured by the Communists. More important, Washington was so concerned by the deteriorating situation in Central China that all Americans in the Nanking-Shanghai area were advised to leave. As if to underline the approaching debacle, President Truman criticized Nationalist China's failure to comply with an agreement on relief supplies and emphasized the many difficulties of extending further effective military help.

By the time the session at Ichigaya was recessed on the eleventh, it was obvious that the reading of the findings was nearing its end.

During the lunch period the defendants were allowed to see their families through wire netting. That evening the prisoners were examined before a fluoroscope at the U.S. Army's 361st Station Hospital to learn if poison or lethal weapons were concealed within their bodies. MacArthur had not forgotten how Goering had foiled the hangman at the last minute. Nothing was found.

Friday November 12 was another sunny, pleasant day with the temperature expected to go above sixty degrees Fahrenheit by noon. After the prisoners were brought into the waiting room they were again allowed to visit with their families.

Tojo was in high spirits as he conversed with Blewett, his American counsel. He laughed and joked, then thanked the lawyer profusely for services on behalf of himself and his family. "Please do not ask MacArthur to save my life if I am sentenced to die," he said, but agreed to let Blewett file an appeal based on the contention that Japan acted in self-defense. "But I do not want to ask any clemency of MacArthur," he reiterated.

There was an air of unreality as the final day of the trial got under way. The twenty-two defendants sat stolidly. Kido slumped in his chair, his eyes closed, opening them only when Webb mentioned his name. Behind him General Itagaki, one of those responsible for the conquest of Manchuria, sat impassively, his long face inscrutable. Tojo, ignoring his comrades, also sat with eyes closed, behind thick glasses. Paler than the others, he still looked in good health. Throughout the morning session his face was almost always utterly without expression.

In the section for prominent visitors the general in charge of the French mission sat erect, listening attentively. Nearby Lady Webb listened as her husband read rapidly without interruption until 10:52, then announced that the court was adjourned for lunch.

"The Tribunal will now proceed to render its verdict in the case of each of the accused," he said when court reconvened. A perceptible thrill of anticipation could be felt throughout the courtroom. Here at last was the moment everyone had waited for so long! General Araki, the first on the list, paled and rocked back and forth when he heard the word "Guilty!" The next man, General Doihara, was also guilty. So was Field Marshal Hata, who seemed unconcerned. The chief secretary of the Tojo Cabinet, Hoshino, rubbed his brow as if he had a headache when he too heard "Guilty!" Kido seemed to be looking for someone in the audience. "Guilty!" An admiral rolled his head from side to side. "Guilty!" The last man, Tojo, was leaning back, the lights reflecting off his bald head, as if ignoring the final, unanimous call of "Guilty!"

Webb called a short recess during which the defendants were taken into the waiting room and their benches cleared away. M.P.'s were stationed around the courtroom. In a few minutes the sentences would be read.

At exactly 3:55 P.M., Webb solemnly said he would now pronounce the sentences. Almost all eyes in the hushed courtroom were on the empty dock. Then Araki was escorted into the room. He walked to the dock and, almost blinded by the glare of photographer's lights, faced Webb who said, "Accused Araki, Sadao, on the counts of the indictment on which you have been convicted, the International Military Tribunal for the Far East sentences you to imprisonment for life." From his seat Tojo's chief counsel, Kiyose, turned around—even though he knew it was rude—to observe the defendants' final attitudes.

Araki bowed and the next man waiting in the doorway came forth. It was Doihara. For the first time in Webb's life, since his native state of Queensland did not have a death penalty, he pronounced the death sentence. Doihara also bowed. In alphabetical order they came forward, received their sentences, and bowed to the court. Kiyose was not surprised that all had refused to look shaken, not wanting to be ridiculed by former enemies or their own countrymen. Yet their tension was all the more evident.

Then the last man came out. Tojo carefully adjusted his earphones, pressed his thumbs against the wooden railing of the dock, and bowed deeply to the court. The other defendants had reminded Kiyose of students standing in front of examiners. Nothing could be less true of Tojo's attitude. On his face was a half-serene, half-smiling expression. *He* was the examiner and he seemed to be listening condescendingly to the answer of an examinee called Webb. To Kiyose it seemed to be an expression of supreme detachment, of complete freedom. His head held high, Tojo listened calmly as Webb pronounced "Death by hanging." He nodded slightly twice as if saying, "Mmmm, the death sentence. I see. I see." Seeing this fleeting expression of sublimity, Kiyose felt relieved, assured that he could now relate how beautifully and nobly the Tokyo trials had ended. Tojo removed his earphones and bowed again. He walked off, thought Maggie, still commander in chief of the Japanese Army. In all, seven, including one civilian—Hirota—were sentenced to be hanged.

During the sentencing Chaucy's own feelings of grief were aggravated by the sight of Will's ashen face. There was little triumph on the faces of most of the prosecution. Although it was a day of triumph for Keenan, Will had been shaken by some of the sentences, particularly the obviously unjust one against Shigemitsu. Blakeney, who had fought so tenaciously for the common defense, went up to Colonel Kenworthy, in charge of courtroom security, and asked permission to talk to the defendants. Recently these same defendants had signed a huge scroll of appreciation for Kenworthy's many kindnesses to them. The colonel had become so fond of his charges that tears were now streaming down his face, and ignoring orders, he admitted Blakeney and Chaucy into the off-limits area.

The defendants had been divided into two groups, those condemned to death in one room, the rest in another. Followed by Chaucy, Blakeney went to those who would be hanged. The condemned men were sitting casually, smoking and chatting as if it were an ordinary day. Blakeney spoke to them in Japanese, a language he had been studying. Chaucy couldn't understand much of what he said but noticed how impressed the Japanese were. Tojo, apparently realizing this was a formal call, stood at attention. The others did the same. "The defense has done its best," said Blakeney, "and you must entrust the court's decision to the judgment of history."

Tojo bowed deeply and, on behalf of the others, thanked Blakeney for everything he and his defense colleagues had done. Tojo then bowed to Chaucy, thanking her for contributions to his own defense. He handed Blakeney a haiku, the classical seventeen-syllable poem:

> Noble are these young men,
> Soundless cherry blossoms that had fallen,
> How precious and peaceful.

The seven condemned men were put in one bus, the rest in another. The two daughters of Hirota—the only civilian to be hanged—in a state of near collapse, waved their handkerchiefs at the wrong bus.

During the final session, Justice Pal of India had filed a dissenting opinion. All twenty-five defendants, he wrote, should be acquitted of all charges. Dissenting opinions were also filed by Judge Röling of the Netherlands who stated that none of the accused should have been sentenced to death, and by the French judge, M. Bernard, who charged that not only was the prosecution carried out in an unequal and unfair manner, but the eleven judges had never been called together to discuss the judgment.

The seven condemned men were taken to a cell block cleared of all other prisoners. Each was placed in a cell eight feet long and five and one-half feet wide. Double wire-mesh screens covered the windows, and the iron bars of the doors permitted eight M.P.'s to keep careful watch. Guard details were changed every six hours.

Tojo, they could see, was serene.

Large crowds in the Ginza were gathering around the extras posted on a wall by Japanese newsdealers. Many were copying down the sentences in notebooks. And almost everyone thought the verdicts were just. So did most of those on the prosecution team, but the defense counsel were just as sure that it had been victors' justice.

McGlynn was dismayed, but the sentences came as no surprise. He caught a glimpse of Mariko in the departing crowd and momentarily thought of trying once more to talk to her. But he realized that it was hopeless in her present state of mind. He disconsolately headed for another lonely dinner.

Will walked out of the courtroom stunned by the verdicts although he thought he had been prepared for the worst. Numbly he flagged a taxi and headed for the Dai Ichi Hotel where he now lived. He could not believe that a civilian was going to be hanged, and that Kido, who had done his utmost to prevent war, would be imprisoned for life. During the past month Will had read and reread in his father's manuscript that President Roosevelt had been so impressed by the last offer of the Japanese that he had written in his own hand a proposed answer in the form of a modus vivendi. Will had shown this answer to both Tojo and Kido at Sugamo. And both had said it would have been accepted. Will would never forget Tojo's big sigh. "If," he said, "we had only received that modus vivendi!"

A concerned Chaucy was waiting in the lobby. "I never thought it would be that bad," she said.

"I'm beginning to dislike the whole damned legal process," he said disconsolately.

"The longer I practice the more imperfect law seems. Let's get a drink." At the bar she began complaining of human progress in all fields but the law. "We're going to break the sound barrier pretty soon, and I bet we even go to the moon. But the law is still an ass. Eighteenth-century legal philosophy rules in our twentieth-century courtrooms."

A young Japanese, out of breath, approached them. "Excuse me, Major. I've been looking all over for Miss Snow." He was a translator on the defense staff of Tojo. "We got an urgent message from General Tojo. He asked to see Kiyose-san, but he's left town, and I couldn't locate Mr. Blewett. Can you come, Miss Snow?"

She quickly swallowed her drink. "Let's go!"

But the translator was terrified at the thought of acting as interpreter. Will volunteered and within the hour they were facing Tojo. He was in a buoyant mood. "I've done what I thought I never would do." He handed Chaucy several papers. "It's my statement to the world. I'll give you the gist of it." He lit a cigarette, took a long drag and put it down. "I apologize for the atrocities committed by my men and ask the Americans to show compassion and repentance to the people of my country who are innocent and have already suffered from terror air attacks and two atomic bombs. I also warn your country not to infect my countrymen with communism." He resumed smoking, then neatly crushed out the butt. "I also prophesy that dividing Korea will lead to great trouble, and that a third world war will break out between you and the Soviet Union. And since the battlefields will be China, Korea, and Japan, it is your responsibility to protect a helpless Japan." He lit another cigarette, enjoyed it for a moment, then picked up the last page. "I close my testament with a poem." Then he read with feeling:

> It is time for farewell.
> I shall wait beneath the moss,
> Until the flowers are fragrant again
> In the islands of Yamato.

He rose and bowed to Chaucy. "I was honored to have you help defend me."

Even while Will was translating his last words tears came to Chaucy's eyes. She held out her hand, and Tojo shook it gently. Then he bowed curtly to Will.

"Kami no goshugo o inori masu," said Will, and extended his right hand.

Tojo's face stiffened. He hesitated, then the ghost of a smile transformed his stern face. He took Will's hand and pumped it vigorously twice. *"Tomoda chi!"*

As she and Will passed down the prison corridor Chaucy asked what he had said to Tojo. "God's blessings." he answered. She squeezed his arm. "He must have been very pleased." What had Tojo replied?

There was a lump in Will's throat. "He said, 'Friend!' "

At the Imperial Palace the chamberlain on night duty, Nagamasa Murai, opened the door to the Emperor's residence to bring a message. His Majesty's face was red, his eyes swollen with tears. Trembling with awe, Murai quickly lowered his eyes so he wouldn't have to see his monarch in such torment. Murai delivered the verbal message and, face still down, left the room.

3.

The accused had until November 19 to submit petitions to MacArthur. Tojo refused to apply. "It was my intention to be the scapegoat," he told the surprised Kiyose. "I am content with the sentence."

MacArthur listened to the opinions of the ten other nations concerned with the trial and then said that no duty had been "so utterly repugnant," as that of reviewing the sentences. "No human decision is infallible but I can conceive of no judicial process where greater safeguard was made to evolve justice." He upheld the sentences.

Even so, the hangings were postponed when the Supreme Court of the United States ordered a stay of execution on requests for review by the defense. But on December 20 the Supreme Court rejected the appeal, six to one, on the grounds that it had no authority over the International Tribunal. There were no more legal steps to be taken and the hangings were scheduled for one minute after midnight on December 23.

The seven at Sugamo were preparing themselves for death. All wore U.S. Army fatigues with a large P on the back. Twice a day they were allowed to visit each other, but only two in one cell. Most of their time was spent in reading, writing, and playing solitaire. Japanese cigarettes were available, to Tojo's delight. But only one could be handed out at a time and it had to be lighted by a guard. All had been allowed to see their families on December first. The next scheduled visit would have been the first of January.

Tojo welcomed the visits of Shinsho Hanayama, the Buddhist chaplain in Sugamo Prison. Religion now dominated the general's life and he was nicknamed *tera-kozo*, the Buddhist priestling. He regarded all the futile efforts of the lawyers in Washington as "something of a monkey show," the outcome of which was preordained from the beginning. Instead of being encouraged when Blakeney and Furness brought news of the stay of execution, Tojo had slapped the table with papers he was holding and exclaimed, "I wish they'd hurry up and get it over with." Then he added with a little grin, "It's no simple matter to avoid catching a cold and staying fit until I'm hanged."

His only request, he told Hanayama at their third meeting, was to have something clean to wear at the end. "We Japanese usually change into clean clothes before we die. Of course, we can't expect the Americans to understand that." Hanayama suggested he write a note of complaint in Japanese.

"I want to hand over these glasses and my dentures and beads at the end," he said and repeated his hope that he would soon be executed. "Then I would be free." Then he mentioned how deeply he was reflecting on the truth of Buddhism.

"Every time I see you," said the priest, "you have something edifying and blessed to tell me."

"Well, everything goes back to Buddha." Tojo smiled suddenly as he glanced at his hand chained to that of the M.P. beside him. "But this is good too. When I raise my hand, he raises his. This is one of the ties of Buddha. When I exercise, he walks with me too. It's all so glorifying."

In the fifth visit on December 10 he startled the priest by remarking he'd had an unexpected visit from the Goddess of Mercy, Kannon. He took out a washcloth on which was the American trademark "Cannon." "Kannon has taken this form and come to me. I thought it very mysterious."

Hanayama feared that Tojo's mind was cracking until Tojo laughed.

He turned to the M.P. beside him. "In English Cannon means big gun, doesn't it? But reading it in Japanese, it is Kannon. That means that the Goddess of Mercy has changed her appearance to come to me." He smiled delightedly. "Tell my children to clasp their hands and chant, *'Namu-Amida-Butsu,'* (Amen, merciful Buddha) whenever happiness comes to their hearts."

On the evening of December 21 the seven condemned men were brought in, in alphabetic order, one at a time, to the chaplain's office. Waiting for them were six men, including the commandant of the prison, a colonel and Hanayama. They were told when the execution would take place. Tojo, wearing his beads as usual, nodded at every word of the pronouncement and then raised the hand with the beads to say, "Okay, okay."

Did he have any last requests? He asked for a religious talk of two or three hours by Hanayama. He also would like the priest to be with him at the end. Then he began criticizing the authorities for taking such strict precautionary measures. "We will never try to kill ourselves. We will show you we can die noble deaths." It was humiliating to have a guard present every time he used the latrine. "To a Japanese this is an unbearable thing. If you were treated this way you would understand." He also asked for at least one Japanese meal. "We are Japanese, after all. Anything—even sushi—will do. And we should like to have at least one drink of sake." He went on to urge help for the families of prisoners in Sugamo who were living in wretched conditions. "Unlike American officers, we are poor and I should like to have some measures taken to enable our families to live."

The weather had been exceptionally warm that December, but on the twenty-second it turned bitter cold. Tojo entered the chapel at 4 P.M. wreathed in smiles. He clasped hands and bowed to the altar. "It is Buddha's summons," he told Hanayama. "And I am grateful for it." He gave the priest a *tanka,* a verse of thirty-one syllables, that he had written for his wife:

> Fare thee well, my dear,
> For today I go, to cross
> The hills of worldly worries
> To find happy repose in Buddha's bosom.

427

He complained of the hundred-watt light burning day and night in his cell. "It's a wonder I haven't had a nervous breakdown. Probably it was only my faith that saved me." He recalled that his father had died on December 26 and his father-in-law on December 29. "It's really quite a coincidence, isn't it?" he said. He was in a mellow mood. "You know I am dying at a very opportune moment. For one thing, I can tender my apologies to the people. Next, I am able to offer myself as a sacrifice to peace and become one stone in the foundation of the rebuilding of Japan. Third, I can die in peace of mind because no trouble has been brought upon the Emperor. Fourth, my death would have had no meaning if it had come through suicide. It will be on the gallows." He was physically weak, with only one or two teeth left, and it was more fortunate to die in one instant than to endure a lingering illness. "If I had been given a life sentence, I should have been tormented with worldly passions and it would have been intolerable." Yes, truly, this was the best time for him to die. "I am very grateful that I can be reabsorbed into the soil of Japan."

At 11:30 P.M. Hanayama hurried to the first floor to see that the Buddhist chapel was in perfect order. He poured wine into cups and prepared the water for the arrival of the seven condemned. Soon the first group, all generals, filed down—Doihara, then Iwane Matsui, Tojo, and Akira Muto. Each was handcuffed and had two guards.

Informed that he had only seven minutes, Hanayama lit the incense and candles in front of the altar. He handed each man a stick of incense which each placed in the incense burner as Hanayama brought it close. With encumbered hands each took an inked brush to write his name on heavy Japanese paper. Then Hanayama helped them drink wine. Tojo smiled now that his request was fulfilled. He was also pleased with the posthumous Buddhist name Hanayama had given him. The Chinese characters for the first syllable meant "light" —that is, wisdom; and the second syllable meant "life"—that is, eternal life, man's most cherished final wish.

"How about some cookies?" asked Hanayama. But three of them declined since they had removed their dentures. The fourth, Matsui, did munch a soft biscuit when the priest placed it in his mouth.

There were but two minutes left and Hanayama read the first three and the last eulogies of the "Sutra of the Three Promises." Tojo and the other three bowed their heads, and with eyes closed all listened in silence. They gave their thanks and then someone said one word, *"Banzai."*

"Matsui-san, if you please," said Tojo.

With Matsui taking the lead, the four men shouted, "Long live the Emperor! Long live the Emperor! Long live the Emperor!" and then, "Long live the Empire! Long live the Empire! Long live the Empire!"

Tojo handed his beads to Hanayama, as did Matsui. The others had left their beads in their cells. They all exchanged good-byes, shook hands with the American chaplain and several American officers, and finally each man grasped Hanayama's hand.

The steel door at the entrance opened. With an officer in the lead followed by the two chaplains, Doihara, Matsui, Tojo, and Muto crossed the courtyard. The four condemned chanted the *"Namu-Amida-Butsu,"* but Tojo's voice was the loudest. At the door of the gallows chamber Hanayama again shook hands with the four and gave them his priestly blessing. They thanked him for all he had done and asked him to take care of their families. All were smiling as they disappeared into the death house.

Inside, each man was individually identified by official witnesses. Secretary of War Royall had suggested the press be present, but Mac-Arthur had vigorously objected. What had been permitted at Nuremberg, he replied, had violated all standards of human decency. Consequently there were present, besides official witnesses, doctors, and essential prison personnel, only four men who had been invited by MacArthur: the American Ambassador and the Chinese, British, and Russian members of the Allied Council.

The condemned men walked up the thirteen steps to the gallows platform where they turned to face the witnesses. Black hoods were placed over their heads, ropes adjusted. The chief executioner on the platform saluted the commander of the execution detail, reporting that the condemned were prepared for execution. The executioner, turning toward the four condemned men, signaled, and the four traps were released simultaneously. It was one and a half minutes after midnight.

Outside, Hanayama was hurrying back to the chapel to prepare the other three condemned men for execution.

The bodies of the seven hanged men were placed in two large trucks and escorted by two jeeps. It was drizzling as the procession rumbled through the floodlit gates of Sugamo where soldiers with fixed bayonets held back foreign and Japanese newsmen. The trucks delivered the bodies to the Kuboyama Crematorium in Yokohama where every precaution was taken to see that the ashes did not fall into the hands of zealots.

The head of the crematorium had already cremated some 125 war criminals. "Well, it's all over," he said upon viewing the ashes of the former chief of the Japanese Army. "It is just what we expected for Tojo."

Time, which had previously ridiculed Tojo and his fellow defendants, wrote: "Last week, at midnight after the winter solstice, the paths of Japan's top leaders ended without glory, but with a dignity that seemed enhanced a little by the doubt and confusion among the victors."

Chapter Twenty-three

1.

Tokyo, December 25, 1948.

At Sugamo Prison, late on Christmas morning, an M.P. read out the names of those Class A suspects not yet indicted. Seventeen were led into a room and told by an American officer that they could go home. MacArthur had decided to initiate no more trials. The prisoners were brought to another room to don their old military or civilian uniforms. Some were ready for freedom but others had made few plans and were like fish which had somehow managed to shake free from the hook in midair and drop back into the water. Like those fish, they were momentarily unable to move.

The Yuletide spirit reigned along the Ginza. By now there were some 125 stores lining Tokyo's Great White Way. All were decorated with Christmas trees, and one tree, advertised as the biggest in the city, had cost 40,000 yen. Despite the holiday air and the great crowds, shopkeepers were complaining that most customers were window-shoppers or were carefully selecting neckties, modest cigarette cases, zori sandals, handbags, toys, animated gadgets, and other low-priced items. Only companies or associations were buying jewelry and precious metalware.

The shopkeepers were gloomy, but Will noted how spirited the shoppers were, with the festive glow of lights, the tinsel and holiday bustle. He was on his way to see Blakeney and Furness at the Foreign Correspondents Club. They greeted him warmly, and proposed that he join the law firm they planned to open once they passed the Japanese bar exams. At the moment they were busy defending Admiral Toyoda, former chief of staff of the Navy, in a complex international military tribunal. This could take another six months, since it involved charges ranging from atrocities committed on hospital ships —a Class B crime—to waging aggressive war—a Class A crime.

Blakeney explained that there would eventually be many cases of illegal seizure of Japanese property by the United States Government. Will would be particularly helpful in these trials because he was at home with both languages. Will had already guessed why he had been summoned and, after thanking them for considering him, said that although he had planned to return to Boston he would think over their proposition. As he walked toward the Imperial Hotel where he was to have a late lunch with his sister and Chaucy, he was puzzled by his reply to Furness and Blakeney. Why hadn't he told them that he had no intention of staying in Japan, and that he longed only for the return to some sense of order and sanity? Was it because he had been intrigued by the cases of illegal seizure of property? Or was it a way to allay the sense of guilt he still felt for participation in what he was convinced was an unfair trial? That was crazy. More likely it was because he was genuinely intrigued by the Toyoda case. But his participation wouldn't be ethical. As a member of the prosecution staff he had been privy to strategy and confidences of that "client." Could he get into the position of even appearing to use his knowledge in the defense of an interest adverse to that of a former client?

He argued with himself. Shouldn't the interests of justice prevail over those outmoded legal conventions regulating professional conduct? But he knew Chaucy would snap back: "You'd be violating the confidence between a lawyer and his client. Don't you remember what we were taught about contracts? 'The lawyer must decide when he takes a case whether it is a suitable one for him to undertake and after this decision is made, he is not justified in turning against his client by exposing injurious evidence entrusted to him.' "

He was not thinking straight. He couldn't afford to make this shift in lawyer-client relationship just to ease his own guilt. His place was back home.

That evening Will escorted Chaucy to a farewell dinner for the remaining counsel in Tokyo. The passions and conflicts of the long trial were not reflected that evening by those who had fought each other so strenuously. There was a sense of euphoria among some of those on the defense, although others like Blakeney were still indignant at what they felt was clearly victors' justice. But even they reserved their indignation for the judges and the system behind them, not for their fellow lawyers.

After the elaborate meal there were impromptu speeches. Though sharing Blakeney's feelings, Furness talked of what *had* been accomplished. "A professor at law school once told us, 'The best case is when there has been a good prosecution and a good defense.' I believe we showed here in Tokyo that there was a very strong defense. What better display of Western justice could there be than for men who had fought against the Japanese to vigorously defend former enemies?" Then he called upon Chaucy to say a few words. "Few outside this room know what an important part Chaucy Snow played in this trial, for she made only one trial appearance. But those of us who worked on the common defense are not only grateful for her contributions, but learned the perils of arguing law with her."

"When I landed at Atsugi," she began, "about all I knew about Japan came from Gilbert and Sullivan. I arrived with the usual baggage of prejudices about the Japanese. Even so I was prepared to use what I had learned at law school and during several years of practice in Boston to give the best possible defense to men I first believed were no better than the Nazis. Within a few weeks I learned my first lesson —that the Japanese shared some of my own New England principles. I believe most of you went through the same change. It was shocking to realize how we had been deceived for years into thinking that the Japanese were completely alien, utterly inscrutable. I learned, as you did, that despite cultural differences we were the same under the skin. The past three years have been the most . . . what word can possibly express what I mean? Never have the days been so full of life to me. Japan has been my university of life. And I believe that when I go back home I will be a better lawyer."

There was loud, spontaneous applause from all but a few, and as she and Will were leaving the room one defense counsel from Cleveland grasped her hand. "For the first two years, every time you opened your mouth at our general meetings I gritted my teeth. I never thought I'd say this, but it's been an honor working with you."

Chaucy smiled. For the first two years she had thought he was a pompous ass. "Thanks," she said.

It took half an hour for Chaucy and Will to get a taxi. She spoke scarcely a word. Will wondered what was troubling Chaucy but was reluctant to ask. Instead, on the way to the Imperial Hotel where

Mark was to meet them, he told her about the offer from Furness and
Blakeney. "I'm debating whether I should take it." He expected pro-
tests but she only said, "Don't wait too long before returning to
Boston."

Mark was waiting for them in the lobby of the Imperial. She had
phoned him to meet her after the farewell dinner, and he had guessed
she had at last made up her mind about marriage. Mark restrained
himself until he and Chaucy were alone in her room. Then he grasped
her but she gently pulled away. "I'm sorry, dear," she said. Her voice
was husky. She had gone through woods and valleys of doubt.

"What do you mean?"

"I—I can't marry you." His jaw dropped. "The law is a jealous
mistress," she said, and explained that she had just accepted the offer
to help defend the six Negro boys in Mississippi.

Mark seized one of her hands. "I'll quit the Marines! I can get a job
near you and . . ." As soon as these words were out, both he and
Chaucy knew he could never leave the Marines in these critical times.
"I love you so much," was all he could say but they both understood.
Each was bound on a different road. They embraced tightly, each
consoled by the other's love, and both knowing it was inevitable they
part. And then they kissed for the last time.

Late that night in Yokohama, a Buddhist priest and one of the
defense attorneys at the Tribunal, Shohei Mimoji, crept into the crematory and—so they later told friends—located the black boxes containing the ashes of Tojo and the other six hanged men. Mimoji and
the priest stole out of the crematory without being discovered, and
hid the boxes in a Buddhist temple.

In the morning Colonel Sullivan phoned Mark to come to his quar-
ters with two other members of his old battalion, Tullio and The
Beast. Billy J. told them he was leaving for Camp Pendleton, and
explained the sad state of U.S. military preparedness despite the Cold
War. Moreover, Nationalist China was on the ropes after defeats at
Mukden, Tainan, Kaifeng, and Suchow.

"But what concerns me most," he said thoughtfully, "is the rapid
disintegration of our armed forces. It took us years and many lives to
get where we were when the war ended. Then almost overnight we

began dismantling our powerful war machine. Why? It makes no sense."

"If we don't shape up," growled The Beast, "we're gonna be caught with our pants at half mast when the next balloon goes up."

Tullio said he'd heard from friends in the States that the Corps was in really bad shape. "But what can we do about it, sir?"

"That's why I'm getting back to Pendleton and the Fleet Marine Force. They need every good man they can get, particularly those with battle experience."

"How about taking us with you?" said Tullio. The Beast was just as enthusiastic.

"I'll see what I can do," said Billy J., and turned to Mark.

He had been listening to all this sunk in depression. But the cheerful faces of Tullio and The Beast brought a wry grin. Those jerks could always be counted on to stick their heads in any wringer. "Count me in too, sir," he said. "Why not?"

There was a knock at the door. It was Major Patterson. "Sorry to barge in," he said. He had some tragic news from Kyushu. "Tomie drowned herself," he said. Her fiancé had learned of the attempted rape and refused to marry her. Mark was devastated. "We're all to blame," said Patterson. "But it had to be done. We had to put Bradford away before he did any more harm."

Mark realized the major was right, but would he ever be able to forgive himself?

2.

A week later—it was January 2, 1949—Mark and Will were driving Chaucy to Atsugi airport in a staff car. Behind them Maggie was chauffeuring the professor and Floss in her battered vehicle. Chaucy couldn't hold back tears as she bade farewell to Mark, but once she started climbing into the plane she could hardly wait for the takeoff so she could read for the tenth time the latest details of the case she was going to try in Mississippi. But she kept waving to the McGlynns. What a wonderful family! Without them she never would have come to know and love Japan—and understand herself.

Mark looked as if he hadn't a care in the world and she loved him for his pretense. McGlynn waved in his own peculiar way as if directing traffic. Chaucy waved in response. God, would the damn crate never take off? It was becoming painful to keep a smile plastered on her face. At last there was a roar and the plane clumsily started forward. Once in the air she opened her briefcase and began reading. She did look up for a last glimpse of Fuji. The sight stirred her as if she had been Japanese in a past life. Then the dramatic peak disappeared, and her eyes and thoughts turned east toward Mississippi.

Mark took Floss to the orphanage in the staff car. Neither was in a talkative mood. She was engrossed in a new project. She must get money for a large addition. In the past month five babies had been left on the orphanage doorstep. Unwanted G.I. babies were everywhere. They were found dead in garbage cans and floating in canals. It was becoming a mass tragedy. Mark told her he had recently seen two Japanese girls, both pregnant, bidding good-bye to their homeward-bound G.I. boyfriends at a Yokohama dock. One girl shouted, "When you come back?" "Come back?" shouted one of the G.I.'s from the deck. "When you Japs bomb Pearl Harbor again! Then we'll both be back!"

Mark was trying in vain to erase Chaucy from his thoughts. The sooner he left for Pendleton the better.

In the other car Will was mulling over his future, and by the time they reached the outskirts of Tokyo he had decided to accept the offer of Furness and Blakeney. He wouldn't touch the Admiral Toyoda case but there was plenty of work helping Japanese civilians get just payment for property seized by SCAP. Remembering what Chaucy had said, he also vowed to return to Boston within a year. He was sure old Snow would realize what good experience this would be.

Maggie had also made a decision. She would accept the offer from Random House to write her World War Two experiences. Fredericks would certainly give her a six-months leave of absence, and she'd stay in Tokyo to write the damn thing.

Her father had also made his decision. He had shown enough patience, and tonight he would go to Mariko's. He would first visit the Todas on a pretext of bringing them the latest family news. It was a Sunday, and Taro always spent that entire evening with his university group and never got home until after midnight. Once it got dark McGlynn would check to see if the boy had left the house.

Maggie pulled up to the Dai Ichi Hotel to let her father off. "I heard a rumor you're going back to Williams College pretty soon."

"You shouldn't listen to those gossips at the Foreign Correspondents Club." First he had to complete research on the pre-Pearl Harbor book. "I'm also thinking of writing a book on the Occupation."

While he was at the Todas' late that afternoon, time dragged. His mind was constantly on Mariko and he listened to the present gossip of the Todas with only one ear. It seemed that Shogo was now a shop foreman at the National Railways, and McGlynn guessed accurately that he must have joined the Communist Party to wangle such a promotion. Those Reds really knew how to operate. It would be interesting to see what was going to happen in the next few months with the Tokyo trial a chapter in history. Sumiko would soon graduate. She had no interest in finding a husband, but was determined to get a job so she would never again have to be dependent on anyone but herself. Others in the family also had high hopes. Akira had just started a subsidiary company of Nippon Steel, and the Todas might soon be living a more stabilized life again. And Ko had come out of the black-market scandal unscathed. He was now working for a silk firm that welcomed his ideas. Although he was starting at the bottom, the firm had already accepted his suggestion that they export a limited quantity of their surplus cocoons to China. This could lead to closer relations with the new China as well as being a preliminary step in turning the industry into a producer of goods for export. That night he revealed to McGlynn that he had an even more revolutionary plan for the future, but he would keep it to himself for several years. What was it? dutifully asked the professor whose mind was elsewhere. "Switch from silk to nylon!" Ko whispered. "With synthetic fabric cheap and durable, who needs silk?"

At last it was dark. The Todas urged the professor to stay for dinner, but he said he had a previous engagement. A friend was going to pick him up at the nearby bus stop. He looked at his watch. "I'd better hurry."

It was bitter cold as he trudged across the Toda garden to the Tajima property. A few lights were burning in the house and he waited several minutes before knocking on the door. Mariko paled when she saw him.

"What are you doing here?"

"May I come in for a few minutes?"

She reluctantly let him enter. They stared at each other with longing. Finally she asked him to take off his overcoat. He was so agitated by the sight of her that he didn't notice it was quite cold.

"I had to see you," he said. She looked anxious. "Is Taro here?" She shook her head. "We've got to talk about our future." She began to weep softly. But he knew this was no time to be soft.

She had trouble speaking. She finally cleared her throat and managed to tell him of Taro's threat to become another Omi. "When I saw that knife I . . ."

He embraced her protectively, inwardly blaming himself for his failure with Taro. "It's just as much my fault as Taro's. I've let emotion take over, and been either condescending or impatient. I know we can work it out." He talked soothingly, and with such confidence that her stiffened body began to relax.

"You know that I love you," he said. "I know you love me. We were meant for each other. In a few years Taro is going to leave you. What kind of a life will you have then? A lonely one, if something happens and I don't come back for you. We don't have too much time."

"Oh, Frank, you make me feel so foolish."

"Please trust me." They kissed and she led him to her bedroom. He lit two candles even though she had always preferred the complete dark. They made love slowly but passionately and a long time passed as if it were a few minutes.

It was almost ten o'clock when Taro got off the bus. Tonight's activity had ended much earlier than usual. The attempt to sabotage a freight train—operated by scabs despite a strike—had failed when the guard Taro had struck with a club regained consciousness and sounded the alarm. Ridiculed by his mates, Taro was in an ugly mood. As he approached the house he was surprised to see there were no lights. Drawing nearer he did notice a flickering in his mother's window. He was puzzled. Usually she stayed in the main room reading until he came home. He unlocked the door and started toward his mother's room. He heard her say something, and then laugh lightly.

The blood rushed to the boy's head. Then Taro heard *him* laughing and he could not breathe. Gulping for air he rushed to the kitchen, grabbed a paring knife, and, quiet as a cat, crept back to his mother's room. When he beheld them together naked in the dim light he saw red. He shouted—not words but an animal roar—and lunged toward McGlynn, who raised up both hands to protect himself, and was slashed across his right forearm. Mariko screamed and this enraged the professor. He swung wildly, ineptly. He had never been in a fight since parochial school but rage and fear gave him unexpected strength. His wild flailing sent Taro sprawling. His mother's frantic pleading aroused new fury, and Taro plunged toward McGlynn, the knife glistening in the candlelight. McGlynn grabbed his wrist and sharply twisted the knife. Taro cried out. McGlynn, to his horror, saw the hilt of the knife at Taro's own breast. He had stabbed himself! Mariko was clutching her throat as if to still her screams.

McGlynn stumbled toward the telephone. He finally reached the Army station hospital, described the wound. Don't touch the knife, he was warned. An ambulance would get there as soon as possible.

Mariko was putting a small pillow under Taro's head, careful not to move him. In the glare of the bedroom lights her face was pale. McGlynn watched in a daze as she softly stroked her son's face. "Forgive me, Taro!" she said over and over. Taro tried to say something. His eyes fluttered, then closed. She knew he was gone, and burst into uncontrollable sobs.

3.

Interrogations by the Japanese police and the M.P.'s were so lengthy that it was dusk by the time McGlynn returned to Mariko's home. He was greeted by Emi Toda who told him Mariko was still in shock and could not possibly see him. The following day, Emi again turned him away, this time with a message from Mariko to leave her in peace until after Taro's funeral. He did get a glimpse of her when she came to the office to collect her belongings, but he made no attempt to follow her. She had, he learned, arranged a transfer to another position away from the Dai Ichi Building.

Each day at the Government Section was an ordeal for McGlynn. Without sparing himself he had told investigators exactly what had happened and why. Mariko testified it was an accident. Nothing of the fight was reported in *Stars and Stripes* or the Japanese press, but half-truths turned the incident into a scandal. Most of the professor's colleagues were sympathetic, but those who had felt the lash of his wit openly welcomed his fall from grace.

He attended the Buddhist funeral at Mariko's home. Mark had

offered to accompany him, but he insisted on facing the embarrassing ordeal alone. He sat discreetly in the background on the tatami floor. The family was coolly polite. When Mariko recognized him with a bow, he was stricken by her face, worn with grief. The agonized look they exchanged sharpened his guilt.

As the priest continued his long monotonous chanting, scenes of Taro as a boy flashed through Mariko's mind. How contented they had been as Taro grew up! The two of them had shared the grief of the death of husband and father as well as the hardships of war. It tore her to remember in her mind's eye Taro as a sweet little boy and what good times they'd had together, and how they'd helped each other in difficult times. Today she would welcome the puzzlement and sadness she had experienced in the postwar years when Taro had become so independent that he was like a stranger, only needing the company of his companions, if she could just have him back!

At last the chanting stopped and the family, relatives, and friends walked one by one up to the improvised altar, sat down and burned incense for the repose of Taro's departed soul. McGlynn had decided it was proper for him to pay his respects, and he was the last in line to sit Japanese-style before the altar. Feeling the stinging gaze of everyone on his back, he thrust three sticks of incense into the candle flame. Then with a wave of his hand he extinguished the flames and stuck the smoking sticks in the ashes of the incense bowl. He took a long look at the large black-ribboned photograph of Taro, and with palms together he bowed and bade him good-bye. How sad that he could ask for Taro's forgiveness and come to terms with him only this way. As he turned and walked back, Mariko and her relatives bowed.

On his way back to the city he could erase neither the painful memory of her face nor his own self-reproach. What agony she must be going through! Over and over he reviewed the scenes of his many clashes with Taro, and wondered how he himself would have reacted if his native country had been destroyed and occupied and his dreams of the future had vanished. How self-centered he himself had been, how thoughtless, how arrogant! He kept thinking that he should have tried to talk sympathetically with Taro rather than reacting with hostility; the young man might have responded to him.

The next day he came to her home. She silently admitted him. He could see she was still in a state of shock. "I've been mulling over and over about Taro and us, and what I could have done for him," he said. "He was so young and I should have . . ."

"Please don't blame yourself, Frank," she said, wiping her tears.

"I wish I could take your sorrow and the burdens," he said in a desperate attempt to reach her.

"It still feels like a dream. I can't believe he's gone." Her voice was hoarse. "I need time by myself to think."

"I don't know how you can ever forgive me," he said.

She abandoned herself to grief, sobbing and shaking. McGlynn didn't know what to do. He wanted to console her by taking her gently in his arms, but he felt she wasn't ready for him to touch her.

4.

The complex military tribunal of Admiral Soemu Toyoda, former chief of staff of the Imperial Navy, was reaching its climax at the Marunouchi Mitsubishi Building in central Tokyo. The paper work was so massive that Will had agreed to help as long as he could stay in the background. Because Toyoda had also been commander in chief of the Combined Fleet, the charges against him were broad. The trial was divided into six segments, five on charges of atrocities and one on conspiracy to wage aggressive war, a Class-A crime.

While Will handled last-minute interrogations and translations, Furness and Blakeney were successfully undermining the prosecution evidence. The presiding judge, an Australian major general, and the six American military justices were upholding the objections of Blakeney and Furness more often than they did those of the American prosecutor.

The most serious charge against Toyoda was the atrocious massacre of thousands of Manila civilians by a Japanese naval unit. But Furness parried this indictment by bringing to Tokyo many of those who had testified at the trial of General Yamashita, and then concluding his argument with this question: How can you try Admiral Toyoda when General Yamashita has already been hanged for those crimes?

On the eve of the judgment Blakeney slipped into the presiding judge's quarters and found a carbon copy of the court's findings. "We won! We won!" he triumphantly told Furness and Will. Toyoda, of course, was not informed, and in court the next day the three lawyers hid their joy. Before announcing the verdict, the Australian judge said to Toyoda, "Do you have anything to say?"

To the consternation of his lawyers, Toyoda said in Japanese, "I apologize for everything." He was about to continue when Blakeney, fearing he was about to take the blame for everything, whispered to Furness, "Pull him down! Shut him up!"

Furness, nearest to the admiral, yanked him to his seat and asked the court's indulgence for his client's interruption. Toyoda was quieted but still felt guilty for not having apologized properly for all the injury and pain inflicted on innocent people by Japanese troops under his command.

Maggie, who was just finishing her book for Random House, took time out to write a news story commenting on Toyoda's acquittal. She predicted that the climate of hate was finally coming to an end, and that in a few years most of those sentenced at Ichigaya to life imprisonment would be set free. Her prediction was deleted by her publisher, even though he had heard a rumor from Washington that pardons were being considered. "There are some things the public shouldn't know," he wrote Maggie.

When the first muggy heat of June descended on Tokyo she left for the cooler elevation of Hakone to make the final corrections in her manuscript. At last she finished it, but she was not happy. She had told of her apprenticeship in California and Hawaii, of seeing war at first hand on Iwo Jima and Okinawa. She had told of her arrest by the U.S. Navy and her triumphant return to Japan in MacArthur's plane. She had written of the brutality of war and the widespread destruction she had found in Japan. But she had said nothing of the loss of the one man she loved, or Will's suffering in prison camps, or the hell Mark went through in battle, or the hardship and tragedy Floss and the Todas had endured. The hell with it, she thought as she dispatched the manuscript to New York. Perhaps in ten years or twenty she could write the real story of the war that had made pawns of the McGlynns and the Todas. And of how by some miracle all of them, except for Tadashi Toda and his two baby daughters, had survived by their own resourcefulness and grit.

5.

When Maggie returned to Tokyo she learned that Mariko had finally agreed to see the professor again. He had hoped he could somehow comfort her, but he felt awkward and Mariko was still too overwhelmed by grief and guilt to think of herself. She saw he too was filled with sorrow and remorse. Never could she have imagined he could be so lost. Now they were bound by a tie of tragedy.

He left Mariko alone, determined to give her more time, but after a month he became so depressed that his children met to discuss what could be done. No one could think of a plausible solution, and Maggie finally suggested that Floss see him alone and try somehow to console him.

She found him in his hotel room spiritless and haggard, but when he saw the tears welling in her eyes he hugged her. "I know how concerned my family is, and I can't tell you how much I appreciate it. I just don't know what to do," he added wearily and told her of his last meeting with Mariko.

"Daddy, losing a child is so terrible for a mother. She'll never be able to get over it. She's blaming herself. The wound is too raw. Seeing you only makes it worse because she realizes what you're going through. You both need time to heal." She put her arms around him as if he were her brother. "You must be patient, Daddy."

Unlike the professor, Floss was far more aware of how strictly Mariko was governed by the code of behavior of her female ancestors. Their ideals, manners, and reactions had become so implanted in Mariko that it was natural for her to do what was expected of a Japanese woman even if she had been educated in the West. Poor Mariko was still devastated by Taro's death, and she didn't have the life-force to rebound.

Each day that passed seemed eternal to McGlynn, but he knew Floss was right and he forced himself to return to work on amnesty for those Japanese industrial leaders who had been purged. He also continued research on his pre-Pearl Harbor book, and contemplated a history of the gathering storm in Asia. But he began losing interest in everything, and he felt so frustrated and worthless late in July that he submitted his resignation. Then he summoned his children to Tokyo and told them he was leaving Japan. In two days he would have a final meeting with MacArthur, he said, and would take off a little later.

All but Floss felt nothing could be done, but she was convinced that leaving Japan without Mariko would be the end of his life. After consulting with the family and Emi Toda, she decided it was up to her to save their father. She would see Mariko.

On the taxi ride she began formulating what she would say. She arrived before she had completely formed a plan, and decided to take a long walk first. But instead she headed straight for the front door, determined to say what came out spontaneously.

Mariko was startled to see her.

"Please forgive me for intruding like this," said Floss in Japanese.

Mariko served green tea. After Floss expressed her condolences they talked of the miserable muggy weather. Then Floss put down her teacup and said in English, "I'm worried about my father." She told of his depression, then revealed how he had taken to drink after his wife died in childbirth, and was forced to leave Harvard.

Mariko avoided Floss's eyes. Reverting to Japanese, Floss told how gaunt and crushed he looked. "He has much to offer, but he's no longer interested in writing, in teaching—in anything. He just re-signed his position and is leaving for home in a few days." Mariko kept staring at the table. "You're the only one who can help him," said Floss earnestly. "My father loves you dearly, and he needs you now. You have so much to offer each other."

Mariko wiped away a few tears and looked up.

"You and I have gone through difficult times," said Floss. "We both lost our husbands during the war. I too have a son, and I can think and feel like a Japanese woman. You have suffered more than I, and yet you have more chance of happiness. You have a good man who loves you. I felt from the beginning that you would never marry him be-cause of Taro. Several times I tried to tell him but couldn't since I made myself believe that something might happen to bring your son and Daddy together." Floss was finding it difficult to speak because of her own feelings. Losing a child, she knew, was the worst thing for a mother to bear, and Mariko was blaming herself. "How hard it must be for you," said Floss.

"*Iie,* no," said Mariko. "You, too, have seen much sadness. So many women have lost their husbands and children in this war."

Floss wiped tears from her eyes. "You know Taro isn't going to return," she said.

Mariko's head jerked up.

"There's nothing you can do for Taro. And life must go on. You are still mourning. So is my father. It's been so difficult for him to endure the sarcasm of those in his office who dislike him and the pity of those who are his friends. Yet he has stayed on and on, still hoping. He can't endure the torture any longer." Floss leaned forward, pleading, "Will you at least see him before he leaves Japan?"

Mariko nodded.

"Can I tell him you will see him tomorrow afternoon?"

Mariko nodded.

The professor was awake most of the night either thinking of Mariko or mulling over the multitude of things he had to tell MacArthur in the morning. By the time he entered the general's office his mind was in a whirl. MacArthur rose from his desk and came forward to shake hands. "We're sorry to lose you, Dr. McGlynn. Even though I haven't taken all of your advice, I have found your suggestions refreshing." He lowered his voice. "I'm deeply sorry about your accident." He motioned McGlynn to the leather sofa as he himself sank into a large leather armchair. After two futile attempts he lit his huge corncob pipe. "I was impressed by your report on our achievements over the past three years." He waved an arm. "We can all be proud of ourselves for bringing democracy to this country."

McGlynn had decided to confine his own remarks to Asia but he couldn't resist saying, "Of course, it couldn't have been done if Japan hadn't been one of the most egalitarian countries in the world."

MacArthur was startled.

"And the war and three years of Occupation have now made her the *most* egalitarian country in the world."

"What do you mean?"

"Rich and poor Japanese now live at the same miserable level. Of course, we helped by purging the powerful, and I believe you'll be best known a hundred years from now for turning over most of the land to the people." A surge of deviltry seized McGlynn. He enjoyed the general's puzzlement, and kept a straight face. This would be his last chance to twist the lion's tail. "You will be known in history as the man who turned Japan into a single class—the middle class. Wouldn't you say at least ninety percent of the people today are middle-class?"

MacArthur was so taken aback he lost the chance to answer. "And what *did* this? The new Constitution you gave Japan! You forbade them to have an army and navy. You encouraged the Diet to tax the wealthy so heavily, particularly through the inheritance tax, that great family fortunes will soon be a thing of the past. Yes, because of you, General, Japan will become the first really socialist country in the world."

MacArthur's face clouded and McGlynn feared he had carried his impudence too far. "No other man in the world could have achieved what you have," he said sincerely. "You have my deep admiration, sir. But what I'd like to discuss," he hurriedly continued, "is the wave of revolution sweeping all over Asia. You are aware of this, I know. But our leaders in Washington are not. They don't realize that by defeating Japan we opened up all Asia to the idea of freedom. And instead of letting the Asians work out their own destiny, Washington is playing a dangerous game with the Soviet Union. As a result, sir, Asia is going to explode with a suddenness that will shock everyone. It may be in French Indochina, or Korea. I don't have to tell you that Chiang Kai-shek is defeated."

It was incredible that the general had allowed anyone to talk at such length, and when MacArthur got to his feet McGlynn expected to be scorched. To his amazement MacArthur began to orate as if to a large audience. "I could not agree more, McGlynn. As you know, I have written off Chiang. The Red Army is breaking through on all fronts." Fixing McGlynn with gleaming, steely eyes, he said, "If *I* were in command of the Communist armies in China—if *I* were Mao —my aim would be"—he peered intently through binoculars made by his forefingers and thumbs, then abruptly flung his arms wide and announced dramatically—*"the Indian Ocean!"*

McGlynn was amazed. What a grandiose concept! It was vintage MacArthur, and the professor wished Chou En-lai and Mao were present. They would gasp at the thought of their gallant but worn forces trying to march across the vast continent. But there was something endearing in the general's grandiloquence. This was the MacArthur who was convinced that Japanese adults had the minds of twelve-year-olds, and who was convinced not only that democracy could only come in Japan through Christianity but that millions had already been converted—when in truth there were still the same small number of genuine Christians in the country as there had been in 1941! This was the MacArthur who truly thought he knew all about Orientals—yet who, next to the Emperor, was the most loved man in Japan today!

"You've been most gracious to give me so much time, General," said McGlynn again with sincerity. MacArthur shook his hand and led him kindly to the door. "I look forward to reading your next book," he said.

After a quick lunch which he consumed without tasting, McGlynn set off in a taxi for Mariko's home. It seemed to take forever, and yet when he reached her street, he seemed to have arrived too quickly. This was going to be the most important moment of his life, and he dreaded facing it. On the trip he had vacillated between despair and hope, and he was now back to despair.

After a single knock the door opened wide. Mariko was standing there. Silently she invited him to enter. Once the door was closed she stared at him for a moment, then said softly, "I've been awake all night." She took a tentative step toward him, then reached for his hand.

His four children brought them to Atsugi Airport. Floss was filled with happiness for her father; Maggie's book had been praised by her editor; Mark had just received orders to ship out to San Diego, and Will was reading to the professor a quote from the Washington *Post*: "It is more and more evident to us that the good name of justice, let alone of the United States, has been compromised by the War Criminal cases in Tokyo." If the *Post* could experience such second thoughts so soon after the trial, said Will with relish, perhaps the law itself was not moribund, just a step behind the times.

McGlynn climbed up into the plane alone, for he and Mariko had agreed that she was still not ready for marriage. She needed more time to put all the pieces together. But McGlynn was convinced that everything was going to work out, and he was once more charged with energy. He found a seat next to the window facing his four children, who surrounded Mariko possessively as if she were already a member of the family. He couldn't help smiling at the thought of that slender figure having such power over him.

Mariko was thinking how much she needed him. Without Frank her life would be barren; with him she could perceive a life of happiness which as yet didn't feel real.

As the plane trundled slowly down the runway, McGlynn's sons waved and his daughters blew kisses. Mariko, who had regained her youthful looks, smiled as he waved in farewell. He loved them all, and vowed to show it more often to his children in the future. He prayed none of them would fall prey to his own stubbornness and impetuosity —a fatal combination. By a miracle he had been saved by the woman in their midst. Ideas and plans flooded his brain. He had already decided not to go back to teaching. Instead he would risk all on his books. It would be too early to write about the fatal months before Pearl Harbor or Occupation, but a cautionary tale on the tempest that could suddenly erupt in Asia must be done at once. Even before the last sight of Japan disappeared, he was scribbling notes. Then he suddenly wondered how Chaucy was faring in Mississippi.

He would not have been a bit surprised to know that, after a long continuance to gather new evidence, she was preparing for another fractious day in court facing long odds in a hostile Mississippi. She was in her element.

Postscript

Tokyo, February 1950.

On the last Sunday of the month the professor and Mariko were married at the same Methodist Church in Aoyama where Floss had married Tadashi sixteen years earlier. All the McGlynns and Todas were there, along with close friends. It was a joyous occasion, a new life for both McGlynn and Mariko. She reminded him more than ever of an elegant, cultured lady of pre-feudal days. But when she looked up at him and smiled she was his phantom of delight. "A dancing shape, an image gay, To haunt, to startle, and waylay."

He thought of the sixteen years since Floss's marriage. During that time the lives of the McGlynns and the Todas had been separated, each family bound to the fate of its own country. Now the McGlynns and the Todas were again united. And Japan and America—bitter, implacable foes for four years—were not only at peace but beginning to understand each other.

Acknowledgments
and Notes

For information on the International Tribunal of the Far East and the B-C War Crimes Trials in Yokohama, I am indebted to the following lawyers: Tosaku Baba, Michael Braun, Valentine Deale, Robert Donihi, John F. English, George Furness, Aristides Lazarus, G. Osmond Hyde, Takahiko Kido, Masatoshi Matsushita, Henry Shimanouchi, Kumao Toyoda, and K. Tokata. Material on Yokosuka Naval Base came from: James W. Brayshay, First Lieutenant, USMC; Walter W. Bauer, Corporal, USMC; James H. Blessing, Staff Sergeant, U.S. Army, Robert P. Borges; William H. Cheney, Sergeant Major, USMC; Alan H. Cole, Gunnery Sergeant, USMC; Mrs. Tomie Cole; Mrs. Edwina Naylor Decker; Lester Dyckman, Sergeant, USMC; Lee Edwards, Master Sergeant, USMC; Merrill Frescoln, First Lieutenant, USMC; James A. Hazard, Corporal, USMC; James M. Jefferson, First Lieutenant, USMC; K. Kobayashi, Yoshio Komiyama; Brigadier General James F. Lawrence USMC (retired); Mrs. Diana Lawrence; Ron Manuel, Gunnery Sergeant, USMC; Alfred A. Mannino, First Lieutenant, USMC; Y. Matsunaga; Clyde McAvoy, Private First Class, USMC; Takao Mochizuki; Francis Modde, First Lieutenant, USMC; James A. Popplewell, Warrant Officer, USMC; Ralph M. Powell, Corporal, USMC; George I. Purdy, Lieutenant Junior Grade, USN; Werner F. Rebstock, Colonel, USMC; Guy S. Rhea, Sergeant, USMC; Eiichi Sawa; Edmund S. Silvestri, Corporal, USMC; Teiji Takemiya; Tatsuo Tamamori; Ichiro Tanaka; Ron A. Whitney, Corporal, USMC.

Experiences of prisoners at Sugamo Prison were based on numerous personal accounts, most notably from those of Shinsho Hanayama, the Buddhist Chaplain at the prison, and Yoshio Kodama. General information on the Occupation came from numerous books, magazine articles, newspaper accounts, official documents, and interviews.

Of particular value were *With MacArthur in Japan* by Russell Brines, *Return of the Black Ships* by Benton and Edwina Decker, *Japan Dairy* by Mark Gayn, *The Kido Diary* (Postwar), *Victors' Justice* by Richard Minear, *The Broader Way* by Sumie Mishima, *War Criminal* by Shiroyama Saburo, *The Honorable Conquerors* by Walt Sheldon, *Stars and Stripes*, *The Nippon Times*, and *Japan's Political Revolution Under MacArthur* by Justin Williams, Sr.

Finally I would like to thank those who contributed most outstandingly to the book: Carl Brandt, Edward Hanify, Lieutenant General William K. Jones, First Sergeant Lewis Michelony, Fred Stocking, Chaucy Bennetts, and my wife, Toshiko.

All the scenes from the IMTFE proceedings are historical except for the appearance of Chaucy Snow in Chapter 19. This incident was based on a one-hour summary to the court made in February 1947 by Mrs. Helen Lambert, the wife of A.P. correspondent Thomas Lambert.

The rescue of President Manuel Roxas by the fictional character Colonel Heijiro Iwata was based on the factual rescue of President Roxas by Colonel Nobuhiko Jimbo as related in detail in my book *The Rising Sun.*

The personal feelings of the Emperor in Chapter Six are based on an article in the January 1987 issue of *Shincho 45* by Akira Hashimoto, whose chief informant was Nagamasa Murai, chamberlain to Crown Prince Akihito and later chamberlain to His Majesty. Other revelations about the Emperor will be published in 1987 by Otsuki Shoten in *Details on the Tokyo Trials: the Interrogatory of Koichi Kido,* by Professor Kentaro Awaya of Sophia University. According to the unpublished postwar diary of Kido, the Emperor made three aborted attempts to abdicate. The first, made soon after the surrender, was prevented by the Japanese Foreign Office and the Imperial Household Agency because the political situation and international relations made this impossible. The second attempt came when the peace treaty between Japan and the Allies was signed in San Francisco in September 1951. Marquis Kido sent a message from his cell in Sugamo Prison to the Imperial Household suggesting that this was the most appropriate time for the Emperor to abdicate since his Majesty was responsible for the surrender of Japan. It was proper that the Emperor take responsibility before his Imperial Ancestors as well as to his people, and by doing so the bereaved families of the war dead and wounded, the unrepatriated, and the families of the war criminals would feel comforted. It would also be helpful in bringing national unity centered around the Imperial Household. "If this is not done," Kido wrote in his diary, "I fear it may leave an atmosphere of dissatisfaction which may leave forever uneradicated the root of calamity." The Emperor welcomed Kido's proposal but Prime Minister Yoshida refused to approve. The third attempt came in April 1952, when the Emperor expressed a wish to abdicate at the ceremony in the Palace Plaza commemorating Japan's independence. This time Yoshida at first approved but then bowed to protests from the Imperial Household and the Foreign Office.

Sir William Webb, who had done his utmost as president of the IMTFE to bring Emperor Hirohito to trial, remained convinced that the Emperor was the chief war crimes criminal. In 1971 he wrote an enthusiastic introduction to *Japan's Imperial Conspiracy* by David Bergamini. According to Bergamini's account, the Emperor ruled pre-war Japan and plotted the course of aggression which led to Pearl Harbor. The Bergamini book, wrote Webb, "supplements and complements the findings of the Tribunal of which I was president. Indeed, it indicates that those findings could have been based on evidence of guilt even more convincing than that tendered by the prosecution." The Bergamini book, he concluded, "will cause a major readjustment in Western views of Oriental history."

Sir William's judgment, commented Professor James Crowley in his October 24, 1971 review of the Bergamini book in the New York *Times Book Review,* "tells us more about the International Tribunal than Japanese history. Mr. Bergamini's brief against the Emperor of Japan, for example, is completely unsubstantiated by any reliable source, primary or secondary."

The fate of General Tojo's ashes remains controversial. According to historian Robert J. C. Butow, "At the crematorium, every precaution was taken to ensure absolute security in the handling of the ashes." But in April 1955, Shohei Mimoji, an attorney for one of the seven hanged men, claimed he had sneaked into the Yokohama crematorium with a Buddhist priest and stolen the black boxes containing their ashes. These were hidden in a Buddhist temple. U.S. authorities ridiculed the story. The ashes, they said, were "long gone with the wind."

But the story of the ashes, even if it is a myth, will never die. In his account of the war crimes trials Ichiro Kiyose, Tojo's Japanese counsel, wrote that he was convinced the ashes were truly hidden in the statue of Kowa Kannon, and in 1959 finally laid to rest in a plot in Mikawa Bay Park in Aichi Prefecture. On a monument in honor of the seven men, General Sadao Araki—now freed from his term of life imprisonment—wrote in his characteristically bold stroke of the brush, "Here lie seven men who died for their country."

In 1980, despite protests from pacifists, the Japanese Government erected on the site of the gallows a simple six-and-a-half-foot monument to Tojo and the other six who died at Sugamo Prison. The monument stands modestly in a pleasant little park in the shadow of an imposing sixty-story building known as Sunshine City. On the day my wife and I visited the park we were the only ones to stop and read the words of memory on the monument. On the front was written, "In hopes of eternal peace," and on the back, "Those sentenced to death by the International Military Tribunal of the Far East at Ichigaya, Tokyo . . . were executed at this location.

"This place is therefore declared an historic site, and this monument erected so that the tragedy of war shall never be repeated."

CC36